An Escape
to Provence

About the author

Sophie Claire writes emotional stories set in England and in sunny Provence, where she spent her summers as a child. She has a French mother and a Scottish father, but was born in Africa and grew up in Manchester, England, where she still lives with her husband and two sons.

Previously, she worked in marketing and proofreading academic papers, but writing is what she always considered her 'real job' and now she's delighted to spend her days dreaming up heartwarming contemporary romance stories set in beautiful places.

You can find out more at www.sophieclaire.co.uk and on Twitter @sclairewriter.

Also by Sophie Claire

The Christmas Holiday
A Forget-Me-Not Summer
A Winter's Dream
Summer at the French Olive Grove

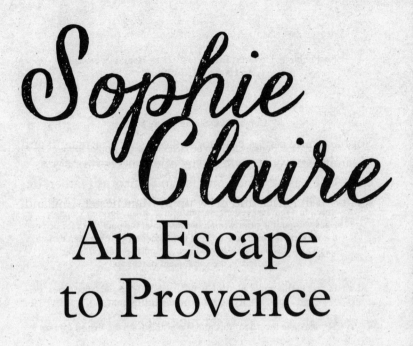

Sophie Claire

An Escape to Provence

HODDER

First published in Great Britain in 2022 by Hodder & Stoughton
An Hachette UK company

1

Copyright © Sophie Claire 2022

A CIP catalogue record for this title is available from the British Library

Paperback ISBN 978 1 529 35006 7
eBook ISBN 978 1 529 35005 0

Typeset in Plantin by Manipal Technologies Limited

Printed and bound in Great Britain by Clays Ltd, Elcograf S.p.A.

Hodder & Stoughton policy is to use papers that are natural,
renewable and recyclable products and made from wood grown in
sustainable forests. The logging and manufacturing processes are expected
to conform to the environmental regulations of the country of origin.

Hodder & Stoughton Ltd
Carmelite House
50 Victoria Embankment
London EC4Y 0DZ

www.hodder.co.uk

To Jacqui Cooper

Chapter 1

'*Still* no progress?' Daisy Jackson gripped the phone tighter as she paced her office. 'At all? Why not?'

'I don't know,' said Christine.

Her thick French accent was deceptive. Daisy knew Christine's English was excellent. 'Have you spoken to him?'

'He's . . . a difficult man to pin down.'

Daisy stopped in front of the window and gazed out over the stunning view. London's rooftops glinted as sunlight bounced off wet glass and slate tiles. 'Difficult to get hold of, or evasive in character?'

Christine hesitated before answering. 'Both.'

'Then fire him. Hire someone else.' Daisy had no time for incompetence. Especially when she was paying him to do a job, which, so far, he hadn't even started. 'It's been months now – almost a year since the papers came through – and that property is just sitting there, empty.'

There was a moment's pause. 'Ms Jackson, I know we came to an arrangement, but I feel I have done what you paid me to do.'

Daisy chose her words carefully. She respected Christine. From the moment Daisy had contacted her Marseille office, she'd been an invaluable help, and Daisy still needed her. She was too far away to deal with this personally. 'You found me a builder as agreed, but he's hardly the right one since he's not actually doing any work.'

'He's the only one who was available.'

'Really? I find that hard to believe—'

'This is Provence, Ms Jackson, not London or Paris.'

'I understand that, but—'

'I've done all I can. You have his contact details, he has yours. I can't do any more to help you.'

Daisy's brows lifted. Christine was washing her hands of this?

'Would it help if I increased your fee?' she suggested. 'How about I double it and you find me someone else?'

'Your fee was already very generous,' Christine said gently. 'And there is no one else.'

'No one? There aren't any other builders in the vicinity?'

'Monsieur Laforêt is the best. His reputation is excellent. And no. No one else is available.'

The call ended and Daisy frowned, her mind working furiously to sift through the options, searching for a solution. She'd made a flying visit to see the property when she'd inherited it and found it shabby, desperately in need of modernisation. She needed the builder to carry out the renovations he'd committed to doing.

She sat down and dialled Monsieur Laforêt's number, but there was no answer. *He's a difficult man to pin down.* How did he have a reputation for excellence when he didn't answer his phone or emails? He'd asked for a big deposit, and they'd heard nothing more. It raised her hackles that she and Christine had been trying to get through to him for weeks now with no success. Daisy didn't like to be ignored or played for a fool. When she'd taken on the house she'd understood that owning a property in another country could be problematic, but she'd hoped that by hiring the right people she'd get a certain level of service in return.

She pushed her chair back decisively and stalked through to the next room. 'Tracy,' she said, 'I need to book some time off.'

Her secretary spluttered coffee over her keyboard. 'Did you just say what I think you said?'

Daisy calmly handed her a tissue to mop up the coffee. 'I did.'

Tracy stared at her, tissue in hand. 'You're taking a holiday?'

'Kind of. There's a problem with the house I inherited. I have to go to France. Can you check my diary for next week and reschedule my meetings? I'm due some annual leave.'

Something had to be done. She had years of experience in dealing with difficult people and was known for being a skilled negotiator. She'd fix this. She just needed to track down Monsieur Laforêt and speak to him face to face.

'Overdue, more like. I can't remember when you last had time off. It's just a shame this doesn't sound like it'll be a restful break.'

'No. Well, perhaps once the building work is done I'll go back to check it and take a few days for myself. In the meantime, I want to meet Monsieur Laforêt and sort this out once and for all.'

Chapter 2

Daisy drove through a pair of tall metal gates and along the gravel driveway. Tall, umbrella-shaped pine trees and slim conifers jutted up into the blue sky, and sunlight bounced off the pick-up truck parked in front of the house. She was relieved to see it. She'd found him, then.

When she'd stopped in the village to ask where Gabriel Laforêt might be, there'd been a few raised eyebrows, a few questions, and perhaps she was cynical but she'd suspected that the *tabac* owner's directions were deliberately vague. 'Take the road up the hill until you reach the grotto,' he'd said, 'then turn left and follow the lane to the end.'

That was it? 'Can you give me the postcode?' she'd asked politely. 'I have satnav in the car.'

The man had laughed. 'I don't know it.'

'The address, then?'

He'd smiled. 'You don't need it. Just look for the grotto and turn left. Gabriel will be there.'

She'd bitten back an impatient sigh, tempted to tell him how ludicrously early she'd had to get up to catch the flight to Nice and make the long drive from the airport. But he had already turned back to resume his conversation with his other customers, so she gave up and left.

Yet now, despite the lack of address or postcode, it seemed she'd finally tracked down the elusive Gabriel Laforêt.

She stepped out of her hired sports car just as a man dressed in a cement-stained T-shirt and shorts came round the side of the house carrying a shovel, a fork and a trowel. His work boots crunched loudly on the gravel. Daisy's breath hitched. So this was the man causing her so many problems? He was younger than she'd imagined. Bigger. More rugged, too. Actually, he was hot. A fizz of awareness made her pulse pick up. She watched as he set down his tools beside the truck. The late-afternoon sun cast shadows over his face, and a dark beard accentuated his strong jaw. He pulled a rag out of his pocket and began to wipe clean the shovel, glancing at her as she approached, but calmly continuing with his task.

Her heels sank into the gravel, and she had to be careful to step around the equipment scattered all over the place. It wasn't easy in a pencil skirt that clung to her thighs in the afternoon heat. The temperature was higher than she'd expected for early May. 'Monsieur Laforêt?' she asked, in her best French.

'Who's asking?' he replied, in English.

She tried not to be offended that her accent was so obvious. At least language wasn't going to be a barrier if he spoke English. 'Daisy Jackson.' She walked round a concrete mixer and offered him her hand. 'I'm so pleased to meet you – at last.'

He seemed amused by this. His hands were grey with dust and his handshake was solid, but his gaze narrowed as if he'd come face to face with the enemy.

She didn't let this intimidate her. But she was equally careful not to antagonise him and kept her smile cool.

'I'm the new owner of Le Mazet up there on the hill.' She nodded in the direction of the next valley. The rooftop of the tumbledown wreck she'd inherited was just visible, and its leaning chimney looked even more crooked from that angle.

His expression turned to stone. 'Le Mazet? There are lots of those round here. Do you know what it means?' He slung the shovel into the back of the pick-up and picked up the fork. He began to wipe the prongs, his movements careful and methodical.

'I thought it was the name of the house,' she said, straightening her glasses. Had she got it wrong? She hated being wrong. In anything.

He examined the fork before throwing that into the truck too. It landed with a loud clang and was joined by the trowel and a paint-splattered spirit level. He wasn't so methodical about storing his tools, she decided, eyeing the messy heap.

'*Un mazet* is a farmhouse,' he said, with a wry smile that set her teeth on edge. 'A smaller version of *un mas*.'

'Right.' Who did he think he was? Superior because her A-level French hadn't been up to par?

Breathe, Daisy.

His muscles bunched as he lifted the concrete mixer into the pick-up, and she tried to hide her surprise at how effortless he made it look. She glanced at the house. Was this where he'd been working the last few months? If he'd told her he was delayed because he had to finish another job she would have understood, but he hadn't replied to any of her messages.

'Well, I'm the owner of that particular farmhouse. The one that needs a lot of renovation. Work I was under the impression you were going to do for me. I sent you a cheque for the initial payment. Did you receive it?'

'I did.'

'But you haven't cashed it.'

'I'm not ready to start work on it.'

Not a hint of apology, nothing. She tried to put out of her mind her frustrations that he hadn't returned her emails or calls. Her experience as a divorce lawyer had taught her that the best way to achieve success in negotiations was to stay detached, identify what the other side wanted, then make them believe they were getting it.

'Because you've been busy here? You've done a good job,' she said, with genuine admiration. The exterior walls looked as if they'd been re-rendered and the wooden shutters were freshly painted in a vivid cyan. No one could fault the quality of his work, but his communication skills left a lot to be desired.

'I always do a good job.' He grinned, eyes gleaming as they met hers and held.

Was he flirting with her? A lick of heat flickered in her centre. 'Monsieur Laforêt, we agreed a schedule. You should have started work three months ago.'

His lip curled a little. '*You* issued a schedule. I didn't agree to anything.'

'I asked you to write one and, when you didn't respond, I put forward a proposal for you to check and amend.'

She'd been careful to word it so his inaction would be taken as agreement.

He didn't look worried, though. In fact, his wry smile made heat rise in the back of her neck. He walked off and scooped up more tools, which had been left haphazardly scattered about. She had to walk quickly to keep up.

'I took your lack of response to mean you were in agreement.'

'A dangerous assumption to make.'

His English was really very good. She tried not to be impressed. She also tried to ignore the way her body responded to his good looks with a fizzing in her blood.

'But a valid one. You left me no option, Monsieur Laforêt. Perhaps you should deal with your paperwork rather than ignoring it.'

Count to ten, Daisy. If only he'd be polite enough to stop and talk to her. Instead, she was following him back and forth as he picked up his things and loaded them into the pick-up, and it wasn't easy. She was breathless from taking a dozen short steps for every long stride of his.

'There's nothing wrong with my paperwork.'

'What's that supposed to mean? That you've been deliberately ignoring me?'

She hated the way he made her sound like an outraged schoolmistress. But she valued politeness, and she believed it was important to behave honourably. Clearly he didn't. She gave up trying to keep up with him and paused, one hand on the truck, to catch her breath.

When he didn't reply, her teeth clenched, her fists curled. 'Don't you want the job, Monsieur Laforêt?' she called after him.

He stopped, and a muscle pulsed in his jaw. 'I didn't say that.'

'You're behaving as if you don't. Ignoring my calls and emails, not sticking to the schedule, not doing anything to begin the job you quoted for. Why did you accept the work if you don't want it?'

He turned slowly. 'Oh, I want it all right.' His features were steely, and his confrontational tone startled her. For the last ten minutes he'd appeared completely unperturbed, yet now she seemed to have touched a nerve. Why?

'Right. Well – good. In that case, when are you going to start?'

'When I'm ready.'

'I'd like a specific date. When will you finish here? Tomorrow? The day after?'

'I'll let you know.'

Her patience wore thin. 'Monsieur Laforêt, I've taken time off work to come here and speak to you. Do you know how much my time is worth? How much I bill clients per hour? I can tell you, it's not cheap!'

He smiled. Which made her blood boil.

'I've already spent –' she checked her watch '– over seven hours travelling here. I'd really appreciate it if we could resolve this as fast as possible so I can get back to London.'

'Don't let me stop you.'

His eyes, treacle dark, glinted and all her intentions of staying calm evaporated. Her pulse hammered furiously.

'You are stopping me! Why are you being so deliberately uncooperative?'

He didn't answer. Instead, the hint of a smile played on his lips. It made her skin prickle. He was laughing at her.

'Fine. Then I have no option but to sack you.' She remembered what Christine had said about there being no one else available, but she didn't believe it. And she couldn't understand how this guy had any business at all if this was how he treated his customers. 'Don't say I didn't try,' she muttered, as she marched off.

She must tell the bank to cancel the cheque she'd sent him. She half expected him to try to stop her, but he just watched as she got into the car, slammed the door and started the engine. She glanced at him before she drove away and did a double take. She frowned, puzzled. The expression on his face didn't make sense.

He'd looked positively triumphant.

So Daisy Jackson was even more uptight than she sounded in her messages, thought Gabriel. Younger and prettier, too, he acknowledged grudgingly, and pictured her long blonde hair and slender legs. Even glaring at him from behind her enormous red glasses, her intelligent grey eyes had snared him. But perhaps he'd succeeded in running her off.

He locked up the client's house and stood back, sweeping his gaze over the front, assessing his work. She'd been right about one thing: he had indeed done a good job here. But, then, he treated every job as if he were working on his own home. Better, in fact, because the old shepherd's hut he'd converted and moved into was only meant to be temporary. His jaw tightened with frustration and he focused on the boundary wall he'd just patched up, making sure the new stones and mortar blended with the old, that his lines were straight, the structure solid. Satisfied, he walked back to his pick-up truck. With any luck, he'd get paid for this job soon, and he'd add the money to his slowly accumulating funds in the bank. And when Miss Uptight from London finally gave up and put Le Mazet back on the market, he'd have enough cash to raise a loan and buy the place. Hopefully.

Once showered, he drove back along the country lane into La Tourelle, where his friends were already at the café. He waved as he passed them, parked in the main square, and walked the short distance back to join them. The café's burgundy chairs and tables were set back from the main road, and Gabriel hadn't even taken his seat before Jacques asked, 'Did she find you, then, the English woman?'

Heads turned. The conversations stopped, and his friends all looked at him expectantly. It was no surprise. When Gilles from the *tabac* had called him to say an English woman was on her way up, he'd known it wouldn't be long before the whole village was talking about it.

He nodded to the waiter, Jean-Paul, for his usual cold beer. 'She did.'

'They say she's beautiful,' said Patrice. 'Tall. Blonde. Fierce-looking.'

He laughed. 'She's nothing I can't handle.' Though now he remembered how determined she'd looked, her brows

11

knotted together when she'd seen him. And when he'd refused to give her the answers she wanted, her eyes had sparked behind those big square glasses.

But he wasn't going to do the renovations she wanted. All those plans to knock down walls and extend left, right and centre. Floor-to-ceiling windows, expensive air-conditioning – no. He'd made a promise to Jeanette. So Miss Uptight could take her silly yellow sports car and drive right back to the airport because she was wasting her very expensive time.

'What did she want?' Patrice drew his chair closer. 'Why is she here?'

Jean-Paul put down his beer and waited, as keen as everyone else to hear his answer. Gabriel lifted his drink in thanks. He took a sip, savouring the icy chill on his lips and the fizz on his tongue before it slipped down his throat. Finally, he said, 'She wants to know why I haven't started work.'

'Ah,' said Jacques.

'What did you tell her?' asked Laetitia, as she rocked the baby in her arms. Her daughter, Giselle, put her doll down and trotted over to Gabriel, arms outstretched. He scooped her up and settled her on his lap, where she began to fiddle with his hair.

'Not much. She shouted a lot,' his lips twitched, 'and then she sacked me.'

Laetitia's sharp scowl told him she wasn't impressed with his attitude. Jacques whistled.

'Is she moving in?' asked Patrice. 'I heard she's up there, at Le Mazet. Arnaud saw a car as he drove past.'

Gabriel took another swig of his beer, amused by this. Le Mazet was barely visible from the main road. Arnaud must either have been craning his neck or he'd taken a detour to check. 'She's there. I don't know if she's staying.' His fingers curled around the beer bottle, squeezing the cold glass dangerously tight. He'd felt a kick in the gut at seeing the hire car parked outside Le Mazet as he'd driven home. The thought of her touching Jeanette's things made him flinch.

Yet the rational part of his brain knew there was nothing of importance left in the house. He'd made sure of that. He'd been through everything half a dozen times, at least.

'Giselle, leave Gabriel's hair,' Laetitia told her daughter.

'It's fine,' he said, waving away her concern.

The little girl giggled mischievously and continued to tug at his hair. Patrice smirked.

'What?' asked Gabriel.

Giselle giggled again.

'My daughter's styled your hair.' Patrice snapped a photo of him on his phone and held it out for him to see.

His hair had been pinned back with a glittery pink hairclip. He pulled a face of mock-horror and Giselle giggled louder.

'So what are you going to do?' asked Laetitia.

'She sacked me. What can I do?'

'You could be straight with her. You could explain the situation.'

He felt a spur of guilt. But then he remembered Miss Uptight's haughty manner, and the way she'd stalked about in those ridiculously high heels, pointing at her enormous silver watch. 'She'll be gone soon. She was

already counting the hours she'd "wasted" coming here.'
He put down his beer with a thud.

'And you'll be happy with that?' asked Laetitia. 'To have driven her away from the house that is rightfully hers?'

Gabriel scowled. Truth was, none of this was sitting well with him. But what choice did he have? He'd given his word to Jeanette that he'd look after Le Mazet.

'So what is she like?' asked Jacques.

Gabriel remembered how her hair had been scraped back into a long ponytail, and how slender her hand had felt in his. 'The city type. Skinny. Full of herself.'

Do you know how much my time is worth? He reckoned she'd last two minutes before she was whinging about the Wi-Fi or the lack of fast-food outlets.

But she was also quick, clever and confident. A woman who knew what she wanted and wasn't prepared to be taken for a fool. He couldn't help but admire that. Even now sparks skittered through his body just thinking about her.

That was only surprise, he told himself quickly, because she'd turned up out of the blue. And her confrontational attitude had woken the gladiator in him. All those clipped questions, that pinched expression. But he'd seen her off and he hoped that would be the end of it. With any luck, she'd soon be gone and the house would remain empty.

'You need to put yourself in her shoes.' Laetitia's brown-eyed gaze met his steadily. 'She's innocent in all this. She just inherited a house. She knows nothing about it or about you.'

'This isn't about her. It's about Jeanette.'

'Jeanette is gone,' she said gently.

'I made her a promise.'

'I know. But you made it thinking you would inherit. Circumstances have changed.'

'So?'

'So you need to adapt too.'

'What – and roll over to the English woman and her demands?'

'Her demands?'

'You should have heard her, talking to me as if I were the hired help. She's superior and bossy.'

'Is that what this is about?' He didn't like the way Laetitia was looking at him – or her slow, dawning smile. 'She's bossy?'

'That's not what it's about, no. I'm just trying to do the right thing – as Jeanette asked me to.'

Laetitia held his gaze. 'But you need to think about the English woman too.'

Daisy finished the last in a string of phone calls, and snapped her laptop shut in frustration. No luck so far.

Still, she wouldn't allow herself to be despondent. Tomorrow she'd carry on working her way down the list of builders in the area. She stretched and checked her watch. Long shadows had crept across the terrace while she'd been on the phone, casting an eerie glow over the neglected house. Creepers smothered the old stone walls, threatening to choke the wooden shutters and terracotta-tiled roof, and the trees at the back of the house waved their branches ominously. She looked at the silent, dark fields in front that stretched to the forest beyond, and shivered. This place was so quiet, so still. So lonely.

She wrapped her arms around herself, more unsettled than she cared to admit. It was nothing like London and she missed the hum of crowded streets and city traffic.

It didn't matter what she thought of the place, she told herself. She was only here for a few days. She'd soon have all the problems fixed and be able to go home knowing the place would soon be generating a healthy profit.

She fetched her case from the car and went inside, wrinkling her nose at the archaic kitchen, doing her best to ignore the musty smell as she got things ready for to-night. She'd much rather have booked into a hotel, but the nearest one of decent quality was an hour's drive away.

Her heels clicked against the stone-tiled floor as she marched through the lounge. If Gabriel Laforêt hadn't put a spanner in the works, she wouldn't have needed to come here at all. Her jaw tightened as she thought of how he'd answered her questions with infuriating indifference. Why had he taken on the job if he had no intention of doing it? It didn't make sense. And why couldn't she shake from her mind the picture of his muscles flexing as he'd slung his tools into the van?

Upstairs, she pushed open all the bedroom doors, quickly identifying which had been the old lady's. Her relative. Family she hadn't even known she had until the solicitor had tracked her down. The thought tugged at her, but she brushed it aside. No point in getting sentimental now. Besides, family wasn't all it was cracked up to be. She knew that better than anyone.

It didn't feel right to sleep in the dead woman's room so she unwrapped the new sheets she'd had the foresight to bring with her and made the bed in the second bedroom. As she did so, she eyed the ancient dressing-table and the imposing dark wardrobe. The old lady might have been able to live in the house like this, but it wasn't up to the standards Daisy was used to. Everything looked so tired and worn, yellowed with age. The builder's first job, when she found one, would be to strip the place of all these horrors, and when the renovations were finished she'd pay an interior designer to kit the place out in a more modern style.

The bed made, she grabbed her car keys and drove towards the village for food, remembering the signs she'd seen for a big supermarket. However, the supermarket was in darkness. She checked her watch. It had closed an hour ago. Daisy sighed. In London there were always lights on somewhere, shops open and traffic rumbling by even at night.

She tried to think: what had she seen when she'd stopped in the village earlier? Hadn't there been a restaurant opposite the *tabac*? There'd certainly been a café next door, although she couldn't be sure if they'd serve food. She hopped back into the car.

Five minutes later, she stood in front of the restaurant and her shoulders sank again. She rattled the door impatiently, but it was no good.

'It's closed!' a man called.

She whirled round. The *tabac* owner who'd given her directions this afternoon was standing outside his shop. She hurried across the street to speak to him, conscious of heads turning outside the café. 'But the sign says they're open on a Tuesday,' she said.

The man waved this away with a flick of his hand. 'Family emergency,' he explained, and nodded at the café next door. 'You can get something to eat there.' He gave a sharp whistle and the waiter turned around.

Daisy's gaze travelled past him to the group of a dozen or so friends seated behind him, and she stilled. In the midst of them, with a toddler on his lap, was Gabriel Laforêt. His gaze met hers, and ice crept down the back of her neck.

'This lady here is looking to eat,' said the *tabac* owner.

The waiter smiled at Daisy. 'I can make you a *croque-monsieur*.'

Her cheeks flushed. 'I – er – I was hoping for a salad,' she said, ruffled at the thought of eating her meal feet away from the builder she'd fired this afternoon.

'Sorry. *Croque-monsieur* is all I can offer you,' he said regretfully.

'It doesn't matter. Thank you anyway,' she said quickly.

Her stomach growled as she drove away, and she cursed this place with its archaic opening times and services. She might as well have travelled back in time to the middle ages.

At the farmhouse again, she got into bed and pulled up the sheets. She'd left the shutters open, but even so the darkness was thick and heavy, the silence overwhelming. Le Mazet was completely isolated. Earlier she'd walked all around the house but there hadn't been another building in sight. Only endless trees and empty fields.

She tried to imagine the sounds of the city and the bright lights that studded the darkness when she looked out of her apartment window. The thought comforted her, and she was just beginning to nod off when she heard a long, urgent scream.

She froze. The noise was bloodcurdling. Too distant to be on her property, but too unsettling to ignore.

Was it a woman? It had sounded human, yet there was no living soul for miles around.

Or was there? She pulled the sheet tighter. She'd locked the kitchen door and the shutters were closed in all the other rooms – but still. She was alone here. What if someone tried to force entry? She tried to remember if there'd been a knife in the kitchen she could arm herself with, or a poker near the fireplace.

She lay still, fingers curled tightly. It had probably been a night bird, she told herself, and a faint memory trickled through from her early childhood but was gone before she could grasp it. The noise had probably been an owl screeching, or its prey screaming.

But she couldn't relax, and she knew it would be a long time before sleep would come.

'Why won't you take the job?' Daisy asked in French.

'I told you – I'm busy,' said Bertrand, turning away. He dropped his small notebook into the pocket of his blue boiler suit. He was old-school, he'd told her, as he'd scribbled her name and number. He preferred a pen and paper to computers, and she'd liked this about him. He'd seemed reliable – until he too had joined all the others in saying he couldn't help her.

'Your first answer was yes. It was only when I gave you the address that you suddenly remembered how busy you are.'

She shot a pointed look at the two men on the building site behind him. Both were perched on a wall; one was eating sandwiches, while the other leafed through a newspaper. They weren't in a hurry to finish shovelling the mound of rubble beside them – and she didn't know how anyone could work in this heat. The temperature seemed to have climbed ten degrees since yesterday.

'Yeah – well, I made a mistake. I have a bad memory.' He pointed a finger at his thinning hair and shot her a weak smile.

She didn't believe him. 'What's going on?'

The builder ducked his gaze away. At least he had the decency to look sheepish, but his wall of silence made her fingers fist around the car keys. 'No one will do it. Why?' she insisted.

'I'm sorry. I have to go now.'

She stood her ground. 'Why?' she repeated firmly. 'Is it the house? Are you superstitious?' Did people believe the place was haunted?

He laughed.

She frowned, her patience thinning. 'Then what is it? Please tell me. I've spent an enormous amount of money on the place and hours, days, of my time trying to get this problem fixed.'

Over the last forty-eight hours she'd contacted every builder within a twenty-mile radius and every single one had told her the same thing: they were too busy to take on the job.

Daisy would have believed them – it was early May after all, probably the busiest time of year for them – if some hadn't initially shown a keen interest then suddenly changed their mind. The words Le Mazet in La Tourelle had the same effect each time: every builder suddenly backtracked, found excuses and ended the call.

Something was going on, she was sure, and she was determined to get to the bottom of it so she'd come to meet Bertrand in person. His was the last name on her list.

She rubbed her temple. 'Please,' she said quietly. 'Tell me the real reason you won't do it.'

He shuffled his feet, before sighing. 'It's Gabriel's house.'

Daisy blinked at him. 'What do you mean? It's *my* house. I inherited it. I don't understand—'

'On paper it might be yours, but it should have been his.' He paused. 'The old lady who lived there, Jeanette Roux, was like family to him. Like his grandmother.'

Startled, Daisy took a moment to process this. He believed it should have been Gabriel's house. Did everyone believe this? Was this why no one would take on the renovation work? 'But if that's the case, why didn't she leave it to him? Why didn't she bequeath him her estate?'

As far as she knew, the old lady had died intestate, which was why the property had passed to Daisy, her only distant relation.

'Everyone was certain she had. She always said she'd written a will leaving it to him – but when she died they couldn't find it.'

She took a moment to absorb this. 'So that's why no one will take on the building work? Out of loyalty to Monsieur Laforêt?'

The man nodded.

She sucked in air, and tried to ignore the spear of guilt. She didn't have any emotional ties with the place or its previous owners, but this place was legally and rightfully hers. And it hadn't come cheap, what with inheritance tax, the solicitor's and architect's fees. She thought back to her conversation with Gabriel Laforêt. Why hadn't he explained the situation to her instead of being so obstructive and arrogant? Come to that, why had he taken on the job? And had there really been a will?

She lifted her chin and looked the man in the eye. 'Well, thank you for being honest with me.'

At least now she understood what was going on. She squared her shoulders. She had to go back and speak to Gabriel, and she dreaded to think what kind of reception she'd get.

Chapter 3

Back at Le Mazet, Daisy went through all her correspondence, hunting for Gabriel's home address. The postcode was the same as her own. She frowned and looked around her. Perhaps in these remote, rural parts the same address might cover a wide area. Anyway, it was lunchtime and too hot to walk, especially in a shift dress and heels. She hadn't counted on the weather being quite so warm or the ground so uneven. She glanced resentfully at the indigo sky, missing London's smooth pavements and temperate climate. Living in the city was so much more civilised than this place in the back of beyond. She set off up the lane, bracing herself as the tiny car bumped and jolted over the bumps and potholes.

Half a mile up there was a tiny turn-off but it looked like a farmer's track into a field so she drove on. The lane, however, came to an abrupt end. Daisy cursed. There was no room to turn the car round so she put it into reverse, but the steep ditch on the left made her nervous and she didn't dare get any speed up. As she reached the little opening, she swung in. Her car juddered along the crude path until a small hut with a low roof came into view. It was made of the same rough stone as Le Mazet, but while the farmhouse was grey and tired, these walls were the pale gold of a sandy beach, and in pristine condition. A couple of chairs and a table stood on a small patio outside, and two empty beer bottles glinted in the sun. The familiar grey pick-up told her she'd come to the right place.

She pulled her shoulders back and strode up to the wooden door. Well, she walked as fast as she could in heels over rocky ground. She knocked loudly and waited. The air was thick and heavy, and the field next door shimmered in the midday heat. She tapped a foot impatiently.

When he finally opened the door, Gabriel looked surprised to see her. Then his eyes narrowed. '*Oui?*'

Daisy faltered, unprepared for the sight of him topless and wearing only shorts. He filled the doorway, and his hair was ruffled. Was it true, then, that people round here napped after lunch? She had assumed it was one of those myths two hundred years out of date, yet he definitely looked as if he'd just got out of bed. There was a sleepy softness about his features and she tried hard not to stare at the ripple of muscles that played across his solid torso. He was disturbingly sexy.

'Can I have a word?' she asked.

The sun was so fierce that she was relieved when he gave a curt nod and stepped back for her to come in. She ducked to go through the low door and wondered how such a big man lived in such a small place. Although once she stepped inside she realised it wasn't as small as it looked. It seemed to be L-shaped and the long section had two sets of French windows, which were open and gave onto a shaded terrace overflowing with pots of colourful flowers.

'I didn't realise how close your house is,' she said. He was practically next door, and she remembered last night's eerie scream with a shiver.

He raised an eyebrow, but didn't reply.

'Did you hear a strange noise last night?'

'What kind of noise?'

'Like – well, a scream.'

'When?'

'Late. It was really loud, really – frightening.' He must have heard it.

He shook his head, puzzled, and she wondered if she had imagined the sound. 'It doesn't matter,' she said quickly. 'That's not why I'm here, anyway.' She gestured at the sofa and asked, 'May I?'

He swept aside a clutter of books and invoices, and pulled out a wooden chair for himself. Straddling it, he sat opposite her. His shoulders bunched, and something about his calm, assured movements made her thighs tug. She remembered the little girl on his lap last night. Did he have a wife or a lover? Yet, as she glanced at the abandoned crockery and clutter, it was difficult to imagine he shared this small place with anyone else.

'So what is this about?' he asked.

'The house.' *My* house, she bit back.

'Do I need to remind you that you sacked me?' he said pointedly.

She didn't rise to the bait. Instead, she said gently, 'I understand that you believe the house should be yours. That you expected to inherit, but no will was ever found.'

His eyes narrowed sharply. 'Who told you that?'

'It doesn't matter. Everyone knows. That's why none of the builders round here will take the job, isn't it? You have a lot of friends, Monsieur Laforêt.' Who behaved like the Mafia, she thought privately.

He didn't respond but his eyes told her everything she needed to know. They glittered like steel nails in the sun. Why was he so angry that she'd found out? What was he hiding?

'Why didn't you tell me how you felt about Le Mazet?' she asked. 'That you have . . . an emotional attachment?'

'Would it have changed anything?' he snapped.

She'd given this a lot of thought during the drive back here, and she could see his point of view, could imagine the injustice he must feel – but it was difficult to have sympathy for him when he was so obstructive and tight-lipped. In fact, she got the feeling his silence had concealed an underhand plan – but what was it? Legally there could be no dispute that the house was rightfully hers.

A slight breeze drifted in through the open French windows carrying with it a sweet floral perfume. The hills in the distance quivered in the shimmering heat.

'I understand you were very close to the lady who lived there previously. Jeanne?' Her tone was gentle. She didn't want to be antagonistic, simply to clarify the facts.

'Jeanette,' he corrected sharply. 'And, yes, I was. Very close.'

'So why didn't she make a will leaving the house to you?'

He barked a laugh and shook his head as if this were the most ridiculous question. Her hackles rose. 'It's a straightforward question, Monsieur Laforêt. I think it deserves an answer.'

'She did,' he ground out.

'There was nothing logged on the national register. The solicitor confirmed—'

'She didn't go to a solicitor. She wrote it herself. *Un testament olographe.*'

A holographic will? She'd never heard of such a thing. But the French had unique laws on inheritance dating back to Napoleonic times.

His big hands gripped the chair. She could see how wound up he was, but she was used to dealing with overwrought clients. She chose her words carefully: 'How do you know?'

'Because she told me. She wanted me to take care of the house.' He looked thoughtfully out of the window at the dry, rust-coloured earth baking in the midday sun.

'You're sure?'

He turned back, and his expression dripped with disdain again. 'Of course I'm sure. I was like family for her.'

'You know it's possible that she *said* there was a will when in fact there wasn't. Elderly people can get confused—'

'How dare you?' He pushed the chair away and stood up in one violent motion that made Daisy start. 'Implying she had lost her mind when you never even knew her! She was completely sane, right up until the day she died! If she said there was a will, then it existed.'

'Okay, okay,' she said quickly. 'I'm just going over the possibilities. Obviously I never knew her so I have no idea what her state of mind was.'

He pointed a finger to his head. 'Up here Jeanette was totally healthy. It was only her heart that was weak.'

She nodded. 'I take it you searched for the will?'

'Of course.' He began to pace the room, his bare feet leaving faint imprints, which vanished instantly, on the tiles.

'There must be something we can do to reach a compromise,' she said carefully.

She wasn't emotionally invested in the house – but he was. Then again, she'd ploughed a lot of money into the place and selling up because of one man with an enormous chip on his shoulder was out of the question.

And, if she was honest with herself, this wasn't simply about the project any more. It had become personal. In blocking her plans, he'd thrown down the gauntlet. He might hold clout in these parts, but she wouldn't let him defeat her. She couldn't bear to lose. In anything. No. She intended to use her negotiating skills to win him round and persuade him to carry out her wishes.

'Monsieur Laforêt, I understand you might find it difficult to see the place go to someone else, but the fact is, I'm the legitimate heir and I paid a lot of taxes for that house – even more in the architect's and lawyer's fees.'

A nerve flickered in his temple, but his mouth remained a flat line. His hands were buried deep in the pockets of his shorts. She wished he would sit down. It was difficult to concentrate while he moved around, all tight muscles and a dusting of chest hair. Emotion still simmered in him, but she couldn't tell what he was thinking. What did he hope to achieve with his obstinate silence?

She tried a different tactic. 'Tell me about Jeanette.'

'Suddenly you're interested?' he sneered.

'Yes. I am.' She met his gaze steadily. 'I don't know anything about her. I wasn't even aware I had living relations on that side of the family.' She added quietly, 'I wish I'd known.'

He looked at her in surprise. 'You didn't know at all?'

'I had no idea. The solicitor told me I was related to Jeanette's husband on my mother's side, but Mum died when I was fourteen and she never mentioned her family.'

Her words were met with silence, and his brow lifted. Was it her imagination or did something shift in his expression?

'That's a shame,' he said quietly. 'If Jeanette had known about you she would have wanted to meet you, I'm sure. Family meant a lot to her.'

She searched his face for sarcasm, but he seemed genuine. 'She had no children of her own?'

'*Non.*'

'So she lived alone?'

'After Benoît died, yes.'

'When was that?'

'A long time – forty years ago.'

Daisy nodded. The atmosphere in the room had at least become less combative, but she felt like she was hitting a brick wall trying to get him to open up. She'd been here half an hour and was no closer to understanding what he wanted. 'What can we do to make this work?' she asked.

Silence. He studied her from beneath his messy fringe with those impenetrable dark eyes. Her gaze dipped to his mouth. She inexplicably longed to run her hands over his cheek and feel if his beard was as soft as it looked, his jaw as hard. Christ, he was so damned attractive. In different circumstances she could have enjoyed meeting him. She could have *really* enjoyed it.

'What are you hoping will happen, Monsieur Laforêt? That I'll give up and leave? Sell the house?' The only sound was the grating noise of cicadas. She could feel the onset of a headache licking at her temples. 'If I sell, you'll never get the house back. Even if the will turns up, the best you can hope for is a sum of money in settlement. Is that what you're hoping for? Cash?'

He didn't reply.

'Or were you hoping to buy the place yourself?'

His features hardened. She could tell she'd hit a nerve – why? She glanced around. His home was small, his possessions few and, those she could see, modest. A sofa, a cheap table and chairs, and on the wall a framed photograph of a family group, discoloured with age. Le Mazet was worth a small fortune. Most likely, he couldn't afford to buy it.

He didn't reply.

Desperation bit at her. She was running out of options. If they couldn't work out a solution to this, what more could she do?

Nothing. It was stalemate.

'You know I came here today to try to resolve this problem, but if you refuse to discuss it with me . . .' Giving up, she stood to leave.

'It's not about the money!'

His bitten-out words made her stop. He raked a hand through his hair, leaving it even more dishevelled than before, and sighed.

His voice was a deep growl as he went on, 'It's not even about the house. This isn't about me or what I want. It's about having respect for a family home that has stood for centuries. It's about keeping it in harmony with its surroundings and not turning it into a concrete box with your ridiculous plans!'

He began to pace again.

She stared at him, noting that his shoulders were rigid with anger. 'You don't approve of the plans?' What on earth was there to disapprove of? The house was a wreck. She was proposing to invest in modernising it.

He swung round. 'They're terrible!' he said, with a strong French accent. His lip curled in disgust. '*Affreux.*'

'What don't you like about them?'

'You want to destroy the character of the house! And make it so big it will be like a hotel. You will ruin its beauty, its *caractère*, its *ambiance.*'

He didn't seem aware that he'd reverted to French, and his expression was fierce.

'I just wanted to smarten it up,' she said. 'The stonework, the roof – they've fallen into disrepair.'

'*Non.* They have not. They are old, yes, but I looked after the place for Jeanette. I did all her repairs myself.'

She visualised how neglected the place looked, with peeling paint, cracked flags and overgrown bushes. Was he really trying to block her from making improvements?

He paced the small room. 'Your modern ideas are not suitable here,' he went on. 'This is France, Provence. We have our own architectural style and traditions. They are rustic – but *authentique*. You don't like them? Don't live here. And why make it bigger? There are four bedrooms already.' He swept a hand through the air. 'Why turn it into a six-bedroom block of cement?'

'Larger properties are more popular for holiday rentals. They allow people to come in big groups with friends or family.'

He stopped dead. 'You don't even plan to live here?'

Why did he look horrified? Her chin went up. 'Of course not. I'm going to rent it. I see it as a long-term investment.'

'An investment?'

She held his gaze.

'Le Mazet is a home, not an investment! Jeanette's family lived there for six generations!' He looked at her with undiluted disgust, then paced away again.

Daisy opened her mouth to defend herself – then closed it. She had come here to find a solution, remember. 'So you don't approve of the renovations,' she said, 'but do you agree that Le Mazet could benefit from some improvements? Some care? It's been empty for a long time. It's looking a little tired.'

'Yes, it needs improvements, but this is not the same as bringing bulldozers and erecting white concrete walls all around the original structure. Can't you see? The house is beautiful as it is. You should be . . .' he searched for the word '. . . *preserving* its beauty, keeping with the old style.'

32

She bit her lip. How were they going to reach a compromise when he saw the place as beautiful and untouchable, and she saw a wreck?

'It needs a little work,' he said, holding up his finger and thumb. 'The terrace, the electrics, the bathroom maybe – but that's all.'

Daisy felt a small lift of hope. Her mind worked fast. Find out what the other side wants and give it to them. He wanted Le Mazet to remain unchanged. She wanted to improve it—

The klaxon ring of her phone interrupted and she automatically reached for her phone, finger poised to accept the call. She saw the caller's ID and stopped.

Her heart thudded. Hurriedly she rejected and silenced it. Christ. Why now? Why here?

She glanced at Gabriel, then back at her phone, which had started flashing as the caller tried again. Sticky heat crawled up her throat into her cheeks.

Ignore it, Daisy.

But memories charged at her, and emotions burst through like a grim jack-in-the-box. She tried to quash them but her heart was banging against her ribs and her hands shook.

Breathe, Daisy. Focus.

She could feel the Frenchman watching her as she fumbled and dropped her phone back into her bag. Emotions were dangerous at any time, but especially here, now, in front of this hostile man who would be perfectly happy if she walked out and never returned.

Chapter 4

Gabriel watched as she blinked rapidly and smoothed her skirt. Her hands were unsteady and her face had turned as pale as milk. Who had the call been from to upset her so much? Not that he cared. He was simply intrigued to know what – or who – had transformed her from forthright and confident to trembling, barely able to lift her gaze from her lap.

She brushed the hair from her eyes and appeared to battle with her emotions. She was slim and delicate anyway, but in that moment she seemed to shrink. He couldn't marry it up with the assertive woman who'd come all this way to convince him to work for her.

'Are you all right?' The gruff question sprang from his lips before he could stop it.

She glanced up, as wary as the stray cat that sometimes skulked around his garden. 'Fine,' she said quickly.

But he recognised bravado when he saw it. 'Who was that?'

'No one.'

He let the silence stretch a moment, gave her room to speak, to explain. When she didn't, he said quietly, 'You seem upset.'

She shook her head. 'I'm fine.'

But her grey eyes contradicted her, and he wasn't sure why he felt a rush of sympathy at this unexpected vulnerability.

He watched as she took a couple of deep breaths, then met his gaze square on. 'How about I revise the plans?' she said.

'The plans?' It took him a moment to realise she was talking about Jeanette's house.

'How about we forget the extension and focus only on renovating Le Mazet? You could work with me to make those renovations in keeping with what you call the old style?'

'You will keep the house as it is?' he asked, eyeing her suspiciously. This was a turnaround.

She nodded. 'On condition that, once you're happy with the revised plans, you start work straight away.'

He considered this. She was making a huge compromise. He could see she would gain from it: she'd get his services when, at the moment, she had nothing. But did he trust her?

'I won't need to reapply for planning permission if I don't extend the house but simply carry out repairs, so there'll be nothing to hold us back.'

Anyone could see she was focused, used to getting exactly what she wanted. Would she really settle for leaving Jeanette's house as it was? Her plans had been dramatic: tearing down walls, installing huge glass windows, air-conditioning . . .

'Don't you think it would be better if we worked together? To keep the house as you would like it to be kept?'

'As Jeanette wished it to be kept,' he corrected.

'Yes.'

He gritted his teeth. She had a point. If it meant Le Mazet was preserved and treated with the respect it deserved, how could he object? And it would give him more time to save money and to keep searching for the will. He refused to lose hope that it would eventually materialise.

'But what you have in mind is not what Jeanette wanted. She wanted it to be a family home.'

'It will be used by families.'

'Holidaymakers. Who will stay two weeks and never return.'

'So? They might treasure the memory of those two weeks in a beautiful place. It might be the only time they get to visit somewhere like this. You're privileged to live here. Why shouldn't other people have a taste of it too?'

He frowned. She was good with words. But he didn't trust her. Laetitia had told him to think about Daisy, but she was only interested in renting the place to strangers, in making money. She didn't give two hoots about Le Mazet.

'I know you're attached to the house,' she said softly, 'but it will be well looked after, I promise.'

His jaw hardened. 'You can't know that. You won't be here.'

'I'll make sure I employ the best agency and I'll keep tabs on it. You have my word.' She smiled. 'And if you see anything untoward, I trust you will inform me straight away.'

He glowered in response. He'd been keeping an eye on the place for the last three years. Of course he would continue to do so.

'So do you accept my offer?' She waited, then added, 'I feel I've met you more than halfway.'

Gabriel sucked in air and tried to push aside the memories crowding his mind of all the times Jeanette had made him promise he'd look after her home. *I'm counting on you not to sell it to people who don't understand, who don't respect the place, the land. I hope you'll keep it in your family.*

If he went along with Miss Uptight, he would be keeping his promise – kind of. At least the house would remain within his control. And he'd be around – until the work was finished, at least.

'I accept,' he said finally.

The English woman searched his eyes. Then, seemingly satisfied with what she saw there, she said, 'Good,' and reached to shake his hand.

Her grip was surprisingly strong, and if she was gloating or relieved she didn't show it. Instead, she got to her feet, brushed down her skirt and said, 'I presume you have work to do this afternoon, so how about we meet this evening, seven o'clock, to go over the plans?'

Her heels tapped against the tiled floor as she stalked towards the door, clearly confident this was done and dusted. Her confidence riled him. Who did she think she was?

'I have plans this evening,' he said.

She stopped. She tried to hide it but he saw her impatience in the rigid set of her shoulders. 'Plans?'

'Thursday night I meet my friends in the village. We eat, we play poker, we catch up . . . ' He shrugged.

Her expression gave nothing away. He had to admit, he'd never met a woman like her, with such a hard outer shell. The women he'd known had been warm and open, easy to read. Miss Uptight here unnerved him with her sharp edges, quick-fire questions and commands. She pressed all his buttons.

Yet the buzz of electricity was unmistakable. She was beautiful. Slim, fine-boned, with hair the colour of honey. And, despite everything, his body was responding to hers.

'We can eat together,' she said tersely. 'Monsieur Laforêt, don't believe that by playing games or intimidating me you will win this. If you drive me away, I assure you I will make sure that the next buyer is warned of your meddling intentions. Which means that the property will either stand empty for years and fall into further disrepair, or it will attract a large-scale property developer who can afford to bring in their own bulldozers and builders. I'm sure that isn't what you want for the place.'

His hands balled into tight fists. He considered his options, but the word 'bulldozers' hung in the air. Finally, he conceded, 'Perhaps I can rearrange my plans.'

'Good. I'll see you at seven.'

He accompanied her to the front door and, as she stepped out into the fierce sun, he murmured, 'It was a fox, by the way.'

She stopped. 'What?'

'The noise you heard last night – like a scream.'

'That was a fox? Are you sure?'

He nodded.

Colour bloomed in her cheeks and she looked a little embarrassed. 'Oh. I didn't realise . . . '

'Yeah, well – you're not from round here, are you?'

Her features hardened and, without replying, she left.

★★★

Damn it, where was he?

Daisy checked her watch again: 7.45 p.m.

She'd definitely said seven, she was sure of it. She shuffled the architect's drawings into a neat pile and tried to swallow her disappointment. She'd really hoped he'd work with her to get plans drawn up for the renovation and commit to them.

She gave the table the once-over: bread, olives, cold meats and cheeses, sundried tomatoes, and a couple of salads from the deli. Enough of everything to feed a hungry labourer. Unbidden, his large hands sprang to mind: those solid chunky fingers, which had felt rough when he'd shaken her hand. Calloused and strong. A hot sensation unfurled from her centre. She ignored it and picked up her phone to scroll through her emails. But there were no new messages since she'd dealt with them all earlier. Only the voicemail message, and she deleted that without listening to it.

Sighing, she sank back in her chair and glowered at the empty drive that stretched away to the lane beyond. The dusty track was punctuated by little rocky outcrops and tufts of weeds.

Face it, Gabriel Laforêt wasn't coming. She should have known he wouldn't. He'd agreed to it under duress, but as soon as she'd left he'd reverted to his stubborn ways, and she was right back where she'd started: waiting for him, and getting only radio silence.

Had she made a mistake in taking this place on? She didn't need the added stress in her life of dealing with a man like Laforêt, or the headache of overseeing building work on a property so far away. In fact, part of her wished the house *had* gone to him, since he and everyone here seemed to agree it should have been his. It would have spared her all this bother, wasted time and money.

But the house *did* belong to her, and she couldn't believe he'd persuaded all the builders in the area to refuse to work on it. That was low. Her jaw clenched. What was he hoping – that she'd give up and sell up? Sell to him? She pictured his delight and cringed. She couldn't bear the thought of him scoring a victory over her. No. She wouldn't even contemplate giving it up. That would be like failing.

Her ears pricked as the sound of a car engine pierced the stillness, and through the trees she spotted a blur of grey on the road. She sat up taller. His pick-up rumbled towards the house slower than a funeral cortège.

She frowned sharply. She'd rarely been an hour late for a meeting in her life, but if that were ever to happen, she definitely wouldn't amble up with one arm hanging out of the window of the car as casual as anything . . . Her fingers curled into fists. There really was nothing hurried about him, was there?

'*Bonsoir*,' she called as he hopped out of his truck. He wore jeans and a T-shirt, plain and simple, and he looked gorgeous. She tried to hide her appreciation but it was difficult not to stare. He filled those jeans, and the navy T-shirt was stretched across his chest and broad shoulders. He was so solidly built, so tall and broad.

He shook her hand and held her gaze. Irritated at the dart of electricity that shot through her, she snatched her hand back and gestured for him to sit down.

'You're late,' she said, careful to keep her tone light.

He planted himself in the chair, completely relaxed, legs apart, his big boots as solid as the stones that made up the walls of the farmhouse. 'I am?'

Earlier, he'd been glowering with simmering resentment. Now he was calm and almost smiling.

'Yes. We said seven. It's almost eight.'

He laughed. 'This is early by Provençal standards.'

'Early?'

He nodded and his chocolate brown eyes sparkled.

'What's punctual, then?'

He shrugged. 'Eight thirty? Nine?'

Her brows lifted. Was he teasing her? Mocking her? 'So, late would be . . .?'

He smiled and creases fanned from the corners of his eyes. 'Tomorrow.'

He was really quite disarming, and she couldn't help but smile too. Relief rushed through her at the ceasefire. Did this mean hostilities were in the past? She hoped so. She wanted them to be able to work together, but she wasn't naïve. Only time would tell if she could trust him.

Her stomach growled – a timely reminder of why he was here. 'What would you like to drink, Monsieur?'

'Gabriel,' he corrected. His voice was so low and deep it sent vibrations through her. 'Call me Gabriel. If we're going to be working together there's no need to be so formal, is there?'

Their eyes connected, and heat pooled in her middle. When he wasn't angry, he really was very attractive, wasn't he? And his self-assured manner told her he knew it.

'I guess not. Call me Daisy.'

'*Daizee*,' he echoed.

Her name sounded unfamiliar from his lips, and he pronounced it like the French word *désire*. Her skin tingled.

He turned to the neat row of bottles she'd set out. 'Let's see. Is this *apéritif* or dinner?'

'Dinner,' she said definitively. It was late, and she was hungry.

'In that case, I'll have a glass of red wine.'

She poured two, and took a deep slug of her own. The sun was low in the sky, but heat was charging the air tonight.

They ate first. He attacked the food with gusto, while she stuck to the olives and salad, and tried not to look at the bread in his hand and the way he chewed it hungrily, with pleasure, brushing the dusting of flour from his hands when he'd finished.

'So you live in London?' he asked.

'Yes.'

He gently spun the wine in his glass. 'Where?'

'In the City,' she said briskly. 'It's handy for work and quiet at the weekend. It suits me.'

'You have an apartment?' He took a slow sip of wine and savoured it.

'Yes.' She pictured her eleventh-storey flat with all the mod cons. She loved its stunning views, the sleek new architecture of the surrounding buildings, and the silver ribbon of river in the distance. There was a coffee shop across the road and a tube station three minutes' walk away. It seemed a world apart from this backward place in the middle of nowhere.

'Do you have a partner in London?'

'Partner?' Her mind automatically turned to the promotion she was going for at work. If she got it, she'd be one of the youngest female partners in the firm.

'A man,' he clarified, his gaze connecting with hers. 'Is there someone you want to get back to?'

'Oh.' Wow. That was forward. Or was he flirting? His eyes glinted in the golden light and she honestly couldn't tell. 'No, there's no man.' She smiled, keen to make that clear. There was an electric charge between them that made the air hum, and it was exciting. She enjoyed the tingle of expectation.

He reached for the bottle of wine and refilled his glass and hers. She was surprised, but she liked it: he felt comfortable enough to help himself. No airs or graces. This was progress from where they'd been when she'd visited him that afternoon.

'Why not? You're a beautiful woman.'

She glanced at him warily, but his smile seemed genuine. 'Thank you,' she said, holding his gaze, letting desire flow through her and savouring its warm sensation. 'But to answer your question, I'm too busy and I don't want a relationship.'

He stopped, the wine glass halfway to his lips. 'No?'

She shook her head.

'Why not?' He put down his glass, his attention focused on what she had to say.

'I see the fallout of failed relationships in my work every day. I decided long ago that they're a waste of time and energy.'

'You're a lawyer.' His tone was disparaging.

She didn't need to ask how he knew – she'd written to him using her work email, hoping it would lend her gravitas. Authority. Hoping he'd be more compliant as a result. It hadn't worked, and now she'd met him, she sensed it had been a pointless exercise. He wasn't a man to let anything or anyone intimidate him.

'Divorce lawyer,' she corrected. His coffee-dark eyes remained trained on her. Intent. 'Relationships don't interest me.' She knew not everyone felt the same – but more fool them. If they did, there'd be far fewer divorces and much less acrimony in the world.

'You don't mean that.' He shook his head.

'I do.'

'Really?'

'Yes.'

He looked flabbergasted.

'Love, romance . . . they're just fairy tales. Beneath the surface we're all selfish, all looking out for ourselves. I think it's better to admit that and behave accordingly.'

'Behave accordingly?'

'Acknowledge attraction when we encounter it, but not pretend it's anything more.' Her eyes held his gaze.

His lips curved in amusement, but she saw curiosity in his expression too. 'So when you meet a man you're attracted to, what happens? You never have relationships?'

'Correct.'

He took a moment to absorb this. 'But you're what – thirty?' She hesitated a second, then nodded. 'So you've had relationships in the past?'

She crossed and uncrossed her legs. How had this conversation got so personal so quickly? 'One,' she conceded, and shot him a wry smile. 'It didn't end well.'

'Why?'

She picked up her glass and drank deeply before replying. 'He turned out to be married.'

'Ah.'

It was a shame, she thought bitterly, because she'd believed they were good together. Fifteen years older than her and successful, he'd understood her professional ambitions and had encouraged her to put herself forward. Over late-night meals they'd enjoyed picking apart complex cases, and their debates had been as fiery as the sex. And because they each had a deep respect for the other's career, they hadn't placed demands on each other. For her, it had been the perfect relationship.

Until she discovered the truth.

He'd been understanding of the long hours she worked only because he was busy with his wife, three kids and dog. She flinched at the memory.

'It's fine,' she said dismissively. 'I prefer to keep things simple and uncomplicated. It works for me. What about you?'

'What about me?' His mischievous grin told her he was playing with her.

She bit back a sigh. 'Are you in a relationship?' She realised, as she waited for his answer, that she really wanted to know.

He gazed into the middle distance. 'No,' he said eventually. And his lips clamped shut.

Delight made her light up inside. Good. A level playing field.

'So. The house,' she said, deliberately steering them back to the topic in hand.

He sat back in his chair, cradling his wine glass, and a screen came down over his eyes. This was the poker face he'd shown when she'd first met him. 'Yes?'

'I think we agree that it needs some care and attention. Repairs here and there,' she said, nodding at the cracked paving near her feet. 'Perhaps we could take a tour to discuss them in more detail, but first tell me about the place. I'd love to know more about the house and its history.'

'What do you want to know?'

'How old is it? Who lived here?'

'There's been a farmhouse on this spot since the sixteen hundreds.'

'That long?'

He nodded. 'This one was built around the eighteenth century, and Jeanette's family moved here around a hundred years later, in 1870 or thereabouts.'

'How do you know all this?'

'Jeanette told me,' he said matter-of-factly. His hand arced through the air. 'All this land around you belonged to them. Farmland and forest.'

The light was fading fast, but she looked at the fields and the trees on the crest of the next hill. Even in the lilac shadows of dusk, she could see it was quite an expanse of land.

'What did they farm? It can't be easy to grow anything in this heat.' The soil was cracked and dry, and the vegetation was wiry and determined rather than lush. In her mind she contrasted it with the green fields she'd known as a child.

'Olives and vegetables, I would imagine. Fruit, too. It wasn't an easy life, and over the years bits of land were sold off. Now there's only one farmer in the area. He cultivates these fields around you, and the travelling shepherds graze their sheep here when they pass through.'

Travelling shepherds? The more she learned about this place, the more backward it sounded, but she kept her thoughts to herself.

'The land is very fertile. It's overgrown now, but Jeanette kept a vegetable garden at the back of the house. Have you seen the orchard?'

'Em – no.' She'd had a quick scoot round, but hadn't paid much attention except to note that the soil was tinged rust-red, and the grounds needed a good tidy, possibly even some landscaping work.

'Come, I'll show you.'

'But it's dark.'

'There's lighting – I installed it myself.'

He flicked a switch in the kitchen, then led her round the side of the house to the orchard, pointing out peach trees, almond, cherry and apricot. Their young leaves glowed in the uplighters, and some were freckled with blossom. But the weeds around them were knee high, and she still couldn't understand why he spoke so reverently about the place.

'The pool needs replacing,' she said, as they picked their way back towards the house.

'The pool? There's nothing wrong with it.'

She stared at the sludge in the bottom of the empty basin and the greyed tiles around the edge.

'I'll clean it,' he said. 'Then you can decide.'

'Is it watertight?' she said doubtfully.

'Of course. Until the day she died Jeanette swam forty lengths every morning every day of the year.'

'Every day? Wasn't that cold in winter?'

The corners of his mouth curled. 'She was – how do you say? – hardy.'

'Right.' Daisy had to hand it to Jeanette: she must have been a tough old boot. As opposite from Daisy as it was possible to be. She was a keen swimmer herself and had brought her swimming costume, but only because she'd been hoping to find a five-star hotel or an exclusive gym with a heated pool. 'Well, this patio needs replacing. See all these cracks? They're trip hazards.'

His mouth tightened and she thought he was going to argue with her, but instead he said quietly, 'Jeanette would never let me replace those paving stones because her husband had laid this terrace with his own hands.'

'I see.'

'She treasured every reminder of him.'

Daisy held her tongue. It was romantic, she supposed, but how did you get sentimentally attached to a patio? And if her husband had died forty years before her, how old did that make these flagstones?

'Well, I think it's time to move on, don't you?' She pointed to the house. 'Shall we go through what needs doing inside?'

They went through it room by room, starting up-stairs, but every suggestion Daisy made was met with objection.

'How about we replace the shutters?'

'They just need a lick of paint.'

'A wet room?'

'What's wrong with a bath and shower?'

'We could knock down this wall and build a walk-in wardrobe.'

'There are plenty of wardrobes already.'

By the time they reached the kitchen, she was worn down with arguing and had decided to save her energy for the important battles – like the kitchen. It just had to go.

'This is where I always found Jeanette,' Gabriel said fondly. 'She was an excellent cook. The best.'

Daisy nodded politely. She couldn't see the point of cooking when food came ready-made from the supermar-ket or restaurant kitchens. Everything in this room was ancient, from the metal range to the ceramic sink. She peered at the uneven flags beneath her feet. They must be original. The stone was smooth from centuries of wear, and whoever had laid them clearly hadn't been in posses-sion of a spirit level. A broom was propped by the door – who, in this day and age, used a broom, for goodness' sake? – and a grubby cream blind hung limp above the window. It must have absorbed decades of cooking fat and dust, she thought, with a shiver.

'Do you agree it could do with updating?' she asked, steeling herself for his inevitable objection.

He shot her a fierce look. 'The kitchen has been like this for decades, if not hundreds of years.'

'Exactly.'

He didn't laugh.

Her smile faded. 'I was thinking stainless steel. Something nice and shiny and new.' Like the kitchen in her apartment. She loved how clean it looked, how the surfaces gleamed.

'A modern kitchen would be completely wrong for this house.' A deep frown cut through his brow.

Daisy clenched her teeth in frustration. 'You know, Gabriel, I get the feeling you don't like change.'

'I didn't say that. You could choose a new kitchen that is not stainless steel.'

'It's not just the kitchen. Every suggestion I've made you've objected to.'

He made a rough sound. 'You wanted to fit big glass windows and air-conditioning. There's no need. This building has walls one metre thick and shutters to keep out the sun's heat.'

'Fine. But all the plumbing is old, and the wiring is unsafe.'

'I can fix those. I'll update them.'

His accepting tone was so unexpected she was momentarily thrown. 'Good,' she said finally.

'And I told you I'd replaster the walls, fit a new bathroom.' He made it sound as if he'd be doing her a favour.

'You did, that's true.'

'It's not that I don't like change. I just want to preserve the authenticity and the beauty of the house.'

'Well, that's a relief,' she said drily, 'because that leaky old shower is definitely not beautiful.'

He returned her smile, and it made her stomach do a little flip. Relief washed through her that they could at least agree on something.

They finished the tour of the house in the lounge, which was stuffed with armchairs and sofas and other old furniture. Every surface was littered with clutter. Daisy wrapped her arms around herself, wishing she'd thought to grab a knitted wrap while they'd been up-stairs. The temperature had plummeted since the sun had gone down.

'You should light the fire,' said Gabriel, seeing her shiver.

She glanced at the fireplace. 'I'll be all right.'

'You do know how to build a fire, don't you?'

'Actually, I don't. At home I have a heating system, which is controlled by a thermostat. It's something they invented around a hundred and fifty years ago. I recommend it.'

The sarcastic bite of her words was met with a calm smile. 'You need to learn how to light a fire. At this time of year the nights are still cool.'

Daisy didn't answer. She'd survive for a few nights without skills that had gone out with prehistoric man.

But Gabriel knelt before the hearth and began to scoop what looked like twigs and sticks out of a basket. 'Come on, I'll show you.'

She took a reluctant step towards him, careful not to get too close. All that ash and dust would be a nightmare to remove if it stained her designer dress. Though she had to admit it was very satisfying to see the stacked logs take light when he'd finished. She stepped closer and warm air snaked around her.

'There,' he said, straightening up and wiping his hands on his jeans. 'That's better, isn't it?'

She nodded and smiled. The flickering golden light cast shadows across his face, accentuating the angles of his features.

'It's old-fashioned but you must admit, it has a special atmosphere,' he said softly.

'I suppose,' she conceded. 'But I expect it'll be messy to clear up in the morning.'

'I didn't mean the fire. I was talking about the house.'

'The house?' A special atmosphere? She looked around at the tired furniture, the terrible paintings on the walls, and thought of how isolated she'd felt last night in the dark. 'It's – ah – different from living in the city,' she said tactfully. She couldn't wait to get this project sorted and return to London.

He was gazing into the flames with a nostalgic smile, and she wondered what he was thinking about. It was a sad fact of life that people became attached to homes but couldn't always stay in them. Time and time again, she'd had to remind a weeping client that what they were grieving was only bricks and mortar. That family, keeping their children close, was what mattered.

Still, she felt a needle of guilt. He was clearly so attached to the place.

'Is there anything in here that you'd like to keep to remember Jeanette by?' she asked gently.

His expression closed. 'I took the important things – her recipe books, a couple of photos. The rest,' he waved a hand dismissively, 'it is of no importance.'

'You understand, don't you, that I'll have to replace all this with fire-retardant furniture? They have strict rules about that in rental properties.'

He nodded, but his mouth was a flat line.

The room fell silent except for the crackling of the fire, and it was difficult not to be mesmerised by the seductive orange and gold flames as they danced and arced and stretched.

'You know, I've done a little research and I wondered why Jeanette chose to write a will herself when she could have gone to a solicitor.'

He blew out a long, slow breath. 'I don't know.'

'If she'd had it logged on the national register, it would never have been lost.'

'I know.' He stared into the flames and in his eyes she saw regret and wistfulness.

Daisy was perplexed. Why tell someone you'd written a will, then hide it? Jeanette had been asking for trouble.

'She hated bureaucrats,' said Gabriel.

Daisy looked up.

'The bank, social services, even hospitals – she wanted nothing to do with officials. She found them intimidating.'

'Why?'

'I don't know. She was always like this. When she took me in she could have adopted me but she delayed the paperwork so long that I became eighteen, an adult, and then it was no longer necessary.'

'She took you in?' She stared at him.

'When my parents died.'

She didn't know what to say. Yes, he'd told her he and Jeanette had been close, but this – this changed everything. She focused on a spot by her feet while she tried to hide her astonishment. No wonder he was feeling sore about the house and the inheritance. He'd lived here with Jeanette. This had been his home.

'She was frugal, too.' Gabriel gave a small laugh. 'She would have resented paying a solicitor's fees. All her life she was fiercely independent. It was typical of her to write it herself.'

'In that case, why didn't she give it to you for safekeeping?'

'I wish I knew. She wrote it a long time ago – perhaps she thought I was too young, or perhaps she mislaid it. Whatever, I'm sure she didn't deliberately hide it. She believed she had put it in a safe place.' He gave a dry laugh. 'In the end it was too safe.'

'I take it you've searched the house for it?'

'Of course.'

'You went through all her papers and documents, page by page?'

The pointed look he threw her spoke louder than words. 'What do you take me for – some kind of *imbécile*?'

She ignored this. 'Did you look in less obvious places – her clothes, socks, pants?'

'Yes,' he said irritably. 'And under the mattresses, floorboards. I turned every piece of furniture upside down. It's not here.'

Regret was etched into his features, and Daisy felt a small tug.

Ignore it, she told herself. In her work she was used to hardening her heart against the many heart-breaking stories she heard. It was crucial to stay detached or she risked losing perspective and making emotional rather than rational decisions. The house was hers now.

Unless the will was found, of course. In which case, she'd have a problem.

'So, how long do you think it will take you to do all this?' she asked.

He ran his dark gaze over the stone walls, and Daisy wondered if he was making mental calculations or just hazarding a guess.

'Around three months,' he said finally.

'When can you start?'

'Next week.'

Damn. She was scheduled to fly home at the weekend. She pulled out her cheque book and scribbled a number before presenting it to him. 'I'll pay you this upfront if you begin tomorrow.'

It was a huge amount. Enormously generous. So she was taken aback when he glared at the cheque, then at her. 'Why are you in such a hurry, Daisy?'

'I expected work to begin six months ago. I think I've waited long enough,' she said, holding his gaze.

'Why the rush? You've told me you're not planning to live here yourself.'

'I took this place on with the expectation of getting a return for my money. Until it's fit for habitation it's only running up costs.'

She held out the cheque for him to take but he shook his head. 'I'm not interested in your money.'

She pressed her lips together, biting back frustration. Hadn't she already made enough concessions? The property might be in her name, but she felt as if he had the upper hand.

Gabriel felt the bite of irritation as he drove away from Le Mazet and headed into the village hoping to catch his friends before they went home. It rankled deeply that Daisy Jackson kept flashing her cheque book about as if it would whip him into doing her bidding. If there was one thing he couldn't stand, it was people who valued money above all else. Money didn't keep you warm or help you through the tough times. Money was lonely: it led you down false paths.

He wouldn't be bought. And she needed to learn she wasn't in control here. Even if she was legally the property owner.

His hands gripped the steering wheel, and he remembered the disdain in her eyes, the curl of her lip as they'd walked through the house. She didn't appreciate Le Mazet. How could she not see its beauty, feel its special atmosphere?

He parked his truck by the main square and got out, pausing to breathe in the night air. Uplighters made the fountain glow gold, and the leaves of the enormous plane trees whispered on a faint breeze. He headed towards the café: it was lit like a beacon in the night, and laughter rang through the air. He didn't just love this place, he was part of it. It was part of him. The perfume of pine trees in the sunlight ran through his blood, and the dusty earth was engrained in the pores of his skin. He couldn't live in a place where the sun didn't beat down, where the colours were greyed and muted by cloudy skies, where there wasn't a friendly face around every corner. This was his home. Nothing would ever take him away from it.

'Aha! Here he is – finally!' said Jacques. 'Where've you been?'

He pulled out a chair. 'Le Mazet.'

'So she's still here, then, the English woman?' asked Patrice. 'You didn't get rid of her?'

'No. She's stubborn.'

'Ha!' said Laetitia.

He ignored her. 'She's not going anywhere.' He heard the edge of admiration in his voice and was as surprised as his friends.

'So you've given up on getting the house back?' asked Jacques.

He tipped his head to one side. 'For now.'

'What will you do, then?'

'New tactic. I'm keeping a close eye on her.'

'Ah,' his friend said knowingly, and winked. 'I see.'

'Not like that,' Gabriel snapped.

Although he had to concede that the attraction was there. And it went both ways: she hadn't disguised her desire at all. It intrigued him, the frank, openly sexual look in her eyes, then her impatient tone and furrowed brow. He could tell she was a strong woman. Determined. She knew her mind.

He found her attractive, but she wasn't his type. Far from it.

Jacques leaned back in his chair and regarded him thoughtfully. 'So you've agreed to work for her?'

'She agreed to do things my way. To keep the house as it's always been, preserving its authenticity.' He wanted to stay close, and not just to the house, he saw now. Daisy Jackson intrigued him as much as she infuriated him with her cheque book and demands.

Jacques was watching him, and smiled. 'Come on, admit you find her attractive and that's why you've done a U-turn.'

He rolled his eyes. 'Don't be ridiculous. Anyway, she did the U-turn, not me.'

'I see it in your eyes. There's a spark, Laforêt.'

'She's a city girl.' His lip curled. 'Always on the phone, barking instructions, thinks she knows best.' He pictured her delicate face and the big, bold, red-framed glasses that were endearingly bookish.

'Thinks she knows best?' laughed Laetitia. 'Who does that remind me of?'

They all chuckled.

'Hey!' Gabriel protested. 'There's a difference between me and her.'

'Oh, yeah? What's that?'

He winked. 'I *do* know best.'

Chapter 5

When Daisy woke it took her a moment to remember where she was. Sunlight tiptoed in through the slats in the shutters and was beginning to infuse the air with gentle heat. She opened them and a pigeon flew away with a frenzied flutter of wings. Although it was still early, warm air rushed in.

She really hadn't been prepared for this weather, not in May. Even when it was hot and sunny in London, she barely noticed, except perhaps to lower the blind against its glare in her air-conditioned office. Why would she notice? She got the tube or taxis to work early, and by the time she came home it was usually dark.

Downstairs in the kitchen, she made an instant coffee and stared groggily out of the window at the empty fields and the forest beyond. Normally she had coffee, showered, dressed and was in the office by seven thirty at the latest. Today she felt . . . aimless. She really missed her busy schedule, the buzz of the city, the satisfaction of being at the heart of things. The first sip made her grimace. She missed her coffee machine, too. This place felt so far away from everything. It would be perfect for holidaymakers seeking a peaceful retreat in the sun, but she couldn't imagine living here – like Gabriel.

She felt torn: part of her wanted to extend her stay and make sure he started work next week as he'd promised. It wouldn't be difficult to arrange – she had a flexible ticket. But the other half of her was desperate to leave this crumbling old wreck and return home. What would she do here for two weeks? How would she fill the days?

She grabbed her phone and padded out to the terrace, the warm air caressing her skin through her thin satin nightie. Other people often remarked admiringly that they didn't know how she achieved so much in a day, how she stayed so calm when her work involved dealing with fraught emotions and highly stressful situations. But she thrived on the pace and intensity. She couldn't imagine life any other way.

Over coffee, she made a quick spreadsheet of jobs she needed to do. She could begin by clearing out the house and planning colour schemes. She glanced up, stroking her chin. The safest option was a neutral cream everywhere, soft furnishings that people would see but not notice, innocuous . . .

The rough growl of an engine interrupted her thoughts and she looked up. It was the grey pick-up. Gabriel.

He stopped, nodded in her direction, then climbed out of his van and began unloading tools from the back. She glanced down at her nightie, torn between wanting to scuttle away and get dressed – or at least fetch her dressing-gown – then worried that she might seem scared of him or as if she cared what he thought. In the end, she lifted her chin and stayed put. She didn't have any hang-ups about her body. Anyway, she told herself, as she approached his van, he'd already seen her, and she didn't want to give him any reason to think she was running away.

'What are you doing here?' she asked, careful to keep her tone neutral.

He pulled out a sledgehammer. 'Starting work.'

'Now?'

His lips twitched. 'Looks like it.'

She felt the prickle of indignation. He was laughing at her, wasn't he? At home, in the office and the courts no one spoke to her with anything but respect. Clients and colleagues alike sought her advice and looked to her for answers. She couldn't think of anyone who'd silently mock her like this – at least, not to her face. 'You said you couldn't begin until next week.'

He shrugged. An infuriating gesture – and he did it all the time. A shrug was neither an answer nor an explanation. 'I changed things around. For you.'

For her? Why? What had changed since he'd left last night? Puzzled, she waited for him to elucidate, but he said nothing. Clearing her throat, she decided to keep her questions to herself: she didn't want to risk another change of mind on his part when this was clearly in her favour. 'Right. Well – thank you.' She hugged her arms, flustered and self-conscious in her nightie. Had he deliberately turned up like this to catch her on the back foot? It was only seven o'clock local time, for heaven's sake. 'Do you always start work so early?'

He reached for a tool belt and clipped it around his waist. 'I do. This is the best time to work, before the temperature rises.'

Her temperature was already high, she thought drily, as he spun a hammer in his hand and slotted it into the belt. If he had any inkling of how masculine he looked in those work boots and shorts, he didn't show it. She ran her tongue over her lips, suddenly thirsty.

'By midday,' he went on, 'the sun will be fierce, too hot to work, and there's nothing to do but take a *sieste*.' He paused and his gaze connected with hers, but his expression remained unreadable.

'I see.' The thought of him in bed made her even more flustered. She tried to sound businesslike. 'So where are you starting? Do we need to move any furniture out of your way?'

'Not unless you've left it in the shed.'

They'd agreed he would take down the ramshackle wooden shed and replace it with a solid structure built out of stone to match, as far as possible, the farmhouse walls.

'The shed? That's the least important of all the jobs that need doing. Why don't you start with the interior or the roof?' She was certain that all the broken and missing tiles must be a problem when it rained. If it ever rained here.

'I'm delaying starting on the house until you've left. It will make your stay less unpleasant.'

She peered at him more closely. Was he genuinely being considerate? It was so unexpected she couldn't help but feel a whisper of suspicion. Did he have an ulterior motive? Don't be so cynical, Daisy.

'Right. I'll let you carry on, then.'

She scurried back into the house, downed her coffee and rushed upstairs. A cold shower was what she needed right now.

As she dressed, she could hear him whistling to himself. Snatches of melody carried up through the air and she tilted her head to listen. She recognised the music – what was it? Memories nipped at her. Was it something she'd heard when she was small? Her mum had loved music. Daisy smiled. Whatever it was, it was beautiful.

She slipped on her navy dress and heels and, moving over to the window, watched him while she clipped the bracelet of her watch in place. He had cleared out the meagre contents of the shed and dismantled the roof, and the muscles in his arms flexed as he swung the sledgehammer, splintering the wall. He broke off a couple of pieces and tossed them onto the untidy heap behind him. His skin gleamed copper in the sun and he wiped the sweat from his brow with his forearm. The sight of him triggered wicked thoughts and made her smile.

He glanced up. His gaze met Daisy's and his lips curved.

She darted back from the window, cheeks burning. Damn. Caught in the act.

Never mind, she told herself. Why hide her appreciation of his good looks?

Once dressed, she returned to the terrace and, under the shade of the plane tree, she rattled through her emails, firing off answers and instructions, occasionally cursing under her breath because the Wi-Fi kept cutting out. As soon as it reconnected, she worked fast and efficiently, completely focused on her clients. The Wrights' divorce was progressing well, but Daisy had concerns about the wife's manipulative streak; she was keen for her client to be granted a residence order for the couple's three children as soon as possible. And Selena Elms had a domineering ex, who was determined to get a share of her catering company. Daisy was determined he wouldn't.

When she'd clicked send and filed the last email, she sat back and smiled with satisfaction at her empty inbox. This was how she liked her life to be: tidy, organised, under control.

The smack of a hammer and the creak of snapping wood made her look up. Gabriel stood back as the last of the shed toppled down. He glanced at her and winked. She bit back a sigh. He was as fascinating as he was irritating. The man was gorgeous, but he knew it, and he was a law unto himself. Obstinate, too, from what she could tell. One thing was for sure: he wasn't going to be as easy to control as her inbox. In fact, she had a feeling that working with him was going to test her more than anything she'd ever done.

Her phone rang and she snatched it up, relieved to hear her secretary's voice. Tracy was apologetic about troubling her with work-related issues, but Daisy reassured her: 'It's fine, honestly. I don't mind at all. I don't have access to a printer here, but if you send me the documents I'll check them.'

When they'd finished discussing work, Tracy asked, 'How's everything going?'

Daisy glanced at Gabriel, who'd walked away from the wood and other debris scattered across the front of the house. He seemed to have stopped for a break. 'We're making progress. Slowly.'

'The builder's decided to cooperate? Does that mean you can come home?'

'Not yet. Let's just say I'm keeping a close eye on him.'

When Gabriel drove away for lunch, Daisy looked up from her laptop and checked the time. She popped out to the village to buy food but the shops were all shut. A three-hour break in the middle of the day? She couldn't believe it. How did anyone get anything done around here?

She went for a drink in the café to wait until they reopened, waving away the waiter's offer of a sandwich. 'Thanks, but I don't eat bread.'

Fortunately she had her tablet with her so she was able to make calls and respond to emails. It wasn't a complete waste of time. She also drew up a spreadsheet detailing all the tasks Gabriel had agreed to do on the house. Even so, an hour and half later she was tapping her foot waiting for the supermarket to reopen.

When she got back to the house it was late afternoon and Gabriel was measuring and marking the empty patch of ground where the shed had stood. She was disappointed he hadn't made a start on digging the foundations for the new *abri*, as he called it. Who knew how long it would take him at this rate? She watched him surreptitiously from the kitchen. He was so relaxed and moved so slowly. He was also incredibly messy. There was stuff everywhere, and she itched to go out and tidy it. Perhaps a neat environment would help him work faster. Then again, when he whistled that cheerful tune, she couldn't help but smile.

She unpacked her shopping, made a few more calls, then checked on him again. He had paused, spade in hand, and was eyeing the half-dug trench in the ground. Her jaw clenched. He was so slow, it was driving her insane. She'd decided to extend her stay to two weeks, but in that time she expected to see results. She scooped up her tablet, got the spreadsheet up on the screen, and went outside to speak to him, hoping to pin him down on timings. It was clear she was going to have to crack the whip and hurry him along.

'Would you like me to help tidy up?' she offered.

He stopped digging. 'Tidy what?'

'All this.' She pointed to the piles of splintered wood, saws, hammers and other sharp-edged tools that were littered everywhere. 'How about I stack this wood over there out of the way, and collect up your tools? It must be difficult for you to work with all this . . .' mess, disorder '. . . stuff around you.'

'I'm not finding it difficult.' He held her gaze in a look of challenge. Or was it mockery?

'They're a trip hazard,' she said, resting her tablet and phone on the low stone wall nearby. She bent to pick up a saw.

'Leave it!' he said, so fiercely that she almost dropped it. 'If you move my tools, I'll never be able to find them.'

She put it down again, irritated. 'I'm surprised you can find them now, among all this mess,' she muttered quietly, and brushed the dust off her hands.

'And they're not a trip hazard if you don't go there,' he said pointedly.

The ring of her phone was a welcome diversion. It was Tracy again with some urgent questions relating to her most recent cases. Daisy replied quickly and decisively, making a mental note to follow up with a couple of emails. It wasn't easy when the Wi-Fi came and went, but she would persevere.

When she hung up, Gabriel was sitting on the wall. 'I'm stopping for a break,' he said. 'Why don't you join me?'

She tried to hide her disappointment. Another? He spent more time having breaks than he did working. But she kept quiet and sat beside him in the shade. To be honest, she was relieved to get out of the sun. 'Thanks.'

He unscrewed a flask of water, poured it into a cup and took a long slug. His Adam's apple rose and fell. She made herself look away.

'It's so hot,' she said, glad of the cool stone beneath her. Aware of him beside her. He was so solidly built, and everything about him was rugged. Immovable. 'Is it always like this?'

'In July, August, yes. Not in May. This is unusual.'

She fanned herself with her tablet. 'How long do you think it will last?'

His features twisted in that particularly expressive French way. 'No one knows.'

She flipped open her tablet and brought up the spreadsheet she'd prepared with the list of work to be done on the property. 'So what have you achieved this morning?' she asked, keen to remind him that replacing the shed was only one task on a long list.

His lips curved. 'You can see what I've achieved.'

She tried to be tactful. 'There's still a lot to do.'

He glanced at the tablet in her hand, clocking her spreadsheet, and amusement danced in his eyes. She felt a spark of irritation – yet even this didn't kill her awareness of him. She looked at his thighs, so big next to hers, and his muscular arm almost brushing hers. She could smell wood and sweat, and it was so easy to imagine him naked in bed, with that penetrating gaze pinning her down. She pictured his body brushing against her bare skin, and her stomach tightened. She flushed, and focused on the tablet in her lap. But immediately her gaze crept back to his hands cradling his cup of water. His long fingers made it look tiny, his skin was grey with dust.

Forcing her thoughts back to the house, she broached the subject of the project. 'How long do you expect it will take to build this shed?' It would have been far quicker to order a new one made of wood, but he'd insisted that a stone structure was more in keeping with the style of the house.

'It depends.'

'On what?'

'Many things.'

'Like what?'

'The weather, deliveries of supplies . . . many things.'

She looked up at the cobalt sky. The weather seemed fairly reliable. Dry and hot was the order of the day. 'Surely you've planned the deliveries so they don't hold up your work?'

'To a point. But the supplier has other customers to think of. Not just me.'

Another evasive answer, she thought, frustrated. Then she had an idea. 'I'd like to make you an offer,' she said brightly.

He lifted a brow.

'I'll double your pay if you cut out some of your breaks.'

'Cut out my breaks?'

'Yes. You had two hours for lunch, correct?'

His eyes narrowed.

She persisted: 'And you're taking how long now?'

He met her gaze steadily. 'As long as I need.'

She glanced at her watch. 'Well, we've been chatting for ten minutes already, so say you take twenty minutes in the afternoon, plus you took at least two breaks already this morning. If you cut all these out, I calculate you could save three hours per day!' She added steadily, 'That's a lot, don't you think?'

His lips pressed together. They were incredibly soft and full, in contrast with his rough dark beard. They made a woman want to run her fingers over them—

She cut short these thoughts and told herself to focus. She'd come out here to get results, not to lust over his rugged looks.

'It's a lot, but it is necessary,' he said. A muscle ticked in his jaw.

'Is it?'

'Tell me, Daisy Jackson, have you ever done physical work? Building, gardening, digging?'

She followed his gaze to her hands and her pale, unblemished fingers, and felt a hot wash of colour creep up into her cheeks. 'No, but—'

'Then you're in no position to tell me when I should take breaks or how long they should be.'

She met his gaze. 'I'm only trying to find ways of speeding up the process.'

'Rest is important,' he said firmly.

'So is productivity. Don't you love the satisfaction of knowing you've worked as hard as possible and given your clients all you can?' Perhaps years of billing clients by the hour had given her this mindset.

'When I go home I know I've done a full day's work. I'm not lazy, if that's what you're implying.'

'I wasn't . . . ' Her words petered to nothing. Okay, perhaps she was. 'I just get a buzz from getting through a list of tasks and knowing I've accomplished so much.'

'But have you done them as well as you can? I find it's better to do one thing well than many things badly.'

She was horrified. 'I never do things badly. I always give my all.'

'Yet you don't appreciate the value of pausing. Of stopping and stepping back.'

'Yes, but—'

'Rest is important – for the body and the mind.' He picked up a piece of wood and flicked open a penknife. He began to whittle, and curls of wood fell to the ground around his boots, like locks of blond hair.

Daisy snapped her mouth shut, not wanting to get into yet another disagreement. Transfixed, she watched his big hands shave the wood, piece by piece. 'Body and mind?'

He nodded. 'Listen. What do you hear?'

'Nothing.' The valley was still, the distant treetops shimmering in the heat. 'Nothing at all. Don't you find it unsettling living somewhere so deserted?'

He lifted an eyebrow as if she'd just failed a test and continued to whittle at the wood in his hands. 'It's peaceful. I love it here. Listen again. What do you hear?'

She tilted her head, concentrating. 'Well, there's the sound of cicadas and the noise of your knife, but I don't think they really count.'

'They count,' he said. 'Look around you. Use all six senses: listen, smell, see, taste, touch, feel.'

'Feel?'

He nodded. 'The spirit of the place, the atmosphere.'

What nonsense, she thought, but kept her mouth shut and tried to focus as he'd instructed. 'I can hear the wind rustling the leaves of that tree over there,' she said tentatively.

He followed her gaze. 'The olive tree, yes.'

He waited for her to go on.

'And I can feel the dryness of the air, the heat weighing everything down.' She looked around and noticed a line of ants busily trundling up and down the wall nearby.

'And can you smell the perfume of the sun on the pines?' He snapped off a twig of conifer and held it out for her, smiling when she inhaled and her eyes widened at the delicious scent. 'See? You wouldn't have noticed these details if you hadn't stopped to rest now.'

She conceded with a faint nod, but she wasn't sure the benefits were all he made them out to be. She'd much rather be at her desk in London, working through a pile of documents, with a computer, printer and reliable internet service. Sitting there she felt restless, her brain longing to be kept busy. She never stopped and did nothing. She ate lunch during meetings or at her desk, checking through documents. Occasionally, she indulged in a little internet shopping for suits or shoes.

'Tell me,' said Gabriel, 'what is a normal day for you?'

She smiled. 'I get up at six. I have coffee, shower, dress, go to work – getting a latte on the way in,' she added. 'Then in the office I see clients, have meetings, and go home by which time it's late so I—'

'Wait a minute, you don't stop to eat? Lunch, dinner?'

'I get salads. Or, rather, my secretary gets them for me. A salad or a smoothie.'

'What is a smoothie?'

She peered at him. Was he kidding? No, his confused expression told her he really didn't know what a smoothie was. 'A drink. You know, with spinach, banana, chia seeds, that kind of thing.'

His dark eyebrows knitted together in disgust. 'Not together?'

'Yes. It's good for you.'

'That's not food!'

'Nutritionally speaking, it's very healthy.'

'Can you hold it in your mouth and chew it and feel the textures?'

'Well, it's a drink so—'

'Can you savour the flavours of the different ingredients?'

'No. They're all mixed together, but—'

'Do you finish it and feel satisfied? Do you feel pleasure?'

Was it her imagination or did his eyes light up as he said that last word? Heat shot down her spine. 'I wouldn't say pleasure, exactly, but when I'm pushed for time—'

'There is no excuse for not making time to eat and enjoy your food.' He shook his head in disapproval. 'This drink is not a meal.'

She ignored that and forged on, describing her routine. 'Anyway, when I get home I'm exhausted so I kick off my shoes and go to bed. And next day I get up and do it all over again.'

'And weekends?'

'I catch up on all the work that's outstanding.'

'You work weekends too?'

'Often, yes.'

'How do you relax?'

She had to think hard. 'I do a mindful yoga class on Fridays. Oh, and I swim. Three times a week.' Although that wasn't relaxing exactly. She liked to power through the water and get her fifty lengths done in the fastest time possible.

'What do you do at weekends when you have free time?'

She shrugged. 'I shop, visit galleries or shows. I don't have much spare time, to be honest. My career is important to me.'

She worked hard. She was proud of all she'd achieved. She'd always been focused. Serious. Driven. Most of her socialising was work-related.

He didn't look impressed. They had seriously different attitudes to work.

She looked at her list. Somehow they'd got distracted. She'd come out here to speak to him about his productivity, not her life in London. She opened her mouth to speak, but he got in first.

'So, have you always lived in the city?'

She bit back a sigh of impatience. 'Recently, yes, but not always.'

'You lived in the country?'

She put her list down. 'A long time ago.'

He continued to chip away at the piece of wood in his hands and glanced her way expectantly.

'When I was a girl we lived in the Cotswolds. It was very rural. Open fields all around, quiet country lanes, sheep and cattle grazing, lots of trees and blue sky. It was very peaceful. Like this.' The memory stirred old emotions. She hadn't thought about that place for so long. It seemed like a lifetime ago. When they were a family.

'How old were you?'

'I lived there until I was thirteen.'

'When your mother died?'

She was surprised he remembered. 'No. That was later. We moved when my parents split up.'

'Tell me about the place where you lived.'

She stiffened, feeling deeply uncomfortable with this topic. 'What do you want to know?'

'What was it called? Where was it?'

'Primrose Farm. It had a thatched roof, centuries-old stone walls, hawthorn hedges, and it was in the middle of nowhere. The nearest place was a small village called Willowbrook.'

She stared into the middle distance. Tiny snippets re-surfaced. Hazy memories of her mother when she was small, smiling and singing, snatches of song carrying on the air.

Daisy cut short that train of thought. It hurt to remember. After the divorce her mum had fought to keep her, but lost. Within a year she was dead. Suicide. But even then Daisy's dad hadn't come for her. She'd remained at boarding school and he'd continued his new life with his second wife and baby.

Her heart squeezed as she remembered how much she'd missed her mum. The feeling had been fierce. A black hole.

She still missed her now. She hadn't let herself think about it in so long, but coming here seemed to have cracked open a box of memories. Events and emotions she was usually too busy to examine. She rubbed her thumb over the hard metal of her watch.

Her mum had been intimidated by her dad. He'd been a strong personality, too strong for her, and from the scant information Daisy had gleaned about their divorce, he must have ridden roughshod over her in court, destroying her and winning residency of their only child. Daisy sometimes wondered how her mum would have fared if she'd had a better lawyer representing her, someone on her side who would have stood up to him, encouraged her to fight, to appeal, to win. Someone like Daisy.

She blinked, making herself focus on the here and now, and realised Gabriel was speaking.

'I don't know what is hawthorn,' he said.

'It's a wild tree or bush with delicate white or pink blossom. It's beautiful, but it has the most lethal thorns.' She'd scratched her arms on it badly and quickly learned not to go near to it.

He smiled knowingly and his eyes creased, gleaming like polished stones. She couldn't imagine that thorns would trouble him. She couldn't imagine he was afraid of anything. His strength, his calm were mesmerising. As if nothing in the world could ruffle him.

'And you lived there with your brothers and sisters?' he went on.

'I'm an only child. But I had friends nearby and I went to the village school. I loved it there,' she added wistfully.

'Where did you move to when you were thirteen?'

'Boarding school,' she said briskly, and rubbed her toes together. Her gorgeous red Louboutins were scuffed, the patent finish dulled with dust.

She felt his gaze on her. Her skin burned as he studied her. 'You preferred living in the country?' he asked.

'I suppose so. I loved the freedom and the open space . . . '

'Yet you don't plan to live here?' His hand circled through the air, indicating the house and the fields.

This sudden switch back to the present day and their marked differences made her back stiffen. Had he steered the conversation to make a point? Her chin lifted. 'No, I don't.'

'What about for holidays? You do have holidays, don't you, in your Very Important Job?' His eyes glinted. Perhaps he wasn't mocking her but teasing.

'The last time I took a holiday was four years ago.'

'*Quoi?* Four years? Why so long?'

She smiled and said simply, 'I love my job.'

'I love mine, too, but in July and August I stop, I have a holiday, I replenish the well, and when I return in September I am re-energised.'

'Unfortunately, people need divorce lawyers even in July and August.' She was conscious of him studying her and her skin burned, despite the cool breeze and the shade of the nearby tree. 'I think,' she said carefully, 'we have different priorities, you and I. We see things – life – very differently.'

'Yes. We do.' His deep chuckle made her body hum. And yet at the same time his presence was calming. In the short time they'd spent talking, her breathing had slowed, her head had cleared.

'*Tiens.*' He handed her the object he'd whittled.

The wood felt surprisingly soft in her hand. She frowned. It looked like some kind of insect with enormous wings and two beady eyes. 'What is it?'

'*Une cigale*. Cicada.'

'Oh.' She couldn't hide her surprise. Why had he given her an insect? And such an ugly one at that. 'Does it have a . . . particular significance?'

'It's the symbol of Provence.'

'Right.' She stared at the delicate pattern he'd carved to show the veins of the wings.

He drained his cup and got up. 'Back to work.'

'Yes.' She clutched her tablet, which she'd forgotten, side-tracked by their conversation, and he scooped up his trowel.

As he turned away, she frowned. How had he done it? She'd come outside with a checklist but it had gone out of her head while they'd been talking. She didn't like that, around him, she was side-tracked, distracted, diverted.

Chapter 6

Gabriel picked up his shovel and went back to digging foundations for the new *abri*. The ground was clay and rock, and he had to resort to using a pickaxe in places. There was no give in it. This was back-breaking work and he hadn't been lying when he'd told Daisy breaks were essential.

His lips curved. Her obsession with speed and her attempts to crack the whip amused him. Those who knew him could have told her she was wasting her time. He worked at his own pace and never compromised on finish or quality. His work was always impeccable.

But perhaps he was guilty of playing with her a tiny bit. He'd started asking questions to distract her, but he had to confess he'd been intrigued by her answers. She was an enigma. She could be so hard, so sharp, with her spreadsheets and big watch and the way she barked instructions down that phone of hers. He'd seen the way her eyes lit up when it rang and she spoke to her secretary. He wiped the sweat from her brow. Yet when she'd described her childhood home her hard edges had softened and for a moment she'd even looked a little lost. He'd almost wanted to wrap an arm around her and comfort her, run his finger over her pale cheek and smooth away her frown.

Not that he felt sorry for her, he told himself quickly.

He stretched his back and flexed his shoulders, then returned to digging. Whatever haunted her, Daisy Jackson was still the imposter here. Materialistic, imperious. Sneering at the place, complaining about the heat when she was dressed for the city. If Jeanette were here she'd be horrified that Le Mazet had fallen into her hands.

The ground gave way and his shovel sliced through, making the earth crumble with satisfying ease.

Jeanette could not have been more different from Daisy. She'd led a simple life, valuing friends and family, not material possessions. She'd adored her husband and had loved children too, though she couldn't have any of her own. She enjoyed growing her own food in the *potager* at the back and, in her kitchen, transforming it into mouth-watering dishes. She had been frugal, but mostly through choice. She'd tried many times to give Gabriel money, but he always tore up her cheques: he'd never wanted her money. She'd given him so much already: a home, an anchor in the world, love. He leaned on the shovel, gazing at the back of the house. She'd been a wise, generous, caring woman. Sane – right to the end. Which was why he hoped that the end had come quickly. That she hadn't lain conscious, hoping help would arrive in time. He hoped her passing had been as sudden and painless as the doctor had suggested.

Gabriel drew back his shoulders and tried to shake off the thought. There was no point in going over the past. Jeanette was at peace now.

He gripped the spade handle tightly and glared at the house where a shadow passed a window. But she'd be furious that her will hadn't been found, that someone like Daisy had inherited. She hadn't even known of Daisy's existence: she'd been quite certain, in fact, that there were no living relatives, which was why she'd feared the estate would pass by default to the government. No, she'd always been certain the will would be found.

So why hadn't it? Where had she put it? He sighed and glanced up again at the house. His lips curved.

He'd caught Daisy watching him – again.

She darted back into the shadows, but he'd noticed how she looked at him: he knew she was trying to suppress the attraction.

He knew it because he was doing the same.

***

Daisy lay in bed waiting for the scream. A fox, he'd said. And yet it had sounded so human, so urgent. Why would a fox scream like that? Was it hurt? Some kind of mating call?

Memories of Primrose Farm crept back to her. The thatched roof that had looked soft as a cushion but was brittle and hard, the black timbers and cream-rendered walls. The garden, messy but colourful, with tall grasses and a jumble of flowers lining the path to the front door. Had she heard foxes' cries as a child, too?

Although she waited for it, tonight there was no scream. The night was silent, the darkness complete. She'd gone to bed early after having spent the evening feeling a little lost, with nothing to do. She'd sat in the lounge for a while, but couldn't be bothered to light the fire so it had been cold and she'd felt uneasy. The countryside around was so still and she couldn't settle in the house. There were shadows everywhere, dark corners and cobwebs, whispers of the past haunting the air. Or was that her imagination?

But she wasn't as isolated as she'd previously believed. She ran her fingers over the satiny wood of the cicada and pictured Gabriel's hut through the trees. The low roof, the terrace crammed with flowers and colourful pots. Had he moved there to be near Jeanette? Had he converted it from a ruin? Had he bought it believing it was a temporary home because one day Le Mazet would be his?

She laid the cicada on her bedside table and lay back. He hated her. He saw her as the interloper who'd stolen his house, his inheritance. She tried to squeeze these thoughts out of her mind and turned over, tugging at the cotton sheet. It wasn't helpful to try to second-guess other people's thoughts or feelings. Anyway, since when did it matter how others regarded her?

It did, though. The realisation surprised her. She pictured his strong jaw and penetrating dark eyes.

What he thought mattered to her, and she couldn't understand why.

Next morning, she woke feeling disoriented. Where was she? It was too dark to be her London apartment. And what was that noise? A really irritating jingling.

Rubbing her eyes, she got up and crossed the room to the window. She'd closed the shutters last night, and once she'd eventually drifted off she'd slept really well. That bed was so comfortable.

She pushed open the shutters and stopped. What . . .? She blinked.

The field in front of the house was filled with sheep, and the noise she'd heard was bells. Hundreds of tiny high-pitched bells all jangling as the sheep moved, hungrily grazing on her land. She looked down and there was Gabriel, calmly getting on with his work as if there was nothing strange about all this.

Daisy grabbed her dressing-gown and ran downstairs. Outside, she almost collided with him.

'Whoa!' he said, his gaze sweeping over her bare legs. 'Where are you rushing off to?'

She pointed at the flock of sheep. 'What's going on? What are *they* doing here?'

'They're grazing. That's what sheep do.' Laughter lines fanned from his eyes. 'You do know what sheep are, don't you, city girl?'

'Of course I do,' she snapped. He found this funny, did he? Well, she didn't. Being invaded by a flock of sheep was the last thing she needed. 'What I don't understand is why they've turned up on my doorstep. They'll destroy everything.'

'Of course they won't. Marianne's put an electric fence up. See?'

She squinted. Right enough, around the perimeter of the field she could see a thin line of orange fencing. The sheep seemed oblivious as they moved, bleating noisily and hungrily devouring the grass or whatever was growing there, their bells clinking. Yesterday she'd resented the place for being too quiet, but this cacophony was terrible. And the smell – well, suffice to say it wasn't going to be bottled for perfume. 'Who is Marianne?' she asked.

'The shepherdess.'

'So these sheep belong to her? Where is she?'

Gabriel smiled. 'They do. And I don't know where she is. She might have gone to get the rest of them. Or she might simply be eating her breakfast.'

'The rest of them? There are more?' The field was already heaving with woolly bodies.

He eyed the animals assessingly. 'I'd say that's about half of her flock, yes.'

'And you don't think it's a little cheeky of her to have dumped them on my land while she enjoys her breakfast?'

Something in his expression hardened, and she instantly regretted her choice of words: *my land*. But it was her land, and surely it wasn't lawful for someone to abandon their flock on it.

'It's what happens every year at this time. This is on their route up to the Alps where they'll spend the summer months. They'll visit again in the autumn on their way back down.'

'What? But – but they'll eat everything! All my plants!' Not that this place was going to win gold at the Chelsea Flower Show, but still. She didn't want to see what sparse vegetation there was destroyed by marauding sheep.

'That's the point. It saves you mowing this field. Unless you had a better plan for how to do that.'

It was clear from his arched expression that he couldn't visualise her doing it herself. And perhaps he had a point.

'This is supposed to be a holiday let. I can't have a flock of sheep turning up when tenants are in the house!'

'Why not?'

'Because – because . . . ' She faltered. They might find it entertaining, she supposed. Curious, at least. 'Because they're noisy! They're disturbing the peace.'

'Yesterday you told me this place was too quiet.'

'That's how I feel, but anyone renting it would *want* peace and quiet. They wouldn't want to be woken at seven in the morning by a hundred sheep bleating and invading the place.'

'They only come twice a year. It's hardly an invasion.'

'It's an intrusion.'

'That depends on your perspective. Round here we see it as something mutually beneficial. The sheep need land to graze, the landholders need to prevent the vegetation from getting overgrown.' His eyes gleamed as he added, 'Plus the sheep fertilise the ground.'

Daisy wrinkled her nose. 'This shepherdess – does she have permission to do this? Is there a written contract in place? Why was I not informed of it?'

'There's no contract,' he said quietly, and if she hadn't looked closely she would have missed the tiny muscle pulsing in his jaw. 'Just a spoken agreement going back decades – centuries, even. It's an age-old tradition.'

His unspoken message was clear. Who was she to upset an ancient tradition?

She looked at the field of shaggy fleeces and pressed her mouth flat. Perhaps she'd give it a few days. She didn't want to do anything hasty.

After an hour the jingling of bells was driving her to distraction, so Daisy decided to go out. Grabbing her keys, she slid into the yellow car. She'd explore the village, perhaps pick up a few groceries before the shops closed for lunch. But as she headed towards the main car park she was met with barriers blocking the road and signs telling her it was market day.

She'd heard about French markets and was curious to visit one, so she turned back, parked a short distance away and walked in. At a guess, she reckoned it would only take ten minutes. She passed a house where the garden had been given over to growing vegetables. She saw strawberries and tomatoes, and other plants she didn't recognise. As her heels tapped loudly on the pavement, she became conscious of heads turning to look at her. The locals were dressed so casually in shorts and summer dresses that she felt a little conspicuous. But she liked her designer dresses and suits and how professional they looked, how empowered they made her feel, and in London they didn't look out of place. Here, they stood out. Still, she wasn't planning to stay long.

She'd only walked a short distance when an elderly gentleman with a walking stick stopped her. 'Hot, isn't it?' he said in French, pulling off his cap and wiping his forehead with his sleeve.

'Boiling,' she agreed, proud that her French was coming back to her. At school she'd been gifted at languages, but she'd been drawn to a career in law because it was prestigious and well paid.

He gestured to the sky and tutted. 'This is not normal.'

'It's not?'

He leaned on his stick and shook his head. 'In July, maybe, but not May.'

'I'm not used to the heat.' She longed for an air-conditioning system she could control with the press of a button, but the sun was beating down relentlessly on the crown of her head. She fanned herself with her hand, but it made no difference and the air weighed just as heavily.

'You must be the English lady, then?' Shrewd eyes studied her.

'Yes. Daisy Jackson. Pleased to meet you.' She held out her hand to shake his.

'Claude. You speak French well. You shouldn't have any trouble settling in. Right. Better be off.'

Trouble settling in? Daisy opened her mouth to tell him she wasn't planning to stay, but he was already hobbling away from her.

She'd walked only another two hundred yards when a woman with a wide sunhat spotted her and waved. She hurried towards Daisy, clutching a straw basket, which bulged with paper bags and a couple of baguettes. 'Ah! You are the new owner of Le Mazet?'

'That's me.'

'I'm Francine. It's good to meet you. I've heard a lot about you.'

Daisy glanced in the direction of the market place. It wasn't far – she could already detect the delicious smell of bread baking coming from the *boulangerie* – but at this rate it would take her hours to get there. In London people didn't even make eye contact, never mind stop to talk to strangers. She'd never spoken to her neighbours in her apartment block, but here in La Tourelle every man and his dog seemed to want to stop and chat.

'How are you liking living there? Le Mazet is a beautiful old house, isn't it?'

Why did everyone keep saying that when it was grey and shabby? 'It needs a lot of work,' she said tactfully.

'And it's so well placed,' Francine continued, with enthusiasm. 'You have those wonderful views, yet you're within walking distance of the village.'

Daisy smiled politely and nodded. She didn't say that she found it eerily quiet and was relieved when Gabriel arrived each morning and started hammering, sawing and whistling as he worked. Nor did she mention today's surprisingly noisy visitors.

'So you're a relative of Jeanette's, hm?'

'Through her husband, yes. But we never met. I didn't know I had any relations left on that side of the family.'

'Really? That's tragic. Jeanette would have loved to meet you. She desperately wanted children of her own but it wasn't to be.'

Francine smiled fondly, and Daisy couldn't help but wonder about Jeanette. Everyone talked about her with such feeling. She'd clearly been well loved.

'Still,' Francine went on, 'at least she had Gabriel.'

'Yes,' said Daisy, and sneaked a look at her watch. She opened her mouth to make her excuses and leave, but Francine continued, 'Are you staying for the summer?'

'Em, no. I'm planning to let the place to holidaymakers.'

'Oh, that's a shame.' Francine's face fell and Daisy steeled herself, remembering Gabriel's horror when she'd told him her plans. But Francine placed a hand on her arm and said, 'For you, I mean. You might find you enjoy it here. And you have a good neighbour in Gabriel.'

Was it Daisy's imagination or did her dark eyes twinkle as she said this?

Francine continued, 'He's a clever man. He could have been anything he wanted, you know. Doctor, lawyer, businessman. But he had no interest in status or money. He came back here to La Tourelle as soon as he'd finished his studies. He just wanted a quiet life.'

Her tone was affectionate. Did everyone see him as the golden boy? Clearly, they didn't know how he'd delayed work on Le Mazet, ignoring Daisy's messages for so long that she'd had to come herself. The devil in her couldn't help but ask, 'He's quite a stubborn character, though, isn't he?'

'Gabriel stubborn?' Francine laughed. 'Ah, yes. Extremely. But this can be a good quality.'

Daisy wanted to roll her eyes. How was stubbornness a good quality? She much preferred dealing with rational people who were willing to listen to reason. Gabriel seemed to have entrenched views – most of which were diametrically opposed to hers. She nodded politely and said, 'Well, I'd better be off. I'm hoping to visit the market.' At this rate it would have packed up and left before she got there.

'Oh, I've just been.' Francine reached into her straw basket. 'I bought these lavender bags. Here, have some for your house. It must need freshening after being closed up for two years.'

'Thanks.' Daisy blinked at the bunch of small cotton bags in her hand. This stranger was giving her a present – why? What did she want in return? She held one up to her nose and the dry perfume filled her senses. 'It smells divine.'

'You can put them in drawers to keep your clothes fresh, or just leave them out to perfume the air. I'd better go. Enjoy the market.'

Daisy watched as Francine crossed the street and waved. Daisy stared after her. Apparently she hadn't wanted anything in return. How strange.

She continued, keeping the church tower in view as she zigzagged through the narrow streets, a little more confident about finding her way now. She passed a large circular fountain where a couple of children were filling their water bottles and splashing each other, then rounded the corner and there was the market. The smell hit her first: cooked food made her stomach rumble, then flowers and lavender as she passed their rainbow-coloured stalls, and finally the sweetness of ripe fruit: cherries, raspberries and melons. She noticed the locals all had straw baskets like the one she'd seen in the kitchen at Le Mazet. She made a mental note to check if it was usable. It would protect the soft fruit from getting crushed or damaged on the way home.

She bought fruit and vegetables and stopped to look at the fish stall, fascinated by the display. She could count on one hand the types of fish she knew, but here there were dozens of varieties with names she didn't recognise at all.

When the stallholder approached, she shook her head. 'I don't know how to cook it,' she explained. She didn't know how to say in French that the fish she ate in restaurants didn't come with eyes and scales like these. This was all too foreign to her.

'Ah,' said the stallholder, knowingly. 'Then take this tuna steak. It's quick and it's easy. And it's ready to cook.'

He gave her instructions, which did indeed sound very straightforward, but she was still reluctant to take it. 'I'm not much of a cook,' she admitted. Though the truth was she didn't cook at all.

'It's a gift,' said the stallholder, pressing the package into her hands. 'And if you like it, you come back for more next week.' He smiled. Daisy was taken aback. Two gifts from perfect strangers in the space of thirty minutes. Granted, the stallholder was hoping for a follow-up sale, but still. She couldn't remember a time when a stranger had done something so generous for her.

By the time she got back to Le Mazet, the sun was hammering down and the air was thick and heavy. It was a relief to retreat inside the house where it was much cooler. She kicked off her shoes and the stone tiles felt refreshingly cold beneath her bare feet.

As she unpacked the shopping, the sound of whistling made her pause. Outside Gabriel was mixing concrete to fill the foundations he'd dug. The sun bounced off his muscular arms as he shovelled sand into the cement mixer. Daisy couldn't help but shiver. There was something about the way he moved that was so self-assured and calm.

Shaking her head, she flicked open her phone to read her to-do list. The skip was arriving soon and a local charity was sending a lorry late this afternoon to pick up all the old furniture. She was planning to shove the contents of the wardrobes and drawers upstairs into bin bags and dump them in the skip, but downstairs there were a few pieces of furniture that she needed to go through before they were removed, which might take more time.

She began in the lounge and pulled open the drawers of a rustic desk, which appeared to have been cobbled together from old pieces of wood worn smooth with age. It was half empty, with just a couple of shoeboxes of papers, and Daisy wondered if Gabriel had taken anything already. He'd told her he'd been through these drawers several times, but she couldn't help checking too.

As she flicked through the old lady's bank records and bills she thought about the missing will. How must Gabriel have felt as he'd searched fruitlessly for it? It must have been devastating for him not only to have lost Jeanette but then to learn he wouldn't inherit after all. Guilt pecked at her, but she tried to push it to one side and carried on. She found an old sewing box filled with a jumble of needles, thread and wool. There was a sock in there, too, with a hole in the heel, which she presumed had been put aside for mending. Daisy held it up to the light, astonished. When her clothes became damaged or worn she threw them away, and if a new outfit needed adjusting she had it done by a professional seamstress. It simply wouldn't occur to her to do it herself, and she didn't even own a sewing kit. She binned a pile of old receipts and empty seed packets.

Pausing, she gazed through the window at the ink-blue sky. What would she do if she found the will? Destroy it? She couldn't do that, and yet that was what she *wanted* to do. Her skin prickled uncomfortably and she returned to sifting through her dead relative's possessions, not sure if she liked what this said about her.

By mid-afternoon she'd finished downstairs and her conscience was clear because there was definitely no will. She picked up a handful of photo albums and carried them outside to Gabriel, who'd just returned from his lunch break. 'Would you like to have these?' she asked him.

He glanced inside the box. 'These photos are of Jeanette and Benoît's relatives. They're more likely to be of interest to you than me, as her surviving family.'

Was that a snide dig? She wasn't sure, so she decided to ignore it. 'I already looked. There's no one I recognise.'

'Get rid of them, then.'

She ran her fingers hesitantly over one of the photo-graphs, yellowed at the edges, the faces in it unsmiling and sombre as they posed for the camera. 'It's so sad,' she said quietly, 'to throw away someone's memories and treasured photos.'

'Yes. It is.' His jaw was rigid, a muscle corded in his neck.

'If there's anything you want, please take it because I need to clear it all.' Which reminded her: what had happened to the skip, which was supposed to have arrived this morning?

As if on cue, a truck turned into the drive and trundled towards them. On the back, a battered yellow skip rattled as the vehicle bumped over the rough ground.

Surprise flickered through Gabriel's eyes. Then he turned back to her. 'I told you, I've already taken all I want.'

***

Gabriel watched as the truck drove away and Daisy threw the photo albums into the skip, then went back into the house. He tried not to think about Jeanette or what she'd feel to see pictures of her relatives dumped in this way, and he set to work mixing more concrete.

On Monday he'd start building the walls of the new hut. He glanced at the pile of authentic old stones he'd sourced locally. They were an excellent match to the farmhouse. Probably rescued from a house some tourist had bought and modified in the way Daisy had planned, he thought wryly, knocking down walls and replacing them with breeze blocks.

Another lorry arrived, this time a tall one with what looked like old furniture inside. A couple of burly men greeted him as they marched towards the house. They emerged a little later carrying a wardrobe.

Gabriel stopped and watched as they manoeuvred it into the lorry. It was the wardrobe from the back bedroom, which had once been his, and watching it loaded onto a lorry stirred up all sorts of emotions. He took a glug of water. He'd told Daisy he didn't want any of Jeanette's things, but she hadn't said she was going to dump it all like rubbish. Okay, he conceded, maybe she'd mentioned a clear-out. But she hadn't told him it would happen now – today.

The men returned with a stack of chairs and a couple of bedside cabinets. Gabriel's eyes narrowed. How much was she getting rid of? Surely she wouldn't throw everything away. When they emerged again, balancing a chest of drawers between them, Gabriel threw down his shovel and stamped off to find her.

He found her in Jeanette's bedroom, stuffing old sheets into bags. The bed linen was slightly yellowed with age, but he recognised the delicate blue embroidery: it had been Jeanette's favourite. His heart gave a violent thump as he registered that the room was empty. All the furniture gone, including the bed. Only the outlines remained where dust had gathered beneath the wardrobe and cabinets and greyed the floor tiles.

'Who are those men? What are they doing?' He pointed at the hallway where they'd just tramped past.

Startled, she whirled round and her eyes widened with confusion, but she quickly recovered her composure. 'Taking the furniture away.' She blew a strand of hair out of her eyes and her brow glistened with sweat.

'What – everything?' He swept his hand through the air. He couldn't believe the ruthlessness of it.

'I'm keeping a few bits and pieces – a bed, the sofa and so on – as a stopgap, but apart from that, yes, everything.' She twisted the bag shut and dusted off her dress.

How could she be so dismissive? He felt winded. He simply hadn't expected this. 'Why?' he asked incredulously. 'Why everything?'

She peered at him as if he'd asked a question with an obvious answer. 'None of this was my style,' she said, gesturing to the empty room. 'I'm planning to replace it all with new modern furniture.'

He stared at her. She was so casual about it, as if furnishing an entire house was nothing to her. How could she afford it, for one thing? And for another, how could she be so callous?

He moved to the window and watched the men lift an armchair into the truck. Jeanette used to call it her grandmother's chair and it had been in her bedroom. A cushion fell off and landed on the ground. One of the men picked it up and slung it into the van without a backwards glance. Gabriel's throat tightened. Who knew where the furniture would end up? Perhaps in landfill if it didn't sell, or on a bonfire.

And along with the furniture, all hope of finding Jeanette's will was gone too.

His hands balled into tight fists. The rational part of his brain knew he'd searched every wardrobe, every drawer and corner of every piece of furniture – yet he still felt a rip in his chest as he watched them carry away Jeanette's belongings. His fingers curled. 'You've only been here a few days and you've emptied the place. How the hell did you manage to arrange all this so fast?'

'I contacted the charity and they said they had a lorry coming by this area today. I just got lucky.'

His teeth clenched. 'You have no respect, no patience at all, do you?'

'Respect for what? Who? This house has been empty over two years now—'

'And you've made the decision to trash all this in the space of three days! You couldn't have waited? Lived with it for a while? If you'd given it time you might have changed your mind or – or found some of it useful.'

'I don't have time,' she said, holding his gaze, her eyes glinting furiously like polished silver. 'I'm only here a few days. And, anyway, I know what I like.'

The heavy tread of boots on the stairs signalled that the men were coming back. Daisy took a deep breath. In a gentler tone she added, 'I also thought it would make your life easier if the place was less cluttered when you came to rewiring, plastering and replacing the plumbing.'

He frowned, caught on the back foot with this – this consideration. 'I suppose.'

'You seem shocked, Gabriel. But I warned you.'

She had, that was true, and he'd said he didn't want any of it. Would he have answered differently if he'd known it would all be whisked away within the hour? They worked on different timescales, him and her. He remembered her pointing to her spreadsheets and tapping her enormous silver watch. He was fuming at how heartlessly she'd emptied the house, but he couldn't help feeling a nudge of admiration for her efficiency and single-mindedness. Clearly she was a woman who knew what she wanted.

The sun slanted in, the lemon-bright light making her blonde hair glow.

He shook his head. 'You're not one for sentiment, are you?'

'Why does that sound like a criticism?'

'I thought you'd keep some of it, maybe give the rest away. There might be people in the village who could—'

The shrill ring of her phone cut him short. 'Excuse me,' she said, quick to answer it. 'I'm expecting a call from a client.'

He pursed his lips, unimpressed.

'Please, Daisy,' a man's voice said on speakerphone. 'Just let me—'

Her face went pale and she jabbed the screen to cut off the call. Her pulse hammered at the base of her throat.

Gabriel frowned. 'What's the matter? Aren't you going to speak to him?'

'No. It wasn't who I thought it—' She stopped as if she'd said too much.

He studied her, noticing how her brows were knotted behind her big glasses, and her eyes flitted nervously about the room. His curiosity was piqued. She was normally so assertive, yet that caller had knocked the confidence right out of her. 'You can call them back, I don't mind. We can discuss this later.'

She blinked rapidly. 'It – it's no one important. What were you saying? That your friends in the village . . .'

He glanced at the lorry. 'It doesn't matter,' he said quietly. 'What's done is done.'

Laetitia was right: he had to accept that the will was not going to be found.

Outside he watched the lorry fill with armchairs, lamps and rugs, and sighed. Gone with all that furniture were memories of his life here, of Jeanette. Had he done the right thing in allowing Daisy to get rid of it all? Should he have kept it? This wasn't what Jeanette would have wanted, was it?

He wasn't sure. Perhaps she would have been pragmatic about it. Certainly if the house had been his she would have told him to do what he wanted. She'd always been understanding.

But it wasn't him throwing everything out: it was Daisy. And she wasn't thinking about what Jeanette would have wanted. She was thinking only of how to generate the maximum money from the place. His fists balled with frustration.

And there was nothing he could do but stand by and watch.

Chapter 7

Daisy pushed her glasses up her nose, then picked up a second box of rubbish destined for the skip outside and balanced it on top of the first. The heat was unbearable. Her dress was sticking to her and she longed to finish the job and step under an icy shower. But she didn't even entertain the idea of asking Gabriel to help with the rubbish – not after their confrontation earlier. Her brow creased as she carefully made her way downstairs and remembered his angry words. *Was* she being disrespectful in emptying the house? She didn't think so. The furniture had been cheap, rickety and riddled with woodworm.

Perhaps she should have waited to replace it, though – for Gabriel's sake. She remembered how his dark eyes had glittered furiously, like a starry night. He'd implied she was cold-hearted, but it wasn't her fault he was the emotional type and she was pragmatic.

She looked at her phone. Was she cold-hearted? She tried not to think about that call – yet another that had got through and left her feeling unsettled. Vulnerable. She wouldn't let him do that. She elbowed open the door to the kitchen. Forget it. Forget him. She refused to give him any place in her life, even in her thoughts.

Outside on the terrace she paused. What with sheep in the field and the removal guys tramping back and forth to their lorry, there was only one possible route to the skip and that was across the side of the house where Gabriel was working. She shifted the heavy boxes in her arms and picked her way around a pile of stones, a shovel and a couple of bags of cement. Why couldn't Gabriel pick up after himself instead of littering the place with tools and equipment? He paused in building the wall and shot her a ferocious look. She didn't know why he was so angry when she'd given him the chance to take whatever he wanted from the house. Lifting her chin, she passed him. She couldn't do anything right by him. Christ, if her solicitor had warned her this house would come with its own personal gatekeeper she'd have thought twice about—

Something caught her foot and she lurched forward. The boxes flew out of her hands, their contents scattering, and she landed face down on the stony ground.

She lay there for a moment, dazed, then heard the rapid crunch of boots on gravel.

'Daisy?' A big hand brushed the hair away from her face and those caramel eyes studied her, dark with concern. 'Are you all right?'

'I'm fine,' she said, wishing he'd help her to her feet instead of peering at her like that. She sat up gingerly. The farmhouse tilted a little, the terracotta roof tiles rippling like waves. She wanted to get up and walk away from this humiliation, but she wasn't sure her legs would cooperate. She glared at Gabriel. 'I told you there'd be an accident if you left your tools lying around!'

His mouth pinched. 'And I told you not to come here!'

'How else was I supposed to get to the skip?'

'You could have waited. But, no, you never wait. With you everything has to be done right now,' he snapped his fingers, 'like that.'

'At least I get things done and a five-minute task doesn't drag out for days or weeks!' she fired back. She wiped her damp forehead, putting her dizziness down to the infernal heat.

He pressed his lips together and bent to pick up her glasses from the floor. 'Your glasses are broken,' he said, holding the two pieces out for her. 'I'm sorry.'

She waved them away. 'Oh, they don't matter.'

He frowned. 'But you won't be able to see.'

'They're only fashion glasses.' She dusted herself off, then noticed a dark stain on her dress and her heart sank. The dirty chainsaw nearby had dripped oil all around. Damn! This was one of her favourite dresses and now it was ruined.

'What are fashion glasses?' asked Gabriel.

'Not prescription. The lenses are just glass,' she explained impatiently. 'To be honest, I'm more worried about my dress. It's a Gucci classic, you know.' She dabbed the stain and her finger came away black with oil.

'I don't know why you're wearing a dress here. Or those shoes. It's no wonder you fell.'

A rush of heat made her neck prickle. She put her hands on her hips. 'What?'

'If you'd been wearing sensible clothes and flat shoes you wouldn't have tripped.'

'Oh, so it's my fault, is it?'

'No, it's mine. I've already apologised.'

'You apologised for breaking my glasses.'

'What – that's not enough?' His lips pressed flat. 'Fine. I'm sorry you fell, too, all right?'

They glared at each other.

'But if you were wearing more suitable clothes you'd be more comfortable and I wouldn't have to listen to you moaning about the heat all the time.'

'I haven't been moaning! Anyway, it's over thirty degrees. Anyone would feel hot – even in a bikini!' Instantly, she regretted saying that. The thought of wearing nothing but a swimsuit in front of him only made her flush even more.

She got up. Gabriel held a hand out to help her, but she ignored it. As she straightened, his expression changed.

'What now?' she snapped. 'Why are you looking at me like that?'

He pointed to her forehead and regret filled his eyes. 'You have a bump,' he said.

Daisy touched her brow. Ouch! The lump felt huge. 'It's nothing,' she said quickly.

He stepped closer. 'Let me see.'

'I'm fine.' She moved to pick up the boxes she'd dropped and their scattered contents, but he reached out and caught her arm. A flash of electricity shot from his touch, which startled her so much that she stopped.

He looked into her eyes. 'Does it hurt?' he asked quietly.

She swallowed, a little thrown by his unexpected concern. 'I told you, no.'

'Do you feel dizzy?'

'No.' Okay, perhaps she did a little, but only because his gaze was trained on her so intently and his face was just inches from hers. Any woman would feel light-headed.

'How many fingers am I holding up?'

'Gabriel, stop it. I'm fine.'

'Maybe. But I think you should sit down just in case. *Allez!* Come into the shade.'

'For goodness' sake, I'm not concussed. It was just a fall.' She spoke these words but at the same time she let him take her arm and lead her to the terrace. His grip was firm, his concern a welcome change from his usual glowering hostility, and she sank gratefully into a chair in the shade.

He disappeared into the kitchen and returned with a glass of water and a small bundle of ice cubes wrapped in a tea-towel. He held this to her head. 'Keep it there for a few minutes,' he instructed, and knelt in front of her.

She lifted her hand to the ice pack and their fingers touched. His gaze connected with hers, unguarded for a moment. Concerned. Tender. Electric.

Then a shutter came down over his expression and he took the seat opposite her.

Daisy held the ice pack in place. It was deliciously cold and her skin tingled with pleasure. Or was that the effect of the man sitting opposite her? He might have gone back to his usual pensive scowl, but she'd seen the desire in his eyes. And she knew it mirrored her own.

He gestured at the broken glasses on the table. 'Why do you wear glasses if you don't need them? I don't understand.'

'Because they're designer, fashionable. And they project the right image.'

Out of the corner of her eye she noticed the men loading the last of the furniture into the van and stopping for a drink.

'The right image?'

'Serious. Wise. Not sexy or frivolous or anything else that might get in the way of my work.'

'What?'

She sighed. He wouldn't understand. 'They help focus minds on what I do rather than how I look,' she said impatiently.

His eyes widened, as if it hadn't occurred to him. 'This is a problem you have?'

'I'm young, blonde and female. What do you think?'

He seemed perplexed. 'But you're a lawyer. An intelligent woman.'

'Not everyone views it like that.'

Silence followed as he absorbed this. If she was honest, it had become less of a problem over time, but when she'd been starting out in her career and trying to prove herself, it had sometimes been frustrating to be judged on her appearance. Since then, her glasses had become part of her uniform, a defence mechanism. Now she felt a little naked without them.

The quiet moment felt like a tiny ceasefire of some kind, so she took advantage to say gently, 'Are you still cross because I gave away Jeanette's furniture?'

'I was surprised, that's all. Now it's done. *Fini.*' He drank his water. 'How is your head? Do you need painkillers?'

'I told you, it's fine.' She took a deep breath. 'Gabriel, I know it must be difficult for you seeing it all go. I'm sorry. I should have warned you . . . '

'Forget it.'

She frowned. He'd repeatedly said that he didn't covet the house, but he'd looked so shocked to see it being emptied earlier. Was it because he'd hoped the will was in there somewhere? Daisy blew a strand of hair out of her eyes. She didn't know what he was thinking or what his motives were, but she remembered the old saying: *Keep your friends close, keep your enemies closer.* Whichever he turned out to be, she had a vested interest in getting to know him better.

'I know you think it's heartless of me to have cleared the house, but I have to think in terms of mass appeal so people will want to rent it. I have to be practical about this project.'

His eyes narrowed instantly. 'It's not a project. It's a house. A home. With a history.'

This was tricky. He was so emotionally connected with the place. She could see it in the tension of his shoulders and the deep frown that cut through his brow, she could feel it coming off him in waves.

Guilt drilled through her. She tried to detach herself as she did in her work, but it wasn't so easy to do here – with him. She kept thinking about the boy he'd been and how he'd grown up here. He'd been promised this place would belong to him, and having already lost Jeanette, he'd then lost the house too.

The clunk of metal doors closing made their heads swivel. The men had finished loading the lorry and one came over to thank Daisy.

'I hope you can find good homes for it all,' she said, and shook his hand, careful not to look at Gabriel.

'That looks painful.' The man was pointing to her fore-head.

'*Je m'en occupe*,' Gabriel growled.

I've got this, she translated. Daisy wondered if he meant the injury or her.

They watched the lorry drive away, kicking up dust as it trundled down the drive.

'It's late,' said Daisy, looking at her watch. 'You probably want to get going too.'

'I'll stay an hour. To be sure you're all right.'

She didn't say no. This place was so quiet and the evenings dragged. Now she'd cleared the house there wasn't much left for her to do, and she simply wasn't getting enough work through from Tracy to keep her busy.

'How about an *apéritif*?' she suggested, and began to get up.

Gabriel held up a hand. 'Let me,' he said firmly. 'I know where everything is.'

'Of course you do,' she muttered, as he headed towards the kitchen. She couldn't help but admire how those shorts moulded his muscular figure, and she wished he'd take his tool belt off, for goodness' sake. It was too damn sexy.

'You didn't clear the kitchen, then,' he said, when he returned.

She didn't reply. Truth was, she planned to replace all the copper pans and mismatched crockery once the kitchen had been updated. She wanted everything to be new for the people who'd rent the place.

'What would you like to drink?' He nodded at the tray of bottles, glasses, ice and olives.

'What are you having?'

He pointed to an unopened bottle. '*Pastis*.'

'I've never had that before.'

'Never?' The corners of his mouth lifted as he poured a little into a tall glass. 'You can't come to Provence without tasting *pastis*.'

She watched, fascinated, as the clear liquid turned cloudy when he added water and ice.

'Here,' he said, handing a glass to her and keeping one for himself. 'Cheers.'

'*Santé*,' she said. She sniffed it, then took a sip. It had a strong aniseed flavour and made her feel tingly. Alive.

She glanced at Gabriel, who was helping himself to a fat green olive. The hills and fields shimmered in the heat and the only sound was the scratching of cicadas. She cleared her throat. 'Gabriel, I have a proposal for you.'

This caught his attention. Was it her imagination or did a hungry look flash through his eyes before they narrowed warily? 'A proposal?'

'I know you feel an injustice has been done regarding the house and Jeanette's will, so . . . I'd like to offer you a lump sum.'

His expression changed to puzzlement.

So she clarified: 'Cash. As – as compensation, if you like, for the house.'

'What?'

She explained again and named a sum, which amounted to approximately one third of the property's value. A significant amount. A week ago she would have scoffed at the idea of offering so much to a stranger who'd staked a claim to the house without any legal grounds. But now, well, her perspective had shifted.

In truth, she wasn't sure any more who was in the right regarding the house's ownership. She felt a little uncomfortable knowing how much the place meant to him. And she was tired of it constantly coming between them: she needed his help and didn't want to fight with him.

He banged his glass down on the table. The sudden noise made her jump. 'You think I want your money? What for?'

'To help you buy another house. Or extend your own, carry out improvements. I just want to help . . . ' Her words trailed away as his expression became thunderous.

'I don't want your money!' He pushed his chair back and began to pace the terrace, just as he had done in his living room that first day when she'd been to see him.

He stopped and pointed a finger at her. 'I told you already. This isn't about the money or the value of the house. It's about this!' He held a fist to his heart. 'It's about Le Mazet and Jeanette and the promise *she* asked me to make.'

Daisy was perturbed. It was rare for her to misjudge a situation quite so spectacularly. 'I know, but I thought you might . . . this money would—'

'You thought money would solve the problem, *hein*?' he cut in. His disgust reached into her and touched something. She shifted in her seat. 'You thought you could be the generous one handing out charity to the less fortunate. You thought if you paid me enough I would go away and stop interfering with your plans for the place. Leave you *carte blanche* to do as you please and not have to think about respecting the house's heritage.'

She shook her head. 'You've misunderstood, Gabriel.' She searched for the words to explain, but his horror, the evidence of how deeply she'd insulted him, was etched into his features and it made words seem futile. 'I wanted to help, that's all,' she finished quietly.

He studied her, his brown eyes intent, then something in him appeared to soften a little. Her heart beat fast, and she was relieved when he sat down again.

'I didn't suggest it to make you go away,' she said, 'and I understand that you want me to preserve the house's authenticity and I will, I promise. I was simply trying to . . . rectify the situation in a small way.'

A couple of sparrows chased each other through the nearby trees, a burst of fluttering wings and high-pitched chirruping. She didn't know how they had the energy. Although the sun was sinking, the light fading to violet grey, the air remained heavy with heat.

'You always think money will solve everything, don't you?' he asked, his tone no longer accusing, but curious.

'No, I don't,' she said carefully, 'but it often does. And if not, then it can compensate. Clearly in this case I misjudged the situation.' Her head throbbed. She lifted her fingers to rub it, but winced when they touched the lump.

'It's painful?'

'A bit,' she conceded. She was suddenly so tired. Tired of the heat, of this place, where everything was so different from what she was familiar with, of Gabriel with his intense emotions and fiery reactions. She couldn't do anything right here – she was constantly floundering and flailing. She missed her London life where her reputation went before her, where people sought her advice and valued her opinion.

'What are you having for dinner?' asked Gabriel, abruptly.

'What? Oh, salad probably.' She glanced at the kitchen and smiled wryly. 'I was given some fish at the market – I might have that. Although I'll probably burn it or find some other way to make it inedible.'

She got up and collected their glasses. The *apéritif* was clearly over and he wanted to get on his way.

'I'll cook it for you,' he said.

She laughed. 'Don't be silly. I wasn't hinting, if that's what you think.'

'I don't think this. I believe you cannot cook.' His eyes creased as he smiled. 'I saw the contents of your fridge when I fetched the olives.'

'What's wrong with the contents of my fridge?' It was well stocked compared with her kitchen at home. She'd learned fast that she had to be organised here and couldn't rely on the local shops and restaurants being open at any predictable time.

'There's nothing in it! Only sparkling water and lettuce leaves. A rabbit would go hungry.' His eyes gleamed in the fading light.

She smiled. 'What does your fridge contain?'

'Meat, cheese, a casserole, fruit, yogurts ... Shall I go on?'

She bent to pick up the tray of glasses and bottles, but he took it from her and carried it into the house. She followed.

In the kitchen he opened the fridge and took out the tuna. 'This is the fish?'

She nodded.

'It will take only minutes to cook. I'll go home, have a quick shower, then come back and make dinner for both of us.'

Her heart gave a tiny jump. She was hungry, and she hated the lonely evenings here. 'There's no need, really. I'm happy with salad.'

'Salad alone is not a balanced meal. You need to eat more or you'll disappear.' His gaze swept over her, but it didn't match the disapproval of his words. It was hot, it was hungry.

A flare lit inside her. 'You're saying I'm too skinny?' she asked, her voice low.

He didn't answer straight away, but dug in his pockets for his keys and weighed them in his hand. 'No . . .' he said, barely meeting her gaze. His cheeks streaked endearingly with colour, and it was a welcome contrast with his sharp frown earlier.

She watched him stride away to his pick-up and smiled to herself. Whatever their differences of opinion and disagreements, they definitely connected on a physical level. The sexual attraction was indisputable and growing with every hour they spent together.

He returned fifteen minutes later, showered and wearing black jeans with a T-shirt that hugged his torso. He smelt of shampoo and his hair, still damp, flopped over his eyes. Daisy had showered too and changed into a clean dress, short-sleeved but made of thick navy stretch material, solid and well-fitting. She wished she had something less clingy because it was still warm even though the sun had sunk behind the hills. If he hadn't been here she would have changed into her satin nightie and let the cool breeze wash over her skin. The secret thought made her thighs tug.

He set to work in the kitchen, calmly slicing the courgettes lengthways and chopping garlic, which he must have brought from home because she hadn't bought any. 'These would be delicious on the barbecue,' he said, with an air of regret.

'Is there one here?'

'No. Jeanette would never have one. She said the risk of forest fire was too great.'

Daisy glanced out at the trees and fields. She thought of the dry twigs and grass that cracked underfoot wherever you stepped. This place was indeed tinder dry. 'You disagree?'

He tipped his head to one side. 'It's fine as long as you're careful. Locals know never to use them when it's windy, and in summer sometimes they're banned. But most of the time it's nice to cook like this. The flavour is better.'

Gabriel fished in a drawer and pulled out a mustard yellow tablecloth decorated with a pattern of olives. He took it out and spread it over the table on the terrace, then went back in and loaded a tray with cutlery, glasses and napkins.

'Here, let me help with that,' she said, and carried the tray out.

She took her time laying everything out just so. Really, she was avoiding being in the kitchen with him. He seemed so at home, so relaxed and in control. There was something . . . sensual about the way he moved confidently from fridge to stove to sink, heating oil in the griddle pan, poking at a pan of white beans, laying out the courgettes so they sizzled and seared, seasoning the tuna. She fetched the basket of bread he'd brought, rosé wine in an ice bucket, and citronella candles he'd pulled out of a drawer.

Just as she finished he appeared, two plates in hand. '*Voilà,*' he said.

'Already?' She couldn't hide her surprise. 'It only took a few minutes.'

He nodded. 'It's quick and simple. The best dishes are.'

He put the plates down and flicked a switch she hadn't noticed by the back door. Tiny lights came on all around the terrace and they'd been threaded through the tree too, electric fireflies in the night.

'Wow,' she said, sitting down and gazing around her. It was romantic, cosy, intimate. She felt heat pool in her centre.

But she held back on letting lust lead her down its predictable path. Things were complicated between her and Gabriel. Their relationship was delicate. Volatile.

'Cheers,' he said gravely, lifting his glass.

She chinked hers against it. 'Cheers,' she said, slightly bewildered by the day's strange string of events. One minute she and Gabriel were arguing passionately, the next . . .

this. A candlelit meal. It made her head spin. Of course, that might be down to the bump on her head.

She tasted the griddled tuna and the cannellini beans, detecting sweet garlic. The courgettes melted on her tongue. Over the years she'd eaten in many expensive restaurants, and this was as good – if not better – than anything she'd been served. 'This is delicious,' she said. 'So simple, yet the flavours are incredible.'

He smiled and broke off a piece of bread. He offered her some. She shook her head, although it was so tempting her mouth watered. She took a quick sip of wine instead.

He ate hungrily and it made her wonder if his appetite would be as voracious in bed, if he'd be as unrestrained, as passionate—

He looked up and caught her watching him. She dropped her gaze quickly, smoothing the napkin on her lap as if it required all her concentration, and hoped the darkness would conceal the fire in her cheeks. What was it about this man that he could unnerve her so?

'What do you plan to do once this place is finished?' he asked.

'I told you. Rent it out.'

'To tourists?'

She nodded.

'So it's a money-making scheme for you?'

'An investment,' she corrected.

'Because you need money?'

'No. Because I want my savings to generate income.'

'You want your money to make more money,' he said flatly.

'Yes.' She met his gaze square on. 'Listen, I know you disapprove, but you have to accept that the house is mine.'

'I do accept it. I'm trying to understand what your plans are, that's all. Your motives, your goals in life. You talk about investments and property and generating income, but these are all ways of saying money. It seems to me that you like money.' He speared a piece of tuna and ate it.

Daisy bristled. She felt he was judging her, but what right did he have? What right did anyone have? 'I *do* like money,' she said. She valued promotions and pay rises and, yes, she valued her apartment, her designer wardrobe and her healthy bank account. 'Money doesn't lie to you. It doesn't break promises or let you down or betray you. You know where you are with money.'

He looked so shocked by this that, for a moment, she thought she'd won the upper hand. Then he said quietly, 'But you can't take it to bed at night.'

The air shimmered with suggestion. A tiny shiver touched her bare arms, and the corner of her mouth lifted. 'Can't you?' she asked. She wasn't naïve. Wealth made her more attractive to the opposite sex. It made men want to linger and infiltrate her life, hoping to profit from it. But she always expelled them without a second thought.

Gabriel shook his head. 'It doesn't keep you warm or take care of you.'

'It pays for people to do those things.' Her gaze locked with his defiantly. 'I'm proud that I've achieved all I have, and the money I earn gives me choices. It buys me nice things and – and it means I don't have to rely on anyone else. I can take care of myself.'

His glass was halfway to his lips. 'This is important to you?'

'Yes. It is. I like my independence.'

He laid his knife and fork on his empty plate and sat back. 'So what do you plan to do with all your money? Will you get married and buy a big house in London?'

Her laughter sounded harsh. 'I have no plans to get married, no.'

'*Ah, oui*. I forgot – you don't do relationships because your job has made you too cynical.'

'Correct.'

'You plan to stay single always?'

'Why not? I'm happy that way.'

'Yes. You have money instead.'

She shot him a hard look.

'What about when you get older? Don't you think you might change your mind and want company?'

'No.'

'Someone to look after you when you're sick?'

'I'll pay a nurse.'

'A nurse won't hold you when you're scared or sad or lonely.'

She shrugged this off. 'I'm not often scared or lonely.' Her words were clipped and dismissive, but a corner of her mind felt a little unsettled. For some reason she thought of Jeanette who'd died alone here, and glanced up at the house, which had stood empty since.

The question that had been niggling since she'd arrived here rose to the surface. 'Tell me, how did Jeanette die?'

He looked a little surprised by the sudden change in topic. 'Heart attack.' His head turned and he gazed absently at the back of the house in the direction of the pool and the orchard.

Daisy waited for him to go on.

'She was in her *potager*. How do you say – where you grow vegetables?'

'Vegetable plot.' She knew where he meant. The area was overgrown with weeds now but the outlines of rectangular beds remained, and a pile of bamboo canes was nestled with a coiled hosepipe against a disused well.

He nodded. 'The doctor said she died quickly, but how can he be sure? I found her in the evening. What if she fell earlier and was still conscious? She could have been there all day. If I'd called earlier perhaps I could have helped.'

Daisy heard the regret in his voice and her heart tugged. He held himself responsible. 'You used to visit her every day?'

He nodded.

'I'm sure the doctors know what they're talking about.' Whatever had happened, it couldn't be changed now. She decided to steer the conversation back to where they'd started. 'What do you see as your future, Gabriel? What do you hope for in life?'

He was single now, but she wondered how many women there had been in his life. She was hungry to know more about him, what made him tick.

'I don't wish for lots of money,' he said pointedly.

'No?' Her tone was defensive. 'What do you want?'

'I hope to find a woman I love and have a family – a big family – of my own.'

'Right.' She might have known, and it was all she could do not to roll her eyes.

'You're pulling that face because you don't believe in love?'

'Correct.'

'You're a cynical divorce lawyer,' he mused, referring to their previous conversation, 'yet you must have witnessed love – in other people, your friends, relatives . . .'

'Oh, I see plenty of people who *think* they're in love, who delude themselves that he's the perfect one, she's their soulmate and so on. But it never lasts. Eventually the novelty wears off, the masks fall away, and it inevitably turns sour.'

The sheep in the field behind her had settled for the night, but every now and then the odd one bleated or a bell jingled. They weren't as irritating now. In fact, there was something quite comforting about having them nearby. Perhaps it was just better than being alone here.

'Sour?' said Gabriel. 'Not always.'

'Ninety-nine per cent of the time.'

He blew out a long, slow breath.

'You disagree?' She smiled at his scowl.

'Yes I disagree. I believe we all have someone out there who is meant for us. We just have to find them.'

'So you haven't found her yet?'

'No. But I will.'

She studied him from behind her glass of wine. His certainty was visible – in the set of his jaw, in the slow, sure way he leaned back in his chair. 'What will she be like?'

'I don't know. Actually, that's not true. I don't know what she will look like, but I know she will want children as I do, and she'll value family and love above all else. Above money or status.'

That stung. It stung more than Daisy cared to admit, but she did her best to ignore it. She wasn't ashamed to put her job and career above all else. It was her passion.

He went on, 'And when I meet her I'll know straight away. It will be – how do you say? *Un coup de foudre.* Lightning . . .'

'Lightning strike,' Daisy translated. 'That's lust at first sight – sex – not love.'

'No.' A deep frown sliced through his brow. 'It will be love. I'll feel it here.' He held a hand to his heart.

She shook her head. 'I couldn't disagree more. You can't possibly know a person when you meet them for the first time. You simply respond on a primitive level – with hormones and so on.' Their eyes met and she felt a hum of awareness. Immediately, she wished she hadn't mentioned sex and hormones because right now her hormones were whirling uncontrollably.

'No,' he said finally, his jaw rigid. 'You are wrong.'

She glanced up as a couple of shadows flitted about above their heads. They moved so fast, darting around at sharp angles, it was hard to focus on them properly.

'Bats,' Gabriel explained. She grimaced. 'They won't do you any harm. They're eating the insects.'

Silence stretched. Then Daisy asked quietly, 'So what will you do when you meet her, this perfect woman of yours?'

'I'll love her for the rest of my life,' he said, as if it was plainly obvious.

He was such a romantic. She had to admire that in him, even if he was naïve with it. Perhaps she'd become cynical because of her job, but she didn't care. She was a realist. She'd never be disappointed in love because she'd never allow herself to be deluded by it.

'Have you never felt it?' Gabriel asked. '*Un coup de foudre?*'

'No.'

'You've never met a man and felt your heart pound, your mouth go dry?'

'Like I said, that's physical attraction.'

'So when you meet a man and feel this way, what do you do?'

Her heart was beating faster, as if someone had doubled its speed, like she did when she listened to audiobooks and was impatient for the story to move forward. 'I talk to him, buy him a drink, and if the attraction is still there two hours later, I go to bed with him.'

He stared at her. 'The same night?'

She laughed at his shocked expression. 'Welcome to the twenty-first century, Gabriel.'

'And then? Something happens? You develop feelings for him?'

She laughed. 'No. I leave.' Before dawn. Always. It was her unspoken rule and it meant things never got messy.

'You leave in the night?'

'Yes.'

'Like a thief?'

'Yes. Like a thief.' She giggled softly.

'So what's the longest relationship you've ever had? The man you said was married – how long were you with him?'

Her mouth hardened. She'd forgotten he knew about that. 'Three months,' she said coldly. For three whole months he'd managed to string her along.

'Is he the reason you don't trust any more?'

'Who said I don't trust? I'm not interested in relationships. It's not the same thing.'

His silent look of pity made her cringe.

'Fine,' she said. 'Believe that if you like. It doesn't make any difference to me.' She took another sip of wine and glanced away, but the image of him, tall and dark, sitting opposite her, remained imprinted in her mind. He was so inescapably good-looking that her body simply couldn't switch off from wanting him.

Yet you don't trust him, do you?

The house, the missing will, their polar-opposite attitudes to life: there was so much coming between them.

She bristled, because perhaps he had been right after all. Perhaps she did have trust issues.

But she dismissed the thought impatiently. She was sensible, that was all. Only a fool walked blindly into open arms. Far better to stick with her approach. She acknowledged the attraction and she acted on it. End of story.

★★★

Gabriel watched her turn away. Candlelight cast gold shadows across her face, highlighting her fine features and peach-like skin.

It was time to be honest with himself. He found her deeply attractive – physically, but also intellectually.

He felt as if they were playing a game, dancing. Every conversation swung between challenge and concession, conflict and the confession of secrets. When she wasn't uptight and armed with a spreadsheet, he found her engaging, challenging, intriguing. His first impressions hadn't been wrong exactly – she was domineering and demanding – but the more he got to know her, the more glimpses he caught of her vulnerabilities. Tiny snapshots of fragility that made him curious to learn more about her.

How could she see the world so differently from him – as if black was white and white was black? He couldn't understand it. Love was beautiful, and necessary. As essential as oxygen or water. Yet she didn't believe it existed. Her world must be a grey place, devoid of hope or happiness. She was a woman who knew what she wanted, who wasn't afraid of her sexuality, and he liked this, but how could her affairs bring her any satisfaction? And what made her so cynical?

'I like you without the glasses,' he said.

'You do?'

He nodded. She'd been cute with them, but she was beautiful without. 'I think you used them to hide. Now I see the real you.'

She laughed. 'You're reading too much into the situation. They were just glasses, not a mask. I haven't been leading a double life or anything.'

He remembered what she'd said earlier and wondered what had happened to make her feel she needed them. Anyone could tell she was intelligent and capable. She wore so many layers of armour: her expensive dresses and dagger-like heels, her enormous silver watch and the iPad that she clutched to her like a shield. All of it made him wonder what lay beneath. Who was the real Daisy Jackson? He itched to unfasten that long hair and run his fingers through it. He'd love to smooth his thumb over those full lips and make her realise she didn't need that kind of armour.

He blinked. He was getting carried away.

She might be beautiful and her conversation, her outlook, might be intriguing, but she was also materialistic and mercenary about Le Mazet. He'd do well not to forget that.

Chapter 8

Daisy stirred, and took her time opening her eyes, emerging from the cocoon of deep sleep. She sat up and gingerly touched her fingertips to the bump on her head. It felt smaller today. And less sore.

If you had been wearing sensible clothes and flat shoes you wouldn't have tripped.

She could hear the quiet crooning of pigeons. The air felt warm for early morning. She looked at her watch and realised with a shock that it wasn't early. She'd slept in. And by the sound of it Gabriel was already at work outside. The tinkling of sheep bells carried on the air, too. She closed her eyes and enjoyed replaying in her mind last night's meal with him. The darkness studded with fairy lights and candles, the delicious food, the meaningful conversation about money and love. They didn't agree on either, but it didn't matter to her. She loved how passionately he held his beliefs. She found him enthralling.

Once she was showered and dressed, she went down. She made coffee and carried it out onto the terrace. The heat of the sun was like a gentle hand on her face.

Gabriel came over straight away.

'I didn't know you worked Saturdays,' she said.

'I don't normally. But my employer is a slave driver.' She smiled. He added, more seriously, 'I wanted to finish concreting the foundations so they have time to dry and I can start building the walls next week. It should only take me half a day. How is your head?'

'It's fine.'

He came close, and she felt a tingle of awareness as he inspected it. 'It's gone down a little,' he said, stepping back. 'What are you doing today? You'll take it easy?'

'It's difficult to do anything else here.' She laughed. 'Actually, I need to go clothes shopping. I only brought enough for a week and most of them need dry cleaning so I'm running short of clean things.' She couldn't bring herself to admit she was going to heed his advice and buy more suitable outfits.

'Is that so?'

His eyes sparked with humour and she knew he saw straight through her. She couldn't help but smile too. 'Where do you recommend I go?'

'For women's clothes? I have no idea.' He pulled his phone out of his pocket. 'I'll ask Laetitia. She'll know.'

After a brief conversation with his friend, he recommended a big shopping centre by the motorway and jotted down directions. 'It's a fair drive,' he warned.

'That's okay. I don't have anything else to do today.'

An hour later, Daisy walked through the shopping centre, disappointed. It wasn't what she was used to. They had none of the designer labels she'd have found in Paris, Nice or Monaco. But she supposed it didn't matter too much. She was only buying enough clothes to last the next week or so. After that she'd probably never wear them again.

She bought shorts, T-shirts, pumps and flat sandals. She was so used to wearing heels that it felt strange to slip on flat sandals. Then she spotted some summer dresses and added a few to her basket, along with a sunhat. Everything was so cheap. And they didn't look bad on her, either. She'd always paid extra for the perfect fit and good-quality fabric, but these dresses swung freely around her knees and the necklines were surprisingly flattering. After she'd paid, she changed into one of the dresses, a white cotton A-line embroidered with a pattern of blue flowers. It felt really comfortable and cool after her tight-fitting work dress, and she wore the sandals for the drive home. Still, without her familiar uniform and glasses, she felt a little unsure, a little out of her comfort zone. But in all honesty, she'd been feeling like that ever since she'd stepped onto this property.

She pulled up outside Le Mazet just as Gabriel was packing up to leave. She saw his brow lift as he clocked her new outfit and she felt a thrill at his appreciative smile.

'Your trip was successful, then?' he asked.

'Very. Please thank your friend for the recommendation. They had everything I needed. I even found a coffee machine.' She glanced at the box under her arm. It would make the next few days here a little bit more bearable.

'Good.' His gaze swept over her again.

'You like my dress?'

He grinned – and were they stripes of colour in his cheeks? 'It suits you.'

His approval triggered a flurry of sparks in her. She glanced down at the cotton dress. 'Thanks.'

'You look more relaxed. Not so . . . uptight.'

'I'm not sure if that's a compliment.' She laughed, then looked around, sensing something had changed since this morning. Surprised, she said, 'The sheep have gone.'

'Yes.' He dropped a shovel into the back of his truck. 'I told you they were only passing through. Your field is nicely trimmed now.'

'And fertilised,' she said drily.

'Yes.' Their eyes met and he smiled.

'Right. Well, I'd better check my emails,' she said briskly, and glanced at the spot where he'd been working. The area was covered with thick plastic sheets pinned down with heavy stones.

Gabriel followed her gaze. 'Yes, I finished,' he said, with mock weariness.

'Why did you cover the concrete?'

'To hide the fact that I haven't done the work.' He winked.

'Very funny.'

'To slow down the drying process and prevent the water from evaporating too fast. It's a problem in this heat.'

'Ah, I see. Well, enjoy the rest of your weekend.'

'And you.' He slung the last of his tools into the back of the pick-up. 'Don't work too hard on those emails.'

She smiled as he got into his truck and drove away, kicking up clouds of dust.

Once he'd gone, she went over to the plastic sheets and lifted a corner to check. He had indeed finished the foundations.

Daisy shut her laptop and leaned back in her chair. She'd done all she could on the Elms case, and she'd read through Miss Newsome's pre-nup twice more than she'd needed to, but now she had to admit there was no work left in her inbox. She gazed around at the quiet, empty fields. Even the sheep with their irritating bells and bleating would have been more welcome than this silence. The back of her neck prickled with unease. The rest of the evening and the weekend stretched ahead of her, long and empty. The rundown house loomed over her with its uninviting bare rooms and shadowy corners, and she wondered if she'd ever be able to relax here.

She touched her forehead where the lump had almost completely vanished. She was annoyed that her thoughts kept returning to last night's meal as if it had been something special. It had simply been a treat to be cooked for, that was all, and perhaps the wine she'd drunk had tinged the evening with gold too. She'd be fine by herself tonight. Perhaps she should drive down to the village and buy a bottle of wine to go with her chicken salad. There was some bread left from last night's meal, too – would it really matter if she broke her diet and had a small piece? Getting up, she grabbed her car keys and purse.

Ten minutes later, she left the shop clutching a bottle of red wine, and headed back towards the car park. As she walked, she glanced across the road and spotted Gabriel with his friends at the café. A collection of empty glasses suggested they'd had at least one round of drinks already. She waved politely and he replied with a quick nod. She heard a murmur of questions to which Gabriel responded and she guessed they were talking about her.

Hurrying on, she glanced right and stepped out to cross the road. The sound of a car horn blared, and she looked left to see a car almost upon her. Heart slamming, she jumped back. The car roared past, barely slowing, and she stared. Her heart thumped. She could have been killed.

Shocked, she stood there a moment, struggling for air. Then hands wrapped around her. 'Are you all right? Are you hurt?' a woman asked.

Daisy blinked. 'What? No – I'm okay, I think.' On the ground were the shattered remains of her bottle of wine, but that hardly seemed to matter compared to what could have happened. She'd been lucky.

A brunette with kind eyes and waist-length wavy hair was supporting her, and Daisy was glad because her legs suddenly felt shaky. Gabriel appeared too, clearly furious. He cursed in French. 'Unbelievable!' he growled.

'I know – it was my fault. I forgot and looked the wrong way.'

'I mean the driver,' Gabriel said. 'He was going much too fast.'

'Oh.' She was conscious of the fury billowing off Gabriel, like a black cloud, as he and his friend exchanged heated words in French. Then he disappeared into the café.

'Come,' said the brunette, and steered Daisy across the road too. 'Sit down while you recover. You're in shock.'

Daisy let herself be led without any arguments. 'Where's Gabriel gone? He's really angry.'

The brunette squeezed her hand. 'The driver of that car is always speeding, and Gabriel gets especially mad because of what happened to his family.'

'His family?'

'They were killed in a car accident. A speeding driver.'

'Oh.' Daisy didn't know what to say.

'He wanted to go after the man, but I told him to ring the gendarmes instead. They will deal with it. That's Gabriel for you, always fighting for what he thinks is right. He's a man who feels passionately. My name's Laetitia, by the way.'

The Laetitia who'd recommended where to buy clothes, Daisy remembered. She was pretty in that effortlessly French way. Long dark hair and deep brown eyes that sparkled conspiratorially.

'Hi. I'm Daisy.' She smiled.

Gabriel emerged from the café with a glass of iced water. He put it down in front of her and crouched so his face was level with hers. 'Are you all right?' he asked.

She looked into his eyes, seeing concern blended with the dark memories of his past, and a rush of warmth hit unexpectedly. 'I'm fine.' Her voice was a thin whisper.

He and his friends did a quick round of introductions and hit her with a volley of names: Jacques, Solange, Alain . . . She forgot most of them instantly, but understood that Laetitia and Patrice were married with two young children: their daughter Giselle was playing nearby while her baby brother slept in his pram.

'You dropped your wine?' the man beside her – Jacques – asked.

She waved this away. 'It doesn't matter. I was going to have it with my dinner.'

'You mean Gabriel did not cook for you tonight?' asked Patrice, with a wink.

Gabriel glared at him. Daisy blushed. Clearly he'd told them about their meal together yesterday. What had he said? Had he bragged? Or had it been an act of charity?

'Gab's a very good cook,' said Jacques, and punched him playfully in the arm. 'You'll make someone a good wife one day, my friend.'

They all laughed. Gabriel, seemingly unperturbed, rolled his eyes and sipped his beer.

'He is a good cook, but he's got enough to do working on Le Mazet,' said Daisy. 'I'd rather he focused on getting that finished.'

When he shot her a dark look she shrugged. It was true.

'Yes, he's extremely slow, isn't he?' said Jacques, with a wide grin.

She looked up in surprise and smiled. 'A perfectionist,' she said tactfully.

'*Comme un escargot*,' said Alain, triggering another ripple of laughter.

'Like a snail,' Laetitia translated, in case she hadn't understood.

In fact, Daisy had understood and she got the feeling that teasing each other was par for the course with this group of friends. They all had a twinkle in their eyes and laughter lines that suggested they didn't take life too seriously.

Jacques told her, 'We never send Gabriel to get ice because by the time he comes back it's melted.'

Alain nodded. 'If he offers to drive you home say no – you can walk faster than he drives.'

Everyone laughed.

'Yes, and if you plant an acorn and ask him to build you a house, the acorn will have become an oak before he's finished.'

Daisy chuckled. Gabriel shook his head, clearly used to this good-natured teasing. 'I do things properly. My walls are built to last for ever.'

Laetitia tipped her head in acknowledgement. 'He is the best, this is true.'

Daisy felt emboldened by the banter. 'Can't you do things well and a bit quicker too?'

'This is the way I am. You want my services? You accept it will not be done overnight.' His eyes glinted.

'Yes, but some time this year would be good,' she countered.

His friends roared with laughter and slapped him on the back. 'You've met your match at long last, *mon vieux*!' said Jacques.

Gabriel smiled. Streaks of plum tinged his cheek-bones.

Daisy relaxed. 'So how long have you all known each other?'

'*Depuis toujours*,' said Jacques. 'Always.'

'Since we were at school,' Gabriel clarified. 'We all grew up here in this village.'

So they knew all about his parents' accident and Jeanette, she thought. They'd been there. She couldn't imagine what it must be like to know people all your life.

Was it stifling, claustrophobic? Or reassuringly familiar? Either way, their laughter made her feel at ease.

'And you live in London, Daisy?' asked Laetitia.

'I do.' She felt a pang as she thought of her apartment overlooking the City.

A few of the men muttered something, then got up.

'Want a game of *boules*?' Jacques asked her.

Daisy raised an eyebrow in surprise. 'Thanks, but I'd better go. It was lovely to meet you all.'

As she drove home the group's warm welcome stayed with her. There were no pretences, no barriers between them. She could see that they shared a special closeness, and she felt an unfamiliar ripple of envy. In London she ate, slept and breathed work. When she socialised it was to celebrate with colleagues or to network. Occasionally, she met up with a couple of old school friends but she hadn't kept in touch with many. Boarding school had been difficult because when she'd started, aged thirteen, everyone else already knew each other. She'd always felt like an outsider.

What would it be like to have friends like Gabriel's? People to talk to and laugh with, who wouldn't judge or calculate how you could be useful to them. She realised she had no idea.

'She's nice,' Laetitia said to Gabriel, once Daisy had turned the corner and vanished out of sight.

'Yeah. Why did you say she's uptight?' asked Alain.

'She's wound as tight as a coil. Didn't you see it?'

'I saw an attractive and intelligent woman,' Laetitia said pointedly.

'An attractive, intelligent woman who's obsessed with money and speed and her Very Important Job, and doesn't give a damn about Jeanette's home.' He didn't mention how, without the big glasses, her soft grey eyes were even more arresting than before. He didn't confess that he found their conversations enthralling and enticing. He'd never been so curious to understand someone before, to get to know what made her tick.

But that was only because he and she had such contradictory views.

They all became quiet. Giselle was chattering to her dolls.

Then Alain said, 'You can't forgive her for inheriting the house, can you?'

Gabriel's jaw hardened. He didn't answer.

'It's not her fault,' said Jacques.

He glowered into his beer. He knew that, but rational knowledge and emotion were two different things.

Jacques leaned back in his chair. 'It'll eat you up, Gab. Make you bitter and twisted.'

'Yeah, he's right,' said Laetitia. 'And I really like Daisy. She's got a spark about her.'

Murmurs of agreement rippled around the group. And he had to concede that she was all sparks and fireworks.

But he thought of the way she'd ruthlessly emptied the house and the hum of attraction gave way to anger. 'She threw out all Jeanette's furniture like it was junk. She talks about the house being an investment, and how she's in a hurry to get back to the city.' He shook his head. 'She's rich and materialistic, and values money and belongings over people . . .'

They threw each other careful glances. No one said anything.

'She's your typical city girl,' Gabriel finished weakly.

'Can you honestly say you've given her a chance?' asked Laetitia. 'Because we all know how impossibly high your standards are. I've told you before, Laforêt, the perfect woman does not exist.'

He sighed.

'Laetitia's right,' said Jacques. 'You should cut Daisy some slack.'

'Yeah, you're not so perfect yourself.'

That made everyone chuckle. Gabriel frowned. Of course he wasn't perfect. But he knew more about her than they did.

However, as he went home, his friends' words trailed him, like a hungry animal. Perhaps they were right and he should give Daisy a chance. Perhaps he was too critical. She thought differently from him – so what? She'd soon be gone, out of his life. Maybe in a few years she'd tire of the place and sell it, and by then he might have saved enough money to buy it.

He sighed. Owning the property didn't matter to him. It was keeping his promise to Jeanette that was important. And he'd do that. He'd watch over the house, albeit from a distance, and if there was any problem he'd be on the phone to Daisy Jackson immediately. One way or another he'd make sure Le Mazet was cared for.

'Uh-oh,' said Gabriel, when he saw her approaching. 'Here she comes with her spreadsheet.'

His eyes gleamed and his lips twitched, which made it difficult for Daisy not to smile too, but she tried to remain serious. Businesslike. 'Just checking where you're up to.'

She knew exactly where he was up to. He was on another of his interminable breaks, sipping water and peeling an orange with his bare hands. But she figured it didn't hurt to show him she was watching.

'You don't need to,' he said mildly. 'I know where I'm up to.'

She looked at her watch and tried to keep her frustration in check. 'Gabriel, it's Monday and so far you've taken a shed down and built a quarter of one wall. I'd really like to see more progress before I leave next week.' She hadn't even asked for the damn shed, and he worked so slowly, choosing every stone with such care that she feared he'd never begin on the house where the real renovations were desperately needed.

One by one, he dropped the pieces of orange peel onto the wall beside him and they built up into a teetering pile. 'I'll do what needs to be done and do it well. I won't compromise on quality or finish. This place deserves love and care and time.'

She looked at the house with its greyed, crumbling stones, broken tiles and weeds sprouting from the gutters. It needed a lot more than love. More like a radical overhaul. But she remembered how well cared-for his cottage was, and bit her lip.

'Why are you in such a rush anyway?' he asked, carefully cleaving the peeled orange in half.

'You said you'd finish work end of June and have two months off in the summer. I'm worried the work won't be done by then.'

'Even if it isn't, does it matter?'

'Yes!'

'Why?'

'Because the house has been standing empty long enough. My plan was to come back this summer, check it's fit for purpose, then start letting it out.' At the rate he was working it didn't seem like that would ever happen.

His mouth flattened.

'If the renovation work drags on into the autumn, the holiday season will be over and the tourists will have gone. I'd really hoped the work on the house would be well under way when I leave next week.'

A flutter of birds sprang from the trees behind them as if something had startled them. She didn't expect Gabriel to understand and, really, why should he? It wasn't as if she desperately needed the income this place would bring. She just found it so frustrating that it was sitting empty and neglected. She hated being unable to control his schedule or make the renovations happen faster.

'If you're so worried about my work why don't you stay longer?' he asked.

His question threw her. She turned to look at him and his innocuous smile unsettled her. 'What are you saying?'

'Why not stay longer? Then you could keep checking my progress, and keep track of how long my breaks last.' He winked and went back to his orange, carefully peeling a segment away from the rest.

He was teasing her. 'I wish I could, but I have to get back to work. I'm extremely busy.'

He popped the orange crescent in his mouth. She swallowed. Her gaze dipped to his biceps. It was tempting to stay. *He* was tempting.

'And I want to get back,' she went on. 'I love the city. I really miss it.' She looked around at the empty fields and endless trees.

'Yet you said you were happy in your childhood home in the country.'

'That's different. I was a child. I loved running around the fields and woods. Now I'm an adult. I have a job and a life I love in the City. This place is too still. Everything's too . . . slow.'

'You prefer fast.' It was an observation rather than a question. He was watching her with that penetrating gaze of his. 'What are you afraid of, Daisy?'

'What?' His question unsettled her. She tugged at the collar of her T-shirt, suddenly hot and uncomfortable despite her loose clothing. 'I don't know what you mean. I'm not afraid.'

'No? When your colleagues and clients ring you look happy, and when you're working too. But when you finish and find yourself alone with nothing to do you look . . . lost.'

She swallowed. He was right. Lost was exactly how she felt. But that was only because this place was nothing like she was used to. She was a fish out of water here. That wasn't the same as being afraid . . . was it?

He went on, 'There's a look in your eyes of . . .' he searched for the word '. . . panic. As if you're afraid to be alone with yourself and no distractions.'

Perplexed, she hurriedly pushed aside the suggestion. 'I just miss London,' she said, a little defensively. 'I really miss it.'

He chewed slowly, studying her. 'What do you miss?'

She considered this a moment. 'The energy, the pace of the city, my job, helping my clients, the way there's always something going on – restaurants, galleries, culture.'

He blew out a breath. 'That's a long list.' He frowned. 'You think we don't have culture here?'

There was nothing here, only the café, the *tabac* and retired men playing *boules*. None of those passed for culture.

'We have restaurants, cinemas, concerts too,' he went on.

'Not many.'

'True. But those we have are quality.'

'Right,' she said doubtfully. 'Where?' She calculated you'd have to drive an hour to the nearest town and two or more to get to Marseille.

'There is a concert every fortnight here in the village.'

'Really?'

He nodded. 'In the church. There's one tomorrow.'

She pictured a group of amateurs playing squeaky instruments accompanied by a local school choir.

'As for restaurants, there's Maman Gilberte's,' he went on, 'the pizza van comes on Thursday and Friday, and we have our own cinema.'

Pizza van? She tried not to laugh. And the cinema? She pictured the tiny place with the art-deco frontage that probably had one showing a day. 'Admit it, that cinema doesn't show the latest Hollywood blockbusters, does it?'

His eyes widened in a look of horror. 'Why would you want that? It shows only French *cinéma*.'

Daisy suppressed a smile. He sounded proud of this, when it only confirmed her argument that the place was backward.

'Just because life here is not like in London doesn't mean it's inferior.' She said nothing. 'You could adapt. Learn to slow down and appreciate what's around you.'

Her gaze settled on his lips and she couldn't prevent the sparking sensation. 'How should I do that?' she asked, her voice low.

He held her gaze. 'I could teach you. Food, wine, a beautiful sunset. These things can all be as satisfying as a Hollywood film.'

She squeezed her knees together, remembering their candlelit meal. She'd enjoyed his company. She'd enjoyed not being alone. 'I'm game for that, if you are.'

'Wednesday, then. I'll show you a sunset you'll never forget.' He nodded, as if it was settled, and put the last piece of orange into his mouth.

She smiled, more excited than she dared to admit by the prospect.

He added, 'And you should go to the concert tomorrow.'

'Are you?'

'Of course. I'm very cultured.' His dark eyes danced with humour.

She laughed. 'Maybe I will.'

A long silence followed, but it was comfortable. A tiny lizard, as slim as a pencil, flashed past and disappeared under a rock.

'I will have the work done before the summer break,' Gabriel said quietly.

She glanced at him. 'What?'

He waved at the house. 'You have my word. It will be done before July.'

'Oh – I mean, that's great.' Her eyes narrowed. 'I hope you're not saying that so I'll get off your back. Because it won't work, you know. I'm a bit of a control freak.'

'A bit?' He grinned.

She smiled.

He went on, 'I'm saying it because you are worried. But you don't need to be. It will be done.' He picked up his water bottle and took a long drink.

She had to force her gaze away from his lips, but she waited expectantly for him to finish. Was he going to want something in return? Make her promise to butt out and stop asking him what he'd done each day?

But he remained silent and got up to go back to work.

She stared after him in surprise. Maybe he didn't want anything after all.

***

Gabriel kept one eye on the house as he bent to pick up a stone. Weighing it in his hand, he decided it was too big and tossed it back on the pile. He scooped up another and reached for his trowel, but his mind was only half focused on the wall he was building. He heard the murmur of voices as Daisy and her visitor came out onto the terrace. Her second visitor this morning. The first had been a notorious painter and decorator from the next town, and now this stranger with the smooth looks of a male model and a twinkle in his eye. He was clearly putting on all the charm for Daisy, and from the sound of her high-pitched giggle, it was working.

Gabriel thumped the stone down harder than was necessary and irritation gripped him. What was she up to? Why was she always planning and organising, intent on getting things done at a hundred kilometres per hour?

Finally, they shook hands and the man got back into his van and drove away. Gabriel marched straight over to her. 'Who was that?'

'What?' she said distractedly, and waved at the retreating van. 'Oh, Paul. He's an interior designer. Look at the colour schemes he came up with. I quite like these traditional colours.' She had a dreamy look in her eyes as she fanned out the swatches of blue and gold Provençal fabrics for him to see.

But Gabriel wasn't interested. 'And why did you get a painter? I can decorate the house.' He jabbed a finger at his own chest.

Surprise made her blonde eyebrows lift. 'I didn't know you did decorating.'

'I do most things.'

She said carefully, 'He might get it done quicker.'

'You're obsessed with speed!' he said, throwing his hands in the air. 'That guy is a cowboy. He'll slap the paint on and splash the floor, the windows – everything. He'll leave brush marks everywhere. When I paint the finish is perfectly smooth. I do it properly.'

'I don't need to decide yet. I can—'

She broke off because her phone began to ring and, of course, she answered straight away. 'Hello?'

Her expression changed to one of horror and she hurriedly jabbed at the screen and put her phone away.

He frowned. 'Who was that?'

'No one.'

Hot colour bloomed in her cheeks and he could see her pulse flickering at the base of her neck. 'Was it the same person you didn't want to speak to the other day?'

'No – yes – it doesn't matter.'

He stepped closer and peered at her. Her gaze darted away, like a trapped bird. 'You're upset.'

'I'm fine.'

He could tell she was she trying to put on a brave face. 'Is it a man?'

She didn't reply. Of course it was. Was it her married ex?

He was surprised by the ripple of concern he felt. Admiration, too. She was determined to manage alone, yet it was clear this man had some kind of emotional hold over her. Gabriel's muscles tightened as a rush of protective-ness hit him.

'Tell me,' he said softly.

She shook her head and tried to get past him. He didn't stop her but he didn't move to let her past either. She looked up at him, her grey eyes clouded with emotion.

After a long moment she sighed. 'It's my dad. He keeps trying to get in touch. He won't take no for an answer.'

'No?' He was confused. 'Why wouldn't you want to speak to your father?'

'You won't understand. I – I just don't want to.'

'Why not?'

She gave a dry laugh. 'All sorts of reasons.'

They sounded like the cold, mercenary words he'd come to expect from her. Yet the hurt in her eyes told another story. She was right, he didn't understand – but he wanted to.

'When the painter gives me his quote I'll make a decision,' she said dismissively. As if to end their conversation.

'What?' He was thrown by the change of subject.

'Whether you should do it or him. And let's see how long it takes you to finish the renovations.'

She hurried back inside the house and he watched her go, troubled by how ruffled she'd looked a moment ago. As if the armour she wore had momentarily slipped, revealing a chink of vulnerability. And it unsettled him.

It unsettled him more than he cared to admit.

Chapter 9

Inside the house, Daisy rested a hand against the broad chimney and made herself breathe. It was cooler here in the lounge, and for once the shadows welcomed her, the bare-plaster wall felt solid beneath her palm.

Why had she told Gabriel about her dad? Why did hearing his voice still have the power to upset her like this? She closed her eyes. It always swept her back in time to when she was thirteen years old, being led up the steps to boarding school, trying to make sense of the news that her parents were separating. She could still feel the queasy churn of her stomach and the clammy fear.

Her parents hadn't sat her down and told her calmly or rationally. They'd never taken the time to explain. No, a car had simply arrived outside Primrose Cottage and her dad had appeared with a suitcase. There'd been screaming, tears and hysterics on her mother's part, accusations and insults hurled across the room, like hand grenades. Daisy had stood, bewildered, in the middle of it all and it was only when she was driven away that it became clear her life was never going to be the same again.

Of course, that had been years ago and she was an adult now. Wise, and well aware of the likely fallout of relationships.

She took another deep breath. Her pulse was gradually returning to normal and the sound of the cement mixer outside reassured her that Gabriel had gone back to work. She didn't want him – or anyone – to see her like this. She picked up her phone. There was an easy way to avoid any future upsets like today's. She'd simply block her father's number.

'Try it,' Gabriel said. 'What do you taste?'

It was evening, and they were sitting side by side at the top of the hill behind Le Mazet on the picnic rug Gabriel had brought, with a basket of wine, olives and salty biscuits. They'd driven here to watch the sunset, but they still had a good thirty minutes to wait. Daisy sipped the wine he'd given her. 'It's delicious.'

His lips curved and he shook his head.

'What? Why are you laughing at me?'

'Because you drank it so fast, you can't have tasted it! Here, begin by looking at it in your glass. What colour is it?'

'Er – red.' She couldn't help adding, 'Red wine usually is.'

He clicked his tongue. 'Not true. Some reds are dark and plummy, others so light you can see your fingers through the glass.'

She peered at hers again. 'This is somewhere in between?'

'Yes. Now swirl it in the glass, then breathe in its aroma, its perfume.' He demonstrated, and she copied him.

'Wow!' she said. 'It smells totally different from how it tastes.'

He grinned. 'Tell me what you smell.'

'Why don't you tell me since I always get it wrong?'

'It's not a case of right and wrong. It's very personal. What you smell I might not. Have a go.'

'Okay.' She brought the glass to her nose again and inhaled. 'Blackcurrant. And something green. Vegetal.' She couldn't find the words to describe it but it reminded her of trees and woodland floors, places where she'd played as a child.

He nodded. 'It's a little woody. Oaky.'

Next, he taught her to hold the wine in her mouth and savour it, thus letting the flavours develop. 'How was it?' he asked, when she'd swallowed.

'It tasted different that time,' she said, astonished.

He nodded sagely. 'Because you have different taste buds at the front and the back of your mouth. You see? If you rush, you miss so much, Daisy Jackson.'

She wasn't sure which was more intoxicating – the wine or watching him run his tongue across those sensual lips of his as he gazed into the distance. 'I should warn you, this might be wasted on me,' she said, gesturing to the sinking sun. 'I don't think I have the patience.' She felt fidgety already. She'd never sat still and appreciated nature before.

'But you enjoyed the concert last night, *non*?'

She tipped her head in acknowledgement. 'That was different. It was culture.' And she hated to confess how pleasantly surprised she'd been by the string quartet. They'd been truly excellent. Even the music they'd performed hadn't been the usual run-of-the-mill popular choices, but more unusual works.

'The sun is beginning to go down,' he said, and pointed. 'See the view?'

She looked over the fields and the forest. They were the same fields and forest she'd seen from the house, just smaller from up here on the hill. 'Yes.'

'Don't you see the beauty in it?'

'Um . . .'

He sighed. 'Look at the colours. The shades of green in the trees, the gold of the fields.'

The fields looked parched to her, the pine trees spindly and grey. Nothing like the luscious green of her childhood. Why was she thinking of her childhood again? She quashed the memories hurriedly.

Gabriel went on, 'Can you smell the sweetness of the sunlight on the earth? The richness of the perfume of the plants and flowers around us?'

She inhaled. She could smell him, his very male scent, which made her long to slide closer and run her hand over the muscles of his arm.

'And listen,' he said, still watching her. 'Can you hear the birds in the distance?'

She craned to hear, but out of the corner of her eye she could see his chest rising and falling and hear the steady rhythm of his breathing. 'Can you hear the wind whispering? The trees murmuring their secrets?'

'Trees don't have secrets.' She smiled. He was teasing her, wasn't he?

He offered her an olive and she took it. It was juicier in her mouth than she'd expected. She licked the oil from her fingers before she realised he was watching. His gaze lingered on her lips, and she felt a sharp thrill.

'Don't they? They've been here a lot longer than you and I will be. Why shouldn't they have secrets?'

She laughed softly and sipped her wine, savouring it – as he'd taught her – before she swallowed. It tasted vibrant, seductive, fiery on her tongue.

'Ah. You're learning,' he said. 'You appreciate wine, at least, even if you don't appreciate what is around you.'

'I thought we were here to watch the sunset, not have a wine-tasting session.'

'We are. But all this,' his hand arced through the air, 'is part of the experience. The colours, the sounds, the smells. Besides, you should not look at the sun just yet. It will damage your eyes.'

'I know.' Her eyes were not the only thing in danger of burning. She felt feverish, impossibly aware of his body, inches away from hers, his long fingers cradling the tiny glass of wine.

She inhaled the evening air. It was still warm, but comfortingly – not oppressively – so. A bird called in the distance. There was something so raw, so primitive about this landscape, and Gabriel looked so peaceful, so at home here. What was it like to feel you belonged in a place? Not just because it was your address, but because your heart was attached to it. He was clearly a sensual, spiritual man, but she'd sensed the same fierce love of the place in the villagers she'd met.

She focused her gaze on the terracotta roof of Le Mazet. Jeanette must have loved it too, to have stayed here all her life. Curiosity stirred in her about the woman and about him.

'How did you meet Jeanette?' she asked softly.

He blinked, clearly surprised by the question. 'She was a family friend.'

'Your parents knew her well?'

'Around here everyone knows everyone. As Jeanette had no children or family of her own she was always happy to help when we were small. She was like a surrogate grandmother I suppose for me, my brother and sister. More so after my parents died.'

He offered her a small cracker, and took one for himself too.

Daisy hesitated, but curiosity gnawed and she had to ask, 'What happened? Laetitia said there was a car accident.'

She half expected him to snap and refuse to talk about it. But he surprised her.

'A speeding car was travelling in the opposite direction and hit them,' he said matter-of-factly. 'These country roads can be lethal.'

'People drive very fast,' she agreed.

'Ah. Look,' he said, and pointed at the horizon. The sun was half submerged in the trees and, as they watched, it sank and swelled and the sky flamed, deepening from a gentle apricot to a velvety rich coral. With each second it changed, like an incredibly subtle firework display.

'Wow,' Daisy said, without taking her eyes off it. Her voice was an awed whisper. 'You were right. It's beautiful.'

'Look at the forest now.'

She followed his gaze. The orange-tinged trees had taken on an ethereal quality. Their edges were blurred, their colours veiled by the terracotta glow, and the air around them shimmered. 'It's . . . magical.'

'And listen. Even the birds have something to say.'

She turned to him, but her smile faded. The special light of the sunset lit his features, accentuating the strong line of his jaw, the fullness of his lips, and made his eyes darken to deep pools of caramel. And it made her thighs squeeze. She ached to touch her palm to his face, she ached to do so much more, but he nodded at the sunset and said, 'Watch. It doesn't last long.'

She turned to look, running her tongue across her lips, trying to quell the longing that gripped her. The sun sank, growing heavier, darker, bigger, and she held her breath. He was right: it was over in seconds. At least, it felt like seconds. And when it finally disappeared, the light dulled again, the trees and the fields were left grey and unremarkable, and all that was left of the spectacle was a memory. Daisy shivered.

'*Et voilà*. It's finished,' Gabriel said softly. 'Until tomorrow.'

'That was incredible. Thank you.'

'It is not me you should thank, but *la nature*.'

'I mean thank you for showing me.' He'd been right – she hadn't appreciated it before. She'd arrived here feeling fidgety and wary, but now she took another sip of wine, not wanting the experience to end.

His eyes gleamed as he smiled. 'You won't be in such a hurry now?'

She laughed. 'Oh, I will. But perhaps I'll pause for five minutes while the sun goes down.' How ironic that his most irritating trait – his slowness – could be so . . . sensual. And attractive.

'This is an improvement. I will work on the rest.'

Hope snagged in her and she made herself ignore it. There were only five days left. Then she'd be gone.

They drained their glasses and when he said, 'Shall we go?' she found herself reluctant to get up.

That night Daisy tossed and turned in bed. The white sheet beneath her felt burning hot, and the air was heavy. Although it was cooler in the house than outside, the temperature was climbing each day. She'd had a cold shower, she'd thrown off the top sheet – she didn't know what else to do to combat the fierce heat.

And her thoughts were as agitated as her body.

She kept reliving that sunset: the colours, sounds, sensations. Gabriel sitting so close and still beside her, the melting desire that had snaked around her, infusing every inch of her body, crowding her mind until she'd been able to think of nothing but him. Naked. In bed. She sighed into the darkness.

Did he feel it too? She reckoned he did. Every now and then their eyes connected and there was no mistaking the hunger in his. It mirrored her own.

Yet at other times he made it so clear he disliked her, disapproved of her lifestyle and her choices. She flicked the light on and sipped the glass of water she'd brought up with her. The ice in it had long since melted.

She switched the light off and lay back. Delayed gratification was foreign to her. Usually when she met a man she was attracted to, they chatted, shared a drink or a meal, and went to bed. Simple. But this wasn't a straightforward situation. Gabriel was working for her.

Then again, she wouldn't be here much longer.

Should she try to ignore the ache? Or should she run with it?

In the cool light of morning, Daisy decided it was definitely wiser to ignore the buzz she felt around Gabriel. It hadn't been easy to get him on board with the renovations, but now he was, and he'd even promised to complete them before his summer break. She'd be a fool to risk that for the sake of one hot night in bed.

But when he started work in the morning, her resolve faltered. The way that tool belt hung from his lean hips and the sun bounced off the muscles in his arms made her thighs tug. She stepped back from the window. Maybe she'd been spending too much time in his company. Maybe the solution was to avoid him.

So, after breakfast she got into the yellow car and drove into town. There, she found a café where she did some work, then had lunch, and in the afternoon she moved on to a shady park where she hid from the sun. And on Friday morning she set off, planning to repeat this.

'Daisy . . .' he began, when she walked past to her car.

'Sorry, can't talk. I'm in a rush.' Just another few hours, she told herself, and then she wouldn't see him again. She was leaving for the airport early on Monday morning.

He nodded and leaned on his shovel, watching as she drove away.

But when she got back that evening he was still there. 'Did you have a good day?' he asked, the lines around his eyes creasing.

Dammit, he was devilishly good-looking.

'Yes, thanks.'

'Where do you go?'

'Oh – just a café in town.' He raised an eyebrow, and she had to think on her feet. 'The Wi-Fi's better.'

'Right.' She thought she heard him snigger, but couldn't bring herself to look at him so she wasn't sure. '*Apéritif?*' he asked.

'Em . . .' It was so tempting, but she had to be strong. 'Not tonight. I have some – paperwork to do.'

Surprise flickered across his face, but he turned away to pack up his tools. Daisy hurried inside and poured herself a large glass of cold water. Through the window, she tried not to watch as he moved the cement mixer into a corner and methodically wiped down his spade, fork, and hammer with a rag. The muscles in his arms bunched as he lifted them into the pick-up. He downed his water and splashed a little on his face. His skin and hair gleamed in the early-evening light. He turned, waved and winked, and her mouth fell open in horror. Damn him, he must have eyes in the back of his head.

Finally, he climbed into the pick-up and drove away, leaving a small cloud of dust in his wake. Her shoulders dropped with relief. She could relax.

But an hour and a half later she was restless, so she unlocked the car and drove down to the village. At Maman Gilberte's she ordered a *salade Niçoise* and a glass of wine, and didn't refuse the basket of bread. The wine was the house rosé, and she thought of Gabriel as she let it sit on her tongue, savouring the rainbow of flavours. Strawberry, lemon, a hint of pepper.

'What is this wine?' she asked, when Maman Gilberte brought her salad.

'It's from the local vineyard two miles down the road. Chateau des Pins. You like it?'

'It's delicious.' She'd never tasted better.

'Would you like more?' Maman Gilberte nodded at her almost empty glass.

'I shouldn't. I'm driving . . .' But she couldn't resist. 'Oh, go on, yes. I can walk home and come back for the car in the morning.'

Maman Gilberte smiled and brought her a carafe.

On her way home, she saw Gabriel and his friends sitting in their usual spot outside the café.

'Daisy! Come and join us!' cried Jacques.

Laetitia smiled and waved too. Daisy's heart gave a little leap at the warm welcome. She hesitated, remembering her resolve to avoid Gabriel – but this was different. It wasn't just her and him alone. Plus the prospect of returning to her empty house filled her with dread. She caved.

The only empty seat was beside Gabriel so she took it.

'You've been for dinner at Gilberte's?' asked Jacques.

Daisy smiled. Nothing escaped anyone round here. 'How did you know?'

'That's the direction you came from.'

'Yes. The food is so delicious I'm finding it hard to stay away.'

'*Ah, oui*. Nobody cooks as well as Maman Gilberte.'

He was right. In London she'd eaten in some of the most expensive restaurants yet they didn't measure up to the robust yet simple flavours she'd enjoyed here. Perhaps she had been a bit quick to judge and dismiss this place. Perhaps it wasn't as backward as she'd originally thought.

'I thought you had work to do?' Gabriel asked quietly, when the others had gone back to their own conversation. His eyes danced with amusement, as if he'd seen right through her flimsy excuse all along.

'I did – I do.' She laughed, embarrassed at how inarticulate she was being. 'Forgive me, I've had too much wine and I can't get my words out.'

'Too much wine?'

'Madame Gilberte recommended the rosé from the chateau down the road and it was delicious.'

'Ah, yes. It's always good, that one.'

'But it's only two miles away!'

'And?'

'This is the middle of nowhere. The sticks! I thought there was nothing here, yet you have the best wine, the best restaurant, market, and that concert in the church was wonderful.'

'Ah, so now you are forced to revise your opinion of us? We are not uncivilised peasants after all?' His lips twitched, and he winked at Laetitia, who'd turned back to listen.

'I never said that!'

'You thought it.'

'Well . . .' she smiled '. . . maybe a little. A tiny bit.'

An Escape to Provence

Laetitia said, 'We all have prejudices based on our experience. Take Gab, for example. He hated New York. How can anyone hate such a vibrant city?'

'He's a country mouse,' said Jacques, with a chuckle.

Daisy stared at Gabriel. 'You lived in New York?' She couldn't hide her astonishment.

'I studied there.' He rubbed the pad of his thumb over his bottle of beer, smoothing away pearls of condensation, and his tone was casual, as if it were of no interest.

But she was intrigued. 'What did you study?'

'Economics.'

She studied him closely, but his expression revealed nothing. 'You dark horse.'

'What does this mean?'

'You're secretive, you didn't say.'

'Does it make any difference?' His gaze, challenging, held hers.

She faltered, recalling their conversations about money. He'd looked so disgusted when she'd talked about it, *You can't take it to bed at night*, he'd told her. Yet he'd studied economics.

'No,' she said finally. It didn't make a difference, but he kept surprising her, kept revealing more layers, each more surprising and intriguing than the last. And that wasn't helping her to fight the attraction. The more she got to know this complex man, the more attractive he became.

At the end of the evening everyone stood up to leave.

'Shall we walk home together?' Gabriel asked her.

'Yes. Why not?' The thought of being alone with him in the moonlight, beneath the stars made her blood pump faster. Why had she tried to avoid him earlier? All the wine she'd drunk blurred her thinking. He was hot and single – what more could she want? A little flirting – perhaps more – couldn't do any harm.

They set off, taking the main road out of the village, then following a disused railway track, which, he told her, was a shortcut.

'I like your friends,' Daisy said, as they used their phone torches to light up the dusty track. 'They know you well, don't they?'

'I guess. We've been friends a long time, all our lives. We grew up together, went to school together. They're like family.'

She felt a pang of wistfulness and was unsure why. Her torch flickered over bushes and flowers growing wild at the edges of the path. The air smelt fresh and cool, and stars fluttered in the sky like pearlescent butterflies.

'You've never spoken about your friends back home,' he said. His footsteps were slow and steady.

She breathed in heavily. 'I don't have such close friends.'

'No?' His brow creased.

'There's just Tracy. She knows me really well.'

'Your secretary?'

'Yes, but she's a friend too.' Or was she? Now she thought about it, she didn't know much about Tracy's private life except that she had a long-term boyfriend, who was away a lot because he drove HGVs for a living.

Gabriel didn't sound convinced. 'Who else?'

They reached the main road and crossed to get to the lane that led to both their houses.

Daisy racked her brain but couldn't think of anyone. She sometimes went for lunch with her colleagues, but they never went beyond discussing work or making small-talk. And she occasionally met up for drinks with her old school friends, but now she thought about it their catch-ups were quite competitive. They were always keen to outdo each other with promotions, incredible holidays or personal achievements, such as engagements and weddings. None of these people knew her well enough to tease her in the way his friends had teased him at the café. 'Like I said, you're lucky to have such good friends.'

They reached the end of her drive, and she stopped to say goodbye, but he insisted on walking her to her door.

'There's no need. I'm a grown woman. What do you think might happen?'

He shrugged.

She pointed her torchlight at the fields around. 'There's nothing round here. No gangs, no knife crime.'

'There are wild boar.' His eyes gleamed in the moonlight.

'I don't think they're likely to hurt me.'

'You never know. A mother with young ones can be overprotective.'

'You're a gentleman beneath that rough exterior.' She smiled, knowing she wouldn't have said this normally, but the drink had loosened her tongue. She felt awash with pleasure: that he was being so chivalrous escorting her home, and at the prospect of an extra five minutes in his company.

'Rough exterior?' he said, pretending to be offended.

Sophie Claire

'You didn't make a good first impression.' Her sandals tapped on the terracotta tiles as they skirted round the side of the house and the exterior lighting bathed them in gold.

'Neither did you, Daisy Jackson.'

They stopped outside the kitchen door. 'But now I know you better I think we can make this work.'

The moment hung in the air, and she smiled up at him, half expecting him to kiss her. She hoped he would. Longing coiled itself around her.

So she was disappointed when he turned to leave.

An idea occurred. 'Why don't you come for dinner tomorrow night?' she asked.

He stopped and slanted her a lopsided grin. 'I'm not sure I want to. You can't cook.'

She laughed. 'I'll buy something. It'll be a slow, leisurely dinner. We can drink wine, look at the stars . . . What do you think?' She held her breath, waiting for his answer.

He smiled. 'A slow dinner would be very good.'

Her heart leaped with joy.

They should get it out of their systems, Daisy rationalised. She was leaving soon anyway, and he knew how she operated. That she expected nothing beyond a pleasurable evening.

She bought wine and food from the deli, put fresh sheets on her bed, laid the table, lit candles, and selected a sultry playlist for background music.

He arrived late, but only half an hour or so – positively early by local standards. She watched as he stepped down from his pick-up. He was wearing jeans and a checked shirt, and tucked under his arm was a bowl of cherries. Dessert. She ran her tongue over her lips, and tried to suppress the shiver of anticipation.

Tonight, she told herself, smoothing down the red jersey dress that swung around her knees, caressing her skin. Tonight she hoped for the release she'd been longing for.

They sat down, uncorked the wine, then began to devour the salads and cold meats from the deli, tore off chunks of bread and dipped the pieces into the tapenade she'd bought, a salty black olive paste.

'You're hungry,' he noticed. His tone wasn't judgemental. If anything, it was indulgent. Pleased, even.

'It's all so delicious.' She gazed at the quiche, pizza and fresh bread from the *boulangerie*. She'd started visiting the bakery every day, lured in by the delicious smell as she passed and the warm welcome the owner, Yvette, always bestowed upon her. Daisy tended to visit just before lunchtime when Yvette was finishing her shift and keen to chat, explaining what she'd baked that day, asking Daisy about her life in London.

He nodded. 'It is.'

'I never ate bread until I came here,' she confessed.

'Why not?'

'Oh, you know – carbs, sugar. They're not good for you.' But this week she'd completely abandoned her regime.

'Pff! What nonsense.'

In the city there were always new trends, and there was pressure to conform to certain expectations, whether fashion or food. But Gabriel wasn't the type to follow the latest fad. He was straight-talking and sure of himself. She admired that about him.

He leaned across the table to refill her glass. 'Everything in moderation. Bread, wine – these are the basics of life.'

And sex, she thought. He woke primitive urges in her. 'Not love?'

'What?'

'I thought you'd maintain that love is an essential in life.'

His lips curved into a slow, sexy smile. 'Yes. Love, too.'

She popped a piece of bread into her mouth. The dough tasted sweet and there was something so incredibly satisfying about the soft chewy texture.

Gabriel asked, 'So what made you change and eat bread?'

'I couldn't resist.' She held his gaze. The air between them was charged with electricity. 'I'm only human, after all,' she added softly.

They finished their meal, chatting easily about everything and nothing, then took their coffees and the bowl of cherries to the front of the house where she'd installed a new outdoor sofa. She'd bought it, telling herself it was an investment and that future occupants of the house would appreciate comfortable furniture. Her arm was almost brushing Gabriel's as they sat side by side, looking up at the glittering canopy of stars.

'It's so peaceful,' she breathed, leaning her head back and gazing at the gauzy moon suspended in the midnight sky.

'I thought it was too quiet for you here.' She heard his teasing smile. He took a cherry and ate it.

'Oh, I'm looking forward to getting back to the city, but . . .'

'But?'

She realised how scared she'd felt when she'd first arrived – of the silence and solitude. It was as if, wrenched from her job, she'd been disarmed. 'Now I understand this place better. I can see why you like it so much, even if it's not for me.' She ate a cherry. It tasted like a burst of sunshine and filled her mouth with juice.

'I don't like it, I love it,' he said, with fire. 'It is part of me, and I am part of the land.'

A week ago she would have raised a sceptical eyebrow at his romanticism. Now she found it charming. She admired how passionate he was about the things he held dear. She sat back, edging a little closer to him. The hairs on her arm lifted. He turned. She held his gaze and the night air became charged. One heartbeat turned into four, five, before she leaned in close and touched her lips to his.

She waited, registering his surprise and the sudden stillness of his body. Then she kissed him again. His mouth was warm. He tasted of cherries and coffee and the wine they'd drunk earlier. Her pulse sped. She brushed her palm against his soft beard and curled her fingers around his nape, her touch light. His breathing quickened, stoking her desire even more. Oh, God, how she wanted this. She'd never wanted a man so much. Then again, she'd never had to wait so long before.

She drew back and her voice was low and husky as she said, 'Gabriel, I'm not going to beat about the bush – there's only thirty-six hours before I leave . . .'

He blinked at her. She swallowed, wondering why she was nervous. Usually she was matter of fact about these things.

She cleared her throat. 'So . . . why don't we take this upstairs?'

A deep crease furrowed his brow. 'Upstairs?'

She nodded and smiled. Her pulse hammered in her throat, a quick light tempo as bright and urgent as a train rattling along a track. She undid a button on his shirt and slipped her hand into the opening, made contact with the heat of his chest. Solid muscle. She moistened her lips. He opened his mouth to speak, but she leaned in and their mouths touched again. As their kisses became increasingly feverish, impatience tore through her. She flicked undone the rest of his shirt buttons, and ached for him to slip off her dress. She wanted to press herself against his naked body and explore the dips and swells of his muscular frame, feel his weight on her, beneath her. She buried her fingers in his silky hair – but he broke off.

He held her away from him, and there was a moment's delay before she realised he was watching her through narrowed eyes.

'*Non*,' he said, sounding shocked. Appalled. He released her.

'What?'

He stood up. He took a couple of strides, then turned back again and blurted a string of French too fast for her to understand. But she understood his tone. Angry. Indignant, even.

'I – I don't understand,' she said. 'What did you say?'

He raked a hand through his hair. 'I won't do – this.' He gestured to the spot where he'd been sitting, and his eyes glittered furiously.

Daisy flinched. Her cheeks burned. 'You seemed willing, just then.'

'You kissed me, I kissed you – yes. But I won't "take this upstairs", as you say.'

His words felt like a hard slap, and it took a moment for his rejection to sink in. 'Why not?' she asked, although she wasn't sure she was ready to hear the answer.

'Because this is not my style. I don't make love to a woman unless it means something. For me, it is not – how do you say? – an itch to be scratched. It is . . .' He searched for the word, then gave up and sighed. 'It is more.'

Daisy took a deep breath and looked at her knees squeezed tightly together while she battled the volcano of emotions erupting inside her. She tried to stay composed, but it wasn't easy. This was unexpected. Unprecedented.

'I didn't mean to offend you,' she said finally, battling humiliation. 'That's the last thing I wanted. I thought you – we . . .' She was still confused. The sunset, and last night when he'd walked her home – she'd been so sure he felt the same attraction. 'I guess I thought wrong.'

He didn't reply for a long moment. She could feel him watching her, but she couldn't bring herself to look up. She sensed the rigid tension in him, glimpsed his balled fists. Anger radiated off him. Her fingers pinched together the fabric of her skirt, making a pleat in the red fabric.

'We are too different, you and me,' he said finally.

She almost smiled. 'Yes. We are.' Even if, on a physical level, she'd believed they were perfectly matched.

His footsteps were heavy as he crossed the terrace, and his pick-up started with a loud growl. The tyres spun and he drove off down the dirt track into the darkness.

He couldn't get away fast enough, Daisy thought, and stared at his abandoned coffee cup, the half-eaten bowl of cherries. How had that backfired so spectacularly?

With hindsight she should have known he wasn't the kind to have flings or one-night stands. If she hadn't been so overwhelmed by desire she could have spared herself this humiliation. She touched her cheeks. They were still hot beneath her fingers.

Oh, God, what would happen to the house now? He'd been so furious, she wouldn't be at all surprised if he didn't turn up for work again. She'd offended him in the worst possible way.

She was mortified, filled with regret and horror at her own misjudgement.

Chapter 10

Gabriel slammed the door of his pick-up and stamped into his house. He downed three glasses of iced water, ran a cold shower and stepped into it. Even having shaken off any lingering effects of the wine, though, he couldn't untangle the mess of thoughts in his head. Fury and indignation chased each other in circles, like trapped bluebottles. He wasn't easily shocked. Some might say he'd led a sheltered life, but he knew how things worked between a man and a woman. He didn't need to visit Marseille's port to understand the seedier side of life. So why had he been so affronted? Why had he behaved like a prude and lashed out? He knew what kind of woman Daisy was, how different her life and values were from his. She'd told him she only did one-night stands.

When he'd seen the care with which she'd set the table tonight – the candles, the music, too – when she'd looked at him with those smoky eyes, had he not guessed where she was leading him?

He shook his head. That wasn't fair. They'd gone there together. He'd simply been slower on the uptake than her. Then shocked when she very honestly articulated what they were both feeling.

Because he *did* want her.

When she'd kissed him he'd been lost. Utterly lost. He remembered the heat of her lips on his, the softness of her body beneath his hands, the rush of desire that had coursed through him, lightning bright. He'd kissed her as enthusiastically as she him, but – but . . .

Sighing, he flicked the shower off. But what, dammit?

He didn't *want* to want her. The realisation hit him with a dull thump.

He knew exactly what he was looking for in a partner and Daisy didn't fit the description at all – far from it. His perfect partner would value love and family. She'd be dependable, looking to put down roots. She'd appreciate the relaxed pace of life here in Provence, the beauty of the place. And he'd know when he found her that she was the one: his heart would tell him instantly.

But Daisy – no. They were too different. Any attraction he felt was only surface deep. Lust. He'd rather fight it than cave in to something that could never last. As she'd said, she was leaving in twenty-four hours. Anything they might have begun tonight would have gone nowhere.

He towelled himself off, but felt uncomfortable with the memory of her bent head when he'd left, and her mortification.

He'd done the right thing in pushing her away, but the way he'd done it – so angrily, so clumsily – had been all wrong. She was leaving soon, but how strained would things be between them next time he saw her? Could he really leave things like this and live with himself knowing he'd hurt her with his bullish rejection?

No. He'd overreacted. He had to fix this.

Daisy stayed in bed the next morning. Sleep eluded her, as it had most of the night, yet she couldn't bring herself to face the day.

Gabriel's reaction last night had made her shrivel. It had reduced her to a pile of crumbs and she felt so small, so . . . worthless. Grotty, too: her throat was burning. At least it was Sunday so she wouldn't see him. And her flight was early tomorrow so she'd have left before he started work.

Her ears pricked at the familiar sound of tyres crunching on the gravel drive and her heart automatically did a little flip – before she reminded herself that he was the last person she wanted to see.

It couldn't be him, surely. Icy dread slipped down her spine. Who was it, then? She jumped up and opened the shutters a crack.

It *was* him. Her heart sank. Oh, God. Why was he here? She remembered his cold fury last night and her skin prickled. She scurried back to bed. Whatever the reason for his visit, he'd soon see the shutters were all closed and leave.

He rapped on the kitchen door. Her heart thumped as she stayed still and quiet. She wasn't up to a confrontation right now. The humiliation was still too fresh and too vivid.

'Daizee?'

She stilled. His voice sounded clear and loud. He was in the kitchen. She remembered too late that she'd forgotten to lock the door last night. What did he want? Was he going to tell her he was quitting? Who would renovate the house then? She cringed. She'd truly blown it.

'Daisy?' His heavy boots sounded on the stairs.

She stared at her closed door. Surely he wouldn't—

A loud knock made her pull the sheet up and hug her knees. Oh, please. She just couldn't face him. Not today. 'Go away,' she snapped.

'Daisy.'

'What?' She held her breath. The cheek of him, the intrusion. She couldn't believe he was standing outside her bedroom door.

'You're still in bed?'

'No shit, Sherlock,' she muttered under her breath. Then, more loudly, 'Yes.'

'Are you all right?'

His concern would have been touching in any other situation. Her eyes felt puffy and sore, her hair was knotted and tangled from a restless, sleepless night. 'I'm fine.'

'Can I come in?'

'No!' She didn't want him to see her like this – naked, vulnerable. She grabbed her dressing-gown, pulled it on quickly, and knotted the belt tight. 'What do you want?' She padded barefoot to the door.

'To speak to you.'

'About what?' Surely there was nothing left to say after last night. Perhaps something had happened, something important that couldn't wait.

In the silent pause that followed, it dawned on her how cowardly she was being. Daisy Jackson did not hide behind doors. She was sure of herself. She was articulate.

Drawing her shoulders back, she made herself open the door and face him.

His expression surprised her. There was no reproach, none of last night's anger. His soft brown eyes were filled only with relief to see her. And was that guilt?

'It's not like you to sleep so late,' he said quietly.

'Yeah – well . . .' she cleared her throat '. . . it's Sunday.'

'Are you all right?'

'Of course I am,' she lied, and gripped the door. 'What is it? Why are you here?' She sounded more curt than she'd intended but he was seriously invading her personal space coming up here like this. Even if he did seem genuinely concerned for her, she grudgingly conceded. What had happened to his indignant fury from last night?

'Would you like to go to the sea?'

It was so off the scale of what she'd expected him to say that she barked a laugh. 'What?'

'I have a small boat. Would you like to go out for the day? We could visit the coast, maybe stop somewhere to eat, swim, play at being *touristes*?' His lips curved in a rueful smile.

She thought of last night. *This is not my style. I don't make love to a woman unless it means something.* His words echoed in her head, but it was the look in his eyes she couldn't forget. 'I can't believe you woke me to ask that—'

'I thought you'd be awake already. Normally—'

'And, no, I really don't think it's a good idea,' she said sharply.

His smile vanished. He even looked hurt. Good. How on earth could he imagine she'd want to take up his ridiculous invitation after he'd rejected her?

'Won't you—'

She cut him off again. 'Listen, I need to get dressed. It's my last day here and I have plans.' She was desperate for an injection of caffeine. Her brain wasn't functioning efficiently enough to deal with this.

She went to shut the door, but he put out a big hand and stopped it. 'Please, Daisy. How long have you been here? Two weeks? And in that time you've seen only building work and dust and this small village. I'd like to show you there is more to Provence.'

Why? Her suspicious mind couldn't find a satisfactory answer. 'That's kind of you but no thanks.'

'Think of it as a mini holiday before you go back to work—'

'Just go, would you?' she cut in, exasperated. 'Get out of my house – now!'

He looked as if he'd been struck. Breathing hard, she waited for the pounding in her ears to subside. He was silent for a long moment. Then, defeated, he turned and left.

Only when the kitchen door clicked shut did she let out a sigh of relief. She sagged against the doorframe. Thank God he'd gone. She'd got rid of him.

But immediately she regretted it.

My house. Why had she said that?

She'd behaved like one of her clients, she realised, appalled – reacting with anger, with damaged pride. Irrationally. Wasn't she better than that? She didn't engage in tit for tat. Still shaking, she showered and dressed, wishing she could rewind and respond in a more dignified way. Rewind last night too.

She pulled a comb through her hair and took a deep breath to steady herself. Never mind. He was gone and she probably wouldn't see him for a long time. When she did, this would be a distant memory. She went downstairs, desperate for coffee. Rubbing her eyes, she opened the door – and stopped.

He was sitting, arms crossed, on the terrace. He jumped to his feet before she could speak and words spilled from his mouth: 'I hurt you last night. I'm sorry, Daisy. But you took me by surprise. I – I wasn't expecting it.'

A stunned silence followed. She stared at his big boots and her heart beat super-fast, like the wings of a hummingbird.

'I overreacted. I'm sorry,' he finished. His expression was earnest. Heartfelt.

Of course it was. Gabriel Laforêt was incapable of anything but honesty. She felt a huge knot loosen in her chest and her shoulders dropped.

Finally she said, 'Apology accepted. And I'm sorry too. I didn't mean to yell at you just now.' What she'd said about the house being hers, that had been low. Really low.

Relief softened his features and smoothed his brow. 'So, will you come?' he asked tentatively.

'To the seaside?' Was he still going on about that? 'You don't have to do this, Gabriel. You apologised. We're good. No hard feelings.'

'I want to.' The stubborn lift of his chin and the hard glint in his eye told her he really meant it. 'I want to show you more of Provence. You haven't seen the coast.

It's beautiful. I promise you'll love it. It will be fun. Relaxing.'

She hesitated, needled by his stubborn persistence, yet at the same time a little intrigued. He had a boat? And the temptation to play tourist, as he'd put it, was compelling. She *was* curious to visit the region, and although she could have done that by herself, she suspected that visiting with a local as her guide would reveal hidden gems that an outsider simply wouldn't find. Something in her began to give. He must have seen it in her expression because he smiled.

'Well?' he said, taking her arms excitedly.

He could really turn on the charm when he wanted to, couldn't he? She sighed. 'Okay.'

'How long do you need to get ready?'

'Um – give me ten minutes to pack a bag.'

'Do you have a swimming costume?'

'Yes.'

'And don't forget sun cream,' he said, with a nod to her arms, which were lightly tanned but still so pale compared to his dark, weathered skin.

'Who are you – my mother?' It was a weak attempt at a joke.

He smiled. 'I'll make you coffee.'

'Thanks.'

'You look like you need it.' He grinned cheekily, as she headed inside.

'Thanks a lot,' she called over her shoulder. Then smiled to herself. At least things had moved on from last night.

★★★

An Escape to Provence

The sun was more intense as they rowed out to sea, but the breeze freshened the air. Gabriel glanced at Daisy. With her dark sunglasses and slender legs, she could have been mistaken for a model in an expensive magazine leaning back on her elbows, drinking in the sights. She would have looked more at home in one of the glossy white craft that powered past them occasionally, but he refused to apologise for his modest fishing boat. On the drive here, she'd picked at the croissants he'd bought and gripped her bottle of water as if it were a lifebuoy, but once they'd got out on the water she had finally relaxed.

'How often do you go sailing?' she asked, tipping her head back to let the sun kiss her cheeks.

'As often as I can. Weekends, mostly.'

'Where do you go?'

'Sometimes I head out there and fish,' he said, with a nod out towards the horizon. 'Sometimes I do like today and sail along the coast.'

He breathed in. The tang of seawater made his lungs expand and his head cleared as it always did here. The limitless blue sea and sky opened around them and made his spirits soar.

'You like fishing?' she asked sceptically.

He laughed. 'I take it from your tone that you don't.'

'I can't think of anything more dull.'

The water tinkled as the oars splashed. 'Have you ever tried it?'

'Never.'

'It's relaxing. Like your mindful yoga classes.'

'But with fish?'

'With fish.' He grinned.

'Even taking a bonus fish supper into consideration, I don't think I have the patience.'

He adjusted the rudder, steering them closer to the land. They were approaching a bay with chalk-white cliffs. The water would be turquoise and clear. He wanted her to see it, to experience the magic of having a secluded bay to yourself. 'You thought this about the sunset, but you enjoyed it. You don't know until you've tried it.'

'Mm.' She sounded unconvinced. 'When did you first try it?'

'My father took us fishing when I was a boy.'

'Us?'

'Me, my brother and sister.'

'As children? Weren't you – I don't know – too noisy?'

He shook his head. 'We loved it. We usually went to the river because it was close and we took a picnic. At the end of the day we brought home fish to eat and Maman cooked it in a simple tomato and olive sauce,' he remembered fondly.

A comfortable silence settled in the boat. She seemed more relaxed than he'd seen her in the two weeks she'd been here. He was glad. It was a stark contrast with this morning when she'd opened her bedroom door clutching her dressing-gown, eyes pink and swollen.

Overhead, a seagull shrieked. Others called back in the distance.

'How old were you when you lost your family?' she asked quietly.

He stiffened. 'Lost? I didn't lose them. They died.'

176

Despite her big sunglasses he saw her eyebrows lift, as if she was surprised by his bluntness. But he didn't see the point in dressing things up. Death was cruel – why talk about it as if it was anything else?

He added, 'When I was fifteen.'

She didn't say anything and he was glad. He didn't need anyone's sympathy. He pulled at the oars, enjoying the energy this took and the soothing repetitive rhythm.

'Here's the first of the *calanques* – do you see?'

'The coves? I've heard about them. Some are accessible only by boat – is that right?'

He nodded. 'They're very beautiful, and this is the time to enjoy them – before the tourists arrive.'

She watched, fascinated, as they sailed past one, rounded a jut in the rocks and another appeared. The tall white cliffs towered over them, some spotted with pine trees, others barren except for the odd nesting bird. The sunlight bounced off them and the clear water had never looked more inviting.

Half an hour later, Gabriel nodded towards an outcrop. 'We'll moor here,' he said. 'There's a nice restaurant at the top of that hill. But first we swim.'

She shook her head and smiled.

'What?' he asked.

'You're so bossy. Not "Would you like to swim, Daisy?" but "We swim."'

He shrugged. 'Fine. I'll swim. You do what you want.' And he dived into the water, deliberately pushing off hard so he rocked the boat and her squeals echoed in his ears as he hit the water.

Daisy clung to the boat as water slapped her and dripped down her face. She watched Gabriel power towards the shore. For a moment she thought about staying primly where she was, but quickly dismissed that idea. The clear turquoise water was too inviting, and she loved swimming. She stripped off her dress and stood up, then dived cleanly into the water.

She swam after him towards the shore. His strokes were smooth and powerful and, although she liked to think of herself as a strong swimmer, she struggled to keep up. Never one to duck a challenge, however, she gave it her all, and when they reached the shore he looked surprised to find her so close behind.

'You idiot!' she said, breathless from the exertion. 'You nearly capsized the boat.'

He made a show of peering out to sea. 'It didn't capsize.'

'It could have. At the very least we could have lost all our valuables – your car keys, my purse and phone.' All were in a bag that he claimed was waterproof and buoyant, but she'd hate to put that to the test.

'That didn't happen, Daisy. It's okay.' She rolled her eyes at his ridiculously laid-back attitude. 'You're fast,' he added admiringly.

She knew he was changing the subject, but she accepted the compliment with a gracious nod. 'I was on the school swimming team.'

'The school team, hm?' Water dripped from his hair and beaded on his bronze skin. She tried not to let her gaze dip below his waist. 'Is there anything you're not good at, Daisy Jackson?'

She laughed. 'Unfortunately, it's in my DNA to try to excel in everything.' She'd never thought of it as a negative trait before, but next to him she was conscious of how highly strung she seemed, of how seriously she took everything. 'I like to swim after work. It helps me clear my head.'

They walked the length of the shore, then swam back to the boat and rowed around to a small pier beneath some steep steps dug out of the cliff. He secured the boat and they towelled themselves dry. Daisy slipped her beach dress back on and he pulled on his T-shirt, but his shorts were still wet and clung to him as they climbed the steps to the restaurant. It was really warm in the midday sun, but pleasantly so, and Daisy wondered if she was finally acclimatising. It would be ironic if she did so on her last day.

The restaurant was relaxed and the waiters didn't blink twice at their casual clothes and flip-flops. They ordered salads, and admired the view. The sea glittered and rippled on one side, and on the other, a park with beautiful planting led to a rocky outcrop with a low fort, which Gabriel said had been a lookout post during the Second World War. The restaurant's outdoor seating area was shaded by a bamboo roof, and vivid scarlet and fuchsia flowers cascaded down all around.

Over lunch, Gabriel chatted to her about fishing. He explained that there'd been a concerted effort by the authorities to clean up this part of the Mediterranean and help the once endangered sea life to thrive again. She listened and nodded. Anyone could have seen how much this place meant to him. It wasn't simply where he lived:

Provence was part of him and he was passionate about it. Rooted to it.

They took their time over the delicious food, neither of them keen to venture out into the midday sun. But by three thirty the sun had shifted a little from overhead. 'Shall we go for a walk?' Gabriel suggested. 'The gardens here are beautiful, and there'll be plenty of shade if you're too hot.'

Daisy reached for her bag.

The gardens were glorious. Palm trees and lush foliage provided the perfect background for brilliant, exotic flowers, which looked as if they'd been imported from distant shores. They followed the gravel path, and its winding course made them feel as if they were the only people around. The plants were teeming with wildlife. Daisy recognised the chirp of cicadas, but she heard the trill of birds, too, butterflies flitted and seed-heads drifted past, carried by the sea breeze.

She felt energised by the boat trip, their swim and relaxed lunch. Her sore throat had vanished and her eyes no longer felt puffy. This trip had done her the world of good. The air here felt so incredibly fresh it was exhilarating. She breathed in deeply, filling her lungs and closing her eyes to enjoy the sensation. Maybe it was because she was leaving tomorrow, or because last night had been such a low yet they'd bounced back, but she felt happy and comfortable.

'I've really enjoyed today,' she said honestly. 'It's hard to believe I'll be back in the office this time tomorrow.'

'Good. I'm glad you've enjoyed it. I wanted to make amends for the way I overreacted . . .' He hesitated and stopped in front of a tall palm with a trunk patterned like a pineapple. He rubbed a hand over his beard before confessing, 'I didn't sleep last night because I felt bad.'

His honesty was refreshing, and her respect for him doubled. 'You were shocked. Your reaction was understandable.'

His gaze held hers, warm and unwavering. 'Maybe I gave out the wrong signals to you. I find you very beautiful, Daisy, but we're too different you and me – in how we see life, how we see relationships, love, everything.'

'I know.' He was right, of course he was. Her desire to keep life simple with no-strings relationships was clearly alien to him, and likewise she wasn't interested in his outdated ideas of soul-mates and love.

She grinned. 'You're so old-fashioned you could have stepped out of the pages of a history book.'

His eyebrows lifted, but his eyes creased good-naturedly. 'Thanks.'

'It's true.'

'Is it? Am I really old-fashioned for believing in love? Or am I just not a pessimist like you, who needs to control everything?'

She tipped her head and gave this full consideration. 'I suppose that's a fair assessment.'

'And the reason you're dead set against relationships is because you can't control feelings – your own and other people's.'

She felt a tremor of recognition. This was spot on. She glanced at him, unnerved that he'd sussed her so accurately. Had she really revealed so much of herself in the short time they'd known each other?

The unexpected ring of her phone sounded too shrill and loud amid the peaceful gardens. Daisy fished in her bag and retrieved it, but it was Sunday so she knew it couldn't be work-related. When she read the number, she rejected the call and put it away. She began to walk again, wanting to leave behind Gabriel's uncomfortable observation of her as much as the unwelcome call.

He easily fell into step beside her. 'Why don't you take his calls?'

'What?'

'Your father. Why won't you speak to him?'

'Because we have nothing to say.'

'He's your parent.' His words were gentle but she heard the unspoken reproach in them.

It washed over her. No one could make her feel guilty. 'No, he's not. He stopped being my parent the day he left.'

His steps fell into time with hers, and the path took a sudden twist to the right. They paused to admire an old stone well, and a bush with exuberant red trumpet-shaped flowers that hummed with insects.

'You say this when you work with divorcees? When you know what it's like for them?' Gabriel waved his hands as he spoke in that very French expressive way. 'When a marriage ends one parent has to leave. It doesn't mean they don't love their children.'

'He dumped me in boarding school,' she said flatly. 'Even a half-decent parent doesn't abandon their child.'

Gabriel heard the bitterness in her voice and it dawned on him that perhaps the sharp tone and the steely look were not signs of hardness or cold-heartedness – but hurt.

He studied her surreptitiously, trying to process this new side of her. Had it been there all along but he hadn't noticed? Her blonde hair was a little frizzy from the salt water and her cheeks were pink. There was a new softness about her today and it was as intriguing as it was contradictory with the hard-edged image she normally presented to the world. Or was it simply his view of her that had changed? His gaze dipped to her lips as he thought of that kiss last night, and he felt another ripple of guilt. He had a feeling he might have been the first man to turn her down. She'd certainly been the first woman to come on so strong with him.

'When was the last time you saw him?' he asked.

'Twelve years ago.'

'That's a long time.'

She nodded. 'When I was eighteen I cut all contact with him.'

He blinked. '*All* contact? Why?'

'Because . . .' she closed her eyes briefly '. . . I decided it was easier that way. For me.'

He waited for her to go on. When she didn't, he prompted, 'How was it easier? I'd have thought cutting yourself off from your parents would be difficult.' He thought of the accident that had changed his life.

'If he'd been your average loving parent I'd agree. But he wasn't. The divorce brought out the worst in him. He fought to take me away from Mum. At first I thought he did it because he loved me. I almost believed what he said about Mum being unfit to care for me because she was ill. But it was all lies. He caused her depression, I'm sure, and he wasn't the caring parent he pretended to be. As soon as he won his court case, he had nothing more to do with me.' She dipped her head. 'The legal battle hadn't been about him wanting to look after me. It was simply about winning. He couldn't bear to lose. In anything.'

'You tried to see him?'

'Many times. I was a child – a teenager. After Mum died I felt . . . lost.' She clamped her lips shut and swallowed hard, but he heard the rawness in her voice and felt her pain.

He pictured a frightened, lonely little girl whose parents' divorce had left scars. Bad scars. Was this why she didn't believe in love or marriage? This, compounded by years of working with divorcees and watching them fight tooth and nail for their money, businesses, children.

A trailing stem of bougainvillaea spilled over the path, and he held it up for her. She thanked him and ducked under the vivid pink flowers.

'What happened to your mother?'

'She died not long after. It was suicide.'

'Suicide?' He cursed in French, and his heart went out to her, to the child who'd been told nothing, left to muddle through the confusion and pain. 'Did you see your father during the holidays?'

'He was always too busy.'

Gabriel stopped walking. Hearing all this made him want to reach out and draw her to him, but he sensed she'd push him away if he tried.

She laughed bitterly. 'I tried really hard to get his attention. I worked my socks off in school to get the best grades, I won awards for swimming and debating, I even won a scholarship – all in the hope that he'd be proud of me and come to a prize-giving ceremony. That he'd notice me. It didn't work. No matter what I did, it wasn't enough to capture his attention.'

She paused a moment, then added, 'Actually, there was one more time I reached out to him. When I was at law school. I was ill, you see. Very ill.' Her brow furrowed. 'But even then he didn't come. So you see? I did the right thing cutting him out of my life.'

Gabriel took a moment to digest this. It was so far from his own experience. How could a parent treat their child like that? 'Is that why you're so driven?'

'And competitive.' Her smile was wry. 'Probably.'

Her words haunted him: *Money doesn't let you down or betray you.* He'd been repulsed by her attitude, but perhaps it was self-preservation.

The strong tang of sea air washed over them, fresh and invigorating.

'Where was he while you were at boarding school? Why do you think he stayed away?'

'That's the million-dollar question. As a child, I thought it was my fault. I wasn't clever enough, pretty enough, funny, kind, outgoing enough. Not lovable enough. But now . . .'

He waited for her to go on. The only sound was the papery rustle of palm leaves in the wind. 'Now?' he said gently.

'I can see that his behaviour mirrors that of many of my clients. They're so busy dealing with their own trauma of a separation that they have no energy left to deal with their children's. Sometimes it's easier for them to break off contact and begin a new phase in their lives. I think that's what my dad did. He made a fresh start, a new life, and I wasn't part of it.'

She shrugged, and her tone was matter-of-fact, dismissive even. She'd reverted to the brisk, hard-nosed manner that had riled him so much when he'd first met her. Gabriel studied her, taking in the proud lift of her chin and the glint in her eyes.

Only now he knew it was a defence mechanism. That steely façade hid her vulnerability.

Chapter 11

Daisy lifted the mosquito net to close the wooden shutters – but paused, her attention snared by the view and the perfume of the evening air. The sun had finished its display of jewel colours, and only a ghost of light remained. The shadowy fields were enigmatically still, and the sweet scent of flowers in the cooling night air climbed the farmhouse walls, making her close her eyes briefly and draw in a long, slow breath. She must have caught the sun despite the factor-50 she'd used because tonight her face felt fiery.

Leaving the shutters open, she leaned on the windowsill and the night air slid over her skin, like deliciously cold water. She couldn't stop smiling and replaying in her head the sunshine and sea air and the sheer pleasure of today. And she was buzzing with – with what? She tipped her head to one side as she tried to put a name to the feeling. It wasn't like the fulfilment of a busy day at work, or the thrill of closing a case. It was more satisfying than that. It ran deeper.

She decided it was happiness, pure and simple.

They'd had a great day together, just the two of them, off duty. Gabriel, the man who suffered no fools, never beat about the bush and didn't hesitate to deliver harsh truths, had smiled and laughed with her. Last night he might have rejected her, but today he'd talked to her as if she were a friend.

Oh, the attraction was still there, but knowing he wasn't interested had made her concentrate on getting to know him and understand him. It had made her feel accepted simply for herself, rather than – well, sex. In fact, she'd never thought she'd say this, but ruling out the physical had opened up a new side to their relationship.

Her brow furrowed as she remembered all she'd told him this afternoon. She never normally spoke about her parents' divorce.

But she'd be gone before he arrived tomorrow, she assured herself quickly, and it would be weeks, months until she saw him again. Perhaps that was what had freed her to open up.

Talking about it had actually felt good. Kind of liberating, as if something she'd kept locked inside had been released, leaving her lighter. Perhaps it was simply because Gabriel was a good listener. She gazed into the distance, searching for the moon, though she couldn't see it. She was glad he'd persuaded her to go with him to the coast. It had repaired their relationship and now she was leaving on good terms. Really good terms.

She frowned. So what was he now – builder or friend? Enemy or neighbour? Suspicions whispered through her mind. He'd said he'd taken her out today to make amends for last night, but could there have been more to it? Was he hoping to keep her on side in order to keep an eye on the farmhouse? She tried to shush her cynical mind. It didn't matter.

Her gaze drifted in the direction of his home and the huddle of trees that separated the two properties. Funny to think that when she'd arrived she'd felt nothing for the place. She'd yearned for the city and been desperate to return to her life, her job. Two weeks later, however, her perspective had shifted. She remembered the sunset and how Gabriel had taught her to appreciate the moment. She thought of all the people she'd met in the village and the evening she'd spent with his friends at the café.

It had been a good holiday, but it was over now, and she'd accomplished her goal of getting the renovations under way. Gabriel had given her his word that the house would be ready for tenants by the summer.

It was time to go home. Her case was packed with all her work dresses and heels. The cheap shorts and sandals were in the wardrobe, probably never to be worn again. She closed her eyes and pictured her apartment, her office, her workload, which would undoubtedly have accumulated in her absence. The city was where she belonged, and tomorrow she'd enjoy being back at her desk doing what she did best.

'Where were you today?' Jacques asked, when Gabriel arrived at the café.

It was late and he was tired after a day in the sun and the long drive home – but he was also buzzing. Too fired up to sleep. So he'd driven down to the village for one quick drink. Laetitia had already left to put the children to bed, and the others were finishing their drinks.

'I went to the coast. Took the boat out.'

Patrice glanced up. 'Alone?'

'No.' Gabriel kept his gaze on the bottle in his hand and tried to dampen down the soaring feeling as he replayed the day in his mind. The swim, the leisurely meal, the walk in the gardens where he'd learned so much about Daisy's past.

'With Daisy?' Jacques said, with an exaggerated wink.

He bit back a sigh. 'Yes.'

Around the table his friends exchanged looks. 'So does this mean the two of you . . .?' Patrice elbowed him.

'No,' he said sharply. 'It's not like that.'

They spluttered with laughter. 'It's not like that,' someone mimicked.

Gabriel rolled his eyes. 'I don't know why I waste my time coming here,' he muttered.

'Remind me,' said Jacques, and held one finger to his chin. 'When was the last time you took a woman out on your boat?'

He pressed his mouth flat. They knew he never had. 'She's leaving tomorrow. I wanted to show her around a bit, that's all.'

'Ah. So you're a tourist guide, now, are you?'

'Shut up.'

They laughed. He couldn't tell them the truth: that she'd come on to him and he'd pushed her away, then felt bad because he'd hurt her.

And he couldn't tell them how close he'd come to not pushing her away, either.

Chapter 12

Daisy woke in the night feeling as if she'd been hit over the head with Gabriel's sledgehammer.

The pain was intense, her throat was on fire, and she was hot – hotter than she'd ever felt, even in this infernal heatwave. Thankfully, she'd left a glass of water beside her bed. She took a sip, wondering if there were any painkillers in her toilet case in the bathroom. She tried to lift her head but it felt heavy as a rock. Everything hurt, and her sheets were sticky and damp with sweat.

What time was her plane?

Was it today or tomorrow?

Her mind was a fuzz of heat and blurred thoughts. She reached to drink again, but the glass was empty.

She slumped back and sleep pinned her down once more.

Chapter 13

Gabriel frowned as he drove up the path. Why was the yellow sports car still here? Wasn't Daisy supposed to have left early this morning?

He parked and walked round to the terrace. Perhaps she'd left in a taxi and the car would be collected – but if that was the case it was strange she hadn't mentioned it. Her bedroom shutters were closed, yet she hadn't shut any of the others as people usually did when they were leaving. Everything looked the same as yesterday when he'd called by early in the morning, yet today something was different. He felt it in his gut.

Perhaps her flight had been delayed or cancelled. He called her mobile. It rang out.

He frowned. Daisy never ignored her phone.

The hairs on the back of his neck lifted. As he hurried to the kitchen door, memories crowded his mind of when he'd found Jeanette collapsed in the vegetable garden. He'd known something was wrong the minute he'd arrived. The water spilling from the hose, which had trickled around the house and down to the drive, the silence, the stillness, the absence of cooking smells from the kitchen.

Now, he found the kitchen door was locked, but he could see the key in the lock inside.

'Daisy?' he shouted, and rapped on the door.

No reply.

He thumped harder. 'Daisy?'

Still nothing. He rattled the door handle and the key fell to the floor with a clatter. He pulled out his own keys. Fortunately, he'd kept Jeanette's.

Inside, the house was silent, the kitchen empty and tidy. He ran up the stairs. He banged on her bedroom door but there was no response. Yesterday she'd been furious. Today, nothing.

'Daisy?'

Hearing a muffled groan, he pushed the door open. Her room was in darkness. Only a splinter of light penetrated the shutters. He flicked the light on and saw Daisy, a small mound in a tangle of sheets, her hair splayed across the pillow, bare legs poking out. She hardly moved when he said her name.

He crossed the room in an instant and gently pushed the hair back from her eyes. Her skin burned beneath his touch and her lips looked parched. The glass beside her bed was empty.

'Daisy, can you hear me?'

She made a tiny noise.

'Daisy, weren't you supposed to leave this morning?'

Her eyes opened briefly, but didn't focus properly. She whispered something.

'What? I didn't hear. Say it again.' He crouched near her so his head was level with hers.

'Don't – feel – well,' she breathed.

It fell into place. She was sick and she'd missed her flight.

'*D'accord. J'ai compris*. Daisy, have you taken anything for the fever?'

But her eyes had already fluttered shut again and she was fast asleep. Gabriel chewed his lip and thought a moment.

Then he picked up the empty glass. There was nothing he could do about the flight she'd missed, but a fever – that, he knew how to deal with.

***

Daisy couldn't tell if the banging was in her head or real. She'd been watching a big bass drum beat an urgent rhythm – or had that been a dream? It started up again and she covered her ears. Go away, she told it. But it persisted. In fact, it got louder.

'Daizee?'

She knew that voice. 'Go away,' she muttered. She didn't have the strength to say it loudly.

'Wake up, Daisy.'

She groaned. She wasn't enjoying this dream. Could she buy a new one? A luxurious designer one that made her feel good. She didn't care about the cost. She'd pay any price, whatever it took.

A hand gripped her shoulder and she reluctantly opened her eyes, squinting. Gabriel stood over her. He rattled off a stream of French, then knelt beside her and gently brushed the hair from her eyes. He was dressed in a clean white T-shirt.

'It's the Angel Gabriel,' she joked weakly.

His frown deepened. Clearly, she was not as funny as she thought. Or perhaps humour didn't translate very well. 'You're awake.'

'Am I? I don't know any more.'

She'd dreamed that he'd helped her sit up and drink water, that he'd put cold flannels on her brow, and when she'd tried to get up, he'd carried her to the bathroom. She'd dreamed that he'd kept asking her questions the whole time and when she stood at the sink watching her reflection swim in circles she'd opened her mouth to say she felt faint, and he'd rushed in and caught her just in time.

'How do you feel?' he asked now, his voice deep and gruff.

She wanted to laugh but it was too much effort. It was difficult to keep her eyes open, and that knocking in her head was like nothing she'd ever known before.

'Don't close your eyes,' he said.

She opened them and scowled. 'Bossy,' she murmured.

'Daisy, I need you to tell me – are you allergic to any medicines? For the fever, I mean. Is there anything you can't take?'

She shook her head. 'Give me drugs,' she joked wearily. 'All of them. Anything to make this headache go away.'

He produced a couple of tablets. 'Here, take these.'

She swallowed them obediently and he nodded as if she'd been a good girl. Then she lay down and let sleep pull her back under.

The next time she woke, he was still there. Or maybe he'd gone and come back because, thinking about it, hadn't he been wearing white before? Now he was sporting a navy T-shirt and his sunglasses were hooked over the collar. He put the book down that he'd been reading.

'How are you feeling?' he asked.

Daisy blinked. The shutters had been half opened and sunbeams lit up swirling dust motes. It made her think of spotlights on a stage. 'I've felt better.' She moved to sit up, but her limbs were impossibly heavy.

'*Tiens*. Let me help you.' He propped her up with a couple of extra pillows then sat down again.

'Oh, my God,' she said, suddenly remembering. 'You helped me to the bathroom, didn't you?'

'I was worried you'd collapse,' he said. 'And I waited outside.'

Was that supposed to make her feel better?

'Do you remember the doctor coming?' he asked. He was sitting with his legs planted wide apart, hands clasped. He looked comfortable: he'd made himself at home. She realised belatedly that he'd moved the big armchair, which had been on the other side of the room, and placed it next to her. She wondered how long he'd been there.

'No.' How could she not remember? 'Was I awake?'

'Briefly.'

'What did he say?'

'You have *la grippe*. Flu.'

'Oh, lovely. How long have I been out of it?'

'Three days.'

She looked longingly at the glass of water on her bedside table. Someone had placed a jug beside it.

'And you've been looking after me?'

'Checking on you,' he corrected. Colour touched his cheeks, though she wasn't sure why. 'You missed your flight.'

'Ah.' She should probably have been more troubled by this news but she couldn't muster the energy. 'Well, these things can't be helped. Although I suppose I should call the office.'

'I spoke to Tracy.'

'You did?'

'She called. Repeatedly. So I answered your phone. She said she'll take care of everything and you should just concentrate on getting better.'

'That sounds like Tracy.' She was privileged to work with such an efficient secretary.

'She also said to let her know if you need her to rebook the flight for you.'

'Right.' She didn't have the energy to think about that now. 'How's your work going?'

His mouth pressed flat. 'I'll catch up, don't worry.'

'Oh, I didn't mean to nag you. I was just—'

He waved a hand through the air. 'It doesn't matter.'

Just making polite conversation, she finished silently. It was an awkward reminder that he was sitting here looking after her as if he was a close friend, but in fact he was her employee.

'You want to drink?' he asked. 'The doctor recommended lots of fluids.'

She nodded and, once she'd heaved herself into a more upright position, he put the glass to her lips. She concentrated hard on trying not to dribble. When she glanced up she was astonished to glimpse a look of tenderness in his eyes.

He put the glass down and his expression cleared. She decided she must be having delusions. Fever could do that. Still, it left her a little perturbed.

'What's that you're reading?' She pointed to the book on the table beside him.

He picked it up and showed her the cover. '*Breakfast at Tiffany's.*'

'Truman Capote,' she read. 'How far in are you?'

'Almost at the end.'

'Is it any good? I've only seen the film.'

'I'm enjoying it.' His expression changed to one of sadness. 'But he's so in love with her. And she just doesn't want to be pinned down. By anyone.'

'Or anything. Not even her cat.'

'*C'est tragique.*' He looked so thoughtful and stricken.

Daisy mustered a smile. She found it endearing that he felt everything so passionately – even a fictional love story. 'Well, I don't know about the book, but the film has a happy ending. He gets her in the end,' she said, remembering a rain-soaked Audrey Hepburn and a long kiss.

'Yes.' He put the book down and gave her a lop-sided smile. 'I'll let you know if the book is the same.'

She smiled. 'What day is it?'

'Wednesday.'

'You don't have to stay, you know. I feel much better now.'

'I'm staying.' His expression was inexorable. There was no arguing with him.

'Really, Gabriel. You're not my mother.' Or her lover. 'I'm sure you have better things to do.'

'I'm staying,' he repeated firmly.

She gave up and pressed her lips together, too tired to continue this argument. Her eyelids were beginning to feel heavy again.

'Are you well enough to eat a little soup?' he asked.

She wasn't hungry at all. 'I can try.'

He nodded. 'I'll bring it up. I won't be long.'

She watched him leave the room and wondered groggily where he was going to find soup. Maybe he was nipping to the shops now.

Gabriel heated the *potage* he'd made earlier from the recipe Jeanette had always used, and carried the bowl up on a tray. He wasn't gone long but by the time he returned, Daisy was asleep again. He put the tray down and watched her for a moment, enjoying the wash of relief that she was over the worst.

He'd been so worried. Her fever had been incredibly high and she hadn't woken long enough to take medication. So he'd stayed with her and done the best he could to bring it down with cold flannels and iced water. He'd brought some sheets and made up the bed in the next room, only nipping home to shower and get a change of clothes, because what if she was ill in the night? Or fell trying to get to the bathroom?

Anyone would think you cared for her, Laforêt.

Digging his hands into his pockets, he walked over to the window and looked down at the pile of stones and his abandoned tools. He should get on with his work. He'd missed three days.

He should. And he would. But only once he was satisfied she was well enough to be left for a few hours.

In the meantime, he picked up his book and resumed his vigil by her bed. She had no one here, he told himself. She was alone. This was what any decent person would do.

Chapter 14

Daisy recognised the smell of lavender first and knew where she was before she'd opened her eyes. Once she had, it took a moment for the room to come into focus: the oak beams across the ceiling, the citrus sun that pushed its way through the half-open shutters, the solid figure sitting beside her bed.

Gabriel looked up from his book.

'You're still here?' she asked.

His lips curved and he pretended to check, looking down left and right, before finally pronouncing, 'I'm still here.'

Daisy smiled. She loved the sound of his voice. Deep and low. It made her feel so . . . secure. Cocooned and safe. Definitely a good feeling to wake up to.

Her tired eyes began to drag shut, but she fought to keep them open. 'I'll feel bad if you catch this,' she said, remembering their earlier conversation – when had it been? This morning? Yesterday? She wasn't sure – but she'd felt so ill. Now she felt a little better at least. 'You should stay away.'

'Trying to get rid of me?'

He offered her a glass of water and she drank gratefully. Her mouth was so dry, her throat burned, and the water was deliciously cold. She sank back against the mound of pillows and watched as he carefully put the glass down. Next to it was the wooden cicada he'd carved and a bunch of lavender in a cup. That was what she'd smelt as she'd woken: the perfume of Provence, of Le Mazet. Who had put it there? It must have been Gabriel.

'I don't even know how I caught it. I mean, flu is a winter thing, isn't it? And I'm on annual leave, too. It's so unlucky to get this now.'

He raised an eyebrow. 'Is it unlucky?'

'Yes. I should have been back at work.'

'Perhaps it's lucky you didn't fly and pass it on to everyone in the plane. Perhaps it's lucky you didn't get it a day later – when you were back in London. Would anyone have been around to take care of you there?'

'I suppose not.' What would she have done? She could get food, wine and meals delivered, but medicine? Water and cold flannels? No.

'Catching flu saved my life,' he said.

She stared at him, her reactions slow and foggy. His eyes creased when he smiled and you knew it was heartfelt. Genuine. She blinked and made herself concentrate on their conversation. 'What do you mean?'

'When I was fifteen,' he said, as if this should clarify everything.

When she still looked at him blankly, he explained quietly, 'My family were out on a day trip when they were killed in the car accident. I was supposed to have been with them, but I had a fever and Jeanette offered to look after me. So I stayed at home.'

Daisy swallowed, feeling a roll of sympathy for the boy who'd lost his family. She had more in common with him than she'd realised.

'So for me,' he went on, 'it was very lucky.'

She could hear the scraping song of the cicadas, the creak of wood in the roof and guessed it must be afternoon, the sun high and at its hottest.

'That's a very positive way of looking at it,' she said, with a weak smile.

'Oh, I didn't see it that way at the time. But now, looking back . . .'

'Hindsight is a wonderful thing,' she agreed.

'And I was lucky in so many ways. Jeanette was a wonderful surrogate parent for me. It can't have been easy for her, taking in a young boy – especially the boy I was then – but she made it seem as if it was the answer to her prayers.'

A fly rushed in and zigzagged frenetically around her. Its furious buzzing made her head hurt. Gabriel batted it away.

'Maybe it was – maybe you were. You said she had no children of her own.'

He bowed his head but not before she'd glimpsed the shadow in his eyes. The same shadow he had whenever he spoke about Jeanette. 'I was a difficult child after the accident,' he said quietly. 'So angry.'

Daisy licked her lips. They were dry and chapped. She was too tired to speak, but she reckoned anger was probably a natural emotion to feel when you'd lost your parents, as he had, unexpectedly and so young.

'I used to wish I had died with them.' He rubbed a hand across his beard. 'I didn't make it easy for Jeanette.'

'I'm sure she understood,' Daisy whispered. 'Grief is complex. It can affect people in such unpredictable ways. And you were young.'

He met her gaze, and his eyes were big and earnest as he told her, 'She was seventy-two, you know, when she took me in.' He shook his head. 'She was a saint. A real saint.'

Her eyelids grew heavy again. His story reminded her of the last time she'd been seriously ill, but her mind was too hazy to think clearly and she drifted back to sleep, lulled by the deep tones of his voice.

'*Alors, comment va la Belle au Bois Dormant?*' Jacques asked. How's Sleeping Beauty?

Gabriel rolled his eyes. He knew what they'd been saying. It was a tired joke that he, the fairytale prince, had been called to rescue his fair damsel.

He couldn't think of a woman less like a damsel in distress. Daisy Jackson had a core of steel and hadn't needed anyone – until she'd fallen ill. 'She's better. Much better.'

'She must be. Her nurse has finally left her bedside to have a drink with his friends.'

Anger flashed through him, hot and fierce, and he rounded on Jacques. 'What else was I supposed to do? She had a temperature of forty degrees! She couldn't even sit up in bed, she was so ill!' He remembered how weak and white she'd been, how she'd weighed nothing when he'd carried her to the bathroom. She'd been delirious, mumbling incoherently. Even the doctor had said it was an exceptionally bad case.

'Hey, hey!' Jacques raised his hands in mock surrender. 'Back off. You know I was only kidding.'

Gabriel sat down again and clamped his mouth shut. But he glared at the others, ready to take on anyone else who provoked him. There were a few smirks but they let it go.

'Anyway, she's better now,' said Laetitia, 'and that's the main thing.'

'Yes,' said Gabriel.

The roar of an approaching car made everyone look up. Jean-Paul, who'd come to take their orders, tutted as the white Renault sped past. Gabriel stared after it and his mind rewound to when he was fifteen.

At first he'd been too sick with fever to understand what was going on. Jeanette told him later that he'd slept through the first few days, occasionally waking and asking for his mother, then drifting back to sleep. 'I lied,' Jeanette had confessed. 'I told you she wasn't back yet. You were so confused with fever that you accepted it at first. I couldn't bear to tell you the truth. Not while you were so weak and ill.' She had sucked in air, as if preparing herself to strike a blow. 'But then you recovered and you knew something was wrong. You sat up in bed and asked, "Where's Maman? And everyone else? Why's the house so quiet?" So I had to tell you.'

He'd been a ball of fury. He remembered wanting to murder the person who'd driven into his family's car, wanting to smash their skull into tiny pieces. Who had done this? Who had killed his brother, his sister and his parents?

He carried that with him for a long time. Jeanette used to watch him and observe sadly, 'You're so full of anger.' But she never judged him. She didn't scold, either. When he flew into a rage, kicking furniture or punching doors, she didn't stop him. Instead, she waited patiently for it to subside, then came to him with bandages and warm water. She cleaned his sore knuckles and held him until the hot salty tears splashed down into his lap.

Sometimes he lashed out at her too. Those were the most difficult memories to stomach. He remembered screaming at her, yelling. The words he'd said had been wiped from his memory, but he'd never forget the hurt in her blue eyes. Once, years later, he'd reminded her of those moments. He was filled with shame.

But Jeanette tutted, as if it had been nothing. 'You were just a boy,' she said. 'You didn't know what you were saying.'

Gabriel straightened and exhaled deeply. He owed Jeanette so much. She'd stood by him when anyone else would have given up. And that was why it was so important that he kept the promise he'd made to her.

'So when is she leaving?' asked Laetitia.

Gabriel blinked. 'What?'

'Daisy. Didn't you say she missed her flight? If she's better she'll be ready to book another and go home.'

'Oh. Yes. I don't know.' He stared into the bottom of his glass.

Of course she would leave. Her illness had only delayed that.

This time, when Daisy woke, it was dark and she was alone. She lay still for a moment, trying to focus, peering at the shadowy silhouette of the wardrobe and her door, which had been left ajar. She heard a noise and realised that was what had woken her.

'Gabriel?' she said quietly.

It wasn't Gabriel. He'd gone home – she remembered now. She was well enough that he'd resumed work on the renovations, but this flu was taking a long time to go. She still didn't have the energy to do much except sleep. Even reading messages on her phone was too much effort. So she slept and drank her water, as Gabriel had sternly instructed, and every now and then he appeared with a tray of food for them both. He'd draped a sheet over the armchair to protect it from the dirt and dust on his clothes.

But she remembered he'd said goodbye earlier and gone home for the night. When she'd learned he'd been sleeping in the next room, she'd been shocked and had insisted she'd be fine on her own. Which she was. The clock beside her bed read 2.30 a.m. She should go back to sleep.

Another noise downstairs made her still. She heard the creak of the kitchen door and slow footsteps. She held her breath. Who could it be at this late hour, except an intruder? She hid her face in the pillow. Of course, the locals probably thought she'd returned to London. Everyone would presume the house was empty, an easy target. They weren't to know there was very little to steal since she'd had all the furniture taken away. She thought of Gabriel's promise to Jeanette to look after the house. What if the disappointed intruder trashed the place? Gabriel would be devastated.

She lifted her head, telling herself not to be such a wimp. She had to go down there and confront them.

She pulled herself up to sitting and got up – slowly because it made her dizzy. She picked up her phone as if it were a weapon and moved slowly towards the door. More noise carried up from the kitchen. Quiet noises, but cat burglars weren't known for being noisy, were they? What were they doing? Probably searching through drawers for valuables. They wouldn't find anything. She would confront them and hopefully that would be enough to see them off. Then she'd go back to bed. She paused at the top of the stairs. Slowly, now. Hold tight to the banister.

When she was halfway down, she heard a car engine start. Damn! She'd been so slow they'd got away.

Finally, she reached the kitchen and had a look round to check they hadn't taken anything that might be of sentimental value to Gabriel. Everything was in place, the drawers and cupboards all closed and as they should be – except for a casserole dish left on the side. Daisy frowned and drew closer.

Cobalt blue and chunky, beside it were a baguette and a handwritten note. She couldn't read it, but she recognised her name at the top, and it was signed from Yvette, the *boulangerie* owner. Daisy lifted the lid. Inside was what looked like chicken stew.

She replaced the lid and didn't know whether to laugh or cry. It hadn't been a burglar. It had been Yvette, dropping this off on her way to work.

'But why?' asked Daisy.

'Why what?' Gabriel poured her a coffee and placed it in front of her.

She'd managed to get up and have a bath today and was sitting on the terrace enjoying the cool morning air. She felt as if she'd been cooped up inside for months, not six days. But her hair was freshly washed, she'd changed into a clean nightie, and brushed her teeth – all of which made her feel more human, if exhausted from the effort.

'Why did Yvette make a chicken casserole for me?'

'I'd have thought that was obvious.' She stared at him blankly. 'Because you're ill.'

'But she hardly knows me.'

'So?'

'I've been here less than three weeks. I'm practically a stranger.' Her eyes narrowed. 'Does she want something in return?'

Perhaps Yvette was having relationship difficulties. Daisy could list countless examples when a meeting over drinks had turned out to be an acquaintance's ploy to get free legal advice – either for their own divorce, a friend or relative's.

His eyes became thin black slits, and he sat down opposite her. 'No, she definitely doesn't want anything. This is called kindness.'

'Why would she be so kind to a stranger?'

He eyed her carefully. 'That's how it is here. There have been other parcels too. Didn't you see the flowers in your room? Cake in the kitchen? That pot of herbs from Laetitia and Patrice?'

She followed his gaze as it rested on the step outside the kitchen where a terracotta pot sat beside the doorstep, spilling over with lavender and other plants she didn't recognise. Her eyes widened. 'That's so thoughtful.'

'Actually, I ate most of the cake,' he confessed, with a sheepish grin.

She pretended to look cross.

'It's my favourite,' he explained. 'Yogurt cake.'

'Yogurt?'

He nodded. 'It's a really simple recipe. People use it to teach young children how to cook. You empty a pot of yogurt into a bowl, then wash it out and use it to measure all the other ingredients. Three pots of flour, two of sugar, one of oil . . .'

'You know the recipe by heart? It must have been really special.'

He grinned. 'It's delicious. There's still a little left if you want to try it.'

She laughed, knowing how voracious his appetite was. 'It's okay, you have it. Who brought the flowers?'

'Arnaud.'

She frowned, not recalling the name.

'The butcher,' Gabriel explained.

'Ah!' She'd only been in his shop once, but she grinned wolfishly as she remembered. 'He's good-looking.'

'You think so?' His mouth pinched, though she couldn't think why. It certainly wasn't jealousy, she thought, remembering his rejection.

It didn't make her smart to think of that night any more. In fact, Gabriel had gone up in her estimation because of it. Now she saw he wasn't one to act on an impulse or cave in to temptation. He was a man of principles, of integrity, and he didn't commit to anything without doing so fully and wholeheartedly.

'But how can I thank all these people for their gifts?' She was used to the gratitude of clients after she'd won their case, but this was different. These gifts were not an expression of thanks: she hadn't done anything to earn or deserve them. No one here knew what she did for a living or whether she was successful, and they didn't care. These gifts were simply for her.

'There's no need.'

'And I want to thank you, too – for staying. And looking after me. It was really good of you.' Today – Saturday – was his day off, yet here he was, and he'd brought fresh bread and croissants for them to share. Unfortunately, she had no appetite and had only picked at hers.

'It was nothing,' he said, propping one foot up on his knee.

'Well, it was to me. And I appreciate it.' She tilted her head back, enjoying the fresh air in the shade of the plane tree, the warm breeze that caressed her bare legs and arms. 'It seems like you're always looking after me.'

'What do you mean?' A wasp flitted around the remains of their breakfast, probably drawn to the fig jam. He waved it away lazily.

'First I bumped my head,' she said, ticking the list off on her fingers, 'then I almost got run over in town, and now I'm ill. It's as if the universe is telling me I'm not as independent as I think.'

The wasp returned, intent.

Gabriel leaned forward to pick the teaspoon out of the jam jar. 'We all need others sometimes. No one can exist alone.' He licked the spoon and put it on his plate, then screwed on the jar's lid. The wasp sniffed around a little longer then flew away.

'I like being alone.' She liked being independent, answering to no one.

'Do you? Or is that what you tell yourself?'

His smile was kind, yet his question unsettled her. She gazed at the pot of herbs, suddenly unsure.

She *did* like being alone, focused on her career. She loved her life in London – although she had to admit that right now she didn't feel in any hurry to return.

But that was just because she was ill. Once she had her strength back, she'd be champing at the bit.

'Usually I'm the one helping others,' she said.

Gabriel drank his coffee and put the cup down. 'Your clients?'

'Yes. They come to me in their darkest moments when they're desperate, afraid of losing their children, house, business.' She provided them with advice, guidance, reassurance. 'I feel much more comfortable giving support than needing it like this.' She swept a hand through the air to indicate herself, weak and washed out.

He raised an eyebrow. 'You said you were ill as a student. Who looked after you then?'

Her stomach tightened instinctively. 'No one.'

It wasn't quite true. In hospital the staff had taken care of her. But afterwards she'd been alone. Truly so.

It wasn't something she talked about.

'What's that you're doing?' Gabriel asked.

It was the end of his working day, and Daisy was curled up in the shade, so absorbed in what she was doing that she hadn't heard him approach. 'Oh, nothing. Just doodling.' Her cheeks heated and she angled her notebook away from his line of vision.

He came closer and peered over her shoulder at her pencil sketches – cameos, really – of the olive tree, the fields, the stone well at the back of the house. 'You're an artist?' he asked.

She laughed. An artist? 'Don't be ridiculous. I haven't sketched or painted for years. Not since I was about fourteen.'

'Why not? You're good.'

His compliment affected her more than it should have done. 'At school I didn't get top marks so I dropped it in favour of Latin.'

He laughed. 'You chose a dead language over a creative activity that could have brought you hours of pleasure?'

She'd never thought of it in that way. 'My teachers told me Latin was well-regarded. Art was seen as less academic.'

'I wonder what da Vinci or Picasso would say about that,' he murmured. 'Has Latin been useful in your life?'

'No,' she confessed, and her cheeks coloured. 'I thought it would for law – but no.'

He arched an eyebrow, as if to say *told you so* and she had to smile. His ability to think for himself and go against the tide won her admiration. He constantly questioned, and made her rethink everything. She liked this in him.

He sat down opposite her. 'How are you feeling?'

'Much better, thanks.' She mustered a smile.

He studied her closely. 'But still tired?'

'A little.'

'Be careful. You mustn't do too much too soon.'

'You're very bossy, you know.' She grinned. 'But thanks.'

'What for?'

'It's nice that you care.'

He shrugged. 'I'm just the voice of reason. You always want to go at a hundred kilometres per hour, but right now your body needs rest.'

Her body had other needs too, she thought wickedly, but kept that thought to herself. 'Talking of doing a hundred kilometres per hour, what have you been working on today?'

His lips twitched. 'I cleared away the ivy, and repointed the chimney. Once I've fixed the roof I'll make a start on the interior. I've arranged for the electrician, Thibaud, to come and rewire the house.'

'That's great. You really did catch up.' She was genuinely impressed.

He held her gaze. 'I said I would.'

She absently added a bit of shading to her sketch of the house. 'Yeah, but lots of people make promises and don't keep them.'

'I am a man of my word.'

She looked at him. His jaw was a strong, firm line; his eyes met hers and held. Yes. He was a man of his word. And she liked that about him too. Actually, she loved it. It was a rare quality in this world.

He went on, 'Oh, and tomorrow I'll start cleaning the pool. It won't need much work and you might enjoy swimming.'

Her heart jumped at the thought. 'That would be great. Thanks.'

He dug in his pocket for his keys. 'I'll go and take a shower. I'll be back in half an hour.'

'Back? What for?'

'To make dinner for us.'

'You don't need to keep doing that. I'm not sick any more. I can look after myself.'

'Can you?'

She scoffed. 'Of course.'

'How? You can't cook.'

'I'll eat . . . em . . . salad or cheese or something.' Her stomach turned at the thought. She still felt a little delicate, but she didn't need him to feed her.

'I think I should teach you how to cook.'

'What?'

'We'll make soup. It's the only thing you've enjoyed since you've been ill.'

'I can't make soup.' She laughed.

He waved this away with a sweep of his hand. 'Of course you can. I'll show you.'

She stared at him as she tried to untangle the unexpected emotions that sprang up inside her. These last few days she'd grown used to having him near, chatting to her, sharing meals with her. She loved his company. And they shared a new intimacy now – although not the kind she'd envisaged that time she'd set the table for two with candles and background music. Now when he turned up each morning, she didn't look out of the window and see a builder who worked for her: she saw a man she respected and trusted, a friend, her equal. And when he paused to discuss with her the layout of the new bathroom or the revamped kitchen, they exchanged ideas and suggestions and came to an agreement they were both happy with.

Yet even now their relationship had deepened, she couldn't shake off the electric charge she felt whenever he was nearby. She had no interest in learning to cook or make soup, but it would mean spending a couple of hours in his company, and that was enticing.

But since he wasn't interested in her in *that* way, wouldn't it be more sensible to let him go home and eat dinner in peace?

She ignored that thought and said, 'Soup? Right. I'll see you soon, then.'

They stood side by side chopping vegetables. Their arms were almost brushing. She was aware of the dark hair on his forearm and the muscles that flexed and knotted as he moved. She was aware, too, of how sensitive she was to him. Her skin tingled, her body hummed.

'I'm not very good at this,' she said, eyeing the mound of diced carrots, onion and leeks in front of him, and her own pitifully small pile of celery. Unlike his uniform cubes, hers were uneven and looked as if they'd been hacked, not chopped.

He smiled. 'You'll get better with practice. Hold the knife low like this and you'll have more control.'

He put an arm around her and his big hand covered hers as he demonstrated to her how to hold the knife tip down and lift the other end of the blade. Her breath caught at the heat of his body so close to hers, and his fingers wrapped around hers. She savoured the sensation even as she told herself to ignore it.

'Now you try.' His low voice vibrated through her, triggering another shower of magical sparks.

Her lips felt dry. She'd never wanted a man like this. So much and so persistently. Her rational mind reminded her constantly that the attraction wasn't going anywhere, yet her body wouldn't listen. She tried to concentrate on dicing the rainbow of vegetables.

'Much better,' he said approvingly, and turned the heat down beneath the pan of boiling water.

'And what happens when we've finished chopping?'

'We just tip it all into a pan with *bouillon*.' He held up a small pot of vegetable stock. 'It adds flavour.'

She nodded, as if she were seriously going to do this, yet she couldn't picture herself cooking in her flat. She couldn't even be sure the oven worked since she'd never switched it on, and she'd only used the microwave to heat ready meals.

'Have you heard from your father?' Gabriel asked. He tipped the stock into the hot water and stirred.

She stopped what she was doing. 'My father? Why?'

'I just wondered. Have you spoken to him in the last few days?'

'No.' Her voice sounded brittle, and she went back to chopping. Her phone had been silent.

She diced the last stalk and passed the celery to him. He tipped it into the big pan with the rest of the vegetables and gestured for her to approach. 'You do it. When it boils, turn the heat down to a simmer.'

She stirred the contents of the pan and a comforting smell filled the kitchen. 'That's all?'

'That's all.'

'How long does it simmer?'

'Until the vegetables are cooked.'

'How will I know if they're cooked?'

'I'll show you.'

She gave the pan a final stir and covered it with a lid. Gabriel was scraping peelings into the bin so she made a start on the washing-up. She hated mess. At home in her own kitchen the metal gleamed and the surfaces were always pristine.

Gabriel picked up a tea-towel and dried. 'I think you should see him,' he said quietly.

The back of her neck prickled. 'Who?'

'Your father.'

'Why?' she asked, scrubbing her chopping board hard.

'It might help you.'

She laughed. 'Help me? I don't think so.' Far from it. Christ, she'd learned that lesson the hard way. She was much better off without him.

'You don't know unless you try.'

She thumped the clean chopping board down on the draining rack and spun round to face him. 'Who are you to tell me what I should do?'

Blood drummed in her temples. Her words sounded more vicious than she'd intended and she regretted them straight away. Yet he didn't look intimidated, and didn't back off even a tiny bit. He simply eyed her with concern. 'I didn't mean to snap,' she said quietly. A gentle gust of wind blew through the kitchen, carrying the scent of baked earth.

'You're upset when you talk about him,' he observed gravely.

'Yes. I am.' Her hands were unsteady as she wiped them dry, and she had to remind herself to breathe.

He nodded as if this were perfectly normal. She knew it wasn't. Normal adults didn't get upset when their parents were mentioned. They didn't hang up on their father.

'This is why it might help you to see him,' Gabriel went on. 'Perhaps there are things you need to resolve, questions you want to ask him.'

Like why he had abandoned her, aged thirteen, and why she had never been good enough to win his attention or his love.

'I think I know the answers,' she said drily, and began to bang open cupboard doors, slotting away the chopping boards, vegetable peeler and knives they'd used.

'Do you? Do you know why he's been trying to get in touch?'

Daisy stopped and looked up at him. His mouth was pressed flat, his expression neutral. Yet she knew Gabriel now. Something about the way his gaze – normally so unflinching – slid away from hers roused her suspicions. She frowned. 'Is there something you're not telling me?'

He hesitated for just a fraction of a second and uncertainty flickered in his eyes.

Her mind spun back through the last few days of fever, sleep, and his vigil. She pictured him sitting in the armchair beside her bed. She saw her bedside table with the jug of water that he'd regularly topped up, the lavender and her phone.

'He called, didn't he? When I was ill.'

Gabriel nodded. His gaze met hers square on. Emotions tangled in her. What had he done? Had he interfered? Rage bubbled up. How dare he? His intention might have been good, but he had no idea what he was meddling with. He had no right.

'You spoke to him?' she asked accusingly. Incredulously.

'It rang,' he said, 'and I thought it might be your work – something important – so I picked up.'

'You answered *my* phone?' Her hands balled. That was a step too far. A huge invasion of her privacy.

And yet she hadn't minded when he'd spoken to Tracy, had she?

This was different. He knew what her dad had done. He knew she didn't want to speak to him. A deep sense of betrayal gusted through her.

'Yes,' he said, squaring up to her in that calm, immovable way of his. 'I also called the doctor and kept you hydrated. You're not complaining about that.' A muscle ticked in his jaw.

'That does not give you the right to answer my phone! How dare you?' She turned on her heel and stamped out onto the terrace. But the evening breeze didn't blow away the indignant heat that seared her cheeks or the fire in her chest. The frenzied scratch of cicadas competed with the urgent beating of her heart. She gripped the stone balustrade and glared at the empty fields.

He didn't understand. He'd had good loving parents, then Jeanette. His experience had been the polar opposite of hers. He couldn't imagine what it was like.

'Daisy, you're overreacting.' His deep voice was directly behind her.

'Am I?' she said flatly, without turning round. She wrapped her arms around herself.

'Yes.' He came up beside her. 'Because you're upset. Talking about him makes you emotional.'

'What are you, now – my shrink?' But even as she said it she knew he was right. She was hurt and upset. And this wasn't like her. Daisy Jackson was calm and always in control. Her clients got upset and emotional, but she didn't. Not normally.

She pushed the hair back from her face and turned to him. 'I'm sorry. I don't know what's wrong with me . . .' She was all churned up inside. A cacophony of noisy emotions that she didn't want to hear was ringing in her ears. She thought she'd left them behind years ago.

'He said he's been trying to contact you for the last three months.'

She nodded.

'But you cut him off each time. You won't let him—'

'I told you why. When I was eighteen I made the decision not to have anything more to do with him.' She glared at him. Whose side was he on?

Gabriel looked at her with solemn eyes. 'Yes, I know. But he needs to speak to you.'

'*Needs?*' Seventeen years after he'd dumped his daughter in boarding school he suddenly needed to speak to her? 'What did he say to you exactly?'

'Nothing. Only what I've told you – that he would like to speak, or meet you.'

He wanted to, did he? Anger flashed up inside her again, like a blowtorch. A more acute, concentrated form of the anger she felt in her work for all the kids whose parents had abandoned them, all the fathers who had to be threatened with court action before they agreed to pay basic maintenance, the mothers who disappeared, turning their backs on the children they'd given birth to. It burned her throat, it made her feel . . . dangerous. 'Well, I won't. He can go whistle.'

'I told him you were ill,' said Gabriel. 'He was concerned.'

'Really?' She gave a harsh laugh.

'*Oui.*' The quiet word landed softly in the still air. 'Perhaps you could text him – just to say you're better.'

'No.'

'Then I will.'

'You will not!'

He raised an eyebrow and she knew he would. He was more stubborn than she'd given him credit for. And yet even as she thought this she wondered. Was he? Or was he decent? Compassionate.

Oh, Christ, she didn't know how to handle this situation. No one had ever breached her personal space in this way before.

No one had ever got close enough.

Her heart hammered in the base of her throat. Talking about her dad only served to remind her of why she didn't let anyone close.

'You don't know why he's calling?' asked Gabriel.

'No, I don't.'

'You don't care?'

'No,' she snapped, then sighed. 'I know it sounds unfeeling, unforgiving, but it's easier this way.' She breathed in, remembering.

'What if he's got something important to tell you?' suggested Gabriel. 'What if he's ill? I mean, seriously ill?'

Her lips pinched. 'It doesn't change anything.'

'Maybe he regrets how he behaved in the past.'

'Maybe.'

'Don't you think you should give him a chance? To apologise, to explain.'

'I owe him nothing.'

'Perhaps you owe it to yourself.'

'What – to get hurt again?' The words flashed from her mouth, and she instantly regretted them. They'd revealed too much.

'He let you down when you were a girl,' Gabriel said gently, 'but it was a long time ago and he might have changed.'

There was a long pause. The last of the cicadas quietened and the evening air became still.

Gabriel said gently, 'I think he cares about you.'

She snorted. 'No. He doesn't. If he cared, he would have been around when I needed him. He probably wants something from me – money, or . . . I don't know.'

She heard the ragged edge of her voice. If she were listening to a client, she'd advise counselling to get this level of emotion under control. So much unresolved anger, and it had been fermenting for so long.

'What do you have to lose, Daisy?' he asked. 'You might even find it helps you.'

She sighed. 'You can't understand. You've no idea what he was like or what I went through. This is none of your business.'

She didn't look at him but she was aware of how still he was and she could feel him watching her.

'You're right, I don't know. But I still think you should reconsider. For your sake, not his.'

His footsteps faded as he went back into the house. She pictured him checking the soup, stirring it, tasting it, heat escaping as he lifted the lid on the simmering pot. And she folded her arms against the sensation that she, too, was boiling and bubbling inside. She could list all the times that her father had been neglectful and selfish, could cite reams of evidence to show how he'd failed her – but she refused to give him that much headspace. To do so would be like going back in time and opening up a Pandora's box of dangerous emotions.

Anyway, she had a feeling that Gabriel would listen calmly, then repeat his assertion: *You should see him.*

She gripped the balustrade and the stone felt warm but rough beneath her fingers. No matter what Gabriel said, she wouldn't see her father. It was out of the question.

Chapter 15

'This is for you,' Gabriel said. He'd left on the dot of nine and driven down to the *librairie-papeterie* in the village. Now, half an hour later, he placed the box with its big red ribbon on the table in front of Daisy.

'What is it?'

There was such a wary look in her eye that he wanted to reach out and touch her, reassure her. It was an unexpected gift, but was she really so unfamiliar with receiving them? Then he remembered her astonishment when she'd seen the get-well-soon tokens from Yvette and others in the village. Apparently she was.

'Open it and see.'

Shooting him another puzzled glance, she untied the ribbon and opened the box. One by one, she pulled out paints, paper, pencils and brushes. Her eyes grew wider, and her blonde brows knitted together. 'What's it for?'

'To paint.'

'I know that.' She rolled her eyes, smiling. Then became serious. 'I mean, why are you giving me this?'

Her question tugged at him and he remembered how upset she'd been last night when he'd mentioned her father. 'Do I need a reason? You're convalescing. You need to take it easy, and this will help you stay occupied. There's nothing worse than feeling bored.'

She opened the box of watercolours and her face lit up. It made him buzz with pleasure.

'Thank you,' she said earnestly. 'It's so kind of you. And unnecessary. But very kind. Thanks, Gab.' She reached up on tiptoe and planted a kiss on his cheek.

He hurried away to carry on with his work, ignoring the sparking sensation where her lips had touched him and definitely not thinking about the time she'd kissed him properly.

In the kitchen he crouched in front of the ancient range he was cleaning and restoring. Most of the work inside the house would have to wait until the electrics had been replaced, but the electrician was finishing another job, and Gabriel had assured Daisy that beneath the grimy black exterior there was a functional range. She'd promised to keep it if he could improve its appearance.

While he worked, he sneaked surreptitious glances at her. He appeared casual, whistling to himself, but he noticed how light her movements were as she settled herself at the table, sketched and painted. Her expression of deep concentration made his lips curve, and when he passed her on his way to the van, what he glimpsed of her paintings made him smile even more.

Why did it matter to him that she seemed happier today? Why did he keep thinking about how upset she'd been last night, how betrayed she'd clearly felt when she'd learned he'd spoken to her dad? As he drove to collect a part for the range, he remembered how her eyes had flashed with fire. From the outside she looked tight-lipped, hard-nosed, fierce. But he could see beyond the steely front. The shine in her eyes, the rapid flickering of the pulse at the base of her throat: these tiny signs all betrayed what she was trying to hide. She was afraid of feeling like that thirteen-year-old girl again, afraid to let her dad back into her life because he might hurt her again. And who could blame her?

So you feel sorry for her, Laforêt?

He gripped the steering wheel and slowed for a roundabout. Perhaps he did. Just as he'd feel sympathy for anyone who'd had a difficult childhood. His jaw clenched. He knew what it was like to find yourself alone.

He swung his truck around the roundabout's central island, planted with a cluster of yuccas that were thriving in the heatwave. Fountains of bell-shaped cream flowers rose from between the dagger-sharp leaves. Heat shimmered from the road ahead as he picked up speed again.

But he didn't feel only sympathy for Daisy. He felt a whole lot of other complicated emotions too. He rubbed his beard as he remembered how it had felt to kiss her, and how happy she'd looked on his boat. In the last week they'd got to know each other so well. It was difficult not to think of her as a friend now, and his respect for her had doubled. She was a fighter. A proud, resilient fighter, who'd turned her experiences into a reason for helping others.

Yet she was also the woman who planned to let Jeanette's house to tourists. Who preferred meaningless sex to relationships. And who would be leaving soon.

When he got back to Le Mazet it was early afternoon, and Daisy was curled up asleep in the shade. He took the opportunity to study her paintings more closely and his eyebrows lifted in admiration. She was seriously talented.

'Don't look at those,' said a drowsy voice. 'They're awful.'

He turned. Her features were soft from sleep, her lips full and pink. 'Sorry,' he said. 'I couldn't resist. And they're not awful at all.'

'I'm out of practice.'

He sat down and held one up. 'I'm surprised. I didn't expect you'd paint the house.'

'Why not?'

'You don't like it.' His gaze ran over her painting of the rustic stone walls and wooden shutters. The lines were patiently drawn, the colours carefully chosen to show the glow of sunlight, the vibrant terracotta of the roof tiles, the red-tinted earth that was characteristic of the area. Looking at this, anyone would think the artist knew and loved the place.

'That's not true,' she said indignantly.

'You said it was rundown.'

She tipped her head in reluctant acknowledgement. 'Okay. Maybe I did. But that was before. It's looking better since you pulled down the ivy and tidied it up.'

He smiled.

She looked at her watch and the big dial glinted as it caught the light. 'What are you doing here anyway? Isn't this lunch and *sieste* time?'

'I had to go to collect a part and I want to finish cleaning the range before this evening.'

'You're working very hard to persuade me to keep that old stove,' she teased.

'I am. It's a piece of history.' As was the farmhouse, but he didn't expect her to appreciate that. She valued what was new and modern, and she couldn't even cook.

'I know.'

He glanced up in surprise. Her expression was warm.

'I won't get rid of it,' she continued gently. 'You needn't worry.'

He didn't know what to say. Relief flowed through him. 'Oh. Well – good.'

★★★

Over the next few days Daisy got steadily stronger. Each morning she got up, showered, had breakfast on the terrace, and Gabriel joined her on his morning break. He also brought food for lunch and they ate together. Each day she felt brighter.

And the house seemed to reflect her mood. It looked sunnier since Gabriel had tidied the exterior, the new storage hut was pretty, and the pool was blue and sparkling. She loved being able to swim again, and she could visualise how it would look once the new patio was laid. Beneath the ivy that had smothered the walls of the house, Gabriel had found a climbing rose, which almost reached her bedroom window. It was straggly after being strangled by the ivy, but he'd tied it up and reckoned it would recover. At night before she closed her shutters she paused for five minutes to inhale its delicious scent and look out at the peaceful fields. Once she'd even spotted a wild boar trotting past with a line of little ones at her tail.

Now Gabriel had started work on the interior there was more dust and disruption, but she didn't mind. She liked to hear him whistling as he worked, and the old range was beautiful now he'd restored it. She remembered they'd had a range in the kitchen at Primrose Farm, too. It had always been warm, even in summer. And in winter her mum used to lay Daisy's school socks on it so they'd be warm when she put them on. She pictured their cottage, the village school, and saw herself running with friends in and out of each other's houses. She remembered when she'd been loved simply for herself. When she'd belonged to and been part of a family, a village, a community. Where had all these memories sprung from? Had she buried them when she'd gone to boarding school? Had she deleted them because remembering what she'd lost was too painful?

One morning when Gabriel stopped for a break she announced, 'I phoned Tracy.'

He seemed to stiffen – or was that her imagination? '*Oui?*'

'Everything is sorted out.' She smiled.

He didn't reply, and took a swig of his water.

'Gab, why do you look so angry?'

'I'm not angry. When are you leaving?'

She brightened. 'That's just it. I'm not. At least, not yet. I've decided to stay on a couple more weeks.'

His head whipped round. 'Why?'

She laughed at his astonishment. 'Were you looking forward to being rid of me?'

'Why?' he repeated.

She chewed her lip, wondering how much to give away. She'd done a lot of thinking over the last few days, but she couldn't tell him the whole truth – not after what had happened between them. 'Because things have changed.'

'Changed? How?'

'I – I'm getting used to this place. I think I might be learning to slow down. It feels . . . right to stay here a while longer.'

She was still so tired. She'd lost the drive she'd been renowned for previously. Yet she didn't think that was simply a physical symptom. She wasn't the same person she had been when she'd first arrived. Something fundamental had shifted. Before, she'd lived with such purpose. Her life in London had been all about chasing from one appointment to the next, accomplishing one task after another, and there'd been no time to think or breathe or simply be.

Then she'd arrived here. She'd felt a little lost at first, afraid of being alone with herself before. But now she was discovering that . . . well, she quite enjoyed the calm. She was beginning to see Le Mazet through fresh eyes. There was an indefinable feeling of calm and tranquillity about the place.

This place had changed her.

'Really?' He smiled and she felt something crack inside. Pleasure leaked through her, warming her. 'That would be a first, Miss Spreadsheet. You don't miss your work?'

His teasing words triggered a tiny thrill that she fought to suppress. He might have shown great kindness in looking after her when she was ill, but he was still the man who'd rejected her.

Yet he fascinated her. And wasn't that also part of the reason she'd decided to prolong her stay? She wanted to get to know him better. Like the well behind the house, she sensed there was so much more beneath the surface.

And she was still attracted to him, wasn't she? That was the heart of the matter, though she didn't like to admit it even to herself.

It wasn't just physical any more, either. She wanted to know how a man could be so inflexible, so fixed in his outlook on life, yet have stayed three days and nights at the bedside of a near stranger. How could a man be so pragmatic in his work and in the kitchen, yet hold such romantic views on love?

'I explained that I've been sick and they were very understanding,' she said. 'They've managed without me the last few weeks. They can manage a few more.'

Gabriel didn't reply but studied her closely. Her cheeks heated a little under his intense gaze. Could he see how she felt? That she hadn't got over her attraction to him? She knew she had to because nothing would ever come of it, but it was proving slow to happen.

'And I made another decision, too,' she said brightly. 'I think it will make you happy.'

He flicked open a penknife and began to slice an apple. 'You're going to stop telling me to tidy my tools?'

She laughed. 'No.'

'Then what?' He popped a sliver of apple into his mouth.

She glanced up at the terracotta roof tiles of Le Mazet, and visualised the rooms inside as they would look once they'd been decorated and furnished. Excitement buzzed in her, but it was all dependent on how he took the news. 'I'm not going to rent the house out. I'm going to keep it for me. As my own private hideaway.'

He stopped and blinked. 'You're planning to come back?'

She could tell from the slow curve of his lips that he was pleased. She nodded, and held her breath, though she wasn't sure what she was hoping he would say.

'But you "don't do holidays",' he said, eyes gleaming as he quoted her. She cringed, remembering the haughty tone she'd taken when she'd first arrived.

'Like I said,' she blushed, 'I think I've changed.'

Chapter 16

So she wasn't going to rent the house out. Still a little taken aback by the news, Gabriel smiled to himself as he stacked the new terracotta roof tiles in a pile. They were rough and warm in his hands, and he balanced them carefully on his shoulder before stepping onto the ladder.

He couldn't express how happy Daisy's decision made him. Jeanette would have been delighted, too: Le Mazet would be a home, just as she had wished. Albeit a quiet one with a single inhabitant. Unless Daisy changed her mind on relationships, but that seemed unlikely: her views were so deeply entrenched.

And she was staying a while longer, too. He was glad. It was sensible. She was far from fully recovered, and this was the perfect place to recuperate.

I'm getting used to this place. She wanted to spend more time here. Why did this thrill him? Had he seen it as a challenge to open her eyes to the attractions of Provence? To teach her to slow down and savour the gentler pace of country life? That must be it. And the satisfaction he felt now was simply the result of having succeeded in changing the city girl's outlook. It couldn't be anything else. Contrary to what his friends said, he wasn't getting attached. Why would he? It would be pointless. She might have extended her holiday, but as soon as she was better she'd return to her life in London with her hot-shot job, fleeting relationships and frenetic schedule.

He reached the top of the ladder and stepped onto the roof. The sun felt hotter up here, the air cleaner. As he lowered himself down a dove landed on the chimney and cocked its head, watching him curiously. He began to work loose a broken tile, and tried to imagine what it would be like having Daisy as a regular visitor next door. No doubt she'd arrive each time with spreadsheets of new jobs she needed doing, and secretly watch him while he worked. A smile tugged at his lips because he still caught her at it from time to time. His mind returned to the night she'd kissed him. He didn't want to want her, but he was nevertheless drawn to her in a way he couldn't explain. They had a . . . connection.

The dove flew off.

But not the kind of connection that mattered, he told himself sharply. Daisy would never be more than a neighbour and friend.

★★★

'Gab?' Daisy stood at the bottom of the ladder and called up through the loft hatch. 'Gab, did you cut the electricity or has a fuse blown?'

She heard a muffled reply.

'What?' she called.

Another reply she couldn't make out. She heard 'won't be long' and '*électrique*', but didn't catch the rest.

She sighed. What was he doing up there? He'd disappeared hours ago. It would be dark soon and she didn't want to be left without power overnight. She decided to go up and speak to him.

It was dark and stuffy in the loft. She climbed the last few rungs of the ladder, and looked around for a safe place to step. 'I wondered if—'

She stopped. Gabriel was kneeling with a lantern torch beside him, sifting through what looked like sheaves of paper.

'What are you doing?' Her tone was flat. She knew what he was doing. The sense of betrayal hit her hard.

She'd never seen him look guilty before. 'I came up to check where the electrics run and I found this trunk. I didn't know it was here . . .' His words trailed off.

The air was thick with heat and dust. A beam creaked, and she faintly registered that this explained some of the noises she heard at night. They'd been so alien and unsettling when she'd first arrived, but now were as familiar as the sound of her own breathing.

'You're looking for the will,' she said flatly.

There was a pause. Then he nodded. At least he had the decency not to deny it. But, then, he was a man who would never lie. She knew that much about him even if she hadn't known what he was doing up there.

'I thought you'd searched the house already.' He'd said he'd searched it from top to bottom half a dozen times since Jeanette's death.

'I had. But I didn't look up here. I thought Jeanette had never come up here.'

There was a scuttling sound and she saw a flash of movement in a corner. Probably a mouse. Or perhaps a rat. Her skin prickled. She wanted to get out fast, but she also needed to know more.

'What have you found?' She nodded at what lay around him. Cardboard boxes and metal tins were strewn around, their contents spilled.

'Mostly old photos, documents, receipts.' He chuckled. 'There's one here for the sale of a plot of land. Jeanette's grandfather sold it in exchange for twelve chickens, six goats and a sack of flour.'

His smile faded when he looked at her, and he put the paper down.

She felt sick. Her heart drummed.

You trusted him, didn't you, Daisy? You let him get close to you. Should have known better.

She looked away, feeling as if a barb had caught in her heart. 'And?' she asked.

'And what?'

'Have you found the will?'

What would it mean for her if he did? She'd be expelled.

It was a shock to realise how much she didn't want to lose this place. Now she'd decided to keep the house for her own use, she'd had visions of holidays and weekends here, trips to the village, the market, sunshine and rest.

He looked despondently at the papers strewn around. 'No,' he said quietly. She heard the disappointment in his voice.

The light blinked nervously. Daisy leaned forward and peered into the open trunk. It was almost empty, except for a couple of unopened boxes. She felt reluctant to go, but she couldn't very well stand over him while he finished searching, could she? 'Well, I'll let you get on,' she said quickly, and retreated down the ladder.

In the kitchen she poured herself a glass of water. Her hand was unsteady as she lifted it to her lips.

What if he found the will? What if he came downstairs with it in his hand? She pictured his expression. He wouldn't be openly triumphant – he'd never be that cruel – but in his eyes she'd see relief, joy. The satisfaction that, at last, the house he felt should have been his finally would be.

Clumsily, she put the glass down. He'd soon tell her if his search was successful, and although she'd previously been confident that it was too late for her to lose ownership of the house, now she wasn't so sure. French inheritance laws were unique, especially in allowing these handwritten wills with no input from a solicitor. Plus, she had the impression that around these parts friends and family might be given preferential treatment. This corner of Provence was Gabriel's home. If it came down to her or him, he was the local, the golden boy, popular and well respected, while she was the outsider. Her spirits sank. All she could do was wait and see what transpired.

But she felt as if she'd been turned upside down and shaken. They'd grown so close since she'd fallen sick. She'd believed they were friends.

Dipping her head, she closed her eyes briefly. Of course he didn't feel anything for her. Calling the doctor and heating soup didn't make someone a friend, just a good person. Kind and charitable. Ultimately, he'd stayed to do his job and keep an eye on the house that meant so much to him. That he believed should be his. Daisy wrapped her arms around herself, feeling chilly despite the heat.

The house was what mattered to him – nothing else.

Gabriel returned to flicking through the dusty contents of the ancient trunk. As far as he could tell, none of this had belonged to Jeanette, it was far older, but he needed to be sure.

He reached into the trunk, pulled out a box and opened it carefully. Peering inside he saw trinkets, a piece of ribbon, a letter and a tiny photograph showing the portrait of a young woman, stiff and straight-backed in a formal pose that looked far from natural. Judging by her weathered face, she wasn't gentry. Most likely, she'd been a local girl who worked the land and had paid a lot of money for a portrait she could barely afford to give to her sweetheart. She'd done it for love.

Gabriel opened the envelope, fairly certain it would not be of any interest. It wasn't, and he replaced it. He sighed and glanced at the loft ladder, remembering Daisy's expression moments earlier.

He recognised the look that had turned her grey eyes flinty and made her jaw jut at a sharp angle. When he'd first met her he'd mistaken it for uncompromising ruthlessness. Now he knew better.

The cold mask was a front, and behind it she was retreating into herself, fighting to hide her hurt. Because he knew she was hurt. And he had hurt her.

He bowed his head. But having found the trunk, what else could he have done? Ignored it? Thrown it out knowing the document he'd been looking for all this time might be in there? His fingers squeezed the fragile paper of an ancient love letter written by someone barely literate and trying to impress. Pretending to be something they were not.

Had he been deluding himself that his and Daisy's friendship meant something? They were from different worlds. His life was simple, rooted in this land and the ancient stones that held up the roof of Le Mazet. Like Jeanette and her ancestors before her, he was a simple man with simple wishes. This house and his promise to Jeanette were what he cared about most. So, yes, perhaps he'd hurt Daisy by searching for the will, but he'd always been straight with her. He'd never deceived her, and had no intention of doing so now.

Still, as he returned the contents to the trunk and lowered the lid, he felt a weight in his chest. And he knew it wasn't only disappointment that he hadn't found the missing will.

'I didn't find it,' Gabriel told her, when he came downstairs a little later.

Daisy was sitting on the terrace, hugging her knees and gazing at the last splashes of peach and apricot left by the setting sun. Candles flickered on the table beside her, and his guilt redoubled because he'd been so engrossed in searching the loft, he'd forgotten about the power cut.

'No?' she said.

The leaves of the fig tree that had seeded itself by the corner of the terrace were like huge outstretched hands in the half-light. They waved eerily in the evening breeze.

He shook his head. 'That was the last possible place it could be, so it's definitely gone. You don't need to worry.'

She seemed relieved. Her features softened and she pointed to the bowl of olives on the table. 'Want a drink? *Un apéro?*'

He nodded and ducked inside to wash his hands and pour himself a glass of water. A barrier had come up between them this afternoon, and he didn't like it. She looked too vulnerable, and he felt responsible. Guilty. He wasn't sure how to put things right.

He went back outside. Daisy shifted in her chair, and fiddled with the hem of her T-shirt.

'I'll check the fuse box,' he said. 'It often trips. I'm sure it's nothing.'

She nodded absently. She seemed distracted as she re-filled her glass, and her movements were nervous, as if she was gearing herself up to ask him something. He chewed an olive, picked a cobweb off his shorts and let the silence stretch, waiting for her to say whatever was on her mind. The last of the cicadas was still singing fervently, a lone voice in the darkness.

Finally, his patience paid off. 'Gabriel, do you still believe the house should belong to you?'

He didn't reply immediately. In the distance a dog barked.

'It doesn't matter what I think,' he said carefully. 'The house is yours, and you've promised you'll look after it.'

It was an evasive reply, but in all honesty he couldn't answer her question. He wasn't sure what he thought any more or where his loyalties lay. When she'd first arrived he would have happily seized the will, waved it in her face and chased her off the property, justified by the promise he'd made to Jeanette. Now, though . . .

He dipped his head and stared at his boots, remembering Daisy's hurt expression in the loft earlier.

He was torn. On the one hand, he couldn't chase her off the property. On the other, the house *was* rightfully his and the will would have proved it once and for all. He tried to push the thought out of his head.

The will was gone. Lost for ever. And perhaps that was the best outcome.

Because if it were to turn up now, he didn't know what he'd do.

★★★

'What are you doing today?' Gabriel asked.

Daisy looked up from eating breakfast. He strode across the terrace to join her on his morning break and reached down to greet her in the local way with a kiss on each cheek. Her heart pounded with excitement at the intimacy of it. She tried to temper this, but it was difficult when her body responded so wildly to his touch.

'Why are you asking?'

'Because I have an urge to draw up a spreadsheet.' He winked. 'If you tell me what you're planning to do, I'll tick off the tasks as you complete them.'

'Ha-ha, very funny.' She cradled her cup in both hands and inhaled the delicious smell of coffee.

'I'm just interested.' He tore off a chunk of baguette, sliced it in half, and dolloped a generous spoonful of apricot jam on his plate.

'Just the usual. I might paint, swim, maybe listen to music.' And watch him surreptitiously, she thought wryly. That was what she did most days. She couldn't resist drinking in glimpses of him as she passed a window or glanced up from reading on the terrace. She loved watching him work: his expression of deep concentration as he laboured, his pensive look as he occasionally drank water or his secretive smile as he read messages on his phone.

'Do you want to come to the café for a quick drink tonight?' he asked.

She blinked. He already stayed to eat with her most evenings. Was he inviting her out too? 'With your friends?'

'Yes. You know them already – Laetitia, Patrice, Jacques.'

She felt a swell of delight. It was tempting. She enjoyed spending time with him, she liked his friends. And the thought of escaping to the village for an hour filled her with excitement too. It would be a change of scene – it would be fun.

But she caught herself. Remember how he rejected you, Daisy? And yesterday, in the loft?

'I'm not sure I'm up to that,' she said, chewing her lip. 'I've been going to bed really early.'

'That's fine. We can have one drink then go home.'

We? Her heart did a tiny flip.

He only cared about the house, the will, a devilish voice whispered.

But the will was gone. She remembered the warmth in his eyes as he'd assured her: *You don't need to worry*. She didn't want the house to come between them. And he'd been so kind to her when she was ill. That couldn't have been the ploy of a mercenary man out to get his hands on a property. In fact, that man would have let her fever rage and hoped it carried her off intestate.

'You go without me,' she said. 'Then you can stay all evening. I don't want you to cut your evening short because of me.' She grabbed her cup and got up to go inside.

'No,' he said fiercely.

She stopped. Something about his tone made her look back at him.

'I don't want to stay all evening,' he said more gently. 'Come with me. Please. It will do you good to get out. You haven't seen anyone but me for days.'

'You don't have to do this, Gabriel. You're not responsible for me. I don't need your charity.'

He muttered a curse in French. 'It's just a drink, you stubborn, proud woman.'

His outburst made her smile. She weighed it up a moment longer. 'Fine,' she relented. 'One drink.'

***

A rare breeze fanned the tables outside the village café, making everyone light up with renewed energy after the day's intense heat. Faces were brighter, their chatter was more animated – even the lights strung across the café seemed to glow more golden.

Gabriel helped himself to a handful of peanuts and sur-reptitiously glanced at Daisy across the table. He refilled her glass with sparkling water and slid it towards her. She thanked him with a smile and turned back to listen to the conversation around her. Pushing the hair out of her eyes, she leaned back in her chair. He felt a spike of concern. He hoped this evening out wasn't too much for her. She looked pale and tired, but she'd been alone for ten days and he'd hoped the change of scene might lift her spirits. Not that she seemed down or anything. He just didn't like to think of her sitting alone in an empty house while he was having fun with his friends.

And you don't like how she's been holding you at arm's length since she found you searching for the will, do you? You want to prove she can trust you, repair your friendship.

He sipped his drink. Perhaps this was true. He didn't want her to believe he was the enemy and she was alone.

Next to her, Laetitia and Jacques were chatting animat-edly, but sometimes they lapsed into rapid French when they weren't talking directly to her – and he could tell that Daisy had zoned out.

Laetitia suddenly broke off and turned to her. 'Daisy, you'll come, won't you?'

Startled, Daisy blinked. 'Come where?'

'To the village *fête*. Next week.'

Gabriel stiffened.

'Village *fête*?' Daisy looked at Gabriel. 'I haven't heard about that.'

'You'll enjoy it,' said Laetitia. 'There will be food and a band and dancing until late into the night.'

'It sounds good. Yes. Why not?'

Gabriel pressed his mouth flat. 'You'll have left by then.'

Daisy blinked at him. 'You don't know that. I told you, I'm going to stay until I feel stronger.'

'It's for locals, not tourists. You might find it dull. Provincial. It'll be nothing like the expensive parties and concerts you're used to.'

Laetitia shot him a querying look.

Daisy smiled. 'I'm sure it'll be fine. Anyway, I'm beginning to feel like a local. All those gifts people brought when I was ill last week. Everyone's so kind here.'

'*Absolument*,' Laetitia said, shooting Gabriel a defiant look. 'You're one of us now, Daisy. Gabriel's friend is our friend.'

He nodded stiffly and tried to untangle the complicated knot of emotions he was feeling. Why shouldn't she come to the *fête*? He'd invited her out tonight with his friends, hadn't he?

A little later, Daisy slipped away to the toilet and Laetitia immediately turned on him. 'What's the matter with you?' she hissed. 'Why don't you want Daisy to come to the *fête*?'

'I didn't say I don't want her—'

She cut him off, imitating his deep voice. ' "It's for locals, not tourists." '

'She *is* a tourist.'

Laetitia rolled her eyes. 'She owns a house here. That makes her as much a part of this village as you are.' She held his gaze in a look of challenge and he knew she was thinking of the will. But that hadn't even entered his mind.

'You're not going to hold a grudge against her for ever, are you, Gab? It's not her fault Jeanette lost the will.'

He gritted his teeth. 'I don't hold a grudge . . .' He and Daisy were way beyond the hostile suspicion he'd felt when she'd first arrived. Now they were comfortable together, could talk about anything – and over the last few days they had. They'd become good friends. And he was happy with being friends for a couple of weeks until she left.

But inviting her to the village *fête* was going one step further. A step he wasn't ready to take.

'She's not planning to live here. Le Mazet is a holiday home for her. She's only extended her stay because she was ill. In a couple of weeks she'll be gone.' He flicked a hand through the air. 'Back to her life in London.'

'She will, if you're rude. What's this really about, Gab? Tell me, because it makes no sense.'

He glowered at the bottle in his hand. If he was honest, it made no sense to him either. 'If she comes, I'll have to look after her.'

'She's not a child!'

'I can't very well leave her on her own while I enjoy myself, can I?'

She'd be all dressed up like he'd seen her once before. Her blonde hair would be loose around her shoulders, her eyes bewitchingly dark. There'd be dancing. He'd be torn, feeling guilty if he left her by herself, but if he danced with her he'd have to fight the urge not to touch her and hold her close.

He couldn't forget the night she'd invited him for dinner or how it had felt when she'd kissed him. And he had to face it: he still wanted her. He was still fighting the attraction, and taking her to the *fête* would make it even more difficult to resist.

'She'll be fine,' Laetitia said. 'We'll all make sure she's not by herself. And Jacques won't mind taking her under his wing if you don't want to.' The devilish glint in her eye triggered alarm bells. He glanced at his friend suspiciously. Did he have the hots for her?

Gabriel tugged at the shoulders of his jacket, suddenly uncomfortable. 'I bet she'll hate it. She'll turn up her nose at it and want to go home early.' The prospect made him uneasy, though he couldn't understand why. Why did it matter to him what she thought of his village and traditions?

'Let her decide for herself what she thinks. It's not right to exclude her. I like Daisy.' Laetitia's eyes glinted. 'And I think you like her, too. More than you're willing to admit.'

Not that again. Gabriel sighed with exasperation. What would it take for his friends to believe there was nothing going on between them?

Except there was, wasn't there?

He stilled. She'd become a friend, too – more than a friend, perhaps. The house and the renovations were not their only point in common any more: her life had become interwoven with his. He knew her vulnerabilities, her scars, her qualities and talents. He looked forward to seeing her each morning.

He cursed himself. What the hell was the matter with him? Surely he hadn't got attached. He knew it was going nowhere. Daisy was a visitor, a tourist who'd come here two weeks in the year at most.

And he'd do well not to forget that.

Chapter 17

When she heard the car arrive, Daisy was on the terrace, relaxing with an ebook.

She'd been doing a lot of reading while she recovered, and in the last few days she'd also been taking short walks, first to the village, then through the forest. Sometimes Gabriel finished work early to go with her, and in this way she was exploring the area and rebuilding her strength.

From the terrace, she couldn't see the car as it slowed to a stop, and she assumed it was a delivery or someone Gabriel knew – he'd been calling in plumbers and electricians to help with the renovations. She went back to her book. Gabriel greeted whoever it was and she heard low voices. Then footsteps crunched over gravel as the two men approached. She glanced up.

Gabriel's expression made her do a double-take. There was a wariness about him that she'd never seen before. She straightened, and it was only as the other man stepped forward that she realised who it was.

She froze.

His blond hair had turned white now, his skin was creased and papery, and he wasn't as tall as she remembered, but his grey-blue eyes were the same. Her eyes.

Horror forked through her, making her skin prickle.

'Daisy,' he said.

Oh, that voice. She'd forgotten how deep and authoritative it was. A flash of memories rushed at her in a whirl of black and red. 'What are you doing here?' she said.

He stiffened. 'I didn't know what else to do. You wouldn't take my—'

'Because I don't want to speak to you.' Rage funnelled through her, making her shake. She pointed to the lane. 'You should leave. Now.'

He hesitated, and Gabriel glanced at him with concern before turning to her. 'He's your father, Daisy,' he said. 'He's desperate to speak to you.'

'Well, I don't want to speak to him. I don't even want to look at him.' She turned away, appalled at how thin her voice sounded.

'No matter what he did,' Gabriel said, 'he's still your father. Don't you think you should hear what he has to say?'

Fury squeezed her chest, as if someone had placed a clamp around her lungs. She should hear what he had to say? She whipped back round. 'How dare you?'

Gabriel lifted his hands. 'How dare I what?'

His calmness only made her angrier. 'Interfere in my life, in things you know nothing about. You did this, didn't you? You arranged for him to come here.'

She couldn't look at her father, but she was conscious of his shoulders slumping.

'No, I di—'

'Of course you did. You spoke to him when I was ill. You took his calls.'

The two men glanced at each other. It was a brief second of complicity, but she caught it and, oh, how it hurt. It sliced through her, deep and painful, the sense of betrayal.

'I took his calls, yes,' said Gabriel, 'but that's all.'

She glared at him, heart thumping like helicopter blades. 'I don't believe you. How else could he have known where to find me? You're so naïve. You think love is the solution to every problem. Well, this man,' she pointed a finger in her father's direction, 'doesn't know how to love! He doesn't have a heart!'

The blood pumped in her ears and she knew she was red in the face.

Her dad stepped forward. 'Daisy, don't be angry with Gabriel.'

She glared at him, fists curling.

'I spoke to your secretary at work,' he went on. 'Tina? Tanya? I can't remember her name, but she gave me your address here.'

Oh, shit. Her heart continued to slug out heavy beats. What the hell had Tracy been thinking of, giving out personal information? And why hadn't she warned her? Perhaps she had, but Daisy hadn't switched on her phone today. She glanced at Gabriel, stricken with guilt.

He threw her a crooked smile that told her no harm was done. Still, she felt bad. Everything had been turned upside down by the appearance of this man.

'Well, it still doesn't change anything,' she told her father. 'I want you to go.'

Gabriel stepped forward and asked him, 'Can you give us a moment?'

Craig Jackson nodded and retreated to the shade of the olive tree. Gabriel led her back onto the terrace, out of earshot. 'It's one hour of your life, Daisy,' he said quietly. 'And can't you see? He's an old man.'

That much was true. He'd aged so much – he looked so small, so thin. Nothing like the tall, imposing man she remembered.

'So?' Yet despite her stony front, she couldn't harden her heart completely against the hunched figure by the olive tree.

She realised she was trying hard not to cry. Why did she feel like a young girl again, lost and at sea, her emotions so much bigger than she was?

'He's just an old man who regrets his actions of the past,' Gabriel said.

'And so he should. I was a child when he left me.'

Gabriel's eyes locked with hers, steady, immovable. She felt their calm strength seep into her.

'It's okay,' he said softly. 'You're not alone, Daisy.'

He held her arms gently and something about his touch affected her. Her pulse slowed a little, and warmth spread from his fingers right through her. Her rage and fear shrank back a little. Was she really going to chase an old man off her property? Couldn't she hear him out? Keep her chin up and let him say whatever he'd come to say?

She swallowed around the lump in her throat. 'Fine,' she said, feeling queasy. 'I'll give him ten minutes.'

Gabriel nodded gravely. 'Do you want me to stay?'

Her mouth opened, ready with an instinctive 'no'. Then closed again. For the last twelve years or so she hadn't needed anyone. She'd built walls around herself. Yet, faced with this unexpected situation, they'd instantly crumbled and fallen away, and she felt exposed. Vulnerable. 'Yes,' she whispered. 'Please.'

He nodded.

She watched him stride back towards her father and steer the older man towards the terrace and a chair. As she ducked inside the house to compose herself, she heard him ask if he wanted a drink.

In the kitchen, she covered her face with her hands but the past rushed back. The hurt when her messages had gone unanswered, when she'd received nothing from him but silence. She'd blamed herself. Believed that, for her own parent to reject her like that, she must be – unlovable.

She took a deep breath and tried to remind herself that she wasn't thirteen any more, but her hands shook uncontrollably.

Gabriel came in. 'He'd like a glass of water,' he said, getting a bottle out of the fridge. 'Would you like one too?'

Daisy nodded and wiped her palms on her shorts. Steeled herself.

'You're afraid,' he observed, and his eyes were deep pools of sympathy.

She couldn't lie. 'Yes.'

He glanced over his shoulder at the hunched figure on the terrace and suddenly looked appalled. 'He's not violent, is he?'

'No. I don't know why I'm so upset. It's not rational.'

He brushed the hair out of her eyes. It was the most tender of gestures, and her heart folded. She was so grateful for his support, so glad he was here. Instinctively, she touched his arms and it steadied her.

'I think I should talk to him alone,' she said. It didn't seem right to sit the two of them against one. And what if things were said that she didn't want Gabriel to hear? She didn't know which direction this conversation might take.

Gabriel nodded. 'I'll stay here, in the kitchen where you can see me. Just say the word and I'll be at your side.'

'Thanks.' She looked at her father again. When the phone calls had started she'd done her best to prevent it but had also feared the day might come when she'd have to confront him. However, she'd never expected her reaction to be so visceral, beads of sweat collecting, her breathing shallow and rapid like that of a hunted animal.

Gabriel must have seen the fear in her eyes because he told her, 'You'll be fine.' And his words were warm, like sunshine on bare skin.

She forced a smile and took another deep breath, then went outside.

'Thank you for seeing me, Daisy,' her father said.

Craig Jackson had always been a confident man. Although age had left him a little shrivelled and shrunken, his voice was the same deep baritone that might be intimidating and certainly demanded respect. She had to remind herself that she worked with barristers and judges. Confidence, eloquence – they didn't intimidate her. Besides, his words might sound confident, but sitting opposite her, in the shade of the plane tree, he kept his gaze low and his hands were clasped tightly in his lap.

She sipped her water, allowing him to go first and speak, steeling herself for what he had to say. What did he want? Was he ill? Bankrupt? In debt?

'I can't believe how grown-up you are,' he said.

'Yeah, well, that's what happens,' she said, more bitterly than she'd intended. He stiffened, and she felt a rush of satisfaction. Immediately followed by shame. Was she going to sit here and fire missiles at him? He'd been a lousy father, but she should be able to rise above the temptation to score cheap points.

He paused, as if to absorb the acerbity of her words, then asked gently, 'How are you, Daisy?'

She glanced at Gabriel's silhouette in the kitchen window. 'I'm good,' she said. Her tone was less combative this time, and the events of the last few weeks whirled through her mind. 'Actually, better than good. I'm really well. Enjoying a long overdue holiday.'

'Yes, you work hard. I've followed your career. It's impressive. You've achieved so much so young.'

She thought of what she knew about his career. He'd worked hard too, and building his business had been his first priority – above her and her mother. Or had it been an excuse to travel and be away from home? Had he found small-town life too stifling? She realised there was so much about him she didn't know.

She swallowed. Perhaps she could use this opportunity to be honest. With him. With herself. 'I tried so hard to impress you,' she admitted, with a bitter smile. Her voice was a little hoarse. 'To earn your admiration.' It took all her strength to keep a lid on her emotions. Like a dam ready to burst, they pressed at her insides, pressure building.

'You've certainly done that. I'm very proud of you, Daisy.'

Really? She stared at him, finding that difficult to believe.

She decided to cut to the chase and asked impatiently, 'Why have you come here . . .' The word 'Dad' hovered on her lips, but she couldn't bring herself to speak it. He didn't deserve the title.

'I was hoping to explain . . .' He dipped his gaze and pressed his knuckles into the palm of his other hand.

'Explain what?' she said. 'Why, when I needed you most, you wanted nothing to do with me?'

He hung his head, looking as if she'd struck him, and she felt a spike of guilt.

But it was the truth. He should have been there for her – after the divorce, and when her mother died. Especially when her mother died. A jagged feeling dug into her heart.

'Yes,' he said softly. He blinked hard. 'I know I let you down, Daisy . . .'

What an understatement. Her heart kicked against her chest as she battled against the hurt and confusion. She hated that it all felt as raw as it had twenty years ago. She didn't dare speak for fear she might stutter – or cry.

He continued, 'And I did a bad thing fighting your mother for custody. I . . .' He bowed his head and swallowed, then met her gaze again. 'I feel responsible for what happened.'

'For her death, you mean?' Her suicide.

'Yes.' It was a whisper.

'What about me? Have you thought about what it was like for me to lose her?' And then lose him, but she didn't say that. Anger coursed through her, like thick black oil.

'I have.' His eyes glistened. The skin around them was papery and creased. 'That's why I'm here. To apologise. And to try . . . well, to make amends in any way I can.' He held her gaze as he went on, 'I hoped you might find it in your heart to forgive me. I hoped we might start again. I – wasn't the father I should have been.'

'Forgive you? Start again?' She shook her head, incredulous, and fury bubbled up. The cheek of him! 'What you did was unforgivable,' she ground out. She felt only contempt for parents who abandoned their kids. Nothing could excuse it.

'I know that now, but at the time . . .' He sighed and his words seemed to evaporate.

'At the time – what?' she snapped.

'I had my reasons,' he finished weakly.

'And you expect me to sit here and listen to them?'

Her father raised his hands in a gesture of surrender. 'I – I don't expect anything. I just . . . hoped.'

The sound of a phone ringing made her look towards the kitchen. Gabriel answered it and disappeared into the shadows of the house.

'Your mum's death was a terrible shock,' her dad went on, speaking slowly and with a distant look in his eye. 'I'll be honest with you, it floored me. Until then I'd been so angry and, I'm ashamed to say, determined to turn the custody battle into just that – a battle. And then she died and it made me realise what I'd done. How far I'd pushed her . . .' His gaze slid away from hers.

Daisy blinked hard. Memories of her mum tumbled back. Daisy had inherited from her father a steely core, but her mum had been gentle, nurturing, kind. No match for him. 'I wanted to stay with her,' she said hoarsely. 'Mum wanted me too. Why couldn't you have agreed to that?'

Remorse twisted his features. 'I can't explain it. Looking back, I know it seems vengeful and vindictive – it *was* vindictive. But at the time I was all hot emotions.'

Hatred barrelled through her. Vengeful – why? *He* was the one who'd had the affair. 'You had to win, didn't you?' she said. 'But why? You didn't even want me. As soon as you won the legal battle you bundled me off to that school and forgot about me.'

A long pause followed. He opened his mouth to speak, then closed it. He swallowed, then began again. 'I was ashamed,' he whispered finally. 'I couldn't face seeing you because I would have been confronted with the results of my own actions. I took the coward's way out—'

'Too right you did! I was a child.' Her hand smacked the table in frustration. Tears burned her eyes. 'After all I'd been through, you were too *ashamed* to see me?' Disgusted, she folded her arms and gave up fighting the tears. They ran silently down her cheeks.

He'd sunk even lower in her estimation. He was even more of a coward than she'd taken him for.

She swiped at her face. 'So, let me get this right. You started a new life with your new woman, and put me out of your mind?'

His lips pressed together. 'I tried to but I didn't succeed, Daisy. I always thought of you.'

'Oh, you did, did you? Well, that's big of you.'

The muffled sound of Gabriel's voice reminded her he was somewhere in the house. She pushed her chair away and stalked across the terrace. When she reached the fig tree, she made herself breathe, and tried to free herself of the winding, tightening anger that had coiled itself around her. She paced up and down. What had Gabriel said? *He's just an old man who regrets his actions* . . . She wasn't perfect herself. Who was? Didn't everyone have regrets?

'So what's changed?' she asked. 'Why have you come looking for me now?'

He sipped his water, then put the glass down with an unsteady hand. 'I'd been meaning to do this for a long time, but then . . .' he took a deep breath '. . . my partner died.'

Ah. There was the explanation. Though she couldn't find it in herself to feel sympathy for the woman who'd stolen him from her. Who'd stolen her childhood.

'I'm sorry,' she said stiffly. Coldly.

He nodded. 'Thank you. It's been a difficult six months, but losing her has forced me to re-examine my life and the choices I've made. That's why I'm here.'

She glanced from him to the kitchen and back again. She couldn't do it. She couldn't be the understanding person Gabriel had suggested she should be. Drawing back her shoulders, she asked, 'What else did you want to say?'

Her father looked up. 'What?'

He seemed startled. Had he really expected her to listen and understand? 'You've said your piece. I think we're done. I want you to go.'

'Daisy, please—'

She held her hand up, flatly refusing to take any more.

He tried again. 'I had hoped—'

'Go,' she said quietly.

Reluctantly, he pushed himself up from the chair and walked slowly back to his car. She followed him, noting he'd developed a slight hunch, and how gingerly he descended the steps from the terrace, gripping the stone balustrade.

By the time he reached his car, she had composed herself again. As he got in, she told him, 'Mum died because of you, and I can never – never – forgive you for that. You wasted your time coming here.'

A short while later, she was in the kitchen, banging about and scrubbing the rim of her father's glass, as if doing so would erase him from her life, when Gabriel came in. She saw him stop in the doorway. 'How did it go?' he asked cautiously.

'I heard what he had to say. That's all.'

There was a pause and she could feel him watching her, trying to gauge the situation. She couldn't look at him, though. She was too angry.

Gabriel prompted, 'What *did* he say?'

She shrugged as if it didn't matter to her, when really she was roiling inside. Smoking with anger, bitterness, resentment – every ugly emotion under the sun. 'He wanted to "explain".' She paused from washing up to make air quotes. 'Or, in other words, ease his conscience.'

He absorbed this and let the silence stretch, left her room to speak, but she wasn't ready yet. Her fingers rubbed the rim of the glass so hard it squeaked. She didn't think she'd ever be ready to talk about it. In fact, she couldn't wait to put this whole afternoon's unwelcome excitement behind her and pretend it had never happened.

'It didn't go well, then?' Gabriel asked gently.

She gave the glass a final rinse with scalding water, and set it down on the drainer with a dull thud. 'No. It didn't. How could it – after what he did?'

Disappointment clouded his expression, but she ignored it. Picking up a tea-towel, she wiped her hands on it with quick, angry swipes. 'I don't know how Tracy could give him my address here. It was totally out of order.'

'I'm sure she did it with the best intentions. Does she know you're . . .' He struggled to find the word in English.

'Estranged? No. But that's beside the point. She should know better than to give out confidential information. I'll have to have words with her. And you were no better.' She waved the cloth at him. 'Taking his calls, speaking to him when you knew I didn't want any contact. You knew what he'd done.' She thought of their trip to the sea when she'd told him everything. Confided in him. Trusted him. The traitor.

'Oh, you're angry with me too?' His cheeks fired up with colour.

Yes, she was angry. The conspiratorial look he and her father had shared had felt like a knife running through her. He'd said he was on her side, but his actions suggested otherwise. Hot tears burned her eyes and she blinked them back furiously.

She finished wiping her hands and smacked the cloth down on the worktop. 'You meddled, Gabriel. You interfered in my life. How could you? I would never do that. Never. Not to anyone.'

'Because there's no one in your life you care about!'

'What?' Her ears rang, and the wind was suddenly knocked out of her. Her hand fell to her side. What was he implying? That she had no friends, no one? That ... he cared about her? She spun away from him, hugging her arms.

'I didn't mean it like that,' he said, quickly appearing by her side. His eyes filled with apology. 'I meant ...' He sighed. 'You're scared of letting anyone get close to you because of him. And I understand that what he did was bad – terrible – and he hurt you. But is that really how you want to live, Daisy? Alone? Afraid?'

Her chin went up. She thought of her life in London, her career, and although the picture was becoming a little hazy because she'd been away a while, it was still the life she'd chosen. How dare he suggest she was afraid?

'What I am is realistic,' she countered, jabbing an angry finger at herself. 'Not naïve with romantic fantasies that love is the holy grail that will solve everyone's problems and – and families are always perfect and happy.'

His eyes flashed like dark stones. 'Of course they're not. Every family, every couple argues and goes through difficult periods, but life's obstacles are easier when you have people you love surrounding you and helping you.'

She wanted to roll her eyes – but then thought of his friends and the tight-knit community here. They'd closed ranks to try to help him keep the house. And when she'd been ill she'd appreciated their gifts, their thoughtful tokens of cakes and casseroles.

A pair of slim doves flew past the window and settled in the plane tree outside. They began crooning to each other. Normally she found their call and response soothing, but today it was irritating, sentimental.

She made herself breathe. 'Promise me you won't meddle any more, Gabriel. You won't go behind my back and call him again.'

He raised his hands in the air. 'How can I promise that? What if you become ill again? He cares about you, Dais—'

'He doesn't,' she snapped. 'He just wants to appease his conscience.'

She saw the silent battle he was fighting with himself to keep his temper in check. And his accent became more pronounced as he became more passionate. 'Okay, I promise,' he said finally. 'Your feelings are more important to me than his.'

Relief washed through her. And their eyes locked. She saw the sincerity in his. Concern, too, and she felt a kick. Having Gabriel's support was something she'd never take for granted. She hadn't known anyone like him before, she'd never had anyone like him in her life. 'Thank you,' she said quietly.

'But I'm sure that he does care. And, you know, if you could forgive him, you might find it helps you.'

With that, he sloped away, back to his work outside, and she stared after him. *Forgive* her dad?

And yet she'd seen in her clients over the years how self-destructive hate and bitterness could be. Moving on emotionally was always the better option.

But in her case it seemed a huge ask. Impossible. She didn't think she could do it.

Gabriel hung his head, thinking of the calls he'd taken when Daisy had been ill, remembering how worried her father had sounded and how Gabriel had reassured him. Had he done the wrong thing? Was he naïve, as she'd said? Did he romanticise love and family life?

He felt a pinch in his chest, thinking of the family who had been ripped away from him. Perhaps he did. And perhaps he'd been fortunate to have had loving parents and then Jeanette. And, let's face it, a whole village looking out for him too.

But Daisy had been alone. No wonder she'd made the choices she had. She'd been hurt by the most important people in her life, losing her parents – her mum who'd died, then her dad who'd abandoned her. It was tragic. Gabriel's chest constricted. He understood, yet how could he – or anyone else – help her? She was so self-reliant – so fiercely and proudly independent. He didn't think anyone would ever be able to pierce her defences. And this troubled him intensely.

Why? What she did was her affair.

Maybe, but he'd seen the fear in her eyes when her dad arrived, heard her furious bluster after he'd left, and seen her wrap her arms around herself – and it had made his heart twist.

He wanted to draw her to him and hold her. No one should hurt like that. No one should be so alone in the world.

Chapter 18

'You're going to have no water or electricity for at least a week while we install the new bathroom,' Gabriel said, as they walked down to the village to spend another evening with his friends. It was almost dark and the sky was inky blue, spotted with the first few stars and a shy wisp of crescent moon. 'Thibaud and Victor are coming to help me and we'll work as fast as we can, but . . .' He shrugged in his expressive way that used to infuriate her but now she found charming. Irresistible, even.

'Oh. Right.' Daisy stopped to pick a small stone out of her sandal, which also bought her a moment to work out how to react to this unexpected news. She'd have to find a hotel room, she thought, and bit back disappointment at the prospect of moving out. She'd spent her first couple of weeks here cracking the whip and encouraging him to work faster. Was she now going to delay the renovations because it was inconvenient for her to move out? There were no hotels nearby, but she supposed she could treat it as a holiday and book somewhere luxurious by the sea. Pamper herself or something.

But she didn't want to be by the sea. She wanted to be here, near Gabriel and the village, with all its friendly faces, and the tranquil countryside, which had got under her skin.

She slipped her sandal back on. 'Were you hoping I'd go home?' she asked.

'What?'

'Back to London. So you can get on with your work?' It would make his life a hundred times easier if he didn't have to clear up each evening, constantly taping off doors and rooms to try to contain the dust and mess as he'd started doing.

He seemed shocked. 'No. Not at all.' A car sped towards them and Gabriel tugged her back from the edge of the road. It was a protective gesture and his hand was warm on her arm.

When the car had gone, he said, 'On the contrary, I think the rest is doing you good. You seem brighter, and you've slowed down a little.'

His lazy wink made her melt. 'You're right.' Being ill had forced her to take things easy, but she'd changed in other ways too.

They set off again, and she took in the moonlit shadows of shrubby forest to her left, and the sparkling lights of La Tourelle ahead. This place had reeled her in ever so gradually, and now she hardly ever thought about her work or London. In fact, if he had asked her to leave, she would have been reluctant. She didn't feel ready.

'So you could stay with me,' Gabriel went on, his tone questioning, 'if you like.'

She stopped again. 'With you?' she said, unable to hide her astonishment.

He gave a low chuckle. 'Would it be so bad?'

'Isn't your place . . . em . . . very small?'

She realised too late how judgemental that sounded, and she hadn't meant it to. But the thought of sharing such a confined space with him, of being in such close proximity to his big frame, to his heat, his *presence*, made her heart sprint with panic.

'It's big enough. I can sleep on the sofa, you can have my room.' He shrugged again.

Her skin tingled with excitement at the prospect of sharing his home with him. 'There's no need to give up your room for me. I can sleep on the sofa.'

In the semi-darkness their eyes connected and held for a long silent moment. '*On verra*,' he said finally. We'll see.

They fell into step again, and Daisy looked up at the moon, trying to calm herself, to take deep breaths. What had that heated look meant exactly? Why did it excite her?

He hadn't meant anything by it, she decided. It was simply her imagination working overtime. Had she forgotten how she'd tried to seduce him and he'd pushed her away?

No, he was just being kind, offering her a place to stay. That was all.

Yet hope rose in her, as weightless as a balloon, and she couldn't stop it.

The next evening Daisy arrived at his house with a small bag and a little trepidation. This felt . . . strange.

'The bathroom's there,' Gabriel said, pointing to one door, 'the bedroom on the right, kitchen through here. That's it. Now you've had the grand tour.' He winked.

She glanced around at his tiny home, all on one level. 'It looks different from how I remember it,' she said, recalling her first visit when she'd found him intimidating, intractable and angry. She'd been astounded when he'd agreed to meet her halfway and carry out the renovations.

He threw her a lopsided grin. 'I tidied.'

She looked at the coffee-table and the sofa, which had previously been swamped with papers, magazines and empty food wrappers. Now they were clear. 'You did that for me?'

'The place looks bigger now.'

'So you'll keep it tidy in future? Have you been converted from your messy ways?'

'I wouldn't go that far.' He grinned. 'Make yourself at home. I'll get dinner ready.'

She went into the bedroom and unpacked her sponge-bag, nightie, dressing-gown and a book. It didn't take long. She'd left most of her clothes at Le Mazet, figuring it would be a good reason to pop in each day. She still wasn't sure how she felt about moving in here, even just for a few days. Sharing a house with a man she was attracted to but who wasn't interested in her might be problematic. She wanted to keep her options open, have an excuse to leave if she needed space.

In Gabriel's bedroom there was just enough room for a double bed, a bedside table, chair and wardrobe. The window looked out onto the terrace at the back of the house, and the fields and hills beyond. He'd told her he'd changed the sheets for her and the fresh smell of laundry powder welcomed her, but his scent lingered in the air. It made her stop and breathe deeply. A masculine, woody smell – she'd recognise it anywhere.

A short while later, she found him in the kitchen. He was standing over a pan with a wooden spoon in his hand. Around him every surface was filled with teetering towers of dishes and pans, some clean, some not. Cupboard doors burst open. Even the floor space was littered with sacks and bottles, and she had to step around them carefully. 'When you said you tidied . . .' she said, with a wry smile.

He looked up from the sauce he was stirring. 'Only the bedroom and lounge.'

'Right. Is this how it always looks, then?' The kitchen was tiny. How could he find anything among all the clutter?

'Yes.'

'If there had been an explosion it wouldn't look much different,' she teased.

His lips curved but he merely carried on stirring the sauce.

As he prepared a simple supper of cod in tomato sauce and she did what she could to help, they chatted. She found herself laughing and smiling a lot, and darting self-consciously around the poky kitchen, trying to put as much distance as possible between them, although it was difficult. The room was so small, and he was mesmerising. His deep voice and calm words had a visceral effect. They lulled and hypnotised her, yet at the same time her pulse danced with excitement, responding to every smile he slanted her way and every gleam of his deep brown eyes.

He was gorgeous, yet he was her polar opposite. They had absolutely nothing in common. Zero.

He was bound to this rural existence; she was a city girl.

He wanted a wife, love and marriage; she didn't believe in love.

He was messy; she craved order.

Slow versus efficient.

Nevertheless, the attraction was there, and sometimes she thought he must feel it too. An electric charge in the air, a silent hum that made every nerve in her body stand to attention, alert with anticipation.

After having dinner outside they went in and settled on the sofa, leaving the French windows wide open so the cool night air could slip inside. It was late, the last of the cicadas had hushed, and a fan whirred quietly in Gabriel's small lounge. Daisy was trying to read, but her eyes were scanning the same line over and over again, not taking in any of the words. She was too aware of Gabriel's muscular arm a whisper away from hers, too conscious of the sound of his breathing, calm and steady, too distracted by his solemn-eyed concentration as he checked his emails.

She glanced at her tablet and realised she hadn't checked her own messages for almost twenty-four hours. Strangely, she had no compulsion to do so. What was the point? It could wait. None of it was important. So what *was* important to her now?

The thought perplexed her. She wasn't sure of the answer.

'Why the frown?' he asked.

She realised he was watching her. Colour filled her cheeks. 'Oh – nothing.'

'You look worried.' He reached out and his fingers touched her brow as if to smooth away her worries.

She stilled. It was electric. All coherent thoughts fled from her brain, and she could only feel. It felt . . . perfect.

Their gazes held and her pulse throbbed so loudly she was certain he would hear it. She tried not to look at his mouth, tried not to imagine what it would feel like to lean in just a few inches and kiss him. Touch him. Run her fingers through his hair, over the square line of his jaw and the dark velvet of his beard—

A quiet miaow made them turn. In the door a tabby cat watched them warily.

Gabriel snatched away his fingers. Were his cheeks a little flushed? A tiny muscle flickered in his jaw, but his expression gave nothing away. 'Zouzou,' he said, and put aside his laptop to fetch something from the kitchen. He returned a few moments later, carrying bowls of water and food.

'I didn't know you had a cat,' Daisy said.

'She's not mine. Not really . . .' He put the bowls down just outside the door, and the cat ate hungrily. He crouched down and scratched the back of her neck affectionately. 'She's a stray. There are a few of them.'

Daisy looked closer and saw the cat wasn't wearing a collar. She was lean and wiry, and the tip of one ear had been clipped. 'You feed them?'

'When they ask for food like this, yes.'

'Is that wise? Don't they carry fleas and diseases?'

'They're still living beings. And they find it difficult during a heatwave when the streams dry up.' He murmured to the cat, 'Don't you, Zouzou?'

'Have you given them all names?'

'Just Zouzou. She's the mother. The others are shy. I don't know them so well.' He straightened up and dug his hands into his pockets. The cat licked the bowl clean, then lapped the water thirstily. 'You don't like cats?' he asked.

'Actually, I do. I had one once. When I bought my first apartment. She was beautiful.' Her name was Lucky, and she was a Scottish Fold. She'd had a regal air and glistening silver-blue fur. Daisy had been living in a basement flat at the time with a shared garden where she'd thought the cat would be safe. She remembered how soft her thick, downy coat had felt to stroke and how, when she came home from work, Lucky would purr and wind figures of eight around her ankles before Daisy had even taken her jacket off. It used to make her heart jump each time to be greeted like that.

'What happened to her?'

She paused, remembering. 'She was run over.'

Within the first month. Not so lucky, after all.

Daisy hadn't wanted another pet.

She cleared her throat and nodded at Zouzou. 'How often does she visit you?'

He tipped his head to one side. 'She comes and goes. Sometimes I don't see her for days, weeks, even.'

'She comes when she needs you,' she observed.

'Yes.' He watched the cat, who was licking her paws. 'She stayed away for a while after I took her to the vet, but I think she's forgiven me now.'

'The vet? Was she injured?'

'No. I took her to have an operation . . .' he searched for the word then gave up and smiled '. . . so she can't have babies.'

'Ah,' she said knowingly. 'Yes, that was probably wise.'

'She didn't see it that way.'

'We can't always see what's good for us in the long-term.' For some reason she thought of her dad and his unexpected visit. And how she'd reacted. She'd been so angry, so unwilling to listen, and she kept thinking about what Gabriel had said. *If you could forgive him, you might find it helps you.*

She didn't think she'd ever be able to do that, and everything in her baulked at the idea of seeing him again. But she was also desperate to be rid of the hot ball of anger she still carried in the pit of her stomach. It wasn't healthy. It felt toxic. And her dad had taken a huge step in coming here and trying to initiate reconciliation.

She picked a loose thread off her shorts. 'Has my dad called you since he came here?'

'No.' He met her gaze and she knew he was speaking the truth. But, then, he'd promised he wouldn't take his calls, and he was a man of his word.

She swallowed, then asked carefully, 'If you were in my shoes, would you want to see him again?'

He thought about this for a long moment. 'It's hard for me to put myself in your shoes. I haven't lived through your experiences. He hurt you.'

She looked away, blinking rapidly. Gabriel understood her so well. Why did that understanding and compassion feel so good? Because she was used to being alone? Because she hadn't acknowledged the hurt? 'He did . . .' she said finally, and her voice was raw. 'But he wasn't always bad.'

Since he'd been here the other day memories had been trickling back, seeping into her consciousness from when she was small and her parents were still together. She remembered helping him rake autumn leaves in the garden, him swinging her in the air, she could hear her own laughter and happy shrieks. She pictured him coming home from trips abroad and enfolding her in an enormous bear hug, the smell of his aftershave like a warm blanket around her. She remembered her birthday party with friends and party games. Her mother had produced a cake and candles, and he'd dressed up as a clown. He was a bit of a showman – he'd always liked a good magic trick. *Now you see me, now you don't*. Gone in a puff of smoke. Her throat squeezed.

She remembered being part of a family, a unit of three. During those years at Primrose Cottage she'd belonged and she'd been loved.

'He loved me once,' she said quietly. And in a way that had made it even harder when he'd turned his back on her. It made it harder now to cast him in the role of villain. No one was evil through and through. She knew that.

Gabriel studied her carefully. Then he said, 'If I were you I would try to see him. He wants to rebuild your relationship. That can only be a good thing.'

She gave a bitter laugh. 'As long as he doesn't hurt me again.'

What a fool she'd be to let him into her life a second time, only to be let down.

He touched her arm. 'I don't think he'll do that.'

His face swam in front of her. 'How can you know?'

'He came all this way to see you, and even when you told him to go, he stayed.'

'Only because he's stubborn.'

'Because he cares about you,' Gabriel corrected. There was a pause and she sensed him weighing up whether to say more or not. Finally, he added gently, 'Seeing him again might never lead you to a perfect father–daughter relationship – but it might help you heal.'

Her head shot up. 'You think I'm broken?'

She hated to think he saw her in that way, hated that he might pity her. She wasn't dysfunctional or damaged. She was Daisy Jackson, high-achieving ambitious divorce lawyer.

Or was she? Had she been hiding behind that façade all these years, refusing to see her own emotional scars? Had Gabriel seen beyond the surface to what even she'd been too deluded to recognise?

'I think he let you down in a way no parent should, and what he did left scars. But it's up to you, Daisy. You'll decide what you want to do.'

'You're up early,' said Gabriel, the next morning.

Daisy was sitting outside, barefoot, in her satin dressing-gown, sipping coffee when he joined her. She loved this time when the sun was still meek, the air fresh with the scent of dew. Gabriel had been in the shower when she'd got up, but she'd found a pot of fresh coffee in the kitchen so she'd poured herself a cup and padded outside with it. Now he joined her, dressed for work in his paint-stained shorts and a white T-shirt.

'*Bonjour*,' he murmured, as he bent to kiss her.

She shivered. This French tradition of greeting each other with kisses was casual and perfunctory when they met his friends at the café, but here, now, in her night clothes, it took on a new intimacy.

He sat opposite her, tore off a chunk of bread and smothered it in butter. 'Did you sleep well?'

'Yes, fine,' she lied.

'You weren't too hot? Le Mazet is much cooler.'

'I had the fan on.'

In truth, she'd lain awake, not because of the heat but because she'd been aware of him just feet away in the next room. She'd lain in the dark, restless, her muscles wound tight, wondering how she'd found herself in this situation: so deeply attracted to a man despite knowing it was unrequited. Her imagination had filled in what reality was missing, and her temperature had climbed, longing coiling within her, making her ache.

Silence filled the space between them, and she realised he was studying her curiously as he ate his breakfast. She reached for her cup. 'How about you?' she asked, to deflect the conversation from herself. 'You weren't too hot?'

'In the house, yes.' He nodded at the nearby trees. 'So I slept in the hammock.'

She spluttered her coffee. 'Seriously?'

'Why not?'

He really was like no one she'd met before. So unfazed by anything – or anyone. His own man. She admired this in him.

'You might have been attacked by a wild boar or a fox or – or mosquitos!'

He laughed. 'This isn't the jungle. Boars and foxes are not predators. And mosquitos don't bite me.'

'Ever?'

'Ever.' He winked. 'I taste too sweet.'

Unbidden, the image of her lips tasting his dark bronze skin sprang to mind, and her mouth watered, heat settling in her centre. She tried to quash it. 'I feel bad,' she said.

'Why?'

'You had to sleep outside in a hammock because I'm in your bed.'

'I don't mind. You can stay in my bed as long as you like.' And was it her imagination or did his eyes gleam with mischief?

***

Gabriel strode through his house and found her sitting on the back patio painting. His heart jumped at the sight of her, and a jab of irritation followed. Irritation with himself – for his response to her.

He'd worked late, hoping to avoid exactly this. When he was with her his body seemed to override his brain. It lit up, wanted to get close, to tease her and make her smile, imagine her in his arms. He'd even started flirting with her and derived a huge thrill from watching her blush in response.

She looked up and smiled casually, then leaned back.

'How are you feeling?' he asked softly.

'Good, thanks.'

Her skin had turned a healthy honey-gold from the sun, but he still searched for shadows beneath her eyes or signs of tiredness and was relieved when he didn't find any. He bent to peer at her painting. She'd sketched in pencil his house with its low roof and sand-coloured walls, and painted the pots of flowers as tumbling balls of primary colours. She'd caught the small details perfectly: the glare of sunlight reflecting in the lanterns on the walls, and the shadowed grooves in the thick oak beam that ran above the French windows. 'Beautiful,' he said quietly.

Her cheeks bloomed a charming shade of pink. 'Thanks. Your pots are so pretty. You must have green fingers to keep all this alive despite the heat.'

He straightened. 'I just water them. It's not difficult.' Although he'd forgotten last night, hadn't he? And this morning. He'd been distracted having Daisy here in his home.

He cleared his throat. 'Would you like to learn how to make *coq au vin* tonight?' It would be the perfect way to keep his mind occupied and off this unhelpful awareness of her.

Her blonde brows knotted. 'Sounds complicated.'

'Not at all. Chicken cooked in red wine. It's very simple. The oven does all the work for you. I'll just get cleaned up, and we can begin.'

Ten minutes later, when he'd showered and changed, he found her in the kitchen, washing her paintbrushes and setting them on the windowsill to dry.

'Here we are,' he said, putting a large stockpot on the stove, and switching on the oven.

'Em – don't we need to tidy a little before we start?' Daisy asked, gesturing to the crowded worktop. 'There isn't much space.'

'*Bof.*' He pushed aside a pile of pots and plates. 'See? Lots of space now.'

She sighed. 'I don't know how you can find anything in all this mess.'

'I know exactly where everything is.' He opened the fridge and lifted out the tray of chicken. 'We're not all neat freaks like you.'

Her shocked expression made him smile. He loved teasing her.

'Better than being a slob,' she teased back, and swiped at him with a tea-towel so he had to duck.

He felt the unexpected urge to snatch the towel from her and pull her into his arms. Quashing it, he made himself focus on the task in hand. Cooking.

'So just heat a little olive oil in this pan and when it's hot you're going to brown the chicken.'

She poured in the oil and switched on the gas, then pointed at the chicken legs. 'You went to the butcher's? Is that why you were late home?'

'I went this afternoon,' he said, avoiding her question, 'and Arnaud sends you his regards.' He clenched his teeth as he recalled the gleam in the butcher's eye as he'd asked how Daisy was.

'She's fine.' Gabriel had shrugged. 'I think.'

'You think?' Arnaud had laughed. 'I heard she's moved in with you. Sounds to me like she's better than fine.'

Gabriel had narrowed his eyes and silently cursed whoever had spread the word – it must have been the plumber, Victor, or Thibaud, the electrician, because Gabriel hadn't even told his friends. It wasn't that he was hiding anything, he just hadn't got round to it yet. 'We're fitting a new bathroom and rewiring her house,' he'd spelled out tersely. 'She can't live without water or electricity.'

'Yeah, yeah.' Arnaud had grinned. 'She's a beautiful woman. Ha. If I was working on her house, I'd make sure to cut the electricity and water too.'

'Oh, that's kind of him,' Daisy said now. 'Next time we cook, let me know what we need and I'll do the shopping.'

His head whipped round. 'Because you want to see Arnaud?' A rush of fiery emotion hit the pit of his stomach.

She looked puzzled. Then, 'No. Because it's not fair that you should pay for all the food.'

'Oh.' He looked away quickly, and told himself to concentrate on making dinner instead of speculating on her relationships with other men. He fished in the drawer for a pair of tongs and handed them to her. 'You can fry the chicken now. The oil is hot enough.'

When she dropped the chicken into the pan and splashed hot oil everywhere, he said '*Non, non, non*. Like this.' Taking her hand in his, he showed her how to gently lower each piece into the pan, nestling it flat, but with enough room around each joint so they'd brown rather than stew. He'd seized her hand instinctively – he'd always been a tactile man – but immediately regretted it. They were so close, pressed up against each other, and his skin sparked where it made contact with hers. An arrow of electricity jolted through him.

He drew back and raked a hand through his hair. This was bad. The awareness he felt was only growing stronger. He'd reasoned that she was just a friend, but the more their friendship deepened, the more his attraction grew.

He had to keep reminding himself that Daisy Jackson was totally wrong for him, and she wasn't here to stay. Soon she'd vanish back to the city and Le Mazet would stand empty. Beautifully renovated and cared for – but empty.

Daisy was sitting in the shade at the back of his house, reading, when he got home on the third evening.

'You're working really long days,' she said. Then immediately cringed at how that sounded – over-anxiously questioning him about his movements as if they were married. But it was six o'clock now and she'd heard him slip out at six this morning. And when she'd popped by Le Mazet at lunchtime to pick up a change of clothes he'd been working through his lunch hour. Yesterday he'd worked a ten-hour day, too. This, the man who usually took two hours off for lunch and a *sieste,* the man who'd told her how necessary rests were for a labourer in the heat.

'I am,' he said. Deep lines furrowed his brow and he looked pensively at the pots of jewel-coloured flowers that spilled over onto the sandstone paving slabs but he didn't elaborate.

His silence did nothing to calm her anxiety. Was living with her driving him to stay away from his home?

When he reappeared after having showered, his wet hair slicked back, he looked brighter and less exhausted than before. He stopped in the doorway of the kitchen. 'Where is everything?'

'Em . . . I tidied.' She glanced nervously at the gleaming surfaces, hoping he wouldn't mind. She'd had to rearrange the contents of his cupboards a little to make everything fit, but doing so meant the clutter had been swept away and there was room to work. It was also spotless.

He opened a cupboard door, then another. He looked at the freshly mopped floor. She held her breath, waiting for his reaction. She'd done it to help because organising was one of her strengths and she'd had time on her hands. But now she realised it could be interpreted as an intrusive act. This was his home and his kitchen.

Finally, he smiled. 'My kitchen is bigger than I knew.'

Relief washed through her.

They set about reheating yesterday's *coq au vin* for dinner, and she dressed a salad of green beans and tomatoes to go with it. As she measured the oil and vinegar, as he'd taught her, then added a pinch of salt, she side-eyed him surreptitiously. He remained obstinately silent, and this only fed her anxiety more.

'How is it coming along?' she asked, whisking in a tiny amount of grainy mustard.

'What?'

'The house.'

'Ah. It's going well.' He tore off a chunk of the baguette and ate it. She loved how he did this. Her life was based around a strict routine and discipline, whereas if he was hungry, he ate. Tired, he stopped to rest. He was instinctive. Sensual.

She waited, but he gazed thoughtfully out of the window and didn't say anything more.

Eventually she prompted, 'What have you done today?'

He gave her a crooked grin. 'Are you checking up on me?'

'Not at all. I'm just curious. You worked twelve hours without a break. You must have got a lot done.'

He placed his hands on her arms to nudge her to the left so he could open the fridge. He often did this kind of thing – stroked her cheek if she looked sad, or brushed her hair out of her eyes. He was so tactile. Her skin tingled where his fingers had touched her. He offered her a cold beer, but she shook her head. He snapped the lid off and took a long swallow. 'What did I do?' he said, thinking aloud. 'I finished ripping out the old bathroom. I began replastering the rooms upstairs where Thibaud's finished rewiring, and I helped Victor replace some old pipework.'

'That's a lot.'

'Yes.' He took another swig of beer, his movements slow and tired all of a sudden.

She fought the urge to smooth the skin around his beautiful dark eyes.

He glanced at the oven. 'The chicken's ready. Shall we eat?'

She nodded, and they carried the food outside. He served himself a generous helping, and she eyed him surreptitiously. Finally, she said quietly, 'I feel bad that you're working so hard.'

Was it because she was here and he wanted to get away from her? The question burned her lips, but she couldn't bring herself to ask it in case she didn't like the answer. Ask Gabriel a question and he didn't wrap things up in tactful lies: he gave only the bald truth.

Perhaps she should leave and go back to London. Then he'd be able to work at his own pace without running himself into the ground, and he'd have his home back. Although he had good friends in the village, she knew he was a man who enjoyed his own company, who was comfortable alone. She didn't need to stay here, did she? The work on the house was well under way and she trusted him to finish it without her.

But she didn't feel ready to go back to London yet.

She didn't have the energy to face returning to work, for one thing, she thought, glancing out of the window at the peachy glow of the evening sun. But she also wanted to enjoy more sunsets, more cookery lessons, afternoons reading in the shade, trips to the market. She wasn't ready to leave. Not yet.

Perhaps she should move out and get a room in the village. Give him more space. But even that thought left her cold.

Truth was, she liked it here. She looked around at the pots of cascading flowers and the golden walls of his cosy house. She'd always been fiercely protective of her own space, yet staying here felt . . . comfortable. She enjoyed their meals outside on the patio, then afterwards curling up on the sofa to read or just talk. Sharing with him had been unexpectedly straightforward.

Except that she was in a constant state of edginess. Living in such a confined space meant they couldn't get away from each other, and her body was acutely conscious of his constant proximity. Tense. Taut. On permanent high alert.

'I'm doing it for you,' he said, breaking her train of thoughts.

'What?'

'I'm working hard, getting everything done as fast as I can so you can move back in as soon as possible.' His hand swept through the air indicating his home. 'You don't want to stay here any longer than necessary, I'm sure, so I've been trying to get the work finished quickly for you.'

She blinked, touched beyond words by his thoughtfulness. 'Oh . . .' she began, then laughed, embarrassed. 'It's not *that* bad here.' She suddenly found herself unable to look him in the eye for fear that he might see the desire in her own, and her gaze dipped to his chest.

But that was a mistake. He was wearing a white linen shirt, the two top buttons undone, revealing a triangle of golden skin and a glimpse of dark chest hair. She ran her tongue over her lips.

'Not that bad?' She heard the smile in his voice.

Her cheeks fired up. 'No – I mean – it's not . . .' She sighed. What was it about this man that he affected her like this? Until she'd come to Provence she'd been an eloquent professional. Right now she felt like a teenager quivering with hormones and the overpowering urge to get naked with him. Christ. She wanted him, but didn't know what to do with those feelings. Ever since he'd rejected her, she'd been trying to suppress her attraction, but it wasn't working. In fact, she felt as if she was clinging to the cork of a bottle of champagne, trying to hold it down while the pressure inside was steadily building. 'What I meant was there's no need for you to work long days or go without breaks. I'm happy here.'

He quirked a brow. 'Really?' The corner of his lip twitched. It was incredibly sexy, and her gaze lingered on it far too long.

She nodded.

'I thought you didn't approve of breaks.'

'I . . .' She blushed, 'I don't mind.'

'And I thought you found this place too messy.'

He was teasing her, she knew, and sparks skittered through her. She glowed. Grinning, she replied, 'Of course I do. But I'm digging deep to overlook your faults.'

His laughter was low and throaty. Her thighs squeezed, and she got up, hurriedly snatching up their empty plates simply to distract herself from her fiery desire.

'Why are you blushing, Daisy? Why the hurry?' He leaned back in his chair, visibly amused.

'You have finished, haven't you?' she asked, her hand hovering over the basket of bread.

'I don't know.' A lazy smile played at his lips. 'Perhaps you want something more? Something sweet?'

Was it her imagination or did his gaze flicker to her lips as he said that. She hadn't thought it was possible for her to blush any more, but her skin burned, like metal in the sun. 'L-like what?' Her voice was soft and rough around the edges.

He held her gaze, and seconds passed. She couldn't forget when he'd pushed her away that night, yet now his eyes were dark with desire. Or was she seeing what she wanted to see?

He blinked and they cleared. 'Ice cream?' he suggested mildly. 'Fruit?'

A cold wave of disappointment washed through her. 'Not for me, thanks,' she said, and hurried off into the kitchen before he could see her humiliation.

As she ran the hot water over the dishes, she gripped the edge of the sink and sucked in air. What was she supposed to do with all this pent-up need? With each day that passed and each hour spent together, the tension was becoming unbearable. For her, anyway.

Yet she didn't want to be anywhere but here.

Gabriel pulled up outside his home and killed the engine. Another long day, another late finish, and here he was dreading going into his home – yet impatient to see Daisy again.

He gripped the steering wheel, confused by the paradox, overwhelmed by the strength of his feelings. And they were gathering force with each day that passed. Sometimes when he was with her, desire – need – grabbed hold of him like a fist. Hot. Fierce. Impossible to resist.

But he had to. He and Daisy were incompatible. Too different, too headstrong. Everyone knew that two strong personalities would end in the most intense clash.

Then again, what was passion but intense emotion? Desire coiled in him, dark and dangerous. He wasn't sure how to handle this. He'd never felt such lust, such misdirected emotion for a woman before. In truth, this was another reason why he'd been toiling long hours at Le Mazet. He'd underestimated what sharing with her would be like. He'd told himself it would be fine, but in his home they were alone, he wasn't occupied with work, and his place was small.

Too small.

Since she'd arrived with her overnight bag, the walls seemed to have shrunk, the air temperature had risen by ten degrees at least, and everywhere he turned she was there. Even when she'd gone to bed at night, she dominated his thoughts, she penetrated his dreams. His muscles were permanently knotted with tension.

While the two of them were sharing a roof, he wasn't going to get any rest, so he might as well work himself into the ground, hammering, mixing plaster and finishing the damn job at Le Mazet so she could leave, and his life return to normal.

Except something in him knew that wasn't going to happen.

He stilled. Because the thought of her leaving was painful.

He enjoyed the intimacy they were sharing here. Teaching her to cook, eating together, reading side by side on the sofa. It wasn't just about desire: it was about making her smile and laugh, listening to her talk about her work, her past, her hopes. It was about sharing happy moments at the café with his friends and walking home together, telling her about his childhood, how it had been to grow up here, and pausing to gaze up at the stars together. She'd become part of the fabric of his life, and as precious to him as – if not more than – Le Mazet itself.

The realisation made him still.

His fist curled around itself. He knew what this meant. He knew what was happening. Daisy Jackson was wrong for him – his head knew it, but his heart wasn't listening.

His heart had decided it was hers.

Chapter 19

'Ready for another cookery lesson?' Gabriel asked. He'd come home late, showered, and now he emerged from the bathroom wearing only shorts and towel-drying his hair. Damp curls kissed the back of his neck. Daisy tried not to stare at the dark hair on his chest or the muscles that rippled as he hung his towel over the back of a chair.

'You're not going to get dressed first?' Her tone was light and teasing, but she felt tense and self-conscious.

'It's too hot.' His eyes gleamed. 'Count yourself lucky. Normally I don't wear shorts.'

Her cheeks flushed. She didn't know what to do with her feelings for him, what to do with *herself*. He was so casual about his nakedness, but this was his home, after all. The fact that she couldn't deal with it was entirely her problem.

'So what are we making tonight?' she asked, trying to move the conversation to a safer topic as she headed into the kitchen. Since her first lesson on soup, he'd taught her how to fry steak and mix her own vinaigrette dressing, how to bake fish, and some basic casseroles. Nothing too difficult and the results had tasted good. But she had to confess she enjoyed spending time with him more than the cooking.

He followed her, and his large frame filled the space around her. No matter where she stood in this minuscule kitchen, she couldn't get away from him.

'Roast chicken and *tomates Provençales*. You had them at Maman Gilberte's, remember?'

She did remember. They'd been melt-in-the-mouth delicious.

He went on, 'They're very easy. But, first, let's get the chicken into the oven.'

She tried to concentrate as he talked her through the simple instructions: drizzle a little olive oil over the chicken to crisp the skin, salt and pepper, then into a roasting tin and oven roast for an hour or so. She tried to concentrate, but her gaze kept being drawn to his bare torso and the solid bulk of his shoulders. Muscles cording and knotting. Even his bare feet made her feel shivery, for goodness' sake. How could the sight of bare feet be so erotic?

She washed the tomatoes and he showed her how to slice them across their equator.

'It's prettier this way,' he explained. 'The seeds do not spill out, and the tomatoes hold their shape, see?'

She nodded and took the serrated knife. It was still warm from his touch. When she'd laid the tomatoes cut side up on a tray, he passed her the garlic and a bunch of herbs to chop while he tipped breadcrumbs into a bowl.

'Now, just mix all this together with some olive oil,' he said.

They worked side by side. His breath whispered across her shoulders, and she was conscious of his thigh next to her hip. Heat crept into her cheeks. He was so big, so gentle in his instructions, and the woody scent of him filled her senses, heady yet paradoxically calming at the same time. How would it feel to be naked with him, to feel those big hands on her, those strong legs entwined with hers?

She tried to push the thoughts back, reminding herself that he'd made it clear he didn't want her in that way, but the fantasies still hovered at the edges of her consciousness, as tormenting as they were tempting.

'*Parfait*,' he said, when she'd made the breadcrumb mixture. His gaze met hers and a rush of warmth swept through her. It was unexpected. Since when had his approval mattered so much to her? Yet it did. It really did.

'See?' he said, when she'd finished spooning the breadcrumb mixture over the tomatoes. 'We'll make a cook out of you yet.'

'I don't know. I'm not sure I could be bothered to cook just for me,' she said, trying to picture her London kitchen, but it seemed so hazy. The only kitchen she could visualise was the one at Le Mazet where the smell of lavender and herbs drifted in through the open door, and the flagged stone floor, worn smooth from centuries of use, was deliciously cold beneath her bare feet.

'Why not?' He looked appalled.

She shrugged. 'Is there any point when you're alone? When there's no one to see how carefully it's been prepared, no one to share it with?' Her gaze fluttered over his bare chest, and her thighs squeezed.

'Of course. It's food. It's going into your mouth. You owe it to yourself to eat well, even when you are alone.'

She was still finding it impossible to imagine herself going to this much trouble for herself at the end of a long hard day at work, and felt an inexplicable pang of sadness.

'So you'll go back to eating takeaway food when you're in London?' he asked.

Her smile was sheepish and she looked up at him from beneath her lashes. 'Probably.'

But she'd think of this. Of him. And she'd miss him.

The realisation made her heart quicken with panic. *Miss him?* Was she getting attached? Surely not.

'This is terrible. I'm outraged!' He shook his head, and she wasn't sure if he was joking or not. She suspected not. 'All these lessons, all this time together, and I have taught you nothing.'

He slid the tray into the oven and straightened up, hands on hips.

She couldn't move. Didn't want to move. She had to fight the urge to reach out and draw his hips against hers. She wanted him so much.

Oh, God, when would this ache lessen just a little? She tried to imagine what it would have been like if he hadn't pushed her away when she'd tried to seduce him three weeks ago. They would have made love and the attraction would have faded. It was only because she couldn't have him that she wanted him so much, that she was feeling so much. Wasn't it?

She swallowed. Perhaps not. She didn't like to acknowledge it, but the truth was this attraction was stronger, deeper, more intense than anything she'd ever known.

'You have,' she said quietly. Her voice sounded huskier than normal. 'You've taught me a lot.'

He'd taught her how to slow down, to savour each of her senses. To appreciate the precious scents and sights, sounds and flavours of this enchanting place. He'd taught her so much. So why did she feel as if there was so much more she could learn from him? So much she could teach him in return? Christ, if only she could quell the unbearable longing and extricate herself from this swamp of sticky emotions.

Half an hour later, the food was ready and they ate in companionable silence.

'It's delicious,' Daisy said. The chicken was golden and tender, the skin sweet and crisp, and the flavour of garlic danced on her tongue as she tried the tomatoes.

'You like it? Good.' His eyes gleamed in the golden lighting.

'I love it.'

He'd put a T-shirt on before sitting down to eat, but the white cotton fabric was stretched so tightly that it teased her with glimpses of hard muscle that knotted and flexed as he reached for the chilled water and filled her glass. A sweet, floral perfume drifted from the pots of flowers nearby.

'It wasn't difficult, was it?' he said.

'Not at all.'

A rustle made her head swivel sharply. She peered at the bushes, but it was impossible to see anything outside the pool of light that surrounded them. Beyond it there was total darkness.

'It's just a mouse or a frog. Don't worry,' Gabriel said, and put his hand on hers.

It had been intended as a reassuring gesture, but she jumped, startled. Then she laughed. 'Sorry. I – I'm on edge.'

He smiled. 'City girl, you're scared of every little sound.'

She stared at her hand. The skin still felt fiery from his touch. She wanted to tell him she wasn't afraid, just acutely sensitive to him. Need coiled inside her. Like light through a prism, it scattered a rainbow of sensations. Her body sparked, her skin tingled. She tried to concentrate on the food and the smooth, light red wine he'd opened to accompany it. But her gaze drifted back to him again and again. She watched his long dark lashes lower, his lips open, his Adam's apple rise and fall as he swallowed. And her thighs squeezed tighter.

Suddenly she couldn't do this any more.

It was too difficult. The perpetual battle with herself was too much. She couldn't spend another sleepless night lying naked and thinking of him, longing for him, needing what she couldn't have.

She pushed her chair back. 'Gabriel, I – I think I'll go home.'

'What?' He dropped his fork and it clattered against his plate. 'Now?'

She nodded.

'Why?'

'To – give you some space.' The words began to tumble from her mouth, fast and clumsy. 'You can't be comfortable sleeping on the sofa or the hammock, and I could still come over and use your shower in the morning – once you've started work. That way I won't disturb you.'

He stood up. Deep creases cut through his brow. 'You're not disturbing me. What makes you think you are?'

'Nothing. I mean I don't think . . .' She swallowed. How had she managed to offend him? Christ, she was making a real mess of this. But she couldn't admit the truth. That she needed to escape the suffocating need that tormented her and kept her awake at night.

'What about your meal?' he asked. 'You haven't finished eating.'

'I . . . I'm not hungry.'

'You said it was delicious.' She heard the confusion and hurt in his voice, saw them in his eyes. Panicking, she went inside and dug in her bag for her car keys. She had to get away before she said something she'd later regret.

He followed her into the unlit lounge. 'You can't drive,' he said quickly, when he saw the keys in her clenched fist. 'You've had wine.'

She stopped. His eyes burned like hot coals in the semi-darkness. He was so beautiful.

'I've hardly had any. It's fine.' She made for the front door. 'I'll see you tomorr—'

'No!' His tone was fierce.

She stopped and blinked at him.

He raked a hand through his hair and seemed as surprised as her. He blew out a long slow breath. Then stepped forward.

His big hands circled her waist, holding her lightly, clamping her with the gentlest of touches. 'I don't want you to go, Daisy.' His confession was raw with emotion.

Her breath snagged. The rueful honesty in his eyes made her want to reach up and touch his cheek.

Confused, she tried to look away, to collect her thoughts, but all she could see was his broad chest in front of her. Even as her heart leaped, she chided herself. He didn't want her: he'd made that clear when he'd rejected her.

And yet his eyes scorched her. His gaze dipped to her lips and another flare of heat shot through her because his body was telling her he did want her.

'Please stay,' he said, his voice so low she felt its vibrations. 'Don't go.'

She was perplexed by the seductive softness of his words. It clashed with her memory of his rejection. He didn't do desire for its own sake. Yet his eyes were drilling into her, pleading with her.

Pride made her want to flee. To tell him the truth would be humiliating. A repeat of her last humiliation.

But since when did she shy away from difficult truths?

'I can't, Gabriel,' she said, keeping her gaze on his chest while she mustered the courage to come clean. Her voice was ragged. 'I can't do this any more.'

'Do what? I don't understand.'

She took a deep breath and made herself look him in the eye. 'I want you, Gab. I've always wanted you, and I can't – can't fight it any longer. Living here, sharing your home with you . . .' She cast about for words to express how strangled she felt by the heat that charged the air whenever he was near her, how in his tiny house it had seemed to grow to formidable proportions. Desire threatened to suffocate her. 'It's too much. Too intense.'

She turned away, embarrassed and angry with herself for revealing so much yet again, for laying her heart bare. Okay, it wasn't so much her heart as something more visceral, but even so. Why couldn't she have had more self-control and mastered her desires? She should have left without giving him an explanation and preserved her dignity.

But that would have been cowardly – as cowardly as her dad's behaviour all those years ago – and Gabriel would have been confused. Hurt. She couldn't do that to him.

Her heart thumped loudly. The house was still and silent. The softest whisper of trees and bushes drifted in through the open doors.

'So?' he said.

Her head lifted. She stared at him. The corner of his mouth lifted in a half-smile. Was he mocking her?

She bristled. Confused, she stepped away from him. 'Don't laugh at me,' she said, blinking hard. 'I've been honest with you. I can't help the way I feel.'

'I'm not laughing at you, Daisy,' he said. She scoured his face and found only warmth in his brown eyes.

Her breath caught. Hope hooked itself around her. 'Then what did you mean, "So?"'

His gaze held hers. 'So you want me – what does it matter?' His hand slipped around her and drew her to him. He cupped her chin tenderly. 'Stay with me. Tonight.'

Shocked, she stared at him, trying to make sense of this. His woody scent made her dizzy.

He dipped his head and his lips brushed hers. 'Daisy,' he said, against her mouth. 'I want you too.'

He did?

Liquid heat spilled through her as he kissed her again, more urgently this time. He cradled her cheeks in his hands and the look in his eyes was fierce. Hungry.

'You . . .' she faltered '. . . you want me to stay?'

'Yes.'

'But I don't understand. You said . . .' she licked her dry lips '. . . you wouldn't – you didn't want to.'

'My feelings have changed.'

But he was immovable, stubborn. He wasn't a man who changed his mind easily or did U-turns. And hadn't he said he'd only sleep with someone he loved?

She searched his eyes and what she saw made her body hum. He kissed her again and it was heavenly. She sank against him, giving herself up to it. God, she wanted this so much she didn't care why he'd changed his mind. She simply had to have him. Now.

Her eyes drifted shut and his breath whispered against her neck before he dropped a trail of tiny light kisses from the base of her ear to her throat. Head tipped back, she couldn't think, couldn't speak. It was exquisite, her body taut with anticipation.

He wrapped one arm around her waist and pulled her against him; the other cradled the back of her neck, his fingers tangling in her hair. How could those big calloused hands be so tender? His touch sent arrows shooting through her. She breathed a sigh of pleasure and his lips sought hers hungrily, growing more feverish with every touch, every breath. She clung to his shoulders, his solid waist. Need coiled itself so tightly within her that she could barely breathe.

He pulled back. His eyes glittered like black diamonds in the moonlight. 'I need to get you out of these clothes,' he said roughly, his gaze sweeping over her, 'and into my bed.'

Her heart soared. Then she realised he was poised, waiting for her assent. She nodded breathlessly. 'Bed – yes.'

He scooped her up and carried her to the bedroom, kicking the door shut behind him. He laid her on the bed, pausing a moment before he joined her – and the look in his eyes as he gazed down at her stole her breath away. Desire swamped her.

He peeled away her top, and began to drop kisses along the lace trim of her bra. His big hand found the dip in her spine and his touch was warm, the sensation of skin against skin too delicious to bear. She twisted and arched against him, breathing fast, trying not to moan with pleasure, but he wouldn't be hurried. His kisses were like the lightest breeze on a warm day: welcome, but not enough. She gripped his shoulders and tugged at his T-shirt, desperate to remove it. He stopped to pull it up over his head and she smoothed her hands across his bare torso, drinking in the caramel tones of his skin, the dusting of dark hair.

'Have you got protection?' she asked.

'I have.' He nodded at the bedside table.

She reached for his shorts. 'Then what are you waiting for?' she asked, when he didn't move.

'Hey,' he said, smiling. His hand closed over hers. 'Slow down.'

'I can't.' She'd wanted this so much and for so long, it was unbearable.

His dark eyes gleamed with amusement. 'Why is everything so fast with you?'

'Because I want you,' she breathed, her voice raw with honesty. 'Now.' She'd never wanted anyone more.

He lifted her wrist and her watch glinted in the pale gold of the bedside light. 'Would it help you slow down if I took this off?' he teased.

'No,' she said, and reached to kiss him impatiently, greedily. She was wound so tight it felt dangerous. No one had ever made her ache so much. No one had ever made her wait.

He pulled back, and the corners of his mouth twitched. 'One day I will teach you to savour each moment, to let time stretch and forget the past or the future.'

Future? There was no future for them, she thought fleetingly. But the thought was swept aside as he began to undo the metal bracelet, and she watched, entranced. His fingers worked slowly, stroking her skin, rubbing it with the pad of his thumb. He flicked the catch open, loosening the watch but holding it in place, then lifted her arm to his lips. His eyes connected with hers and held. Her breath caught as he kissed the pale, tender skin on the inside of her wrist, never taking his gaze off her. It was the most erotic thing she'd ever known. Sparks scattered where his lips touched her skin. Seconds stretched endlessly. Taking all the time in the world, he eased the metal clip through and the diamond-studded clock face glittered as it caught the light of the moon. Her heart was pumping so hard she thought it might burst. Still Gabriel held her gaze, his eyes gleaming with heat and unspoken promises. Finally, he removed the watch and laid it on the bedside table.

'If you're going to take that long over every little thing, I'm not sure I can do this,' she whispered, her thighs squeezed tight, every muscle coiled.

'Oh, you can, Daisy,' he said. 'And I promise you it will be worth the wait.'

Chapter 20

This is bliss, was Daisy's first thought when she woke in the night. Perfect. At long last she had relief—

The fog of sleep abruptly cleared and she turned to look at Gabriel. Fast asleep beside her, his features were relaxed and peaceful, his long lashes fanned against his cheeks. Panic made her throat tighten.

She looked at the window and saw the moon glowing, swollen and serene, surrounded by a cluster of glistening stars. Its light flowed into the room, bathing everything in liquid silver.

Her heart beat fast. She shouldn't have done this. Three weeks ago he'd pushed her away. Last night he'd said he wanted her, and they'd had the best sex of her life. What had changed? He'd told her he'd only make love to a woman he loved—

Her throat closed. Alarm filled her. No. He couldn't—

Skin prickling, she pushed back the sheet as softly as possible. The sex had been incredible, but she'd already stayed longer than she ever did. She had to go. When she got home and there was space between them she'd be able to think clearly. She'd work out how to deal with this because she'd never expected last night to turn out as it had. Carefully, she slipped out of bed. The tiles were shockingly cold beneath her toes–

'*Non.*'

Gabriel's deep voice made her freeze.

'Don't tell me you're planning to sneak away in the night like a thief, Daisy.'

She sucked in air. That was exactly what she'd been planning.

The sheets rustled as he reached over. He took her hand and gently tugged her back towards him. She shook it off, afraid to get too close to his electrifying heat and his body, which had moulded so perfectly against hers. Afraid she'd lose her resolve and succumb again to temptation.

'What are you afraid of, Daisy?' he asked calmly. 'That you'll turn into a pumpkin? You're not Cinderella.'

Despite herself she smiled in the darkness. But she couldn't speak, couldn't answer his question. How did she explain without hurting him?

'Why are you leaving?' he insisted.

'Because I – can't stay.'

'Why?'

She swallowed. 'I never stay.'

'No? You think that by creeping away from me now I'll become like the rest of them – all your other one-night stands?' In the darkness he was a grey silhouette but his eyes gleamed like stars. And his gaze held hers, immovable, unwavering. 'We both know that isn't going to happen, Daisy. Not this time.'

She swallowed. He was wrong. 'Gab.' She cleared her throat and began again. 'This can't – I don't do relationships. I don't do—'

Love.

Why couldn't she say it?

And he'd said he'd only sleep with a woman he loved. Did he love her? The question stuck in her throat. She couldn't ask for fear of his answer.

'Try it.' His hand squeezed hers.

Her heart thumped against her ribcage. She shook her head. 'We're not compatible.'

'You weren't saying that three hours ago.'

Heated memories smoked through her. 'But we want different things,' she said finally. Her words were weak and so was her attempt to push herself away from the bed. He wanted love. A lasting relationship. She didn't.

Then a thought occurred. The memory of him in the attic, searching through the trunk for the will – and looking despondent when he hadn't found it.

She'd felt so hurt, betrayed.

Perhaps he didn't love her after all. A curious mixture of relief and familiar cynicism washed through her. Perhaps he was doing this to keep her close, to keep himself close to Le Mazet. After all, the house meant more to him than anything else. It made sense. A man with rigid principles like him wouldn't suddenly abandon them. Yes, he was probably still hoping to find his soul-mate, but in the meantime he'd chosen to follow his desires. To take what he wanted – sex – as she did.

'Come back to me, Daisy,' he said.

She hesitated. It was so tempting.

He went on, 'It doesn't have to be complicated. We can just take one day at a time.'

Really? She glanced at him, and his gaze met hers steadily. His earnest expression reassured her. It was just sex?

'I want you and you want me.' The low purr of his voice sent vibrations through her and her shoulders sagged. 'Don't be scared, Daisy.'

As she stared into his eyes, her heart hammered. Thoughts swirled, dark and guilty. It was difficult to resist when he was looking at her like this, as if she were the centre of his universe. As if nothing else mattered but the two of them and the magic they'd shared tonight.

Because it *had* been magic. She'd been with enough men to know this had been special. Exceptional. His hands, as he'd shaped her waist, her hip, her thigh, had been so gentle. And his eyes had been filled with tenderness. Desire. Concern. Checking, silently asking, did she like this? And this? Watching, listening, gauging her reactions, her pleasure mounting to almost unbearable proportions.

Yes, it had been the best sex. And she wasn't ready for it to end yet.

The last threads of her resolve snapped. Longing wrapped itself around her, entwined itself in her limbs, and she sank back onto the bed and into the heat of his arms.

Gabriel watched as Daisy got up, murmuring that she needed coffee. Her satin nightie whispered over her bare legs, her blonde hair swung about her shoulders, glowing like gold metal in the newborn light. Then she disappeared. He lay back, hands behind his head, staring unseeingly out of the window.

His heart felt full. Brimming with emotion.

What they'd shared last night had been intense. Incredible. Unforgettable. She'd felt it too, he was sure of it. But her instinct had been to flee, and even now she was still holding back.

And he was disappointed.

He'd hoped this might be the key to unlocking her. That it might bypass her cynical, analytical mind and take him straight to the part of her she kept so well guarded. Her heart, her soul.

But it seemed her defences were harder to break down than he'd anticipated. She would have left in the night if he hadn't woken and stopped her. She reminded him of Zouzou, the stray cat. Wary. Fiercely independent. He'd had to coax her back to him, reassuring her, trying to calm her fears.

I don't do relationships.

He understood. Her heart had been left in shreds by her parents' divorce and her father's abandonment. She said she didn't believe in love, but was she really so hardened? He suspected she was protecting herself. She didn't want to make herself vulnerable by allowing anyone close.

And, ironically, her reticence left *him* feeling vulnerable. Exposed. He'd given her everything last night. He hadn't planned to – she'd caught him off guard when she'd suddenly got up to leave – but it had been waiting to happen. He'd been tired of fighting the temptation. So he'd given her his body, his soul, his heart. Laid himself bare. A less passionate man might have settled for sex, but he'd never been that man. He'd always felt things acutely.

He loved her completely. For always.

Of course, he couldn't tell her how he felt. It was too soon, and he couldn't risk frightening her away. Still, he knew she was the woman he was destined to love for the rest of his life.

And yet she was so far from the woman he'd been searching for. He wanted love, fidelity, permanence. Daisy wasn't interested in any of those. He rubbed a hand over his face. She couldn't be more unsuitable for him.

Yet his heart wasn't listening. Instead, it was hoping she'd return his love. He needed her to return it.

But she didn't love him. She didn't do love at all.

She might, if she felt safe. He'd make her feel safe. He'd protect her, cherish her, give her all the love and stability she'd missed out on growing up. He'd show her that she didn't have to be alone any more: she could rely on him.

He hung his head. But until the day came when she felt ready to open her heart, there was nothing he could do to make her love him.

Like when he went fishing and sat waiting for a fish to bite, he'd just have to be patient – and hope.

He hadn't said he loved her. Two days later Daisy clung to this thought as if it were a lifebuoy.

She'd walked down to the village to do some shopping, but as she waited in the queue at the *boulangerie* her mind was stuck at Gabriel's little house where they'd spent a third hot night in each other's arms. Yet he hadn't said a word to explain how he felt about this, and she was worried.

He must have come round to her way of thinking and realised that sex was enough, she decided. It was simple, straightforward, and no one would get hurt.

She tried to push away the niggling doubt in her mind that contradicted this. She should end it. Tell him it had already lasted too long, and it had to stop.

But you can't, can you, Daisy? The devilish whisper in her mind was right. Her previous certainty that once she'd made love to a man the attraction would fade had been well and truly blown out of the water. If anything, her awareness of Gabriel had deepened, and the intimacy they shared had grown. He'd got under her skin.

And she was scared. Scared that Gabriel might love her, that she'd hurt him. Scared of her feelings for him. One-night stands were her comfort zone. This fling, or whatever you called it, was unfamiliar territory. And seeing her dad the other day had been a brutal reminder of how destructive relationships could be. She didn't need anyone else to hurt her. She didn't need anyone.

A customer left the shop carrying a big white cake box, and the queue shuffled forward. The smell of freshly baked bread warmed the air, and Daisy's gaze drifted to the display of mouth-watering tarts and pastries. They weren't good for her waistline, but she'd given up trying to resist the temptation. Just as she'd caved in to Gabriel.

She bit her lip. Sex aside, Gabriel had become a good friend, and she didn't want to spoil their friendship. Yet she couldn't mislead him into believing this was more than a fling.

He wouldn't think that, she assured herself. He didn't know everything about her, but she'd always spoken openly about her views on relationships. And Gabriel was frank: if he'd felt anything . . . deep, he would have said so. But he hadn't.

So it was fine. This was just sex and that was all it would ever be.

'Want to see the new bathroom?' Gabriel asked, the keys to his truck in his hand. He'd just got home, he was still dusty from a full day's work, but he was impatient to show her the result of his toils.

Daisy's eyes widened as she looked up from watering the pots of geraniums. 'It's finished?'

'It's finished.' Excitement fizzed inside him. He hoped she'd like it. Not just because she was an exacting customer, but because he cared. He'd worked so hard to make it perfect for her.

She twisted the hosepipe shut and put it down, wiped her hands on her hips. 'Of course I want to see it – let's go now.'

A few minutes later they parked outside Le Mazet, and went in.

As they neared the bathroom door, he covered her eyes with his hands. 'What are you doing?' she asked, smiling.

He steered her slowly towards the open door. 'Stopping you peeking. I want it to be a surprise.'

'You're building this up too much. It's just a bathroom, and I chose everything, remember? You can't surprise a control freak.'

No? He smiled to himself and dropped his hands, then waited for her reaction.

She blinked. He felt a ripple of satisfaction when her mouth fell open and her eyes grew big and round. 'It's –

amazing,' she gasped. 'But – I don't understand – how does it look so different from before?'

He tipped his head. 'The plumber and I played around with the layout.' The result was they'd made room for a larger shower, the walk-in kind she preferred, and after a lot of searching he'd managed to find all the fittings and finishing touches that gave the room an ultra-modern look. Glass screens, a wet-room-style tiled floor, a sleek mirror with ambient lighting and all sorts of other unnecessary and expensive embellishments.

She took a few steps inside and spun round. 'I love it. It's so . . . modern.'

'That's what you wanted.'

'But you said traditional suited the house better.'

'I can live with chrome taps and modern tiles.' He grinned. If they made her happy, he was happy.

He gestured to her bedroom across the landing. 'The electrics are safe throughout the house now. Thibaud replaced all the light switches and plug sockets, and I have some replastering to do where he ran the cables but your bedroom is fine.'

'So . . . I can sleep here tonight?'

He stiffened. Was that what she wanted? He tried to keep his tone casual. 'You can sleep wherever you want.'

Their eyes connected. The air simmered with heat. Hope rose in him – but he saw her hesitation.

He asked quietly, 'Where do you want to sleep?'

'Here,' she said, looking around her with a fond smile. 'I can't believe how I've missed this place.'

His heart sank. So he *had* been just like her other one-night stands, then.

She continued, 'You probably don't remember, but when I first arrived here you told me this house has a special atmosphere.' She laughed. 'I thought you were mad. I just saw a rundown old wreck with empty fields all around. But now . . .' She ran her palm over the wall beneath the small window. The stone was almost a metre thick, solid and cool. '. . . now I know exactly what you mean.'

Gabriel didn't say anything. All he could think was she wanted to move out, wanted to leave him already.

She went on, 'So, yes, I'll move back here tonight. There's more space, a gorgeous new bathroom, and it's cooler.'

He nodded politely, and when he spotted a minuscule splash of dried paint on a tile, concentrated hard on scraping it off with his thumbnail while he wrestled his disappointment to the ground. Wrestling a bear would have been easier.

'Gab? Would that be okay?'

He realised she'd stepped closer and was peering anxiously at him.

'*Oui.*' He jammed his hands into his pockets and shrugged.

'You don't seem happy.'

'I'm fine. It's fine. Whatever you want.'

A short silence followed. The house made settling noises, small creaks and sighs as the temperature dropped and the structure shrank and contracted. He looked around, everywhere but at her. He'd been foolish to believe the last few nights had meant anything to her, foolish to think that with time she might change. He'd been a hopeful fool.

Daisy said, 'There's some space in the wardrobe, if that's what you're worried about.'

He glanced at her. 'What?'

She swallowed. 'You could . . . stay with me. Here.'

It was his turn to stare, wide-eyed.

She reached into her handbag and patted the book of Jeanette's recipes, which he'd let her borrow so she could pick their next dish to cook. 'Well, if you're going to work long days on the house, then stay late to give me cookery lessons, there's not much point in you going home, is there?' Her grey eyes shone mischievously. Seductively.

And his heart exploded with joy.

Gabriel absently stroked Daisy's hair, his gaze tracing the faint cracks in the ceiling while he tried to assimilate the galaxy of emotions he was feeling. Her leg was curled around his, and her hair was splayed across his chest. He could feel her heart beating against him. When they made love it felt so powerful, so overwhelming, he was certain each time that this would be the moment when she finally lowered her defences and let him in.

Yet each time silence followed, and he found himself pressing his mouth shut again, biting back the words he longed to say – and longed even more to hear.

'Tell me about when you lived in New York,' she said, unexpectedly breaking the silence.

'What do you want to know?'

She drew a circle on his chest with her fingertip. 'What was it like? Was it exciting? Did you enjoy your studies?'

'No and no.' He felt the flutter of her eyelashes against his skin and pictured her rolling her eyes.

'That's all you have to say?'

'I didn't enjoy it. What more do you want to know?'

'Tell me why you didn't enjoy it.'

A pause followed while he considered this. The memories crowded his head like noisy rush-hour traffic. 'I couldn't stand living in the city. It was too loud, too big, impersonal. Concrete and bricks everywhere. No beauty, no nature. People looked right through you as if you were not there. And I kept asking myself, What's the point? Why am I doing this?'

She propped herself up on one elbow to look at him, frowning as if she didn't understand. But it seemed obvious to him. He'd been so lonely, felt so isolated and insignificant. He'd known it wouldn't be anything like life in La Tourelle, but he hadn't known how important it was to him to feel part of something bigger. Surrounded by people who mattered; not busy strangers clutching coffee cups as they hurried, heads down.

He finished, with a shrug, 'So I came home and I was happy again.'

'Home to La Tourelle?'

'Yes.'

'Have you ever lived in Paris? Or Marseille?'

'No.' Why would he want to live in a city? 'This is where I belong.'

A long thoughtful silence followed, and she continued to trace shapes across his chest. Figures of eight. He felt the stir of desire.

'Do you know what I can't understand?' she asked.

'What?'

'Why you haven't settled down already.'

He tensed.

She continued, 'I mean you're what, thirty-six?'

'Thirty-five,' he corrected.

'And you've had other relationships?'

He nodded, unsure where this was going. She was asking questions so dispassionately, as if she were in professional divorce-lawyer mode.

'So when you're clearly someone who wants to settle down, why haven't you done so?'

'I'm not sure,' he said quietly. 'My friends always tell me I'm too . . .' He searched for the word.

'Pig-headed?' she suggested teasingly. 'Opinionated?'

He smiled. 'I have high expectations. They think I expect perfection.'

'Perhaps they have a point. The perfect woman doesn't exist. We're human and humans have flaws.' She smiled and held his gaze in a silent challenge. 'Even you.'

'I never said I didn't. And I'm not looking for a perfect woman. Just someone who's perfect for me.' He stroked the hair back from her face and his chest ached. It was getting more and more difficult to dampen this down, to hold back. But if he told her his true feelings for her, he suspected she'd leap out of bed and run.

'So what would she be like?'

'Intelligent, interesting, loving, kind. She'd know her own mind. She'd be sparky.'

'Sparky?' Her eyes gleamed.

He nodded. Like Daisy. He loved her fire, her independent spirit. He went on, 'And she'd want to live here, in the country, and settle down, have a family.' He smiled and said ironically, 'That's all.'

Daisy's gaze slid away from his and she lay down again. He couldn't see her face when she asked quietly, 'Why is it so important for you to marry and have children? I mean, you seem happy with your job, your life.'

Silence followed before he took a deep breath and admitted, 'When my family died, I felt so alone. So lost. The people who knew me and loved me better than anyone were gone. Yes, Jeanette took me in and became my family, and I had all my friends in La Tourelle too, but . . .'

'They couldn't replace your family?'

'*Voilà*. I never want to feel alone like that again. I want my life to be filled with noise and laughter and little feet. People who need me as much as I need them.'

She didn't respond. Her hand on his chest had become still and he covered it with his own.

His voice was rough as he said, 'Family is what's important, love is what's important. More than air and food and water.'

Without a family, what did life mean? Without love, what was it all for? Family – those close-knit bonds, those blood ties – was the most precious thing, and he yearned for the day when he could look into the eyes of his own child. A woman he loved, a family, and a place like Le Mazet to call their home: this was what he wished for more than anything.

Daisy was silent. She'd softened since she'd first arrived. She'd changed, adapted, learned to slow down and live more sensually, more appreciatively. Was he wrong to hope her values might have changed too?

'Can't you see that?' he prompted.

Perhaps she heard the hope in his voice because she said gently, 'You know my views on love.'

'They haven't changed?'

'No . . . Well – maybe slightly. The family bit.' He held his breath and waited for her to go on. 'I thought I might contact my dad. Ask to see him again.'

Disappointment flattened his hopes. 'Really? That's good.' He tried to sound as if he meant it. As if he wasn't inwardly screaming, *What about us? The last few days together, all the times we've made love – hasn't that meant anything to you?* 'What made you decide this?'

'I don't know. I just . . . He's the only family I have.'

Her voice had a vulnerable edge that made his chest constrict. Perhaps seeing her father again would help her heal. Perhaps it would be an important step and he should be more patient. He cupped her face with his hand and looked into her beautiful eyes. *But he doesn't need to be your only family*, he thought sadly, and kissed her.

The afternoon sun was a shimmering ball of fire in the cobalt sky, but Daisy was comfortably cool sitting in the shade. She'd come outside because Gabriel had asked her to choose a recipe from Jeanette's old recipe book, but her mind wasn't on French cooking. It was restless, buzzing with questions and worries. Mainly, what had she got herself into?

The sex last night had been amazing. Again. Far from fizzling out or turning sour, this fling had only got better, stronger, deeper since he'd moved in with her here at Le Mazet. She looked up at the cornflower-blue sky. What had she been thinking, inviting him to stay here?

She couldn't explain it. She'd never behaved so irrationally or impulsively in all her life. But she was hooked. The pleasure was so intense she couldn't live without it. She rubbed her temple, trying to quell the panic.

Her world used to be a wall of neatly stacked bricks. Order ruled. Routine. Discipline. Success. Now those bricks had been knocked sideways. Lying in Gabriel's arms was both exquisite and terrifying. What was she going to do? They couldn't carry on. He wanted love and long-term, a family. She didn't even want to get involved. But she didn't want to hurt him, either.

She blew her fringe out of her eyes. He wouldn't get hurt. No promises had been made. Nothing about this was permanent. It had been just a few nights together.

Trying to hold on to that thought, she picked up Jeanette's recipe book and began to flick through. It was a plain black hardback notebook, the kind you could buy from any stationery shop or supermarket, its pages yellowed with age and not lined but squared in the characteristically French tradition. It was swollen with magazine cuttings and scraps of paper, which had been stuck in with sticky tape. As she turned a page a loose one fell out, and Daisy reached to pick up the recipe for *tarte au citron*.

Jeanette must have begun her recipe collection as a young woman because her handwriting progressed from small, neat loops and curls, to looser, more confident strokes of the pen. The first dozen or so recipes were named after family members who, presumably, had passed them down to her. Grandmère Laure's *gratin de courgettes*, Mamie Suzie's *potage*, and Tata Aurélie's *omelette à la confiture*. That last one made her stop and pause – jam omelette? She made a mental note to ask Gabriel about it.

Daisy wrinkled her nose because the next page was splashed with sauce, and creased where the corner had been bent to mark a favourite recipe. Seeing the handwritten notes made her think about the woman who'd written them. Gabriel had adored Jeanette and talked about her a little, and Daisy was curious to know more. What it had been like to grow up in this house and live here all her life? Would Daisy have liked her too? The inheritance business aside, what would Jeanette have thought of her, a distant English relative on her husband's side?

She made herself refocus. She was supposed to be choosing a recipe to make with Gabriel. *Daube de boeuf, soupe au pistou* . . . How to choose? Perhaps she should go for the one with the shortest list of ingredients. The *ratatouille*, maybe? Or roast lamb? She turned another page and stopped to examine a photograph of a young Gabriel holding a cake. The pride and satisfaction in his expression made her smile and she felt a tug for the young boy. Presumably this had been taken after he'd moved in with Jeanette. The recipe was for *gâteau au yaourt*. Yogurt cake? Hadn't he said that was his favourite? Idly, she ran her fingers over the photo of him and peered at the ingredients. But her fingertip hesitated over the edge of the photo.

She looked more closely and noticed something poking up from behind it. Curious, she tugged at it, revealing a thin envelope. It was sealed, and she turned it over in her hand.

Then froze.

On the front, in the same handwriting as all the recipes, were the words *Testament de Jeanette Roux*.

Daisy's heart juddered. The missing will.

She slid it back where she'd found it and snapped the recipe book shut. Heat crawled up her cheeks as she glanced at the house, looking for Gabriel. She couldn't see him, but the sound of whistling told her he was still painting inside.

Her fingers were clammy as she pressed the front cover of the book. What should she do? Her mind worked fast. She didn't need to open it to know what it said. Gabriel had always been adamant the will existed, that Jeanette had left everything to him.

Did Daisy tell him she'd found it?

She swallowed. She remembered when she'd found him in the loft, searching through the contents of the abandoned trunk. He would be ecstatic the will had been found. This was the miracle he'd been hoping for all along, the document that legally reinstated him as the rightful owner of the property.

Or perhaps it was too late. There must be a cut-off date after a will's execution when the decision could no longer be reversed. But she couldn't be sure. She'd tried to research it and hadn't found a definitive answer. Five years was one possibility she'd read, and they were still within that timeframe.

How had he not found it sooner? She guessed he hadn't thought of looking in a recipe book, and if he had, the envelope had been wedged behind the photo, almost imperceptible.

But if the house was handed over to him, Daisy would be left with nothing. She'd have no links with this place, no reason to come here any more. Her chest tightened.

This was the first place where she'd felt happy for years, since she was a child, before her parents' divorce. It was selfish, but she didn't want to give it up.

Her fingers pressed the spine of the book as she thought of the nights she'd spent with Gabriel, and how it felt to drift asleep, warm in the circle of his arms, to wake with his soft beard pressed against her hair. Their evenings alone together on the terrace or in the café with his friends. Her friends too, she thought, remembering Laetitia's words. *You're one of us now, Daisy.*

She loved her trips to the *boulangerie* where Yvette always took a few minutes to talk to her, the butcher's where Arnaud greeted her with a cheeky smile. She loved the colours and delicious smells of the weekly market that drew all the villagers, and how everyone stopped to say hello.

Her spirits sank. She couldn't be sure how Gabriel would react to finding the will, but everything pointed to him choosing the house over her.

Of course, she didn't have to tell him. She could keep it quiet, or even destroy it. That would be illegal, immoral, her lawyer's brain informed her. Still, how would anyone know?

But she'd be betraying him. Could she live with herself, knowing she'd robbed him of the one thing that meant the world to him?

Heavy footsteps approached, echoing in the kitchen. In a panic, she glanced around, looking for somewhere to hide the book. Her laptop was open on the table, perhaps she could slip it underneath, but before she had time Gabriel stepped outside. He spotted her and smiled. She kept the book firmly shut on her lap.

'*Ça va?*' he asked casually, drawing near.

She forced a smile. Her pulse was beating fast at the base of her throat and she hoped he wouldn't notice. 'You've got paint in your hair,' she said. It was true, but it was also a weak attempt to distract him from the book on her knees with the envelope inside.

'Does it suit me?' He winked.

She smiled fondly. 'You look like an old man with white hair.'

It was like a glimpse into the future, she thought. This was how he'd look in twenty-five years' time, and she wasn't sure why her heart gave a small lurch.

'What are you doing?' he asked.

'Oh – working.' She waved a hand at her laptop, willing him to go and get on with whatever task he'd come outside for.

But he peered at the recipe book. 'Ah. Jeanette's recipes.'

Her heart thudded like a bass drum.

'Have you chosen one?' he asked.

'Not yet.' The words felt sticky on her tongue.

He reached for the book. She wanted to snatch it back. Instead, she held her breath and watched as he laid it on the table and began to turn the pages. His movements were as unhurried as usual, but to her it seemed like they happened in slow motion. His eyes lit up as he read the words. 'Ah, yes – *gratin de courgettes*. That's a good one. *Coq au vin* we made already . . .'

He was going to find it, she was sure of it. Her cheeks burned. It would be over. All this – him, her, the house – would end in a flash.

Her throat was tight as she watched him turn a couple more pages. '*Gâteau au yaourt*,' he said. 'How about that one?'

She nodded, unable to speak.

'It was my favourite and it's very straightforward. Ah – look, there's a photo of me. I remember that day . . .'

She didn't hear the rest, but tracked his gaze, feeling sick, waiting for the moment she dreaded.

He shut the book and handed it back. 'I shouldn't influence you. You choose the recipe that *you* want to make.'

She blinked at him.

'I was on my way to get more paint and a new roller,' he said, jangling the keys for the truck. 'When are you going to see your father?'

'Oh – tomorrow. I'll leave early.'

'Are you sure you don't want me to go with you?'

'I'm sure. But thank you.' This was something she had to do alone. Her father was staying in Monaco, just a few hours away.

'*D'accord. À tout à l'heure.*' He waved as he walked towards the pick-up.

She stared as he started the engine and drove away, the chunky wheels kicking up dust as he went.

Relief made her sway in her seat. Wow. That had been a close call.

Her hand shook as she retrieved the envelope containing the will and went inside. She'd hide it somewhere safe while she decided what to do.

Chapter 21

'Goodbye, Daisy. And thanks for coming here today. I can't tell you how much it means to me.'

Daisy looked into her father's grey eyes and saw the man he'd become. Aged. Humble. Solitary. So different from the formidable businessman who'd behaved so callously all those years ago.

He walked with her to her car in the grounds of the sleek Monaco hotel. Palm trees reached over them like giant green fans against the cobalt sky, and the air carried the salty tang of the sea. They stopped beside Daisy's yellow sports car. It looked small and understated next to the enormous Bentleys and super cars.

'I'm glad I came, Dad,' she said quietly. Genuinely. In fact, she was amazed at how well the meeting had gone, how frankly they'd talked – and how she felt as a result.

It felt like a real step forward. She hadn't been so angry this time. Today she'd come prepared, and met him with the goal of wanting to learn more. And spending time with him, talking, and hearing his perspective had dislodged something in her. Something that had previously been stuck fast.

Oh, this wasn't a fairy-tale ending, and although she respected him for being honest with her and could tell his remorse was heartfelt, nothing he said or did could alter the past. What he'd done, hadn't done, and the loss of her mum. But something had changed nevertheless.

During the last decade there'd been times when her anger had been like a ball and chain. Now, she felt lighter.

'We'll keep in touch?' he asked. 'I'd love to hear your news. Perhaps we can meet again when we're back in the UK.'

'Yes. That would be good.'

'And I hope things work out with Gabriel.'

'Oh, it's not like that,' she said quickly. 'He – I – we're not going anywhere.'

His smile was warm. 'That's what you say, but—'

'We're not,' she insisted. Then bit her lip, thinking of her guilty secret. 'There are things he doesn't know . . .' Her hand instinctively squeezed her handbag where the will was safely hidden, and she asked herself for the hundredth time what she was going to do about it. She knew what she *should* do, yet she couldn't bring herself to confess. What kind of person did that make her? She finished quietly, 'And once he does, it will be over.'

Her dad considered this. Then, 'I'm sure that's not true. Whatever it is, you'll work it out.'

She shook her head mutely, wishing he was right. Wishing things could be different. The will had come between them at the start, and its reappearance would only resurrect all their differences.

'Anyone can see you two have something. He's a good man.'

That she could agree with. 'He is.'

He smiled and tweaked her chin. 'Take care, Dayday.'

A shock of emotion hit her, like a warm wave. 'Dayday,' she repeated. 'I'd forgotten that.'

It reminded her of her mother, and that loss would never lessen, no matter what happened with her dad.

'Your self-appointed nickname,' he said affectionately, 'because you couldn't say Daisy when you were little.'

She swallowed a lump in her throat. 'Bye, Dad.'

She got into her car and rolled down the window, waving as she left. As she drove away, she saw him in her rear-view mirror, one arm raised, a small figure standing alone in the shadow of the enormous hotel.

Daisy drove home along the motorway with the car roof down, sunglasses on, and her hair streaming behind her in the wind. She kept her speed low, enjoying the sun on her face and wanting the experience to last.

Perhaps a small part of her was also putting off arriving home, too – although, at the same time, she couldn't wait to tell Gabriel about her day.

She tilted her face up to the sun as her car swallowed the last few miles of motorway before the turn-off and the country roads that led back to La Tourelle.

By the time she got to Le Mazet, the sun had sunk low, the sky was tinged with peach and salmon. She parked next to the olive tree, reached for her handbag, and wondered at herself. How could she be so excited to see Gabriel and share with him all her news, yet also dreading being with him for fear of spilling her secrets? There wasn't just the will. There were other things he didn't know about her, and the thought made her stomach twist.

'Gabriel?' The terrace and kitchen were both empty.

'*J'suis là*,' he called. I'm here. 'In the garden.'

She followed the sound of his voice to the orchard. She could tell he'd just showered because his hair was still damp, and she found him picking apricots. His left arm cradled a basket that was already three-quarters full. Her heart did a little spin. She was so pleased to see him. The evening light cast a golden glow over him, and she felt a sweep of emotion. Affection. Joy. Guilt.

Mostly guilt. He looked so at home here, picking the fruit of the land. The land he'd grown up in.

He put the basket down, eyes creasing when he saw her, and greeted her with a hug, a kiss, and a quiet 'So how did it go?'

Her heart pummelled against his. She didn't deserve him.

She let out a long slow breath. 'Okay.'

'Want to tell me?'

She took an apricot from the basket and bit into it hungrily. 'Mm,' she said, surprised by how deliciously sweet and sticky it was.

Gabriel smiled. 'It's a good year for fruit, a big harvest. You might have to give some away, or learn how to make jam.'

She laughed. 'Me? Make jam? I don't think so.' And her insides twisted because he talked about the apricots as if they belonged to her.

But she knew better.

'Look,' he said, pointing to the fruit he hadn't yet picked. 'There are so many.'

The trees were indeed dripping with fruit, and it made her curious to know what other crops were waiting and ripening in the orchard. 'Let's walk,' she said, gesturing away from the house. It would be good to burn off some energy after the long drive.

They fell into step together, the orchard so peaceful after the noise and bustle of Monaco. A twig snapped beneath Gabriel's foot, and a grasshopper leaped away from them, a blur of green amid the scratchy yellow grass.

Gabriel asked, 'Did you find the hotel okay?'

'Yes, without any problem. And he was there, at the time we'd arranged.' She smiled wryly, because one of her fears had been that her father wouldn't show up – just like he hadn't shown up at countless school events. But he'd been early. He'd greeted her with a warm smile, and they'd had lunch together.

'Do you remember that his partner died and that's what prompted him to get in touch?'

He nodded.

'Well, he told me it's because of her that he broke off contact when I was a girl. She was a jealous woman and insecure, and after the divorce she didn't want him to have anything to do with me or his past life.'

'Do you believe him?'

'Strangely, I do.' Although she'd always find it hard to trust him completely after what he'd done.

A dove swooped down from a tree ahead, its wings gracefully outstretched.

'Anyway, because my dad had one failed marriage be- hind him already, he was eager to make that one work no matter what. So he went along with her wishes. He regrets it now, of course, but he wanted to explain.'

Gabriel let out a low whistle. 'It's not the best explanation. He could have stood up to her. You were his daughter, his responsibility.'

Daisy nodded. 'But you know what? I've seen it so many times. A weak man, a controlling woman, and he tries so hard to please her. . .' Her throat squeezed and she blinked hard. 'It still hurts – that he didn't stand up to her, that he put her first before me – but I kind of understand.'

Gabriel drew her to him and wrapped his big hands around her. He felt so solid and safe, and she knew he would never allow anyone to control him. He had strong principles, and when she'd first met him she'd thought this was a negative thing, that it made him unbendable, but now. . . Now she saw it could be positive too.

'Daisy,' he whispered into her hair.

'I'm fine,' she said, her voice muffled against the wall of his chest. She drew back and looked up at him. 'Really I am. I think it's been harder for him in a way.'

'Harder? How?'

She nodded. 'All those years of being conflicted and haunted by his conscience – not knowing what to do for the best. It explains why he intermittently made contact, then went silent for long periods.'

'That made it worse for you, though.' His voice was a low growl.

'Yes. That's why I broke contact with him in the end. It was easier than having my hopes raised then dashed repeatedly.' But now she knew she hadn't been to blame for his rejection. She hadn't done anything wrong. It had been nothing to do with her and everything to do with him and his second wife. And that knowledge came with the most enormous sense of relief. The damage he'd done would take longer to heal, but at least now it could begin to do so.

'So he wants to resume contact with you?'

She nodded.

'And how do you feel about that?'

She swallowed. 'I will – but on my terms. Not too much too soon.'

'That's understandable.'

'You were right about seeing him. It did help me – kind of.' It was difficult to describe, but she felt as if a heavy weight had been lifted and the world was brighter. She turned and stared at the last splashes of the setting sun. 'You know what was weird?' She blinked rapidly.

'What?'

'Even after all he's done, it still felt . . .' She blinked again, but couldn't prevent the spill of tears. 'He's still my dad, and I actually enjoyed seeing him.'

Gabriel pulled her to him again. He held her as she sobbed into his chest, and he kissed the top of her head. When she drew back he told her, 'You've been so brave. It can't have been easy to meet him after all those years and after what he did. I'm happy for you, and proud of you.'

Her smile flickered. There was no one in the world who understood her like this man did. But her guilty conscience cast an ugly shadow over this. Was the closeness they shared becoming more than friendship? And what would happen when she went back to London?

When – if – she told him about the will? What had she got herself into? She should be keeping him at arm's length, not burrowing into him and confiding in him about her most private emotional battles.

She had to tell him about the will, she decided. She'd tell him tomorrow. First thing.

Dread filled her, but she knew it was the right thing to do. The honourable thing. Even if it would spell the end of the idyllic days they'd spent together.

Gabriel studied her a moment longer, then asked tentatively, 'Has meeting your father changed your views on love?'

She tensed. 'What?'

His gaze danced away. 'You didn't believe in love. You said people delude themselves and think they're in love when what they're feeling is lust.'

Ah.

She looked down. Her sandalled feet were small and pale next to his. She'd heard the edge of hope in his question, but she had to be honest with him. There were already too many secrets and lies coming between them.

Seeing her dad had been cathartic and in time would perhaps help heal old wounds, but it had also served as a reminder of how much damage people could do to one another. She stood by her beliefs. She'd never fall for fairy-tale nonsense.

'No,' she said quietly. 'I haven't changed my views.' And she had to steel herself against the hurt in his eyes.

Gabriel woke early. The sun was still shy at this time, tiptoeing in through the wooden shutters, feeling its way into the darkened room and casting a haze of light over the crumpled sheets. He instinctively turned, checking Daisy was still there. She lay facing away from him, curled up in the crook of his arm. He felt a small wash of relief, but it was short-lived.

Every morning he went through the same ritual – woke early, searched anxiously for her, then lay back, wrestling with the deep-seated sense of unease. The foreboding that this joyous explosion of emotion would not, could not last. When they made love it was perfect. But the rest of the time there was a haunted look in her eyes. Sometimes he caught her watching him with the wary expression of a hunted animal. It made his heart fracture each time.

I haven't changed my views.

His love was growing stronger, but would she ever love him in return? He wished he could read her mind and know what was worrying her. What was she so scared of? Hadn't he proved to her that she could trust him? That he wasn't like her father or her married ex.

She stirred. Sleepily, she turned to him and he drew her closer, breathing in the scent of her as he kissed her hair, savouring her softness, her slender legs that wrapped around his.

The trill of a phone made him tense. He turned and checked, but it wasn't his phone. His was switched off and lay inert on the bedside table.

Another trill.

He spotted her handbag on the other side of the room. Daisy murmured something in her sleep and tugged the sheet up around her neck but slept on. She was tired. Yesterday's emotional meeting with her dad had left her exhausted. And last night – well, they hadn't had much sleep. She needed to rest.

He eased himself out of bed and padded over to her bag. The screen of her phone was illuminated with a message from her dad: *Hope you got home safely. Here's my home address. Let me know when you're back in London and . . .*

Gabriel didn't read the rest. He only wanted to silence the gadget so it didn't disturb her. He flicked it to 'silent' and bent to put it back in her bag.

Then paused. An envelope, slightly yellowed with age, lay face up. Gabriel frowned. Something about it was familiar, and it was only as he crouched and parted the bag a little more that he recognised the handwriting.

He froze as he read the words. His blood chilled.

The envelope was sealed, but he didn't need to open it to know what was written inside.

He stared at it, thoughts swirling. Jeanette *had* written it. She *had* left him the house. He hadn't made it up or misremembered. He felt vindicated. He felt a whole lot of other emotions too. Anger. Joy. Suspicion.

But anger was the fiercest.

'Gab?' He heard the fear in her voice.

He turned round. She was sitting up in bed, and her face was as pale as the sheet. He could barely look at her.

'Where did you find this?' he asked. The envelope burned his fingertips.

Her guilt was etched into her knotted brow. 'I was going to tell you . . .' she began weakly.

Meaningless words. Fury steamed through him. How long had she had it – kept it from him? 'Where?' he repeated.

'In her recipe book. I found it the other day.'

The recipe book? How had he missed it? He'd searched through all Jeanette's belongings – including that book – many times. But he'd probably only flicked through it. He'd never expected to find the will in there. Never. What had Jeanette been thinking?

'It was slotted in behind a photo of you,' Daisy went on, as if reading his thoughts. She slid out of bed and crossed the room, put a hand on his arm, but he shook it off. Stepped away from her.

'A photo?' He was confused.

'With the recipe for yogurt cake.'

Understanding dawned.

She went on, 'I don't know why she thought that was a good place to hide a will.'

But Gabriel knew. It had been his favourite recipe.

Memories crowded his head and he pictured himself, fifteen years old, awkwardly tall, standing beside Jeanette in the kitchen, watching her clean out the empty yogurt pot. 'Now use this to measure the flour and sugar,' she'd told him.

A flash of anger had made him snap, 'This is stupid! I'm not a baby.' And, if he remembered correctly, he'd stormed out of the kitchen, refusing to take part.

Yet he must have returned, because he could see himself measuring the ingredients, mixing and baking the cake, sliding it out of the oven. And once he'd mastered that, she'd taught him more bakes and more dishes. She'd taught him everything he knew.

Damn it, Jeanette. Why didn't you tell me? What were you thinking, hiding the will there? A clamp tightened around his chest.

He held up the envelope, pinching it hard. 'You kept this from me,' he ground out. 'How long have you had it?'

Daisy blanched. 'Two days. I was going to tell you today, I promise.'

'Oh, really.' He blinked hard as what she'd done hit him square in the chest.

'Yes! I – I've thought of nothing else. Gab? Where are you going?'

He didn't reply. He couldn't stay here a second longer.

'Gab, please!'

He didn't listen. Snatching his shorts, he flung open the door and thundered down the stairs, carried by a wave of fury.

And the deepest sense of betrayal.

Chapter 22

Heart clattering, Daisy's footsteps were slow and clumsy on the stairs.

In the kitchen she went through the motions of making coffee, but her mind was caught up in a whirlwind of anxiety. Gabriel's pick-up was still there, but he'd disappeared. She didn't know where he'd gone, and there was no point in going after him. Not while he was so angry.

She couldn't blame him. She knew how it must look.

She knew how much Le Mazet meant to him.

Blinking hard she padded outside to the terrace and leaned against the stone balustrade, cradling her coffee cup. She took a deep breath and listened to the frenzied chatter of sparrows in the nearby bushes and the whisper of the breeze on the fig tree. The shadows of the plane leaves caressed her feet, and the air felt fresh on her face. But all the details she'd learned to appreciate over the past weeks brought her no comfort now.

Her stay here was over.

Le Mazet was no longer hers, and the sense of loss was profound. All the holidays she'd hoped to spend here in future would never happen.

She stared into the coffee cup and tried to comfort herself with the thought that now the house would belong to its rightful owner. And it was a weight off her mind, at least, to have it out in the open. Perhaps if she told Gabriel her other secret, she'd feel the same sense of unburdening.

No, she doubted it very much. Anyway, their time together was over so there was no point in going there.

'Daisy?'

She jumped at Gabriel's deep voice, and knocked her cup over. Coffee spilled everywhere.

He held his hand out. 'Sorry.'

His eyes were filled with remorse, too. She relaxed a little because his anger had died back. But it didn't change much. Her time was up.

He approached and righted the cup. The coffee had already soaked into the stone. 'It's not broken at least,' he said.

Daisy didn't care about the cup. Cups could be replaced. Perhaps she'd look for another house here, something smaller, more suited to her solitary status. Perhaps Gabriel would sell her his little home since he'd no longer need it, she thought wryly. Perhaps not. Now he had what he wanted most, he might lose interest in her. And, anyway, she didn't want to live next door, did she? She looked up at the golden stone walls of Le Mazet. Only now she'd lost it did she realise how attached she'd grown to the house.

It's just bricks and mortar, Daisy. She glanced at Gabriel. *It's just sex.*

He was barefoot and wearing only shorts. Normally she'd have nestled up to his warm body and stroked her fingers through his soft beard. Instead, she tugged the belt of her dressing-gown tighter around her waist.

Standing next to her, he rested his elbows on the wall and gazed thoughtfully at the fields and forest ahead. The envelope was in his hands.

The silence stretched. If only he'd never lent her that stupid recipe book. If only she'd picked the first recipe on the first page. She looked up and saw an eagle drawing lazy circles in the sky. Its grace and size filled her with awe.

'I'm sorry,' he said again, his voice rough. 'I lost my temper.'

'I can't blame you. But I *was* going to tell you.'

'I know.'

Her head jerked up. 'You do?'

He nodded. 'I believe you. If you'd wanted to stop me seeing it, you could have destroyed it. But you didn't. You were keeping it to give to me.' He held her gaze. 'I trust you, Daisy.'

She was surprised. And touched. Something glowed inside her, but she hurriedly pushed it aside. 'I won't appeal against it or make life difficult for you,' she said quietly.

He studied her intently. 'Is this why you've been preoccupied the last couple of days? Distracted?'

She shrugged, and stared at the field in front of them. A cockerel crowed in the distance. A joyous uplifting sound, but Daisy's heart was heavy.

'You must have been tempted to burn it,' Gabriel went on.

She studied him warily, expecting to see signs of anger, but his expression gave nothing away. 'It crossed my mind, yes.'

'Why didn't you?'

She wrapped her arms around herself. 'I couldn't.'

He turned his head and she felt his gaze on her. Those beautiful deep brown eyes burned into her. 'Why?' he said softly.

She let out a long, slow breath, knowing he wouldn't let this rest until she gave him an answer. 'Because Le Mazet is yours. It was always yours.'

He tutted. 'No. I think you kept the will for a reason.'

'What do you mean? I kept it to give to you.' Sadness began to give way to frustration.

But Gabriel was calm as he said, 'Why did you want to give it to me?'

'You're not making sense. I don't know what you're—'

He cut in, 'Is it because you want to stay? With me.' The look in his eyes was so tender it made her breath catch. 'Is it because you have feelings?'

'No!' she said, on a rush of air. She stepped back, appalled that he'd come to such a conclusion. 'No. You love this place. And Jeanette wanted you to have it. That's all. It's yours. You're family.'

There was a beat's silence. Then, 'So are you.'

She shook her head. 'No.' Legally she might be the nearest relation, but that wasn't family. Not in the way that mattered.

Tears burned the backs of her eyes and the field ahead became a patchy blur. Dammit, she was a wreck without coffee. Her throat knotted and she frowned hard, annoyed with herself. She'd never been the emotional type before.

The violent tearing of paper made her head turn sharply. She gasped. 'What are you doing?'

Gabriel had torn the envelope in half. Now, slowly and deliberately, he took each half and tore them once, then twice more. The tiny shredded fragments fluttered down over the wall. Daisy snatched at the air to catch them, but they jumped away from her and darted through her fingers. The breeze carried them, making them spin and fly, scattering them like confetti.

She stared at Gabriel, open-mouthed, knowing that even if she retrieved them all, it would be pointless. The will would be invalid because it wasn't intact. Damaged beyond repair. He'd just ripped up his one and only claim to the house he loved.

'Are you mad?' she asked. A curse escaped her lips. 'Why the hell did you do that?'

A faint smile played around his lips, but his expression was grave. Like a teacher explaining to a small child, he said, 'Because I don't want it.'

Anger rushed at her. 'What utter bullshit!' He was going to regret this, she was certain. How many times had she seen clients behave impulsively, emotionally, then backtrack, only to find it was too late? And he'd resent *her* for it. 'Why are you even saying that? We both know it's not true!'

'It *is* true,' he said steadily. His words were calm and measured as he said, 'I don't want you to leave.'

She blinked, trying to make sense of this.

'Nothing matters to me as much as us,' he went on.

'What?' The pulse pounded in her temples. *Us?* No . . . 'You can't – this isn't— What about your inheritance?'

'I thought Le Mazet was all I wanted, but then you came into my life and my priorities changed.' He held up his hands as if he'd had no influence over any of it.

She stared at them and the blunt, strong fingers that were so gentle when they slid over her naked body. Her stomach was a tight knot.

He turned and, smiling, cupped her face. 'I love you, Daisy,' he said firmly. 'I love you more than any house.'

Joy sparked in her, but immediately she quashed it.

Love? Icy white panic zipped down her spine and she closed her eyes, unable to look at the unabashed adoration in his.

Oh, God, how had it come to this? She thought she'd been clear that she didn't do commitment. She'd believed that sex was enough – for both of them. She had to remind herself to breathe, and realised he was waiting for her to respond.

'Why does it have to be either/or?' she managed finally, and stepped back, away from him. 'The house or me?'

His hands fell to his sides and he looked stricken. Telling herself it was kinder to be honest, she forged on. Her hand swiped through the air, indicating the few remaining fragments of the will that lay on the ground. 'Couldn't you have taken the house, then waited to see where our relationship goes?'

The land and the trees were silent. Nature held its breath, listening, waiting. Why had he done such a stupid thing?

His eyes shone and he blinked hard. A sky-blue butterfly fluttered near him and he briefly watched it, then turned back to Daisy. He drew breath and said again, 'I love you. I don't want the house. Just you.'

She shook her head, wishing he'd stop saying those words, and she stepped back even further.

'I thought – hoped you might love me too,' he said.

Guilt made a deep gash in her heart, but she stood firm. 'Gab, I was always upfront with you,' she said hoarsely. 'Love was never on the cards.'

'Maybe, but my heart had other ideas.' He held her gaze steadfastly, refusing to be cowed, and she had to admire him. He was no coward, this man. This wonderful, loyal, obstinate man, with all his idealised romantic notions that were so damned unrealistic. 'I love you,' he persisted.

She recoiled in horror. 'Don't.'

He laughed. His eyes were warm with emotion. 'Why? You're afraid, but I am not. Love is what we all need – more than bread or water. Without love we are not living but existing.'

She backed away. 'We're too different, you and me.'

'Are we?'

'Yes. I have my own life back in London.'

'But you love this place.'

She did. It was true. 'And I can't – I can't give you what you want.'

'You are all I want.'

'That's not true.' She blinked hard, fighting for composure. 'You want marriage and long-term and I can't give you those.'

'No?'

341

'No . . .' Memories bubbled up inside her, wakening jagged emotions – but she couldn't put any of it into coherent words. There were things he didn't know about her, secrets she'd never shared.

He stepped forward. 'You're afraid,' he said gently.

'No.' Her heart pounded frenetically, her head buzzed with panic. 'I told you, I don't do relationships.'

'Because of the man who hurt you – the one who was married?'

She shook her head.

He took another small step towards her and she backed away, fighting a primitive urge to turn on her heel and run. 'Gab, I can't do love—'

'Because of your father,' he cut in, 'who broke your heart when you were a child. Who let you down when you needed him most.'

Her back hit the wall of the house and she flattened her palms against the rough stone. Her throat closed and it felt as if a tiny bird was trapped in her ribcage, flapping wildly to be let free. Gabriel's face blurred in front of her, and she couldn't find the words: she was a hot tangle of fierce, unwelcome emotions. He reached her.

He drew her into his arms and she pressed her fists against his chest, wanting him to stop, yet wanting him to hold her tight. She felt the heat of his body and his solid strength, and she was tempted to lean in. He *loved* her?

Wouldn't she love not to be alone? To be with someone, have someone to share weekends and holidays with. Share dreams, memories, make plans with. To have something other than work in her life. Wouldn't it be a relief not to have to work so hard, not need the long lists of cases won or grateful clients to prove that she was worth something? Simply to be accepted and loved for herself.

But it would also be terrifying. To open her heart.

Confused, she bowed her head, feeling as if something solid was crumbling around her, leaving her exposed and vulnerable.

He held her close and kissed her forehead, his deep voice murmuring soothing words. 'I know you're scared. And I understand why. But we can do this – together. You just need to trust me and let me in – here.' He touched her heart, and it drummed beneath his fingers. 'Don't be afraid. I won't hurt you, Daisy. I promise.'

And the astonishing thing was that she believed him.

Gabriel would love with his whole being, and as stubbornly as he approached everything else in life. He was unshakeably loyal, committed. He'd do everything in his power never to hurt her.

But *she* would hurt *him*, she thought wretchedly.

That was what she was afraid of.

Chapter 23

Daisy stayed in the shower longer than was necessary. When she'd finished and dressed and Gabriel came in, she deliberately ducked out of the bedroom, doing her best to avoid him for as long as she could – but she couldn't avoid him for ever, could she? And there were things they needed to talk about.

Finally, she mustered the courage, and when he came out onto the terrace, she asked, 'What would Jeanette think about what you've done?'

'What?'

'With the will,' she prompted. 'She wanted you to have the house.'

He considered this for a moment. Then, 'You're looking after the house. She'd be happy.'

'I don't believe you. She wanted you to make it your home.'

A long silence followed. Then he said softly, 'I still could.'

Her insides knotted, and she shook her head, trying to find the words to tell him, *Don't go there, don't.*

He must have seen the panic in her eyes because he quickly added, 'Forget about the house, Daisy. And the will. None of this is important.'

'It is to me.' His reaction this morning had been so un-expected. She'd thought the house meant everything to him. She had expected to have to pack her bags and leave – not for him to announce that he *loved* her.

He pressed his lips flat. 'I have to go.'

Her head flew up. 'What? Where?'

She was totally thrown, and noticed for the first time that he was holding the keys to his pick-up. 'To help prepare for the *fête*.'

'That's tonight?'

'Yes. Had you forgotten? It starts at seven. Be ready.'

'You'll be gone all day?'

He glanced at his watch. 'Yes. I'll go home to get changed, then pick you up. Okay?'

She nodded.

He hesitated, then dropped a light kiss on her cheek. And she watched him leave, wondering why, when twenty minutes ago she'd been desperately avoiding him, she was now distraught to watch him drive away, leaving a cloud of dust.

She spent the day flitting about the house, trying to keep busy by finalising her choices of paint colours and new furniture, then getting ready for the evening. But all the time, her mind kept rewinding back to that morning, replaying his words.

He loved her? He loved her. The realisation exploded in her like an enormous firework display. It was overwhelming and terrifying, yet intoxicating too. It made her glow and tingle with excitement. It made her heart sing. Gabriel Laforêt didn't give his heart easily. He wouldn't sleep with a woman unless he was fully committed.

So how could he be committed to her, Daisy Jackson, city girl, outsider, imposter in his dear Jeanette's house?

He couldn't. He knew they were wrong for each other in so many ways. Perhaps he'd come round to her way of thinking and was indulging in a short-term affair.

No. She believed that he loved her. She'd seen the silent pledge in his eyes, heard it in his voice when he whispered her name. She'd felt it in the way he'd touched her and held her. No one had ever made love to her like that, with such intensity, with a passion that burned furnace-like from his soul.

But when he knew her secret he'd regret it all. He'd feel deceived, betrayed. He'd say he wouldn't have let any of it happen if he'd known.

She shouldn't have let it happen. She should have pushed him away – or confessed. But she'd done neither. She'd chosen to go to bed with him, knowing they had no future. And she'd told herself she would leave, but she was still here.

She closed her eyes. She was a bad person. Selfish. Yet even now she couldn't regret it. These last days – weeks – had been the happiest of her life. She'd carry the memory with her always. Like that special sunset, it would glow inside her, and she was certain it would never fade, no matter how much time went by.

But it had to end. She had her own life back in London, her own plans. And they were very different from Gabriel's. Their lives might have intersected tonight, but tomorrow or the day after or at some other point in the future, they would diverge again.

And there was nothing she or Gabriel could do to prevent that from happening.

Rainbow-coloured bunting and fairy lights crisscrossed the village square and danced in the evening breeze. In the main village square a stage had been set up with drums, guitars and microphones. There was a bouncy castle, and Yvette had brought a candy-floss machine for later. But just now everyone was seated, ready to eat. Colourful tablecloths had been laid over long rows of trestle tables and everyone had contributed food – homemade, if the assortment of mismatched plates and platters was anything to go by. Quiches, pastries, cold meats and jewel-coloured salads were passed around and shared, and wine poured into small glasses. It was a feast, thought Daisy, glad that she'd contributed a case of wine to compensate for her lack of cooking skills.

She and Gabriel were among the last to arrive so they squeezed in where there was space – Daisy next to Laetitia and her family, and Gabriel a little way down on the opposite side. Although she was disappointed, perhaps it was good that they were not together. This wasn't the place for the kind of conversation they needed to have.

No one seemed worried about who they were sitting with: the old sat next to the young, teenagers next to little ones, and everyone knew everyone else. There were smiling faces all around and Daisy couldn't believe how well behaved the children were, only leaving the table when a band went up onto the stage and invited them to come and dance so the adults could linger over the cheese and wine.

'Your French has really improved,' Laetitia told her, after they'd chatted a little.

Daisy blushed. 'Gabriel's been talking to me in French.'

'Has he?' Laetitia's eyes sparkled.

'He's teaching me to cook, too. I think he just likes telling me what to do. He's very bossy.'

'*Ah, oui*,' Laetitia agreed, and the two of them eyed him, then shared a smile. 'I'm happy for you two. He hasn't had a serious girlfriend for a few years. Not since Marianne.'

Daisy opened her mouth to say it wasn't serious, but that name threw her off. 'Marianne?' She realised she'd never asked him about his past relationships. Then again, she'd never intended to become a current relationship, so avoiding that subject had seemed wise.

'The travelling shepherdess – you know?'

Daisy's eyes widened as she remembered the flock of sheep that had appeared overnight.

Laetitia went on, 'She wouldn't settle down and couldn't commit. It broke his heart. He dated once or twice but nothing lasted. It's as if his standards became so high he was impossible to please. But now he's found you, and I'm glad to see him so happy. Have you thought about what will happen when you go back to London?'

Daisy's smile suddenly felt plastic. She'd got into deeper water than she'd previously thought. Not only did Gabriel love her, but everyone in the village believed they were in a serious relationship. 'Em – no,' she said, and a prickly hot sensation spread across her chest and up her neck. 'I haven't thought that far ahead.'

'Well, I'm sure you'll find a solution,' Laetitia said cheerfully. 'You two are made for each other.'

Once the meal was over, the band invited people to dance, and everyone got up from the table and formed pairs.

Gabriel appeared at her side. 'Sorry we couldn't sit together. Did you enjoy the meal?' he asked, in that grave voice of his.

'It was lovely,' she said, her body sparking because he was close. He looked gorgeous tonight in black jeans and a smart shirt. She glanced over her shoulder at the musicians on the stage. 'Do you want to dance?'

'In a minute,' he said, frowning at something over her shoulder. She followed his gaze and spotted Patrice struggling with a crying baby and a toddler. 'It looks like Patrice needs a hand.'

They went over. 'Here, let me help,' Gabriel said. 'I'll take the baby.'

'Thanks, Gab,' Patrice said. 'He's just hungry, but this one doesn't know what she wants.' He picked up Giselle, who was sobbing. 'I think she's overtired, and we forgot to bring her teddy. I'll take her home. Will you tell Laetitia?' He gestured at his wife, who was dancing with a couple of friends.

'When she's finished. Let her have fun,' said Gabriel. 'Have you got a bottle for Théo?'

'It's there, warming. It should be ready now. Will you test the temperature?'

'Of course. I know what to do.'

'Thanks, Gab.' Patrice shot him a heartfelt smile and left.

A short while later Théo was contentedly guzzling milk, propped in the crook of Gabriel's arm. Daisy watched as the baby sucked and his eyes began to drift shut. 'You have the touch,' she said, impressed, and trying to hide how uncomfortable she felt in contrast to him. 'Have you done this before?'

He smiled. 'Many times. I like to help when I can.'

She felt a squeeze of emotion, though she didn't know why. Babies were not her thing. Théo looked small and delicate against Gabriel's broad shoulders; perhaps that was why. Gabriel was very different from the men she'd met before, his undisguised tenderness contrasting so strongly with his physical size. It was easy to picture him married with children of his own, and a wife who'd be nothing like her. Shifting awkwardly from one foot to the other, she focused on the villagers dancing, having fun.

She couldn't understand why Gabriel wasn't already settled. He was a real catch. Handsome, hard-working, reliable. One day she'd arrive here in La Tourelle and find him holding his own son or daughter. She plucked a thread from her dress, suddenly feeling a little queasy.

When the milk had all gone, Gabriel reached into a bag, pulled out a white muslin cloth and slung it over his shoulder. He lifted the baby onto it, his movements confident and relaxed, and gently rubbed Théo's back. The baby looked around with solemn brown eyes, blinked hard, then nuzzled sleepily into Gabriel's shoulder.

He kissed the baby's head, and the tender gesture made Daisy stiffen. A sharp pain flashed through her. He'd make such a good father. The best. Patient but no-nonsense. Loving, devoted, dependable. Always dependable. He'd never allow anything or anyone to come between him and his family.

Unlike her dad.

'He seems very content,' she said, trying not to look too closely at the baby's velvety cheeks. 'But I don't know how he'll get to sleep with all this noise.'

'Oh, he'll be fine. Babies sleep through anything.'

The gulf between them widened. 'I'll take your word for it.' She felt awkward. Everything about this was a glaring reminder of how ill-suited she and Gabriel were.

'You want to hold him?' asked Gabriel.

'No, thanks,' she said quickly, and stepped back. 'I mean, he's happy – and sleepy. I don't want to spoil your good work and make him cry.'

'He won't cry. Théo's very chilled. Go on. Hold him.'

She shook her head. 'No – thanks. It's fine. Really.'

'*Bonsoir*, Gab! Daizee!'

They sprang apart, and Daisy was relieved at Arnaud's interruption. '*Bonsoir*,' she murmured.

'Want to dance?' the butcher asked, with a wide smile.

She didn't hesitate. 'That would be lovely.'

'Good!' Arnaud said, delighted. He turned to Gabriel. 'You don't mind, do you? You're busy anyway.'

Was it her imagination or did Gabriel shoot him a daggered look? He rocked the baby and waved his free hand. 'Go ahead.'

Gabriel watched as Arnaud winked, then swept Daisy away into the crowd, beaming at her and making her laugh. The butcher was a flirt – he knew that and could deal with it. But what really cut deep was the relief he'd seen on Daisy's face.

She'd looked so uncomfortable, so disinterested in Théo. Sneaking longing glances at the dancers, she'd clearly been itching to get away and enjoy herself. She didn't want to waste her time babysitting. And she'd positively recoiled from his offer to hold Théo.

He shouldn't be disappointed. He knew who she was. Successful career woman with no interest in relationships of any sort.

He rocked the baby and watched as the dancers whirled faster. His gaze automatically sought out the blonde of Daisy's hair as she tipped her head back, laughing with delight as Arnaud kept her there for dance after dance.

Eventually, the music switched to a slow number and Arnaud slid his arm behind her back and drew her close. Gabriel tensed.

She blew a lock of hair out of her eyes. Her cheeks were a little flushed and she suddenly looked tired. He wanted to rush over and ask if she'd like to sit down. He had to ball his hands into fists, the urge was so strong. He despaired at himself. *Leave her alone, Laforêt. Give her space.*

How could he, after he'd bared his heart earlier? Told her exactly how deep his feelings ran.

For nothing.

He'd hoped she might say she loved him too – but no. She'd looked terrified. Horrified.

And yet he hadn't imagined she had feelings for him too, had he? Yes, he had. The time they'd spent together – and the nights – had felt special. As if they meant something. He understood that opening her heart to someone would be a huge step for her, but he'd hoped.

He lifted the baby a little higher on his shoulder. Théo was a dead weight now, fast asleep.

Perhaps it wasn't just fear making Daisy tight-lipped. Perhaps she simply didn't have the same feelings for him.

He swallowed. He'd always felt she was holding back part of herself, guarding something, yet he'd hoped. He shook his head despairingly. Maybe he'd been a fool.

Still, it didn't change the way he felt. He couldn't dilute the intensity of his love or turn down the volume.

He loved her. Always would.

A while later, Gabriel lowered the baby into his yellow pram, then tucked the muslin around him. A night like this was too warm for a blanket, but he knew babies liked to feel swaddled and safe.

As he straightened up, Daisy appeared by his side, still breathless from dancing. 'Everything okay?' she asked.

'Yes. Fine.' He glanced around for Arnaud. 'You've had enough of dancing?'

'With Arnaud, yes. Do you want to get a drink? If you're not busy with the baby, that is.' Her gaze darted to the pram, then back to him.

He had a quick word with Laetitia, then returned. 'Come. The bar's this way.' He led her to the far end of the square. It was quieter there, which made it easier to talk. They watched the scene as they sipped their drinks. The bouncy castle was now busy with children, Yvette's candy-floss stall too. And some people had returned to the tables to sit and chat while they rested their feet.

'Did you enjoy yourself dancing with Arnaud?' The instant he'd spoken, he hated himself for asking the question.

'It was okay.' She looked up at him and smiled. 'I'd rather dance with you.'

His spirits soared. He confessed, 'I was jealous – watching you with him.'

She laughed.

'No. Really,' he said.

She looked up at him in surprise. Then, realising he was serious, her expression softened and she said, 'Don't be. I can't think of him like that. He's just a friend.'

His heart beat hard. Their gazes locked. The band finished their song with a flourish, and as the last note faded, he asked silently, *And me? What am I?*

But she simply smiled. The band played the opening chords of the next piece and Daisy's eyes lit up. 'Have you finished your drink?' she asked. 'I love this song.'

Gabriel placed a hand on her waist and it was all Daisy could do not to jump at the electricity from his touch. His other hand held hers. His skin was rough but reassuringly warm. He spun her round to the music, and she felt high. The atmosphere tonight was relaxed and joyous. Everyone around them was dancing and smiling. Their laughter lit up the night.

Daisy felt a strange twist in her chest. A tug she couldn't identify. It was the same feeling she'd had when she'd first arrived at boarding school as a thirteen-year-old. Homesickness? She couldn't put her finger on it.

Later, when the music slowed, Gabriel drew her close. They swayed in time to the song, and she was glad of the chance to savour the closeness. Dancing with Arnaud had been exhausting. He'd told a lot of jokes, but he wasn't as funny as Gabriel. He'd flirted madly, but sparks didn't fizz through her, like they did with Gabriel. Arnaud had slow-danced with her like this, but her body hadn't shimmered like it was doing now, and the air hadn't felt charged with energy. And the whole time, her gaze had kept searching out Gabriel in the sea of faces. As if he was her magnetic north.

'What do you think of the *fête*?' he asked.

'I'm really enjoying it.' The pang of longing still lingered and she couldn't understand it or explain it. 'Everyone's so . . . together, aren't they?'

'What do you mean?'

'Does everyone here know everyone else?'

He looked around at the faces. 'More or less.'

She was amazed. 'It's incredible.' Joy nudged against unease, and she tried to identify what she was feeling. She shivered. 'Why are you looking at me like that?' she asked.

His eyes gleamed. Damn. He was so handsome when he smiled like that. 'I didn't think this would be your thing, that's all.'

'The *fête*? Why not?'

'You're always telling me about the grand concerts and glamorous parties you're used to in London. I'd have thought this wouldn't be on the same scale.'

'No, it's not.' She smiled. 'It's better.'

The scene around her was idyllic, and she was acutely aware of how privileged she, an outsider, was to have a glimpse of village life in this warm, loving community. The connections here were so strong – it was like an enormous extended family, really. There was the occasional bickering, but mostly there was humour, and because everyone knew everyone, they could depend on each other.

His brows lifted. 'Really?'

'Yes. Everyone's having a wonderful time. Look. And not an ulterior motive in sight. There's no networking going on, no softening people up with the hope of striking a business deal or calling in a favour later.'

'Is that what your life is like?'

'Yeah.' She sighed. 'Oh, God, I don't miss any of that at all.'

It was almost midnight now, but the bouncy castle was still busy with children squealing and jumping, pretty dresses flying up, little bumps and knocks causing momentary tears, which were soon forgotten. Those who were flagging were carried off for cuddles or to be rocked to sleep in pushchairs by grandparents, leaving the parents free to dance. Laetitia waved goodnight and wheeled Théo home in his yellow pram. The music got really slow and smoochy, and Gabriel held her close. She let her head rest against his chest, savouring the weight of his hand in the small of her back, the scent of him, his heat.

She realised that the tug she'd been feeling was a longing to be part of this community. To belong. She'd had a taste of it when she'd been ill and the villagers had left her thoughtful gifts and food parcels, but she yearned for more.

All her life she'd striven to prove herself, to stand out and be the best, but here she was nothing special, just one of the community. And it was a relief to be accepted for herself and not have to earn acceptance. It felt good. In fact, being here tonight, and being part of the celebrations, had made her realise how barren her life in the city was. How isolated she was amid a million anonymous faces.

She stopped herself, appalled by this train of thought. She loved her job, loved her life in London. Gabriel's heart beat steadily against her ear.

Anyway, wishing for something didn't make it happen. Like a thief casing their next target, she might want all this – but it wasn't hers to have.

She could never belong here, no matter how much she yearned to.

It was the early hours by the time they got back to Le Mazet. They locked the house, closed the bedroom shutters, and Daisy slipped off her shoes. She eyed her bed, remembering the conversation they'd had early this morning. They needed to talk, she thought, bracing herself.

'You looked beautiful tonight,' Gabriel told her, as he drew her against him.

She smiled and spots of colour warmed her cheeks. 'It's just a cheap dress,' she murmured, closing her eyes as he trailed kisses down her neck.

'It's not the dress that counts, but the person inside it.' He slid the zip down and let it fall to her feet. 'I wanted to do that all night,' he said, with a crooked grin.

Desire stirred, making her breathless, and she kissed him. His lips were soft and warm, and he tasted of sweet lemonade. Kissing him felt different knowing he loved her. It wouldn't be just sex now that she knew how deep his feelings ran.

She waited for the familiar panic to seize hold of her, because she didn't do love. She didn't want him to love her.

And yet she did want this. He stroked the hair back from her face tenderly, adoringly. She wanted it more than anything. There was so much they needed to talk about, but right now she couldn't think. Need blurred everything, and as they fell into bed she thought, Why complicate this when it worked so well, the two of them, naked together? Why spoil it?

But lying in bed afterwards, reason prevailed again, and as Daisy snuggled in to him, she plucked up the courage to whisper, 'I think you might be right. I'm afraid to be close with anybody ever again.'

He squeezed her. 'You don't need to be afraid, Daisy. I won't hurt you.'

'You don't know that. Your feelings could change at any time. My dad loved me – until that woman turned his head. Took him away from us, from me.'

She tilted her head to watch him. His lips pressed flat, his eyes were alight with passionate emotions. 'I'm not a man whose head is easily turned, Daisy. You have my heart. Always.'

She dipped her gaze. She had to put the brakes on this. She should never have allowed it to get this far.

He rolled onto his side and on top of her, supporting his own weight on his elbows. Her body instantly responded to his, but lying beneath him she couldn't escape his gaze.

'I know this isn't easy for you, but you can trust me, Daisy. I won't let you down.'

But what about her? She couldn't give him what he needed.

Tell him.

'Gab . . .' She took a deep breath, then tried again, 'There are things you don't know about me . . .'

He waited. The words stuck on her tongue. She couldn't say them. She knew if she did, he'd pull his hand back and those dark eyes would become black shards of ice and she'd be frozen out of his life for always.

You must tell him.

'Of course there are.' He smiled gently. 'But I know you well enough to know I will always love you.'

'No,' she said quickly, then squeezed her eyes shut, afraid he'd see her dark secret, afraid he'd know and this would end.

Because it would end when he knew.

She had to tell him – she had to. But she was caught, snared in this no man's land of being with him but not, in this wonderful, sensual, magical place and she couldn't bear to shatter it all.

He reached out to her. 'Daisy, please.'

She placed a finger on his lips. 'Shush.' While they were together, the physical worked so well. Words only spoiled it.

She didn't want to hear him say he loved her, and she couldn't bring herself to tell him why there was no future for them. So, pulling his head down to meet hers, she kissed him until he surrendered, and desire became a fireball that consumed their words.

Just let this be, her mind silently pleaded with him, as their bodies came together and his eyes bored into her, feverishly, intently. *Let this be enough.*

Chapter 24

With every hour that passed, her secret grew inside her like a tumour.

He didn't need to know. He didn't.

He did.

It hovered on the tip of her tongue – during the pauses in their conversations, in the breathing spaces, the silences and full stops. Perhaps it would be a relief to get it off her chest.

No. It wouldn't. She could picture his reaction. She knew him so well now.

No.

And just like that, her mouth snapped shut. Fear silenced her. Each time.

Chapter 25

'Did you enjoy the *fête* last night?' Laetitia asked, rocking the yellow pram to get the baby to sleep.

'I had a wonderful time,' Daisy said honestly.

She and Gabriel's friends were seated around the bistro's small circular tables, chatting and laughing.

'You and Gabriel were looking very happy.' Laetitia winked. She picked up her drink. 'I saw you dancing together.'

Trying to feign nonchalance, Daisy shrugged. She wondered if he'd told his friends about the will and how he'd ripped it up. She glanced at him just as he turned, and the smile he gave her, the intimacy of it, the promise, stole her breath away.

But guilt followed hot on its heels. As time was going by, her secret was burning, brimming inside her, determined to be told. She had to tell him. And she would. She just had to find the right moment.

Laetitia continued, 'I haven't seen him smile so much for a long time.' Théo let out a little cry and she jiggled the pram again.

Daisy rubbed the back of her neck, suddenly feeling hot and uncomfortable. 'No?'

'Certainly not with any of his past relationships. But we could tell from the moment you arrived that you were different. He pretends he is strong with the heart of a lion, but inside he's a lamb.'

Daisy laughed and dropped her gaze, knowing what Laetitia meant. Gabriel did everything so passionately – he gave all of himself and held nothing back. And right now he believed he was committing to a new relationship, she thought grimly, to something lasting.

'Don't look so worried. You two are made for each other. It's obvious.'

'I don't think—'

'Of course you are!' Laetitia frowned. 'Daisy, what's wrong?'

'Nothing.'

'Are you sure? You seem—'

'What do you think, Daisy?' Gabriel interrupted, turning from his conversation with Jacques.

'What?'

'We're planning a trip to the beach tomorrow. It's last-minute, but while the weather is good and the tourists have not arrived, this is the perfect time to go.'

'Sounds great.' She glanced at Laetitia, relieved at the change of subject. 'Who's going?'

'Everyone.'

'You don't really mean everyone.'

'I do.' He turned to his friends. 'Don't I?'

They nodded.

'We'll meet here in the square and drive down together. It should be great fun. Want to come?'

'Yes,' she said brightly. She could feel Laetitia studying her, but she didn't dare look in her direction. 'Why not?'

The beach trip was disorganised, slow, laid-back. All the things Daisy hated. Yet it was possibly the best day of her life.

The sun shone, the sea was warm, children's laughter rang in the air, grandmothers sat in the shade knitting and minding the babies asleep in prams and pushchairs. Daisy looked left and right, up and down the beach. All around, people laughed and chatted over games of cards or plates of food.

When Gabriel had said everyone would be going, Daisy had assumed he was exaggerating. But when she'd arrived at the village square at some ungodly hour that morning, one glance at the dozen or so cars, people-carriers and a mini-bus had told her he was right. She'd spotted Yvette and her partner, Arnaud, Patrice and Laetitia with their little ones. In fact, she'd recognised most of the faces around her. The car park had filled with excited noise as they'd organised the sharing of lifts, making sure every car was filled and everyone had a seat, before they'd set off in convoy to the coast.

The beach, when they'd finally arrived, was quiet and like something from an expensive travel brochure: a curl of sand around turquoise water that shivered and sparkled in the sun. A rim of pine trees separated the beach from the tarmacked parking area beyond, and the only building to speak of was a shack selling chilled drinks and ice cream. There were a handful of families scattered around, and they'd watched, round-eyed, as the big group from La Tourelle laid towels on the sand, erected parasols and planted cool boxes in the shade.

Daisy breathed in the tangy sea air and gazed around her in wonder. All the usual teasing and joking was going on, and just as with the village *fête*, everyone was involved.

'*Allez,* Daisy!' Patrice shouted. He was wrestling with a parasol and used his free hand to beckon her over. 'Don't just stand there. Come and help!'

She felt a stab of trepidation, but went over, her feet sinking into the powder-soft sand. 'What do you need me to do?' She prayed he wouldn't ask her to look after Théo. She had no clue what to do with babies.

He paused from his task and nodded at Laetitia, who was crouched behind him, soothing an impatient Giselle with one hand and feeding Théo with the other. 'Can you help Giselle?' he asked. 'She's impatient to swim but needs armbands before she can go in the water.'

Patrice cursed in French as the parasol jammed again.

Giselle, hearing her name, trotted over to Daisy, arms outstretched. '*Tu viens dans l'eau avec moi, Daisy?*' she asked. Will you take me for a swim?

'*Oui, bien sûr,*' Daisy said.

Laetitia smiled gratefully and pointed to a pair of deflated armbands on the picnic rug. 'I've got my hands full with the baby,' she explained, and turned back to Théo. It was all so casual that Daisy could have been an aunt, a sister or at least someone they'd known a long time. Without a second thought, she knelt in the sand and blew up the armbands, then helped Giselle out of her cotton dress.

The day passed in a blur. She and Gabriel swam and splashed about with Giselle and the other children, played volleyball, sunbathed for a while, then swam out to deeper water where Gabriel trod water and kissed her – until they went under. They resurfaced spluttering and laughing. For lunch everyone grouped together so the lines of families and couples blurred. They ate a picnic of *pan bagnats* – delicious baguette sandwiches stuffed with tuna, egg, tomatoes, olives and vinaigrette dressing. Afterwards, Daisy crept under a parasol with Laetitia and Giselle, and they napped in the shade. When Daisy woke, Laetitia and her daughter had vanished, and Gabriel was sitting beside her eating an ice cream. She sat up. He offered it to her, and watched with hooded eyes as she licked it.

By evening, Daisy's cheeks glowed from a day spent in the sun. As the sea air began to cool, people had built a small bonfire in the sand and gathered around it to eat supper. Bottles of wine were passed around and poured into plastic cups. Daisy sipped hers and looked around at the smiling faces. The sound of laughter and chatter rang through the air, everyone relaxed and happy and together. And she felt part of it. She belonged.

The thought filled her with a glowing warmth. She couldn't remember the last time she'd felt like this – certainly not during her adult life. Oh, after a victory at work she might have fooled herself that she and her colleagues were a close-knit team, that their closeness was exceptional and they were like family. But now she saw how deluded she'd been. Her work colleagues admired and respected her professionally, but they'd always behaved with a certain element of self-interest. They wouldn't have teased her for her spreadsheets, and they wouldn't have brought her soup when she was ill.

Gabriel and his friends, on the other hand, didn't give a fig about her status or professional life. They accepted her for herself, without any conditions. They made her feel she was part of this enormous family. Friendship, trust and love

– she'd never expected to find those here. She swallowed, feeling choked. She hadn't expected to find them anywhere.

And it made her heart squeeze. Knowing all this could have been hers if things had been different.

She leaned against Gabriel's shoulder, and he put his arm around her and drew her close. His warmth and his touch had a soothing effect, and she closed her eyes, trying to imprint all this on her mind, knowing she'd treasure the memory.

Because a memory was all it could ever be.

She had to leave. It was the right thing to do – for everyone.

The beach began to clear, the young families with sleepy children first, followed by the older villagers and those who had work the next morning. The fire shrank down, the branches collapsing into powdery embers. Daisy steeled herself for what was to come, but it wasn't easy. Her heart tugged as if it had become rooted in this place.

Jacques topped up her wine. 'There's rain on the way,' he said.

Gabriel looked up at the sky. 'You think so?'

The moon was shining, but in the distance out at sea thick black clouds were rolling in.

'I know it,' Jacques said.

'I hope we get it back home too,' Gabriel said. 'The land needs it.'

A box of dates was shared around, but Daisy handed it on.

'You don't want one?' Gabriel asked.

'I'm not hungry.' There was a tightness in her chest, a heavy weight. Perhaps she'd drunk too much wine, or it might be indigestion. She set down her plastic beaker, pushing it into the sand so it wouldn't topple over.

The conversation around her was lively, but she zoned out, distracted by the prospect of leaving. She tried to picture her return to work, to muster the enthusiasm for the promotion she'd been hoping to get. Except 'hope' wasn't the right word any more. She couldn't even remember why she'd wanted it so much. The Daisy who'd come here six weeks ago seemed like a different person.

Once she was back in London her drive would return, she reassured herself. Her passion would be reawakened, she was sure of it.

'This would be the perfect place to get married, don't you think?'

Gabriel's question was directed at Jacques, but Daisy looked up, immediately on guard.

'Barefoot on the beach,' he went on, gazing out to sea, where the moon was a rippling white disc in the water. 'Nothing fancy or formal, with everyone from the village gathered here. It would be perfect.'

Jacques rolled his eyes. 'You're such a romantic, Gabriel.'

Gabriel shrugged. Daisy's gaze slid away from his and she hugged her knees and buried her toes in the sand.

Jacques went on, 'You say it's perfect, but there'd be sand in the champagne and your bare feet would get stung by a jellyfish.'

The others laughed. Not Daisy.

He *was* romantic, she thought. Romantic, perfectionist, idealist. She loved all these traits. She loved him.

She drew in a sharp breath and stared at the fading embers of the bonfire. *She loved him?*

The realisation settled like hot ash. The ache in her chest wasn't caused by indigestion or too much wine. It was love. The one emotion she'd believed she was immune to. The one she'd vowed never to allow herself to feel again. She dragged in a slow, ragged breath. Yet it had burrowed into her heart, silently sowing its seeds during every conversation and every look they'd shared, each smile and touch and night they'd spent together.

She'd told herself it was purely physical, but she'd fallen for him, hook, line and sinker, and her heart knew that the pain of leaving him would be excruciating. Crippling.

Because she had to go.

He might think he loved her now, but when he learned the secret she'd kept from him, he'd think again. He'd push her away just as he had done when she'd tried to seduce him.

And she couldn't put off telling him any longer. Tonight was the end of the road.

She closed her eyes against the sting of tears.

'Daisy?' His liquid brown eyes were creased and his concern made her heart turn over. 'Are you sure you're all right?'

By the time they got home to Le Mazet it was really late, but Daisy had made her decision: she wouldn't put it off any longer.

Gabriel pulled up outside the house and turned off the engine. The countryside was still as they gathered their belongings from the back of the pick-up. She shivered. The air was cooler than she'd ever felt it here before.

'Jacques might have been right about a rainstorm,' Gabriel muttered, as they trooped through the darkness towards the house.

Daisy's throat felt tight. They reached the terrace and she put the icebox down while he slotted the key into the kitchen door. 'Gabriel, can we talk?'

He stopped. 'Yes. I'll just open—'

She put her hand on his to stop him.

Surprised, he blinked at her. 'Now? Here?'

She nodded and gestured for him to sit. 'There's something I have to tell you.'

He left the key, and concern furrowed his brow. 'What is it?'

She sat beside him, perched on the edge of her seat. The outside light cast a syrupy gold filter over them. She dipped her head, but could still feel his chocolate eyes boring into her. Her chest squeezed hard, making it difficult to breathe.

This was the end, she thought. She had known this moment would come, but that didn't make it any easier.

'I – I . . .' She swallowed and tried again. 'I have to go, Gabriel.'

Silence followed. 'To work?'

'No. I have to go home.'

There was a pause before he said calmly, 'But you'll be back.'

She didn't reply. He must have seen the apology in her eyes because his expression changed.

'What? You won't come back?'

She dragged air into her lungs and shook her head.

He got up. 'What are you talking about? You're happy here. Why leave? *We* are happy, you and me, together.' His words echoed through the darkness. Crouching beside her, he touched her arm. 'Aren't we?'

She had to close her eyes because all she could think of was how perfect it had felt when he'd held her and made love to her. 'There's something I haven't told you,' she said finally.

The sound of a cat's angry snarl in the distance made her turn. But beyond the terrace lighting she saw only thick darkness.

Gabriel's gaze remained fixed on her. 'What?' he asked.

'Something you need to know.'

'Tell me.'

'I should have told you before . . .' The words sat, like concrete blocks, on her tongue, refusing to budge.

He gripped her arm with both hands. Those big blunt hands that were so gentle, so tender. 'Daisy, you're scaring me. What is it?'

'I . . .' She blinked hard, fighting the burn of tears, and had to force herself to meet his gaze as she told him, 'I can't have children.'

His hands fell away – as she had known they would.

A fat raindrop landed on her arm, startling her. A moment later, she felt one on her head, then a whole barrage of them began to fall. They were cold, and they smacked down, quickly drenching everything. 'We should go inside,' she said.

But he was frozen to the spot, staring as if he didn't understand. Rain splashed over him. '*Quoi?*'

She repeated it as slowly and gently as possible. 'I can't be the woman, the partner, you need,' she finished, on a lame whisper.

The torrent of rain bounced off him. He stood up and paced away from her, shocked and furious. She felt his love roll back, leaving an icy vacuum in its place.

Rain hammered down on the roof, the terrace, her. Her beach dress was saturated, and her hair dripped down her back. For the first time in weeks, she felt properly cold. She clutched her arms and watched him, waiting what felt like an age for him to respond. The sheets of rain added to the dark of night so she could barely make out his features: only the pale gold of his face and the whites of his eyes. Everything else was a wet blur.

'How do you know you can't have children?' he demanded, his voice ragged with desperation. 'You're thirty. There's plenty of time . . .'

She shook her head. 'I was very ill – when I was at law school. I had an operation. They had to . . .' She drew in breath, remembering.

At the time it had been no big deal. She'd had no plans to settle or have a family. She'd long ago decided that path wasn't for her so she'd been accepting of her fate. She hadn't known back then that one day she'd meet this man for whom having a family was so important.

She should never have let things get this far. But so much of it had felt beyond her control. The feelings he'd ignited had caught light despite her best efforts to stop them, to smother them. 'I can't, Gabriel. It's not physically possible.'

Chapter 26

What was she saying? She couldn't – she'd—?

Gabriel made himself breathe but all he could see was Daisy turning away from him, arms wrapped around herself, shoulders hunched. Her hair hung in twisted tendrils and she trembled. He thought of the woman who'd first arrived here six weeks ago with her enormous silver watch, designer glasses and spreadsheets. She'd appeared so calm and focused on her work when inside she'd been hugging this secret. It couldn't have been easy, no matter what she said.

'You should have told me,' he managed finally. His voice sounded hoarse. 'Why didn't you tell me sooner? All this time we spent together—' He'd given her everything, laid himself bare. He'd made love to her, admitted he loved her. Yet she'd kept this enormous secret from him.

He felt betrayed. Her silence had been a betrayal and it tore through him. Why hadn't she told him? The rain fell even harder now. It hurled itself at the house, ricocheting off the roof tiles, overshooting the gutters and firing off explosions of water everywhere. Pools collected around the edges of the terrace where it couldn't drain fast enough.

'I'm sorry,' she said.

'You didn't say anything. Not a word.'

'I didn't think you and I would . . .' Her words petered out.

'We made love,' he ground out. 'I told you I loved you – and still you said nothing!'

She flinched as if his angry words had struck her. Then dipped her head. His chest tightened. She'd been carrying this secret all along. How lonely it must have been for her. How heartbreaking. Why hadn't she confided in him? Trusted him?

Part of him wanted to go to her, but shock steamrolled everything else. 'You –' he struggled to find the words '– you know how important it is to me to have children of my own, a family.'

His sense of loss was profound.

Her chin lifted. 'I told you all along I don't do commitment.'

This was true. And he'd chosen not to listen because he believed in love. He believed that if two people loved each other any problem was surmountable.

He still did. But at the same time he felt her retreating from him. There was a look in her eyes, a coldness.

'You're right,' he said quietly. His throat felt raw. 'I thought – I hoped – you might change. Grow to love me.' He heard the desperation in his voice and hated himself for it. Every time he'd said he loved her, he'd hoped she would respond with the three words he longed to hear. But she hadn't. Her lips had pressed together, and her gaze had slipped away from his.

Ice slid through him. He suddenly became aware that he was soaked. Cold, too. His T-shirt and shorts clung to him.

Her eyes glinted in the moonlight. 'I don't love you, Gabriel,' he thought she said. 'This is the end.'

'What?' Thunder grumbled in the distance.

'I don't love you.' She had to shout to make herself heard over the rain. Her gaze held his defiantly even as water streamed down her face.

He didn't think it was possible for him to hurt more, but hearing her say those words was brutal. They crushed him, they extinguished the tiny spark of hope he'd been nurturing.

Lightning flashed, like a broken lightbulb. Desperately, he searched her face for a trace of the woman who'd smiled at him earlier this evening in the light of the bonfire, who'd whispered his name in the dead of night and roused him from sleep with petal-soft kisses countless times. Had he really misjudged the situation so badly when he'd hoped – believed – she felt something for him?

The woman standing before him now showed no sign of emotion. Her expression was steely, and her shoulders were stiff and straight as metal bars. He imagined this was how she must look in court, representing her clients. Stony. Determined. Unapproachable.

'You're soaked,' she said. 'You should go home.'

Her words echoed through his head. 'Home? This is—'

She turned and hurried inside. Thunder rumbled again, louder and more menacing this time.

'Daisy!' He started after her but the door slammed. 'We haven't finished—'

'We'll talk in the morning,' she said, her voice muffled through the glass pane. 'When it's had time to sink in.'

She turned the key, shutting him out, then vanished from view, swallowed by the shadows.

He waited a moment, but the old farmhouse remained dark. Lightning flashed, so close and so bright it made him start. The house, the fields and forest lit up and flickered, like a black-and-white film. He pressed his face against the glass of the door and banged with his fist. 'Daisy!' he called again.

But there was no answer.

And Gabriel felt his heart splinter into hundreds of tiny pieces.

Daisy didn't sleep at all that night. Instead, she lay in bed listening to the storm. The thunder made the shutters shake, and the rain was so heavy it sounded like gravel spilling onto the roof. Rivers of water flowed down the gutters and drainpipes. She shivered and clutched the sheets.

When did you tell someone you couldn't have children?

When you first met them? No way.

When they became a friend? A good friend? No. It was too private, too painful.

When you slept with them for the first time? That fragile, exciting getting-to-know-each-other-intimately stage?

Perhaps her infertility was another reason why, with past lovers, she'd always left before dawn. It had been simpler. For her and for them.

She remembered her first night with Gabriel, and how he'd held her hand and persuaded her not to run. She could have told him then, or at any point after, but what they'd shared had felt so rare, so new, so unlike anything she'd known before that she hadn't wanted to risk damaging it. When a beautiful butterfly fluttered near, you didn't try to grasp it. You didn't crush those delicate wings with clumsy fingers. You let them spread and fly so the brilliant colours and patterns could shine, radiant in the sun.

And then there'd been the will. Why tell him her secret when she'd been so certain that Jeanette's will would spell the end of their relationship? She'd expected Gabriel to evict her from the house, from his life, and she wouldn't have blamed him if he had.

But of course he hadn't, she thought dully. He loved her.

The only point in her defence was that she'd been upfront that relationships and family did not feature in her plans. A solitary tear leaked out onto her pillow. It had always been easier to say she didn't want children than to explain the truth.

She should have told him sooner, though. Regret made her squeeze her eyes shut, but it wasn't enough to block out the picture of him and his shocked expression earlier, how he'd pounded at the kitchen door, rain coursing down his face as he'd shouted her name. She hugged her knees, remembering her words. *I don't love you.* At the time she'd believed it was kinder to say them, that it would be better for them both in the long run.

But as lightning had illuminated his stricken face it had felt so wrong.

What else was she supposed to have done? How could she have made it less painful for him? She didn't want him to suffer. She'd rather take the hit herself than hurt him. She curled up smaller.

In the end, she'd hurt everyone.

Early next morning, she pushed open the shutters as the damp night became smudged with the faint grey and duck-egg blue of dawn. It had stopped raining, but she could still hear water dripping. It sounded like a ticking clock.

She had to get back to the city. She had clients waiting, cases to win, a promotion to pursue. Her heart thudded like a hollow drum. Yet she wanted to stay here. After last night's rain the landscape glowed with a new brilliance. The leaves gleamed emerald, and the damp earth was dark as rust. She leaned out of the window and looked around her, taking in the fresh hues of the newborn sky, the first notes of birdsong, and the magical stillness of nature drawing breath before a new day. She pictured Gabriel's place beyond the trees, and her heart ached.

Blinking hard, she took a deep breath and opened her suitcase. Time to go, Daisy. There was no point in staying.

A short while later she closed the door and fumbled clumsily with the key, unable to see the lock through her tears.

Chapter 27

The door was locked. Gabriel knocked loudly and shouted Daisy's name.

Silence.

The yellow car was gone. All the shutters were closed. Frowning, he dug in his pocket for the key and let himself in. In the kitchen he called her name again. There was no answer, no noise at all. He glanced around, noting the absence of a coffee cup on the draining board. Her phone charger wasn't anywhere to be seen. His pulse picked up. He took the stairs two at a time and checked her room.

Empty. Her alarm clock was gone, her suitcase too. He moved quickly from one room to the next. In the bathroom there was no toothbrush. No trace of Daisy anywhere.

His temple pounded. *We'll talk tomorrow*, she'd said. She couldn't have gone. She couldn't.

Regret filled him. He should have insisted she let him in last night. They should have finished the conversation, not left it hanging. But he'd been shocked. Hurt. He'd driven home dazed in the lashing rain, and her suggestion that the news needed time to settle had seemed sensible.

He went back into the kitchen, and that was when he saw the note. Folded and propped up against the coffee machine in the corner, it bore the logo of her law firm and beneath that her elegant, confident handwriting:

I'm sorry. For everything. For not telling you sooner, for allowing things to develop between us when I knew we could have no future. I said we'd talk, but I've realised talking won't change anything. It will only be painful and hurtful, and I always think it's best not to put off the inevitable. Goodbye, Gabriel. I hope you find the person you're looking for, and the love you so deserve.
Daisy

'Gabriel! You're here already.' Laetitia smiled. When he didn't get up, she bent to kiss him on each cheek. As she straightened, she read his expression and frowned.

Behind her Patrice was staring open-mouthed at the collection of empty glasses and beer bottles Gabriel had accumulated. The couple exchanged a look of concern before Patrice said drily, 'You've started early, *mon vieux*.'

Jean-Paul came over to take their orders. Gabriel asked for more beers and vodka shots. His friends' eyes widened and Jean-Paul shrugged, as if to say what could he do?

Gabriel gripped his beer bottle and glared, willing any of them to challenge him – because he was ready. He was spoiling for a fight tonight.

But they didn't. Instead Laetitia began rabbiting on about how her mother-in-law had the kids tonight and she was looking forward to time alone – blah blah blah . . .

'He's not listening,' Patrice told his wife. He turned to Gabriel and said bluntly, 'What's the matter? You look like shit.'

Gabriel drained the last of his beer. 'She's gone,' he said, and smacked the bottle down on the table.

'Who? Daisy?' asked Laetitia.

'Yes, Daisy.' He spat out her name. 'Who else?'

They exchanged another look and remorse stung him. It wasn't his friends' fault his world had been upended.

'She went home,' he added quietly, and stared into the bottom of his glass.

'But she lives in London,' Patrice said, as carefully as a bomb-disposal expert approaching his task. 'Isn't this what you expected?'

He shook his head. 'No.' When he'd made love to her, it had been a turning point in their relationship. A pledge of his love. So, no, he hadn't expected it.

But he should have. All the times he'd said he loved her she'd remained tight-lipped. *I don't love you, Gabriel. This is the end.*

Their drinks arrived. 'Three vodkas,' Jean-Paul said, with a sniff, and left them to it.

'Why did she go?' Laetitia asked, and the gentleness of her tone almost made him crack.

'She doesn't love me.' He bowed his head, feeling as if his heart would never beat again. Even when Jeanette had died it hadn't hurt as much as this. He'd only ever known grief like this once before in his life.

'Ah.' Patrice picked up a beer mat and absently tapped it.

'She doesn't love me and she doesn't want this life.' He couldn't tell his friends Daisy's secret – it wasn't his to tell – but it preyed on his mind and had done ever since she'd told him.

So she couldn't have children? It didn't matter.

Well, okay, it did. Having a family had been his wish for as long as he could remember – since the day he'd lost his. But would he have turned his back on Daisy because she was unable to have children? Of course not. No way.

He loved her. He loved her for who she was, exactly as she was, not for what she could or couldn't give him.

I don't love you, Gabriel.

But she didn't return his feelings.

His shoulders dropped. He'd been naïve to hope that someone so cynical could change and open her heart. Perhaps love had made him blind, or perhaps she'd been right all along and he'd led a sheltered life – while she was worldly-wise. Realistic.

He felt as if his heart had been shattered. Someone had taken a sledgehammer to it and only broken fragments remained. He didn't think it would ever beat fast with joy or laughter again. At best, it would survive. Because that was how life without Daisy would be – bare existence.

Despair sucked him under. He'd given his heart to the woman who'd told him right from the start that she didn't do love. What had he expected?

There was a long pause. Arnaud passed in his truck and waved, but Gabriel only glared at him.

'That's what she told you?' Laetitia asked. 'She doesn't love you?'

'Yes,' he said, losing patience. He snatched up a vodka. Beer alone wasn't enough to numb this.

'That's strange,' Laetitia said, 'because she seemed really happy here.'

Glass in hand, he frowned at her. 'You know her. Her career means everything to her.' Only he'd been stupid enough to believe she'd changed. Idiot.

'Does it?' Laetitia said sadly, as if he was missing the point. Her question hung in the air, like the sour smell of alcohol.

What was that knowing look for? What was she implying? His brain was too befuddled to understand.

Frustrated, he gave up trying to work it out and lifted the glass to his lips. He downed the vodka in one go and thumped the glass down angrily.

Jacques arrived. He threaded his way through the tables and chairs, taking in the scene and staring at Gabriel as he reached for another vodka, and a third.

'Wow! What's got into you?' he said, when he reached them. 'You haven't drunk spirits since you were an angry teenager.'

'Welcome to Heartbreak Hotel,' said Patrice.

'What?'

'Daisy left,' Laetitia explained.

'Ah.' Jacques sat down heavily.

Gabriel raised a bottle of beer to him. 'Cheers,' he said bitterly.

Chapter 28

Daisy caught the train from the airport, then the Tube. She decided to walk the last half-mile or so to her apartment. It had been a long day travelling with lots of waiting around before she'd managed to get a seat on a flight, and the walk might clear her head. But the tarmac felt hard beneath her feet, and she was tired. Her suitcase felt heavy as bricks as she dragged it behind her and heaved it up onto the kerb.

Why had she never noticed before how grey everything was in London? The pavements, walls, roads, and endless rows of front doors and windows overlooking one another. The smell of diesel hung in the air, and she rubbed her temple. The relentless noise of traffic was a buzzing irritation.

She passed a florist and stopped to stroke a stem of lavender. It felt silky and made her think of Le Mazet. As she carried on walking, she lifted her fingers to her nose and the scent transported her there.

Frowning, she forced the memories out of her mind and stopped outside her apartment block. She was home. Finally.

Once inside, she waited for the quiet sense of peace she'd expected to feel at being back in her flat, her life, where she was a respected lawyer, a consummate professional, a success.

And alone.

She sank into her sofa, thinking of Gabriel and her heart squeezed, as if firm hands were wringing it hard. God, she missed him. She hadn't expected it to knock the breath out of her quite so much.

She lifted her chin and gazed out of the window at the view over London, and tried to be positive. It would get easier. Tomorrow she'd go back to work, and her head would fill with clients and cases and documents all needing her full attention. She wouldn't have time to feel sorry for herself. The pain would fade. It would.

'Tracy, I can't find my file on the Daltons,' Daisy told her secretary. 'Have you seen it?

'Yes, it's here. I found it this morning. Perhaps you left it out last night.'

'Um . . . I don't remember.'

Tracy eyed her curiously. 'It's not like you to misplace things, Daisy.'

She laughed, embarrassed because this was the third time today. Normally she would have been fired up and eager to proceed with a new case but she felt . . . indifferent.

Tracy said carefully, 'You seem a little distracted. Is everything okay?'

'I – I don't know.'

There was a short pause. 'You don't know?'

She'd believed that she'd slot back into her old life as easily as zipping up a favourite dress, but it had been four days now and she still felt like a fish out of water. Each morning when she opened her wardrobe it was like look-ing at a stranger's clothes: the dagger-heeled shoes, the rail of tailored jackets and trousers in bold shades of scar-let and navy. They were all top quality, sophisticated and elegant, but they didn't fit any more. During her stay in France she must have gone up at least one dress size, if not two. And the tall heels she used to find emboldening rubbed and pinched.

'I just can't seem to stay focused . . .' She rubbed her forehead. 'Did you call that solicitor in France?'

Tracy nodded. 'He said it's very straightforward. He'll have the documents ready by the end of the week.'

'Good.'

A couple of her colleagues went past in the corridor, their footsteps purposeful, their conversation loud and cheerful. Daisy shivered. 'Is it me or is it freezing in here?'

Tracy glanced down at her short-sleeved shirt. 'It's just . . . normal.'

Daisy pulled her jacket tighter and stared past Tracy at the slate-grey sky crazed with dull clouds. She missed the heat of Provence. She missed the laid-back, gentle pace of life. She couldn't seem to keep up with the frenetic rhythm here. Everything felt . . . wrong, somehow.

Tracy peered at her curiously. 'I'd recommend a holiday, but you've just had one.'

There was no malice in her words, but Daisy knew that eyebrows had been raised at how long she'd been away. She knew her dedication had been called into question, and she'd almost certainly scuppered her chance of pro-motion. 'Yes. I don't know what's the matter with me.'

'Maybe you're coming down with something,' Tracy suggested.

She thought of when she'd been sick with a fever and Gabriel had nursed her. Her heart folded. 'Maybe.'

'If I didn't know better, I'd say you were lovesick.' Tracy laughed.

Daisy poked at a stain in the carpet with the toe of her shoe. Was it that obvious? She'd always prided herself on being dedicated and driven, objective and rational in her work, never ruled by emotion, exemplary. Yet now she could barely stay focused on the simplest of tasks.

'But of course that would be ridiculous,' Tracy went on, turning back to her computer monitor. 'I mean, you've always said you don't believe in love.'

Daisy left work early. Well, early by her previous standards – on the stroke of six. Once she got home she slipped off her heels, grabbed a bottle of rosé and a glass, and padded out onto the balcony.

She left the pile of mail unopened, she ignored the buzz of her phone signalling new emails and switched it off, relieved at the silence. Her shoulders dropped, and she sank into a chair. Leaning back, she watched the clouds drift, bumping into one another, joining and breaking up to create new shapes, painting pictures for her. She closed her eyes to inhale the wine's perfume, and when she sipped it she tasted sweet berries, sun-drenched peaches and the zing of lemons. She pictured the coral-pink sunsets of Provence, the turquoise of the Mediterranean Sea, the cobalt sky. She remembered the buttery-gold sunlight streaming down on the ancient landscape, baking the clay-red earth. She heard the sound of sheep bells, the rustling of the forest in the wind. She could smell sweet garlic cooking and the perfume of pines in the arid heat. And she could see Gabriel's solid frame, his cement-stained hands. She could feel his gentle touch on her in the dark of the night. She heard his loving words whispered against her neck.

Her throat thickened, making it difficult to swallow, and she reached into her pocket for the tiny cicada he'd whittled. She ran the pad of her thumb over the smooth, warm wood.

She'd done the right thing, she told herself. Gabriel would move on and find his perfect woman. She dipped her head and squeezed her eyes shut against the hot sting of tears. But it would take her a long time to get over this.

Because she'd left a piece of her heart in Provence.

***

'You can't go on like this,' said Laetitia, 'not eating, not sleeping or communicating with anyone – even us.'

'No?' Gabriel said bitterly. 'Watch me.'

She glared at him, then turned away as Giselle approached. Laetitia lifted the child onto her knee.

'You're like a zombie,' Patrice said. 'A ghost.'

His short laugh was acerbic. 'So what's the solution? Tell me.'

Jacques sipped his beer. 'It's obvious. You need to go after her.'

'Watch my lips. She. Doesn't. Love. Me.'

'How do you know?'

'She told me.'

'And you believe her?' Laetitia asked.

'She's an intelligent woman. She knows her own mind.' He picked up a beer mat and absently flicked it between his fingers.

'This isn't about her mind, though, is it?' said Jacques. 'It's about her heart.' He held a fist to his chest.

Gabriel scowled. 'Believe me, her mind is made up. Look.' He dug in his back pocket and produced a creased letter. He slapped it down on the table. 'She's giving me the house.'

'What?' Jacques's eyes became round.

Laetitia gasped. They all leaned in to read it.

'Wow,' said Patrice, a moment later.

'So you got what you wished for,' Laetitia murmured sadly.

'Yes.' He gave a bitter laugh. Except he *didn't* want it. The thought of gaining the house but losing her made him sick.

He was relieved when they turned away and the conversation moved on, leaving him to nurse his beer.

But Jacques's words tugged at him. *It's about her heart.*

He remembered the tear that had slipped down her cheek, how she hadn't been able to meet his eye as she'd said, *I don't love you.*

Had she really meant it?

Of course she had. She'd always said she didn't believe in love. Love was for fools.

And yet when he'd held her in his arms it had felt like love. He'd looked into her eyes and seen all her dreams, talents, hopes, vulnerabilities, fears—

He stilled.

She was afraid of love.

What if she'd fallen in love despite herself? *I can't be the woman you need.*

What if this was what she'd believed? He'd told her time and time again how much he wanted a family. Her childhood experiences had hardened her and taught her to expect rejection. He'd been shocked when she'd confessed her secret. He'd been angry. Had she seen this as the rejection she'd expected? Was that why she'd retreated from him?

What if she'd said she didn't love him to make it easier to leave? What if she'd done it to set him free?

He downed his beer and scraped his chair back.

'Gabriel?' said Jacques.

'I have to go,' he growled.

'Where?'

'To London.'

His friends exchanged a glance. Jacques asked, 'Right now?'

He nodded. 'I have to speak to her.'

On the Tube people piled in, pushing, squeezing, their faces hostile. The air became thick and heavy, and Gabriel's palms were sticky. He tugged at his collar, glad that in his rush to get here he'd forgotten to bring a jacket.

An Escape to Provence

Staring at the map above the doors with its spider's web of primary colours he reminded himself of why he was there. For Daisy. He was doing this for her. Because the alternative was unbearable. Life without her was greyer even than this city.

He got out one station too late, but shrugged off his mistake. He had legs, didn't he? Walking would do him good. As he traipsed the pavements, he gazed up at the tall buildings and tried to picture himself living there. He didn't doubt he could find building work, but the rest – could he hack it? Raindrops began to fall. Not the warm and welcome rain that was so refreshing in Provence. No. This was as chilling as a sharp blade, and it sliced down the back of his neck, under his collar and soaked up his trouser legs. He put his head down and quickened his pace. Could he live with this? The weather, commuting, climbing scaffolding, adding floor upon floor to high-rise flats and offices? He swallowed the growing sense of dread. It might not be the kind of work he was used to and it might not be rewarding, but he'd have Daisy. He'd come home to her each evening and her eyes would light as she told him about her day and all the people she'd helped. He'd cook her a meal and they'd sleep wrapped in each other . . .

He stopped and looked up at a glass-fronted building. This was it. Daisy's home.

He found her name among the rows of buzzers and pressed. MS JACKSON, it said, and although it was written in block capitals, he recognised her handwriting.

There was no answer so he buzzed again. And again. He called her mobile – trying not to remember how she'd refused to take her dad's calls. Was she staring at his caller ID with the same horrified expression now? She was scared of getting hurt and she responded by shutting people out, cutting them out of her life. It was how she protected herself.

Her mobile went to voicemail. It was almost 7 p.m. – was she still at work?

The door to her apartment block suddenly swung open, and Gabriel stepped back as a man strode out, head down, not even glancing at him. Gabriel hesitated only a second, then grabbed the door and slipped inside.

She lived on the eleventh floor, and he called the lift. Upstairs, he rapped at her apartment door, but there was no answer. He tried the apartment next door. A middle-aged woman answered. 'Who?' she said.

'Daisy Jackson. Your neighbour.'

She shook her head. 'Sorry. Don't know her.'

He looked around. The sumptuously decorated hallway was deserted and silent. He went to the next apartment.

'Daisy Jackson?' the man said, puzzled.

'Slim. Blonde hair. Well-dressed.'

'Oh, her. How should I know where she is?'

The occupant of the third and last apartment answered angrily, 'You banged on my door to ask me that? Who do you think I am? Her personal assistant?' before shutting the door in Gabriel's face.

Startled, he stepped back. No one knew her here. Not one of her neighbours.

Early the next morning he waited at the reception desk for Shaw and Stone's offices. He'd found the name of the firm she worked for: it had been on the emails she'd sent him before she'd come to France. He shifted from one foot to the other, impatiently watching the lift. The receptionist had offered him a seat but he was too restless to sit. Daisy's secretary, Tracy, was on her way down to speak to him in person, but he suspected this was a polite form of gatekeeping.

Daisy didn't want to see him, did she? The sickening realisation was gradually growing more likely. He'd blown it. He'd lost his temper and now he'd lost Daisy. He should have listened. He should have asked more questions and shown more understanding – instead of flying off the handle because she hadn't told him sooner. She couldn't have children. No matter how much bravado and indifference she showed, this was monumental stuff. She'd needed him – but he'd pushed her away.

And he realised now that his friends had been right all along: he'd had unrealistic expectations. The perfect partner he'd pictured didn't exist, and he couldn't recreate the big happy family he'd had as a child, which had been torn away from him. Or, rather, he didn't *need* to recreate it to be happy. But he did need Daisy.

The lift pinged and the doors opened with a hushed swish. A young woman emerged.

'Mr Laforêt?' she began.

'Where is Daisy? Can I see her?'

Her expression twisted in a look of regret. 'I'm sorry . . .'

His heart sank. A river of disappointment swept through him. He pictured Daisy upstairs in her office, arms folded, stubbornly refusing to see him.

'I'm afraid she's left,' Tracy finished.

'Left? To go where – to court?' He'd wait for her. He didn't mind how long he had to wait.

She shook her head. 'Daisy resigned. She doesn't work here any more.'

He blinked at the secretary. 'What?' The blood drained from his face and the room tilted. 'Why did she resign? Where has she gone? Where is she working now?'

Tracy shrugged. 'As far as I know, she had no job to go to. She just . . . quit. She said she was going away, taking time off.'

Minutes later he stepped out into the street, dejected and despairing. Unless Daisy answered her phone, he had no way of finding her. He jammed his hands into his pockets and stared at his boots.

He had to face it: he'd lost her.

Chapter 29

Daisy steered the Jeep along the lane towards Le Mazet, slowing to gaze at the landscape all around. The forest was unchanged, but everything else had lost its greenery and looked even more golden than she remembered in the late-afternoon sun. It was July. Four weeks since she'd last been here, but it evidently hadn't rained in that time. In the fields all around the crop of *sainfoin* had grown, and the red-gold earth was cracked and dry. Heat shimmered, blurring everything.

She got out of the car, took a deep breath and closed her eyes. The familiar perfumes punched the air: lavender, pine, sunshine. The sound of the cicadas' simple song chimed like bells. The warm breeze wrapped itself around her bare arms like a cashmere shawl.

The shutters of the house were all closed, the outdoor furniture bare of cushions or any other sign of life, but she felt a spark of joy as she ran her gaze over the undulating terracotta roof tiles and stone walls. They gleamed pale gold in the sun, and she remembered that Gabriel had talked about sandblasting them.

Squeezing the car keys, she glanced warily in the direction of his place. She supposed she ought to go round and speak to him, let him know what she'd decided. But she was dreading the prospect. She'd leave it until tomorrow.

The deep growl of a diesel engine made her turn. As if she'd conjured him with her thoughts, the pick-up came into view on the lane, and the noise grew louder as it approached. She watched it trundle past, a flicker of grey through the trees and bushes. Her heart jumped at the sight, even though it had no right to, but she was relieved when it passed the end of her drive.

However, the screech of brakes made her still. A cloud of dust rose up as the pick-up reversed back along the lane, then stopped at the end of her drive. She watched as it paused there, then turned in and hurtled towards her. She wondered if Gabriel was at the wheel and not someone else because she'd never seen him drive so fast. Joy and dread warred with one another inside her. Her mouth dried. This wasn't going to be an easy conversation.

Gabriel jumped out of the pick-up, and strode towards her. His hair had grown long and unruly, and as he approached she noticed there were new lines beneath his eyes. Her fingers itched to smooth them away. Was he all right? She hoped he hadn't lost sleep over her. She hoped he'd moved on.

He stopped in front of her, his expression fierce yet unreadable. 'You're back,' he said. 'Why?'

Direct as always, she thought fondly, and wished she'd had time to shower and change out of the jersey dress she'd travelled in. It had been a long drive all the way across France from England. Then again, his clothes were grey with dust and there were flecks of white paint in his hair so perhaps it didn't matter.

'I missed the place,' she said honestly. Her throat felt raw.

Their gazes held. She'd missed him, too, but kept that thought to herself.

His brow pulled into a deep frown. 'What have you missed – the house? The people? What?'

She gave a watery smile. 'Everything,' she said, and let her gaze sweep from the fields to the forested hills and back again. 'The sunsets, the food, the peace and beauty of it all.'

His shoulders sagged as if in disappointment.

She licked her lips, nervous about how he would take her news. He'd be justified if he reacted angrily. Taking a deep breath, she told him, 'I resigned from my job and sold my flat.'

His eyes widened. She'd forgotten how beautiful they were. Deep pools of the most indulgent chocolate brown.

'I know you resigned – I went to your office to look for you. But why did you sell?' he asked, clearly shocked. 'You love the city, you love your job. I don't understand.'

He'd been to London? She shook her head, emotions bubbling up inside her, making it difficult to speak. 'I found it . . . different when I went back. Too much had changed. I had changed.'

He scoured her face, as if he was baffled by what he saw. 'What are you going to do?'

'I'm going to set up my own small firm. It will give me the freedom to work part-time and take on the clients I choose. Those who need me the most rather than those who can afford to pay the highest fees.' She looked around her. 'I'll also be able to work remotely.'

'Remotely? Where from? Where will you live?'

She glanced at her car, filled with her belongings. 'I – ah – I'm planning to look for another house. I want to live here.'

'Here?'

She nodded. 'I've applied for a residence permit.'

'You want to live here, in La Tourelle?' he said incredulously.

She steeled herself for his reaction. It was the most emotional and irrational decision she'd ever made, and now she was here she realised how selfish it was. She couldn't justify it. If he objected – as he surely would – she didn't know what her plan B would be. She loved La Tourelle. She loved Provence. 'Yes.' She gave a nervous laugh. 'We'll be neighbours. If that's all right?'

His brow creased even more. 'Neighbours?'

She hoped and prayed he could accept her living here – so near, yet no longer part of his life. 'Gabriel, I don't want any trouble. I won't interfere in your life, I promise—'

'No?' His expression was grave. 'And what if I want you to interfere?'

Now it was her turn to look puzzled. 'What?'

'What if I *want* you to be part of my life?'

She held her breath and her heart drilled out the milliseconds that followed. He stepped closer. Took her hand in his.

'But I told you – I can't—'

'I don't care,' he said. His eyes shone, brilliant and warm, instantly reminding her that with Gabriel his emotions were never far from the surface and burning strongly. 'I wanted children, but I want you more.'

She blinked and lit up inside.

He went on, 'I'm sorry I reacted the way I did. I should have listened. I want to know everything about when you were ill, what happened. It can't have been easy for you.'

She stared at him, then shook her head. 'You had every right to be angry. I was a coward. Should've told you sooner, but . . .'

His finger hushed her. Then he brushed her cheek wondrously, as if he couldn't believe she was standing here before him. 'I love you, Daisy. I can't live without you.'

Emotion swelled up in her, enormous and overwhelming.

'You would be such a great father,' she said. 'I don't want to prevent you from having a family. Maybe we could adopt. If you're happy to, that is.'

'Would you want that?' His words hung in the air.

Daisy thought of how it had felt to help little Giselle at the beach, and she remembered her early years growing up in the country, how happy she'd been. 'Yes,' she said. 'I would.'

His features lit up. 'We could give a home to a child who needs a family as I did, or we could simply be the best babysitters for our friends' children. Surrogate auntie and uncle. Like Jeanette was for me.'

She smiled and nodded.

His eyes creased. 'I love you, Daisy. And I know you love me too.'

'What?' She laughed. 'You're very sure of yourself, Monsieur Laforêt. *How* do you know I love you?'

'I feel it here.' He held a fist to his heart. 'You said you didn't love me to protect me. You wanted me to hate you and move on. Love someone else . . .'

She smiled and bowed her head, glowing with the knowledge that this man knew her better than anyone else in the world. He had the measure of her and he'd never let her be anything but honest with him. He was her equal, her perfect match.

He drew her to him. 'But I could never love anyone except you, Daisy.' She heard the smile in his voice. 'No one else could tempt me with her spreadsheets or neat-freak tendencies.'

She touched her fingers to his face, savouring the warmth of his skin and seeing the sun reflected in his eyes. 'I love you so much, Gabriel ...'

He rested his forehead against hers, and she closed her eyes. She felt . . . as if she'd come home.

All her life she'd longed for this. Finally, she'd found it. But it turned out that home wasn't a place: it was his touch, his words, his heart.

'I want to stay with you here for ever,' she whispered.

The low croon of a dove made them both look up at the chimney where a pair of pale grey birds were nestled up close.

Daisy and Gabriel smiled at each other, and the future stretched ahead like a promise.

Recipes

Grandmère's soup

This is a really easy, comforting *potage*, perfect for a cold winter's day. I've listed ingredients, but really you can use whatever quantities you have. It's not set in stone at all. And although it's usual with soup recipes to begin by softening the onion in oil, this one is even simpler because the vegetables are simply boiled.

When I was small my mum used to add a swirl of milk or cream to my bowl of soup, and my husband loves to add a sprinkle of curry powder to his (Grandmère would approve because she loved strong flavours), but I prefer it plain and simple.

Serves 4

Ingredients
8 carrots, sliced
2 leeks, sliced
1 onion, chopped
3 cloves of garlic, chopped
4 celery sticks, sliced
3 potatoes, peeled and chopped

1 litre vegetable stock
1 bay leaf (optional)

Tip all of the vegetables into a large pan and add the vegetable stock and bay leaf, if using. Cover with a lid, bring to the boil, then simmer until the vegetables are soft (around 25 minutes). Season with salt and black pepper, then remove the bay leaf before blending to a smooth consistency. Serve with crusty bread.

Tomates Provençales

These are simply sunshine on a plate! I like to serve them as an accompaniment to any summer dish, but they're particularly good with roast chicken, and bread to mop up the garlicky juices. Of course, the tomatoes grown and sold in Provence have much more flavour and sweetness than those we get here in the UK, but if you choose the ripest tomatoes you can find, these will still be delicious.

One final thing: Grandmère's secret ingredient was to add cracker crumbs to the breadcrumbs. This gives a little more crunch, and I highly recommend it.

Serves 4

Ingredients
6 large tomatoes
2 tablespoons olive oil, plus a little extra for oiling

salt and pepper
2 cloves of garlic, crushed
30g breadcrumbs
15g fresh parsley or thyme, chopped finely

Preheat the oven to 200°C/180°C fan/Gas 6.

Cut the tomatoes in half across their equator and place cut-side up on an oiled oven dish. Season with salt and pepper. In a bowl mix the garlic, breadcrumbs, herbs and 1 tablespoon of the olive oil. Sprinkle a teaspoon of this mixture over each half tomato, then drizzle with the remaining olive oil. Bake for around 25 minutes or until the breadcrumb topping is golden.

Gâteau au Yaourt

(Yogurt Cake)

With love and thanks to my godmother, Marie-Luce Larget, for this recipe.

Ingredients
3 eggs
Small pot, approx,100g, natural yogurt (use the pot to measure the other ingredients)
2 pots caster sugar
3 pots plain flour
1 pot sunflower oil

1 teaspoon baking powder
½ teaspoon vanilla extract

Preheat the oven to 200°C/180°C fan/Gas 6. Line a 500g loaf tin with baking parchment. Whisk together the eggs and yogurt, using an electric whisk or by hand. Then whisk in the remaining ingredients in the order they're listed. Pour into the tin and bake for 45 mins or until a skewer comes out almost dry.

Acknowledgements

I owe huge thanks to Glenys White and Marie-Luce Larget for their help with research into French wills. This turned out to be a minefield (any mistakes are entirely mine), but I was so excited by the idea that someone could write their own will and hide it that I just had to base a plot around it.

Thanks to Cath Staincliffe, Livi Michael, Jennifer Makumbi and Jacqui Cooper, whose feedback on this book was invaluable. I'm also very grateful to Ros Ashcroft for checking the legal terms.

As always, thanks to my mum, Brigitte, for checking the French. To Amy Batley, Kimberley Atkins and all the team at Hodder who work so hard behind the scenes. And to Megan Carroll, my favourite agent.

And finally, thank you, my wonderful readers, for buying my books and making it possible for me to keep writing. I love hearing from you and there really is nothing more magical than sharing the stories in my head and seeing them go out into the world.

Discover more from Sophie Claire . . .

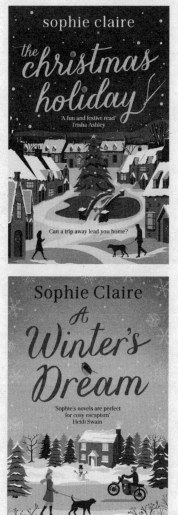